Only
Begotten
Daughter

NOVELS BY JAMES MORROW

The Wine of Violence
The Continent of Lies
This Is the Way the World Ends
Only Begotten Daughter

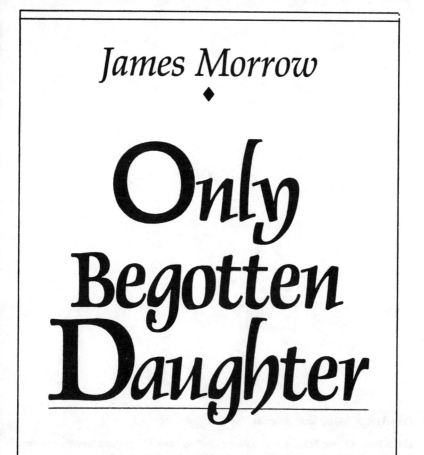

James Morrow

Only Begotten Daughter

William Morrow and Company, Inc.
New York

For Jean

ISBN 0-688-05284-3

BOOK DESIGN BY PATRICE FODERO

ACKNOWLEDGMENTS

◆   ◆   ◆

Throughout the writing of this novel, my companions included several extraordinary books dealing with the scientist's search for God, the evolution of Christianity, and other pertinent topics. Let me here acknowledge my debt to Paul Davies's *God and the New Physics*, Edward Harrison's *Masks of the Universe*, Stephen Hawking's *A Brief History of Time*, Richard Dawkins's *The Blind Watchmaker*, Thomas Sheehan's *The Second Coming*, Hyam Maccoby's *The Mythmaker*, Ian Wilson's *Jesus: The Evidence*, Hans Küng's *Does God Exist?*, and Edward Peters's *Inquisition*.

I am grateful to the wide circle of friends and colleagues who commented on the manuscript during its various systolic and diastolic phases: Joe Adamson, Linda Barnes, Michael Bishop, Jon Burrowes, Shira Daemon, Denali Delmar, Margaret Duda, Joan Dunfey, Alexander Jablokow, Ellen Kushner, Geoffrey A. Landis, Elissa Malcohn, Chris Monroe, Jean Morrow, Resa Nelson, Steven Popkes, Peter Schneeman, Brett Singer, D. Alexander Smith, Kathy Smith, Sarah Smith, James Stevens, Bonnie Sunstein, and Michael Svoboda.

Finally, I must thank my agent, Merrilee Heifetz, for her continuing moral support, and my editors, David Hartwell and Susan Allison, who provided the kind of intense line-by-line attention most novelists only dream of receiving.

Philosophy has succeeded, not without struggle, in freeing itself from its obsession with the soul, only to find itself landed with something still more mysterious and captivating, the fact of man's bodiliness.

—Friedrich Nietzsche

PART ONE

• • •

Signs and Wonders

CHAPTER 1

♦ ♦ ♦

On the first day of September, 1974, a child was born to Murray Jacob Katz, a celibate Jewish recluse living across the bay from Atlantic City, New Jersey, an island metropolis then famous for its hotels, its boardwalk, its Miss America Pageant, and its seminal role in the invention of Monopoly.

The abandoned lighthouse on Brigantine Point that Murray had taken over, claiming it for his own as a hermit might claim a cave, was called Angel's Eye. It was wholly obsolete, which he preferred; as a sexually inactive hermit living in the highly eroticized culture of late twentieth-century America, Murray felt somewhat obsolete himself. During its heyday, the kerosene-fueled lamp of Angel's Eye had escorted over ten thousand vessels safely past Brigantine Shoals. But now Murray's lighthouse was fired up only when he felt like it, while the business of preventing shipwreck passed to the United States Coast Guard's new electric beacon on Absecon Island.

Murray knew all about Angel's Eye, its glory and also its shame. He knew of the stormy July night in 1866 when the kerosene ran out, so that the British brig *William Rose*, bearing a cargo of tea and fireworks from China, had smashed to pieces on the rocks. He knew of the foggy March morning in 1897 when the main wick disintegrated, with dire consequences for *Lucy II*, a private pleasure yacht owned by the Philadelphia ball-bearing tycoon Alexander Strickland. On the anniversaries of these disasters, Murray always enacted a commemoration, climbing the tower stairs and, at the precise moment when *William Rose* or *Lucy II* had pulled within view of Angel's Eye, lighting the lamp. He was a devout believer in the second chance. To the man who asked, "What's the point of closing the barn door after the horse has been stolen?" Murray would answer, "The point is that the door is now closed."

At the time of his child's conception, Murray's sex life revolved exclusively around a combination sperm bank and research center known as the Preservation Institute. Its scientists were doing a longitudinal study: how do a man's reproductive cells change as he ages? Murray, broke, signed up without hesitation. Every month, he drove to this famous foundation, housed in three stories of weatherworn brick overlooking Great Egg Bay, where the receptionist, Mrs. Kriebel, would issue him a sterilized herring jar and escort him upstairs to a room papered with *Playboy* centerfolds and pornographic letters mailed to *Penthouse* by its own staff.

Not only did the Preservation Institute harvest and scrutinize the seed of ordinary citizens, it also froze that of Nobel Prize laureates, making their heritable traits available for home experiments in eugenics. As it happened, thousands of women had been waiting for this product to come on the market. Nobel sperm was cheap, reliable, and simple to use. After acquiring a turkey baster, you injected yourself with the rare fluid—the *crème de la crème*, as it were—and nine months later out burst a genius. The laureates received nothing for their donations beyond the satisfaction of upgrading the human gene pool. Murray Katz—retail clerk, involuntary celibate, Newark Community College dropout—received thirty dollars a shot.

And then one afternoon a message arrived—a telegram, for like most hermits, Murray had no phone.

YOUR LAST DONATION CONTAMINATED. STOP. COME IMMEDIATELY. STOP.

Contaminated. The word, so obviously a euphemism for diseased, made a cold puddle in his bowels. Cancer, no doubt. His semen was riddled with malignant cells. STOP: indeed. STOP: you're dead. He got behind the wheel of his decrepit Saab and headed over Brigantine Bridge into Atlantic City.

When Murray Jacob Katz was ten years old, he'd begun wondering whether he was permitted to believe in heaven, as were his various Christian friends. Jews believed so many impressive and dramatic things, it seemed only logical to regard death as less permanent than one might conclude from, say, coming across a stone-stiff cat in a Newark sewer. "Pop, do we have heaven?" he'd asked on the day he discovered the cat. "You want to know a Jew's idea of heaven?" his father had replied, looking up from his Maimonides. "It's an endless succession of long winter nights on which we get paid a fair wage to sit in a warm room and read all the books ever written." Phil Katz was an intense, shriveled man with a defective aorta; in a month his heart would seize up like an overburdened automobile engine. "Not just the famous ones, no, *every* book, the stuff *nobody* gets around to reading, forgotten plays, novels by people you never heard of. However, I profoundly doubt such a place exists."

Decades later, after Pop was dead and Murray's life had been relocated to Atlantic City, he began transforming his immediate environment, making it characteristic of heaven. The whole glorious span of Dewey's decimal system soon filled the lighthouse, book after book spiraling up the tower walls like threads of DNA, delivering intellectual matter to Murray's mammalian cortex and wondrous smells to the reptilian regions below—the gluey tang of a library discard, the crisp plebeian aroma of a yard-sale paperback, the pungent mustiness of a thrift-store encyclopedia. When the place became too crowded, Murray simply built an addition, a kind of circular cottage surrounding the lighthouse much as three hundred noisy, unraged, and well-dressed Christians were now surrounding the Preservation Institute.

Three hundred, no exaggeration, brandishing placards and chanting "It's a sin!" Even the seaward side was covered; a flotilla of yachts lay at anchor just offshore, protest banners fluttering from their masts: PROCREATION IS SACRED...SATAN WAS A TEST-TUBE BABY...A GOOD PARENT IS A MARRIED PARENT. Murray crossed the sandy lawn using the cautious, inoffensive gait any prudent Jew might adopt under the circumstances. AND THE LORD STRUCK DOWN ONAN, declared the placard of a gaunt old gentleman with the tight, reverent carriage of a praying mantis. GOD LOVES LESBIANS, GOD HATES LESBIANISM, proclaimed a large-eared adolescent who could have starred in the life of Franz Kafka. Murray studied his goal, a ring of sawhorse-shaped barricades manned by a dozen security guards anxiously stroking their semiautomatic rifles. Protestors pawed Murray's coat. "Please

keep your sperm," urged a pale, toothsome woman whose placard read, ARTIFICIAL INSEMINATION = ETERNAL DAMNATION.

As Murray passed the barricades, a hand emerged from the
mob and trapped his shoulder. He turned. A leather patch
masked the protester's right eye. To fight God's battles, God had
equipped him with massive arms, a body like a Stonehenge meg-
alith, and a riveting glint in his good eye. "So what will your
spilled seed get you, brother? Thirty dollars? You're being un-
derpaid. Judas got silver. Resist. *Resist.*"

"As a matter of fact, my last donation wasn't acceptable,"
said Murray. "I think I'm out of a job."

"Tell those people in there it's wrong—a *sin*. Will you do
that? We're not here to condemn them. We're all sinners. *I'm* a
sinner." With a sudden flourish the protester flipped back his
eyepatch. "When a man takes out his own eye, that's a sin."

Murray shuddered. What had he expected, a glass orb, a
fused lid? Certainly not this open pit, dark and jagged like the
sickness he imagined gnawing at his gonads. "A sin." He
wrested free. "I'll tell them."

"God bless you, brother," muttered the man with the hole in
his head.

Shivering with apprehension, Murray entered the Institute
and crossed the glossy marble floor, moving past a great clock-
face with hands like harpoons, past spherical lamps poised on
wrought-iron stands, at last reaching Mrs. Kriebel's desk.

"I'll tell Dr. Frostig you're here," she said curtly, arranging
her collection jars in a tidy grid. She was a stylish woman, decorated with clothes and cosmetics whose names Murray didn't
know.

"Have they decided what's wrong with me?"

"Wrong with you?"

"With my donation."

"Not my department." Mrs. Kriebel pointed across the lobby
to a sharply angled woman with a vivid, hawkish face. "You can
wait with Five Twenty-eight over there."

The lobby suggested the parlor of a first-class bordello.
Abloom with ferns, Greek vases anchored the four corners of a
sumptuous Persian rug. On the upholstered walls, set within
gold frames, oil portraits of deceased Nobel-winning donors
glowered at the mere mortals who surveyed them. Well, well,
thought Murray, perusing the faces, we're going to have Keynes-

ian economics in the next century whether we want it or not. And a new generation of astrophysicists writing bad science fiction.

Glancing away from a dead secretary of state, Five Twenty-eight offered Murray an ardent smile. Black turtleneck jersey, straight raven hair, scruffy brown bomber jacket, eye shadow the iridescent green of Absecon Inlet: she looked like a fifties beatnik, mysteriously transplanted to the age of sperm banks. "I don't care whether I get a girl or a boy," she said abruptly. "Makes no difference. Everybody thinks dykes hate boys. Not true."

Murray surveyed the lesbian's offbeat prettiness, her spidery frame. "Was it hard picking the father?"

"Don't remind me." Together they ambled to the next portrait, a Swedish brain surgeon. "For the longest time I was into the idea of either a painter or a flute player. The arts are my big love, you see, but with science you've got a more reliable income, so in the end I settled on a marine biologist—a black man, they tell me, one of their own staff. Mathemeticians were in the picture for a while, but then they ran out. Actually, there was one. A Capricorn. No way. Let me guess—you look like a Jewish novelist, if you don't mind my saying so. I considered having one of those, but then I started reading their stuff, and it seemed kind of dirty to me, and I decided I didn't want that kind of karma in the house. You a novelist?"

"Matter of fact, I have been working on a book. Nonfiction, though."

"What's it called?"

"*Hermeneutics of the Ordinary.*" Upon turning forty, Murray had resolved not only to collect obscure and profound books, but to write one as well. Within six months he had three hundred pages of ragged manuscript and a great title.

"*What* of the ordinary?"

"Hermeneutics. Interpretation." Through his employment at Atlantic City Photorama, where he collected exposed film and doled out prints and slides, Murray had discovered that snapshots afford unique access to the human psyche. A lawyer photographs his teenage daughter: why the provocative low angle? A stock broker photographs his house: why does he stand so far away, why this hunger for context? Snapshots were an undeciphered language, and Murray was determined to crack the code;

his book would be the Rosetta stone of home photography, the Talmud of the Instamatic. "It's about my experiences serving Photorama customers."

"Oh, yeah—I've seen that place," said the lesbian. "Tell me, is it true people are always shooting each other screwing?"

"A few of our clients do that, yes."

"That confirms my suspicions."

"It gets even stranger. We have this real estate agent who does nothing but animals who've been . . . well, squashed."

"Gross."

"Squirrels, skunks, groundhogs, cats. Roll after roll."

"So you can really get into human nature by seeing what everyone brings to Photorama? I'd never thought of that. Heavy."

Murray smiled. His book might have a readership after all. "I also run that lighthouse on Brigantine Point."

"Lighthouse? You really run a lighthouse?"

"Uh-huh. We don't light it much anymore."

"Could I let the baby see it sometime? Sounds educational."

"Sure. I'm Murray Katz." He extended his hand.

"Georgina Sparks." She gave him a jaunty handshake. "Tell me honestly, do I strike you as insane? It's insane to try raising a kid alone, everybody says, especially if you're a dyke. I was living with my lover and, matter of fact, we split up over the whole idea. I'm real big on babies. Laurie thinks they're grotesque."

"You're not insane." She was insane, he thought. "Isn't 'dyke' an offensive word?"

"If *you* said it, Murray Katz"—Georgina grinned slyly—"I'd kick your teeth in."

A rhythmic clacking intruded, Mrs. Kriebel's heels striking marble. She held out an insulated test tube with the numerals 147 etched on its shaft.

"Oh, wow!" Georgina seized the tube, pressing it against her chest. "Know what this is, Mur? It's my *baby!*"

"Neat."

Mrs. Kriebel smiled. "Congratulations."

"Maybe I should've held out for a mathematician." Georgina eyed the tube with mock suspicion. "Little Pisces mathematician tooling around the apartment, chewing on her calculator? Cute, huh?"

The elevator door opened to reveal a pudgy man in a lab coat.

He motioned Murray over with quick, urgent gestures, as if he'd just found a pair of desirable seats at the movies. "You made the right choice," Murray told Georgina as he started away.

"You really think so?"

"Marine biology's a fine career," he called after the mother-to-be and stepped into the elevator.

"I'll bring the baby around," she called back.

The door thumped closed. The elevator ascended, gravity grabbing at the Big Mac in Murray's stomach.

"What we've essentially got here," said Gabriel Frostig, medical director of the Preservation Institute, "is an egg identification problem."

"Chicken egg?" said Murray. A bell rang. Second floor.

"Human egg. Ovum." Dr. Frostig guided Murray into a cramped and dingy lab packed with technological bric-a-brac. "We're hoping you'll tell us where it came from."

Dominating the dissection table, chortling merrily like a machine for making some particularly loose and messy variety of candy, was the most peculiar contraption Murray had ever seen. At its heart lay a bell jar, the glass so pure and gleaming that tapping it would, Murray imagined, produce not a simple bong but a fugue. A battery-powered pump, a rubber bellows, and three glass bottles sat on a wooden platform, encircling the jar like gifts spread around some gentile's Christmas tree. "What's *that*?"

"Your most recent donation."

One bottle was empty, the second contained what looked like blood, the third a fluid suggesting milk. "And you're keeping it in a, er . . . ?"

"An ectogenesis machine."

Murray peered through the glass. A large wet slab of protoplasm—it looked like a flounder wearing a silk scarf—filled the jar. Clear plastic tubes flowed into the soft flesh from all directions. "A what?"

"Artificial uterus," Frostig explained, "prototype stage. We weren't planning to gestate any *human* embryos for at least five years. It's been strictly a mouse and frog operation around here. But when Karnstein spotted your blastocyte, we said to ourselves, all right . . ." The doctor squinted and grimaced, as if examining an ominous biopsy drawn from his own body. "Besides, we thought maybe you *expected* us to let it die, so you could go running to the newspapers—am I right?—telling 'em how we like to butcher embryos." He jabbed his index finger contemptuously toward the front lawn. "You one of those Revelationists, Mr. Katz?"

"No. Jewish." Murray cocked an ear to the protesters' chants, a sound like enraged surf. "And I've never run to a newspaper in my life."

"Damn lunatics—they should go back to the Middle Ages where they belong."

"Wait a minute, wait a minute, are you saying there's a *baby* growing in that thing?"

Frostig nodded. "Inside that uterine tissue."

Murray pressed closer. The glass widened his face, making his already considerable jaw look like a sugar bowl.

"No, don't go looking," said the doctor. "We're talking about a cell cluster no bigger than a pinhead."

"*My* cell cluster?"

"Yours and somebody else's. You didn't by any chance introduce an ovum into your sample?"

"How could I do that? I'm no biologist. I don't even know very many women."

"A dead end. We figured as much." Frostig opened the top drawer of his filing cabinet, grabbing a stack of printed forms, carbon paper sandwiched between them like slices of black cheese. "In any event, we need your signature on this embryo release. We weren't born yesterday—we know people form weird attachments in this world. Last weekend I spent about twenty hours convincing a surrogate mother to hand a newborn over to its parents."

A baby, thought Murray as he took the embryo release. Someone had given him a baby. He'd feared it was cancer, and instead it was a baby. "If I sign, does that mean I—?"

"Forfeit all claims to the cluster. Not that you *have* any. Far as the law's concerned, it's just another sperm donation." Frostig pulled a fountain pen from his coat as if unsheathing a dagger. "But that egg's a real wild card—inverse parthenogenesis, we're calling it at the moment. On the whole it never happens. So for the protection of all concerned..."

"Inverse partheno...what?" An unprecedented situation, Murray thought, and what accompanied it seemed equally unprecedented, a strange amalgam of confusion, fear, and the treacly warmth he reflexively felt around puppies.

"In conventional parthenogenesis, an ovum undergoes meiosis without fertilization. Aberrant, but well documented. Here we're talking sperm development without an ovum." Frostig ran his fingers along the tube connecting blood to womb, checking for kinks. "Frankly, it's got us spooked."

"Isn't there some scientific explanation?"

"We're certainly looking for one."

Murray examined the embryo release, dense with meaningless print. Did he in fact want a baby? Wouldn't a baby pull his books off the shelves? Where did you get their clothes?

He signed. Georgina Sparks's lover had called it right. Babies were grotesque.

"What will happen to the cell cluster?"

"We usually carry frogs to the second trimester," said Frostig, snatching up the embryo release and depositing it on his desk, "a bit longer with the mice. The really key data doesn't come till we sacrifice them."

"Sacrifice them?"

"Ectogenesis machines are still very crude. Next year we might, just might, bring a cat to term." Frostig guided Murray toward the door, pausing to retrieve a sterilized herring jar from the clutter. "Do you mind? As long as you're here, Karnstein would like another donation."

"The cell cluster." Murray accepted the herring jar. "What sex?"

"Huh?"

"Is it a boy or a girl?"

"I don't remember. Female, I think."

As Murray entered the donation room, a reverie enveloped him, a soft maelstrom of cribs, stuffed animals, and strange nonexistent children's books by his favorite authors. What the hell kind of children's book would Kafka have written? ("Gregor Samsa was having a really yucky morning...") He stared at Miss October for 1968. Meiosis was obviously the last thing on her mind.

Sacrifice. They were going to kill his embryo. Kill? No, too harsh a word. At the Preservation Institute they did science, that was all.

He looked at his watch. Five-seventeen.

They were going to butcher his only baby girl with a scalpel. They were going to tear her cell from cell.

Dr. Frostig's staff had probably left. The decision was actually quite simple: if the lab were locked, he'd go home. If not, he wouldn't.

He crossed the hall, twisted the knob. The door swung open. What was he going to do with a baby? Twilight leaked through the lab's high, solitary window. The liquid thumpings of the glass womb synchronized with Murray's heartbeats. He flipped on the light, picked up the wooden platform and its contents, and staggered back into the hall. A baby. He was holding a damn baby in his arms.

Slipping into the donation room, he set the machine beneath the furry crotch of Miss June for 1972. Best to wait until the Revelationists were gone. If mere artificial insemination were sinful by their standards, inverse parthenogenesis would give them cat fits.

He checked the plastic tubes for kinks, just as Frostig had done. What made him think he could get away with this? Wasn't he the first person they'd come looking for? A good thing his cell cluster was too young to see the dozens of naked women surrounding her. All those breasts, they'd put her in a tizzy.

The door squealed open. Murray shuddered and jumped. His heart seemed to rotate on its axis.

"Oh, I'm sorry," said a tall black donor with a rakish mustache. Sauntering forward, he pulled a herring jar from his sports coat "Thought the place was empty."

"That's all right." Feebly Murray attempted to cover his crime, sidling toward the stolen womb and standing before it in a posture he hoped was at once protective and nonchalant. "I'm finished."

"With all those grants they keep getting"—the donor grinned slyly—"you'd think they could put some *black* chicks in here." He pointed to the womb. "Are the fancy ones just for white folks? All I ever get is a herring jar."

"It's an ectogenesis..."

"One Forty-seven."

"Huh?"

"I'm Donor One Forty-seven." The black man clasped Murray's hand and shook vigorously. "Actually I wear several hats around here. Up on the third floor I'm Marcus Bass."

One Forty-seven. Murray had heard that name before. "You're a marine biologist, aren't you?"

"Western civilization's top man in mollusks, I'm told."

"I met one of your recipients today. She decided on you after—"

"No, buddy, no—don't tell me anything about her." Dr. Bass gestured as if shooing a fly. "A man can't trust himself with that sort of knowledge. You start trying to find your kid—just to see what he looks like, right?—and you end up doing everybody harm."

Murray sighed sharply, exhaling a mixture of disappointment and relief. So: his caper was over; he might have smuggled his embryo past an ordinary donor but not past a clam expert. It was all right, really. Fatherhood was nothing but work. "Then you know this is really an—?"

"Ectogenesis machine, prototype stage." Dr. Bass offered an ambiguous wink. "Frostig would be awfully upset if it disappeared."

"I just wanted to *be* with it for a while. This time they've got a human embryo inside. The egg's a mystery, but the seed came from me. Inverse partheno . . . you know."

"You're Katz, aren't you?" That wink again, mischievous, subversive, followed by a friendly squeeze on the shoulder. "Quite a dilemma, huh? Know what I'd do in your socks, Mr. Katz? I'd pick up this womb and walk out the front door."

"You mean—take it home?"

"It's not *their* inverse parthenogenesis, buddy. It's *yours.*"

Murray shook his head dolefully. "They'd guess right away who stole it."

"Stole it? Let's work on our vocabulary, man. You're *borrowing* it. For nine months, period. Don't worry, nobody'll take it away from you." Marcus Bass gesticulated as if setting up his words on a movie marquee. " 'Sperm Bank Seizes Dad's Embryo.' Frostig would kill to avoid that kind of publicity. He'd *kill.*"

Heartburn seared Murray's chest cavity. Sperm bank seizes dad's embryo: he could actually get away with it.

Assuming he wanted to . . .

"Thing is, Dr. Bass, I'm not sure I—"

"Not sure you want to be a pop?"

Had Marcus Bass used a different word—*father* or *dad*—Murray would not have been moved. "With inverse parthenogenesis, there's no mother," said Murray. Till the day he died, Phil Katz was Pop. "I'd have to do everything myself."

"I'll tell you my personal experience. Before it actually happens, you never realize being a pop is what you always wanted." Marcus Bass pulled out his wallet and unsnapped the fanfold photographs. Four small grinning faces tumbled into view. "A little boy is the greatest thing in the world. Alex, Henry, Ray, and Marcus Junior. They can all swim."

"These ectogenesis machines, are they hard to operate?"

Dropping to his knees, Marcus Bass caressed the pump. "See this cardiovascular device here? Make sure it stays connected to the battery. Ordinary room air oxygenates the blood, so keep the entire unit in a warm, well-ventilated place, and don't let anything block this intake valve."

"Right. Lots of air."

"Every thirty days these liquids should be replenished. This bottle takes regular infant formula, but for this one you need whole blood."

"Blood? Where do I get *that*?"

"Where do you think?" Gently Marcus Bass punched Murray's arm. "From the father, that's where. Just hang around your local fire station—make friends with the paramedics, okay? When the time comes, slip 'em a twenty and they'll gladly stick their transfusion needle in you."

"Fire station. Right. Transfusion needle."

"This third bottle receives waste products and should be flushed clean when full. Baby's first dirty diaper, kind of . . ."

"Regular infant formula—that something I get from a hospital?"

"Hospital? No man, the supermarket. I prefer Similac." Marcus Bass tickled the glass womb with a kitchy-koo finger. "You mix it with water."

Murray joined Marcus Bass on the floor. "Similac . . . how *much* water?"

"Just read the can."

"It comes in a can?" How convenient.

"Uh-huh. A girl, isn't she?"

"So they tell me."

"Congratulations. I imagine girls are the greatest thing in the world too."

When Dr. Bass smiled, Murray had a sudden flash of a two-year-old sitting astride her pop, the horse.

The Reverend Billy Milk, chief pastor of the First Ocean City Church of Saint John's Vision, reached inside his sheepskin coat and caressed his steel detonator. God's wrath was sticky and cold, like an ice-cube tray just removed from the freezer.

Dusk washed across the Institute grounds, bleeding the colors from his flock's protest signs, turning them from angry shouts into moans of discontent. A soft rain fell. Billy looked at his watch. Five o'clock: the demonstration permit had expired. He nodded to his acolyte, Wayne Ackerman the insurance wizard, who in turn signaled the others, and the righteous host disintegrated into a hundred separate suburbanites drifting through the December mist.

Ever since gouging out his right eye, Billy Milk had been burdened with the ocular equivalent of a phantom limb. Just as amputees endured pain and itch in their missing legs, so did Billy endure visions in his missing eye. For six months straight the phantom organ had been showing him God's wishes concerning the Preservation Institute. The jagged flames and billowing smoke. The cracked rafters and broken bricks. The rivers of boiling semen rushing from the shattered foundation.

Ambling past their leader, Billy's flock acknowledged him with discouraged nods and exhausted smiles. A lonely enterprise, this business of being against evil. To see the moral shape of things, to say this is right but that is wrong, was a habit long out of fashion in the United States of America, land of terminal relativism. But wait, brothers and sisters. Have patience. In the next morning's *Atlantic City Press*, Billy's congregation would finally be reading some good news.

Planting the bomb had been harrowing, but since when was God's will an undertaking for the timid? Billy didn't mind telling the receptionist he was a donor—sin happens in the soul, not the tongue—but then came that awful room papered with naked women and obscene letters. The bomb fit neatly under the middle pillow of the couch, right below Miss April for 1970. In what kind of society was it easier to find a full-color photograph of a woman's private parts than a Bible? A diseased society, to be sure. Only the Parousia could cure it—Christ's Second Coming, his thousand-year sojourn in the New Jerusalem.

Rain drumming against his eyepatch, Billy strode down the wharf and peered, Godlike, into his flock's little worlds. Cabin cruisers were paradoxical, wholly private when at sea yet here with their sterns backed into port they baldly displayed a thousands intimacies—Oreo cookie package on the table, paperback Frank Sinatra biography on the bunk, Instamatic camera atop the refrigerator. Reaching *Pentecost*, her white hull shining like the ramparts of the New Jerusalem, Billy scrambled aboard, steadying himself on the three-hundred-dollar marlin rod he'd fixed to the transom. What did it mean to have great wealth? It meant you owned a yacht and a big house. It meant your church was the largest building in Ocean City. It meant . . . nothing.

The Lord tested Revelationists more severely than he did other believers. If a Revelationist's pregnant wife died delivering a premature baby, the ordeal did not end there. No, for Billy's infant son had been subsequently placed in an incubator, where the supplementary oxygen had choked the undeveloped blood vessels in his eyes; his son had been scarred by air. When Billy first heard that one-day-old Timothy would never see, he had reeled with the incredulity and outrage of Job, puncturing the delivery room's plasterboard wall with his bare fist, penetrating all the way to the nursery itself.

Billy Milk had a yacht, and a church, and a sightless son, and nothing.

No sooner had he entered the cabin when dear old Mrs. Foster sashayed over, waving a supermarket tabloid called *Midnight Moon* in his face. "The coming thing," she exclaimed, pointing to an article about a British zoo that trained pets for visually impaired children. In the accompanying photograph, a harnessed chimpanzee led a blind girl across a playground. "By the time Timothy's three, he'll be ready for a seeing-eye ape," she insisted. A smile spread across her flat face, its skin brown and crinkled like a used tea bag. "Orangutans are the cheapest, but the chimps are smarter and easier to care for."

"I appreciate your concern," said Billy impatiently, "but this isn't for Christian children." Mrs. Foster was a good nurse, a devout Revelationist, but she lacked discretion.

"I'm going to ask God about it. I'm going to pray."

"Yes. Do that." Billy stalked off, certain the Lord would forgive him his snappishness with Mrs. Foster. He hadn't seen Timothy since lunch.

Creeping into the forward stateroom, he approached the little berth. Two-year-olds slept so cleanly, not like men with their snores and tossings, their foul dreams. Gently, he brushed Timothy's blanket, his stuffed bunny, his diapered rump pushing up from the mattress like a cabbage. What a wonderfully squishy world the Lord had made. If only Barbara . . . but she *was* seeing it, she *was*.

Bending over the berth, Billy kissed his son's nape. A mere seventy years or so, and Timothy's tribulation would be over. There was no blindness in heaven. Eternity knew nothing of retrolental fibroplasia.

He went to the wheelhouse and took the broken binoculars from their place between his Bible and his nautical charts. During a temper tantrum, Timothy had shattered the lens in the left-hand barrel. Billy turned the binoculars upside down, aligning its functional eye with his own, and focused on the Institute, cloaked in drizzle and fog. A light burned in a second-floor window. A late worker, most likely. Billy shut his good eye and propped his forehead against the binoculars. So: there would be a boundary to cross after all, that terrible seam along which the laws of God and the ordinances of men parted like halves of the Red Sea. A Revelationist always knew which waves to ride, however turbulent and high.

He yanked the detonator from his sheepskin coat. On both sides of the wharf, his congregation's yachts churned across the darkening bay.

Over a year had passed since Billy had tried making his deal with God. It had seemed so reasonable, so symmetrical. I'll destroy one of *my* eyes, God, and then you'll give Timothy back one of *his*. That's all I ask, an eye for an eye.

Billy had violated himself with Timothy's christening spoon. Infection followed, then surgery. Afterward, Billy had decided against a glass eye. He preferred the feeling of a hole inside himself, a gap reifying the incompleteness of his faith.

But God was not to be trifled with. God did not make deals. The heavenly father, offended, had given the earthly father a second, well-deserved cross to bear, a phantom eye spelling out the exact duties of a believer. *Smite this sperm bank, Billy Milk, remove it from my creation, even if . . .*

Even if there's a lighted second-floor window?
Yes.
Billy pushed the plunger.
Like a seraph's silent whisper the radio command leapt from the wheelhouse to the Institute. The explosion was thunderous and majestic, filling the night with blast-wave overpressures and, if Billy heard correctly, appreciative cheers from heaven. His phantom eye showed him the glorious fruits of it, the *Playboy* centerfolds and *Penthouse* letters bursting into flame, the tainted semen turning to steam. The building's hot guts, its pipes, cables, ducts, and girders, rained down as nameless smoldering shapes.

Mission accomplished! Gomorrah erased! Sodom slain!

The thorns that grew on the path of righteousness did not cut a Revelationist's feet only; no, sometimes they sliced his brow, and sometimes they slashed through his eyepatch and lodged in his brain. Billy determined to inspect the rubble not from guilt— a crusade was not a crime—but only because after you enacted God's will, you were obliged to redeem whoever inhabited the aftermath.

The burning clinic pulsed hotly against his smooth-shaven cheeks as he marched down the wharf and jumped onto the sand. He removed his sheepskin coat, resting it on his shoulder like a soft cross. Ashes swarmed everywhere, a million airborne holes.

The black man was upright, encircled by charred fragments of wall rising from the beach like grave markers. His posture was most peculiar. Had he been pounded into the ground? Either that, or...

The apocryphal climax of Daniel blazed across Billy's inner vision. The two lustful elders falsely accusing Susanna of lying with a young lover... their treachery unmasked... Daniel demanding they be cut in two.

A sharp section of wall had struck the black man's abdomen, bisecting him and simultaneously pinching the wound shut, sealing his torso as if it were a piece of ravioli. "Are you a donor?" Billy asked. What terrible things God's servants were called upon to behold. "'For even now the angel hath received the sentence of God to cut thee in two,'" Billy quoted somberly. People were wrong about angels. Angels were not androgynous choirmasters with lutes and wings. Angels spread judgment and doom.

"Gahhh..." The man's jaw flapped up and down like a grouper's. A strained articulation, but it definitely sounded like *yes*.

"Were you contributing, brother?" The smoke sucked tears from Billy's good eye. The fire bellowed like the Red Dragon of the Revelation.

"Urggg..." The sinner surveyed his divided self with a combination of horror and incredulity. He was losing only a little blood: a surprisingly neat mutilation. He nodded.

"A harsh lesson."

"Never...happened...before..." Tears rolled down his dark cheeks.

"The Savior awaits your acceptance, brother."

The donor was opening up now. Relief blossomed on his face as the heavy bleeding started. Sinful flesh on the outside, and now his sinful colon spilled forth, now his sinful liver. Had he found Jesus? It seemed so—Billy could feel it: the donor had lost his seed and gained his soul.

A foulness clawed the air as the saved man's bowels gave up their contents, and suddenly he was dead.

Marcus Bass was right, Murray decided as he piloted his Saab down Ventnor Avenue—you didn't know you wanted certain things until they became yours. His cell cluster slept beside him, her ectogenesis machine constrained by a seat belt. He whistled a *Fiddler on the Roof* medley. Matchmaker, matchmaker. If I were a rich man. He slapped his palm joyfully against the steering wheel. Inverse parthenogenesis did wonderful things for you; it hit you like music, like an idea, like a kiss from God.

Rain spritzed out of the sky. Murray turned on the wipers. The blades sketched ugly muddy streaks on the windshield. He didn't care. The glorious day kept rushing at him, bright memories refracted through the bell jar of his newfound fatherhood. Regular infant formula, is that what Dr. Bass had said? Yes, yes, all it could eat, a hundred meals a day for a ravenous placenta.

As he entered Margate, an explosion shattered the dusk. He pulled over, stopping by a boarded-up drugstore. Had his cell cluster heard the blast? Was she frightened? He got out. A red

glow filled the seaward sky like a misplaced sunset. Undoubt-
edly this disaster mattered to someone, to lots of people, but not
to him, not to a man with an embryo.

Driving away, Murray patted the jar. The glass vibrated with
the comforting thumps of the oxygenation process. Hush, little
girl. Don't be afraid. Pop's here.

He maneuvered through the bleak urban battlefield called Atlantic City, then headed over the bridge. Across the inlet lay the
northern arm of the famous Boardwalk, at one time a prestigious
site for vacations, but then had come jet travel and cosmopoli-
tanism, and the wealthy had begun summering on the Riviera.
There was talk now of resurrecting the place through Las Vegas-
style casinos. Legalized gambling, people said, would save Atlantic City.

Lured by the full moon, waves grabbed at the rocks along
Brigantine Point, as if trying to gain purchase. Harsh winds
wrapped around Murray's lighthouse, peeling a shingle from the
cottage roof, hurling it across the bay. Hunching over his embryo
to shield her from the rain, he ran into the cottage and set the
womb beside his propane-gas heater.

Fatherhood changes you for the better, Murray realized. In
the old days, he'd always climbed the tower at a measured pace,
but now he took the steps two at a time. And this too was his
embryo's doing: filling the tank to the brim, raising the clockwork lens, and igniting the four concentric wicks—*Baruch atah
Adonai elohanu melech ha-olam* . . . "Blessed art Thou, O Lord our
God, King of the Universe, who has taught us the way of holi-
ness through the Mitzvot, and enjoined upon us the kindling of
the Sabbath light." Always the flame bedazzled him. How like a
living creature it was, a high-strung pet sharing his habitat,
barely tolerating his presence. He wound the lens motor and, as
the cut-glass prisms threw twirling spiderwebs on the floor,
looked south. A fire raged somewhere near the Preservation Institute.

Heart pounding, he descended to the cottage and got his embryo, bringing her up the helix of stairs and setting her before
the beacon's nourishing warmth. As the fifty-pound lead piston
glided downward, forcing kerosene into the wick chamber, the
glow filled the whole room and turned the jar into a golden ark.
It would be tough having a baby around. How would he know

when to start feeding her? When to stop? More wick. The beam shot from the tower. He tracked the light as it passed over the bay, skewering fog, melding with stars; look here, the light said to all the ships at sea, look at me, Murray the hermit and his beautiful embryo. See: inverse parthenogenesis has come to Atlantic City, and I thought you all should know.

Piloting his cabin cruiser away from the burning sperm bank, Billy Milk watched as God calmed the bay and sucked the storm clouds up into heaven. *Pentecost* retreated under a clear sky. The northern shore shimmered with the fall of the Preservation Institute. All across the peninsula, fire sirens screamed—machines in pain, technology judged and punished.

Somebody had turned on the old Brigantine Lighthouse. An empty gesture—the Coast Guard beacon on Absecon Island had ten times the intensity and range. Yet the Brigantine lamp burned brightly, a candle blazing upon an altar of rock.

The December stars were like the lights of a great city. Rome, Damascus, Antioch. But the greatest city of them all had been foretold in the Book of Revelation. The New Jerusalem, whose glow was like a jasper stone's.

What did it mean to have great wealth? It meant you could obtain things. A yacht, a mansion, a church, perhaps even . . . a city? Yes. Quite so. A city. Between his publishing royalties and his seminar profits, his stocks and his real estate, Billy could actually build the New Jerusalem. Not as a bargaining chip— God did not make deals . . . but surely Jesus would be more inclined to return if proper accommodations awaited him, a metropolis shaped to biblical specifications. The thought stunned Billy. Might he actually trigger the Second Coming?

Slowly, ever so slowly, his phantom eye painted the New Jerusalem across the speckled sky, the seven bejeweled foundations, the twelve gates of pearl, the sparkling river in which Christ would baptize the entire world. Tonight Billy had merely saved a sinner and purged a clinic, but one day . . . one day he would raise up God's city and lure down God's son! Oh, yes, he could practically hear the Savior's booming voice, feel his fiery breath, see his torn feet walking golden streets commissioned by Billy himself!

Phantom eyes cannot be closed, and cities cannot rise until

their sites are cleared. What ground might prove holy enough? A once wicked place, a place whose raw festering sins had been cauterized by Jehovah's hot sword?

Yes.

A battle was coming, then. Babylon besieged and sacked. Billy's brain shook with it, the smoke of her burning, the cries of her slain citizens. Your typical denominational Protestant could never face it. Every Sunday millions of them sat in their pews staring at Bibles, refusing to confront the final book, but there it was, in every tepid little Episcopalian and Methodist church: the Revelation to Saint John, that compendium of apocalypse and slaughter, of blood-robed armies marching on Babylon, of sinners cast into the lake of fire and crushed in the winepress of the wrath of God. But Billy's Revelationists could face it. Oh, yes, oh, yes...

Alas, alas that great city Babylon, that mighty city, for in one hour is thy judgment come!

The Brigantine beacon flared brighter than ever as Billy brought *Pentecost* about and headed for the open sea.

CHAPTER 2

◆　　◆　　◆

Because the mere presence of his embryo brought Murray great joy, he decided to keep her in his bedroom, right on the dresser next to the Instamatic photo of Pop and him riding the now defunct merry-go-round on Steel Pier. Every evening, the minute he got home from Photorama, he would dash up to the glass womb with the eagerness of a twelve-year-old boy visiting his electric trains. Staring at his developing baby through her amniotic sac felt like an invasion of her privacy—but did not parenthood of any kind ultimately invade its object's privacy? And so he watched, a voyeur of ontogeny.

From Stephen Lambert's *Evolution in Action*, Murray had learned ontogeny did not really "recapitulate phylogeny," that is, there was no appearance *in utero* of adult forms from other phyla. Nevertheless, his embryo had a sense of history about her. If only Pop could have been there. Look, Phil Katz would have said, just look at my little *tsatske* growing up. See, she's a herring. Now a turtle. About now we should have...I was right, Murray, an anthropoid ape! Hey, she's a disc jockey already. What's the next stage? A Neanderthal, I should imagine. Yep, right on schedule. Look, a high-school dropout, we've got. A lawyer, Mur. She gets better all the time. And now—am I right?—yes, she's finished. All done. A Jew.

Unfortunately, Angel's Eye was a conspicuous and alluring installation, forever attracting bored teenagers from town and nosy adults from the Brigantine Yacht Club. Whenever he was away, serving Photorama customers or running to the Stop and Shop for a stack of Swanson frozen TV dinners, Murray was haunted by images of goonish intruders peering through his bedroom window, plotting to steal the strange machine on the dresser.

He decided she'd be safer in his laundry room, and so one frigid February morning he drove to Children's Universe and purchased a hundred-and-fifty-dollar crib, the Malibu Natural Babybunk, complete with hardwood endboards, a mobile of plastic geese imported from Sweden, and the Consumer Product Safety Commission's highest rating. After assembling the crib and the mobile, he set the machine on the mattress, then wedged the whole affair between the washer and the drying rack. He felt better. He'd done right. His baby would mature in a secluded and tropical world, its soapy air warmed by the sultry pulse of his electric heater as it dried his clothes and bedding.

As it happened, the day Murray relocated the machine was also the day Georgina Sparks came lumbering up the path to Angel's Eye, laden with a U.S. Army backpack, dressed in a baggy yellow T-shirt asserting that MEN HAVE UTERUS ENVY, and pushing a rusted and spavined bicycle. At first he didn't recognize her. Only after focusing on her pregnancy, which bulked before her like an ectogenesis machine, did he recall the friendly lesbian from the Preservation Institute.

"See?" she said, proudly extending her occupied womb. "I brought it off. Five months down, four to go, and then—pop!— my very own marine biologist."

"You look great," he said admiringly. She did: the second trimester, with its bright complexion and ripe contours.

"You weren't kidding, you really run this thing." Georgina spun toward the lighthouse tower, making her long raven hair swirl. "How very phallic. Can I watch you fire it up?"

"I use it only to commemorate wrecks."

"Tonight we'll commemorate the wreck of the Preservation Institute. You ask me, it was those Revelationist idiots who bombed the place. Hey, wow—you've got your own private ocean here." Murray followed as Georgina wheeled her bike past the tower and headed for the point. "Weird, isn't it?" she said. "If I'd tried picking up my semen a day later, it would've been blasted halfway across South Jersey, and I wouldn't be having this particular baby. Which to my mind raises all sorts of cosmic questions, such as how did you end up being the person you are instead of, I don't know, some turkey who got killed in the Franco-Prussian War?"

Murray grabbed the bike seat, jerking Georgina to a halt. "Somebody blew up the Institute?"

She removed her backpack and pulled out a tattered newspaper clipping. "I could tell you're a person who doesn't keep track of the outside world. Here . . ."

BABY BANK ABORTED, ran the headline. "Longport, New Jersey," Murray read. "Police report that a homemade bomb has destroyed a sperm bank here, killing a forty-one-year-old marine biologist and leveling . . ."

A cloud of hot gas drifted up Murray's esophagus.

Was his reaction at all reasonable? Had the bomb in fact been meant for his embryo?

He kept reading. The First Ocean City Church of Saint John's Vision was cited as a possible suspect, but an indictment seemed unlikely, the case against the protesters being entirely circumstantial. Dr. Gabriel Frostig, interviewed, praised the University of Pennsylvania for offering the Institute a new home, then went on to lament that a valuable piece of technology, the world's only prototype ectogenesis machine, had been vaporized by the explosion.

Vaporized. Good news, Murray realized. Five months ago he'd stolen a glass womb, now suddenly he was just another bookworm with a locked laundry room. Off the hook. Saved. Except he couldn't enjoy it. BABY BANK ABORTED. Somebody was out to get his child . . .

No, a silly notion. Self-centered and paranoid.

He read on. Shock and outrage welled up in him. The murdered biologist of paragraph one was Marcus Bass. He checked and rechecked. Yes, Marcus Bass, whose four boys, sandwiched in his wallet, could all swim.

"Dinner," he croaked. Would any good be served by telling Georgina her fetus's father was dead?

"Huh?"

No. None at all. "You want to stay for dinner? I have spaghetti but no wine."

"I don't drink these days." Georgina patted her biologist. "The pregnancy."

That night he made them an entirely dreadful meal, the spaghetti so overcooked it broke under its own weight, the salad soggy and self-contradictory, part Greek, part tuna. Georgina liked it, or so she said, and subsequently there were other dinners, two or three every week. In Murray, she'd clearly found the ideal audience—for her pregnancy, for her crazy interventionist theories of child-rearing (every baby a latent genius), for her grandiose questions about human existence. She was a non-practicing Catholic and a dabbler in feminist paganism. She was a dreamer and a pragmatist, a hardheaded mystic who used numerology to find her perpetually misplaced keys and pyramidology to keep her Swiss Army knife sharp. She covered her bases. For Georgina Sparks, a brilliant child was at once something you calculated into existence through preschool stimulation and something you allowed to happen through cosmic openness. Don't attempt parenthood before placing both cognitive psychology and the Spirit of Absolute Being in your camp.

After each dinner, Murray, Georgina, and Murray's cat Spinoza would sit on the lighthouse walkway watching sailboats and Revelationist cabin cruisers glide across the bay.

"I have a present for you," she said one evening as the fading sun marbled the sky with reds and purples. She opened her backpack and removed a set of novelty condoms from Smitty's Smile Shop, the Boardwalk emporium she managed, their wrappers emblazoned with portraits of famous discredited clerics: William Ashley Sunday, Charles Edward Coughlin—collect all twenty-six. Murray was touched. Once, before he even knew Georgina, he'd bought a pornographic candle at Smitty's, a birthday gift for Pop, who collected such things. Georgina's life was measured out in paraffin penises, whoopie cushions, latex dog vomit, and windup chattering teeth. She spoke often of getting into real estate. The town was changing, she would note. The casinos were coming. "You got a girlfriend?"

"I'm not very successful with women," Murray confessed.

"I know the feeling." Georgina stood up, her pregnancy eclipsing the moon. She was in her seventh month, Murray in his eighth. "I was nuts about Laurie, I really was—but, Jesus, so noncosmic. I mean, get dinner on the table at six o'clock or the world will end."

Murray contemplated an Aimee Semple McPherson condom.

"In college I slept with quite a few dental hygiene majors. What I really want these days is a child."

Georgina scowled. "A child? You want a child? *You*?"

"You think it would be wrong for me to adopt a baby, raising it all by myself and everything?"

"Wrong? Wrong? I think it would be *wonderful*."

Murray started toward the tower stairs. Good old Georgina. "In my laundry room there's something that'll interest you."

"I've seen plenty of dirty laundry in my time, Mur."

"You haven't seen this."

They descended.

Surrounded by glass, tethered to bottles, sitting fast asleep in her crib, Murray's fetus looked less like a baby-in-progress than like one of the toys she would play with once she arrived.

"What on earth is *that*?"

The glow of the naked light bulb bounced off the bell jar, speckling the fetus's head with stars. Such a face, Murray thought, all flushed and puffy like an overripe plum. "What does it look like?"

"A goddamn fetus."

"Correct." Murray tapped the nearest bottle, abrim with his own blood. "*My* fetus." He'd followed Marcus Bass's instructions exactly, dropping by Brigantine Fire Station No. 2 several times a week and eventually earning sufficient trust among the three paramedics—Rodney Balthazar, Herb Melchior, Freddie Caspar—not only to avail himself of their transfusion rig but to be included in their poker game. "Female."

"But where'd you *get* it?" Georgina asked.

"The Institute."

"And it's alive?"

"Alive and developing. I stole it the day we met." The oxygen pump chugged soothingly. "The semen was mine—nobody knows where the ovum came from. Inverse parthenogenesis."

"What the hell are you talking about?"

"One of my sperm began meiosis without an egg."

"It *did*?"

"An egg of indeterminate origin, at least."

Instantly Georgina's dormant Catholicism awoke. Crossing herself, she whispered "Mother of God" and, quavering with awe, approached the crib. "Wow—I knew God had eggs, I just *knew* it." She grasped the teething rail and took a deep Yogic breath. "You know what we're looking at? We're looking at one of those times when God herself comes barging into human history and gets things cracking."

"God?" Murray spun the Swedish mobile. "You say God?"

"Not *God* God, I mean GOD God. The God beyond God." Georgina splayed her fingers, ticking off her pantheon. "The Spirit of Absolute Being, the World Mother, the Wisdom Goddess, the Overmind, the Primal Hermaphrodite."

Murray said, "I don't even believe in God."

"Listen, there's no way to account for an event like this without bringing in God. This child has a mission. This girl has been *sent!*"

"No, there are other explanations, Georgina. A God hypothesis is going too far."

"Growing a baby in your jism—in a bell jar—you think that's not going far? You've already gone *far,* Mur." Georgina wobbled pregnantly around the room, pounding piles of dirty laundry. "A virgin conception—sensational! Ever see *The Greatest Story Ever Told*? Jewish people probably didn't catch it. John Wayne's the centurion, right, and he gets up on the Mount of Skulls and he says, 'Truly this man was the son of God.' The son—and now the *other* shoe has dropped. Just sensational!"

"Some joker put an egg in my donation, that's all."

"We've got to tell the world about this! We've got to telegram the Pope! First the son, now the daughter! Get it?"

Now the daughter. God's daughter. Murray cringed. He didn't believe in God, but he didn't believe some joker had put an egg in his donation either. "The Pope? The *Pope?* I don't want to tell *anybody,* I'm sorry I even told *you.* Baby bank aborted—remember? Whatever's going on, somebody almost killed her. Already she has enemies. Enemies, Georgina."

His friend stopped pacing; she sat down in his laundry basket.

As she usually did about this time of day, the fetus woke up, yawned, and flailed her stubby arms.

"Hmm," said Georgina at last, absently harvesting socks from the drying rack and pairing them up. "Mur, you're absolutely right—the Mount of Skulls and all that. Jesus Christ's very own sister would certainly have to watch her step, at least till she figured out her mission."

Murray's heartburn returned, a fire-breathing worm in his windpipe. "She's *not* Jesus' sister."

"Half sister." Georgina slammed her palm on the washer, startling the fetus. "Hey, friend, your little advent is safe with me. As far as I'm concerned, she's just the kid down the street, she's never even *heard* of God. Got a name picked out?"

"Name?"

On the morning of Murray's fourth day at Newark Senior High she'd suddenly appeared on his bus, Julie Dearing, wealthy and spoiled—a Protestant princess, Pop would have called her—with a face so gorgeous it could have started a broken clock and a body that should not have been permitted. She had dropped her geography book in the aisle. Murray had picked it up. The relationship never got any deeper.

"Julie." Murray pointed to his fetus's opulent black hair. "Her name's Julie."

"Nice. You know, you've got a golden opportunity here, with Julie out in the open like this. You can begin her preschool education. Talk to her through the glass, Mur. Play music. Show her some flash cards."

"Flash cards?"

"Yeah. Pictures of presidents. Alphabet letters. And fix up this place, will you? It looks like an outhouse. I want to see animals on these walls. Bright colors. This mobile's a step in the right direction."

"Sure," said Murray. "Gotcha. Animals." A smile appeared on Julie's face—ethereal, there and not there, like a cat weaving through the dusk. What enormous potential for intermittent happiness the world offered, he thought. Aberrant or not, *this* was the child that was his, no other, this one, whether she came from a cabbage patch, the Overmind, or the brow of Zeus. His. "I'm scared, Georgina. Baby bank aborted. I want her to have a life."

"The kid down the street. She's just the kid down the street."

"But you really think . . . God?"

"Sorry, Mur. She's a deity. She's here to shake things up."

Bong, bong, bong, came the glassy cadence from the laundry room, like a crystalline clock tolling the hour. They were dining by candlelight, all the electricity between Brigantine and Margate having succumbed to a thunderstorm. Georgina looked up from her plate and smiled, a noose of spaghetti dangling from her mouth. "Something is on the wing," she said. The storm was blowing out to sea; the world seemed scrubbed, the air squeaky clean. "Wing of angel." Georgina the neo-Catholic. "Wing of phoenix." Georgina the pagan priestess.

Tree branches ticked against the kitchen window. Murray retrieved the Coleman lantern from the pantry and ignited the two testicle-shaped mantles. Georgina's swollen belly, so tense and electric beneath her artsy tie-dye smock, bumped against him as together they marched to the laundry room.

And there she was, caught in the Coleman's roaring glow, an aborning baby, battering the glass with her tight little fist. Her sac had ripped, filling the jar to belly depth with amniotic fluid. Hard-edged shadows played across her resolute face. Condensed breath drifted through the machine, so that Julie's efforts to enter the earth suggested the mute gyrations of a creature in a dream. A fissure appeared, then a fretwork of cracks.

"Julie, no!" Murray lurched forward. The jar exploded like a teapot under a hammer, glass fragments hailing against the washer, the amniotic fluid gushing onto the mattress. "Julie!"

On her forehead, blood.

He lifted his wet, squalling baby from the broken womb, and, sliding her over the teething rail, held her to his breast, her cut leaking onto his white wool sweater. The more blood he saw, the happier he felt. His child had a heart. A real heart, like any other baby's, not a ghostly spark, not a supernatural vibration, but a pumping lump of flesh. She was a child, an incipient person, somebody you could take to an ice-cream parlor or a Nets game.

The umbilical cord, he saw, still joined her navel to the placenta. She was not entirely born. But now here came Georgina, Swiss Army knife in hand, cutting the funiculus and tying it off with the dexterity of a boatswain.

"We did it, Mur. A natural childbirth." She yanked a pillow case from the drying rack and pressed a corner against Julie's snake-shaped gash. "Nice Julie, sweet Julie." The baby's squalling subsided into a series of hiccuplike pouts. "It's just a scratch, Julie, honey."

Murray felt embarrassed to be crying this much, but there he was, awash in the arrival of his firstborn. Hefting the dense wriggling bundle, he realized mass was an art form, it could approach perfection: Julie's every gram was correct.

"Hello," he rasped, as if she'd just called him up on the telephone. His hugs should have fractured a bone or two, but love, he sensed, had a high tensile strength; the harder he squeezed, the calmer the creature became. "Hello, hello."

"You'll need a pediatrician," said Georgina. "I'll tell Dr. Spalos to expect your call."

"A woman, no doubt."

"Uh-huh. You should also send for a birth certificate."

"Birth certificate?"

"So she can get a driver's license and stuff. Don't worry, I've been through all this with my midwife. In the absence of an attending physician, there's a form you fill out. Mail it to Trenton, Office of Vital Records, along with the filing fee. Three bucks."

He looked at Julie. Her wound had stopped flowing; the blood on her cheeks was dry. When he pressed his face toward hers, the air rushing from her lungs pushed her mouth into a facsimile of joy.

Three bucks? Was that all? Only three?

Georgina's marine biologist arrived exactly thirty days after Murray's alleged deity—a female marine biologist, her skin the color of espresso beans, a wiry and spirited little bastard who, Murray argued, looked exactly like Montgomery Clift. Together the new parents went to the registrar in the Great Egg Township Department of Health and obtained the necessary filing forms.

"I have to put her name down," said Georgina. "Nothing sounds right."

"How about Monty?" Murray suggested.

"We need something cosmic here."

"Moondust?"

"What's your opinion of Phoebe?"

"Sure."

"You really like it? Phoebe was a Titaness."

"Perfect. She's entirely Phoebe."

Phoebe, Georgina wrote.

That a Spirit of Absolute Being or a World Mother or a Primal Hermaphrodite may have influenced Julie's conception did not stop Murray from worrying about his parenting abilities. Her runny nose, for example. Dr. Spalos kept saying she'd outgrow it. But when? Then there was the milk question. The two dozen parenting books Murray had exhumed at garage sales and flea markets were unanimous in censuring mothers who didn't breastfeed. Every time Murray mixed up a new batch of Similac he read the label, wishing the ingredients sounded more like food and less like the formula for Tupperware.

On clear nights, he and Georgina always fed their infants on the lighthouse walkway.

"Up here, Julie's closer to her mother," Georgina noted.

"I'm her mother. Mother and father—both."

"Not a chance of it, Mur." Georgina transferred Phoebe from one nipple to the other. "Julie was sent. The age of cosmic harmony and synergistic convergence is just around the corner."

"You're guessing." Murray started Julie on a second bottle. What an earnest little sucker she was. Her slurpy rhythms synchronized with the incoming tide. "Nobody knows where that egg came from."

"*I* do. She break any natural laws yet?"

"No."

"Only a matter of time."

Whenever Georgina dreamed up some bizarre new project for fattening Phoebe's brain cells—a carnival, a street fair, a Bicentennial parade—Murray and Julie went along. "They're putting up a casino on Arkansas Avenue," Georgina would say. "I think the girls should see what girders and jackhammers and all that shit look like, don't you?" And so they were off to the Boardwalk, watching a great iron ball swoop through the sky like a BB from heaven and bash down the Marlborough-Blenheim Hotel in preparation for Caesar's Palace. Or: "Trains, Mur! Noise, smells, movement, adventures starting—trains have it all!" And so they drove to Murray's hometown of Newark and toured the terminal, letting their infants soak up the presumably enriching chaos.

The Primal Hermaphrodite—whoever—did not spare Murray the dark side of parenthood. Julie's dirty diapers were no more appealing than any other baby's, her ear infections no less frequent, her cries in the night no less piercing and unfair. Often he felt as if his life had been stolen from him. *Hermeneutics of the Ordinary* was a lost cause, not one sentence added since Julie's birth. Day-care helped, saved Murray's sanity in fact—Farmer Brown's Garden, the best in the business, according to Georgina, who sent Phoebe there three afternoons a week—though the women who ran the place made him uneasy. They were all swooners and gushers, and of course the Katz child, so cute and precocious, gave them plenty to swoon and gush about.

Precocious. Murray couldn't deny it. Only five days after her birth, Julie had rolled over in her crib. By Yom Kippur she was tooling around the cottage on hands and knees. She uttered her first word, *Pop,* at a mere twenty weeks. By eight months she could walk upright, spine straight, left arm swinging back as the right leg went forward, an achievement that proved particularly disturbing to Murray when in the middle of her second year he noticed that among the several media on which she walked— sand, eel grass, the cottage floor—was the Atlantic Ocean.

It was really happening. They'd come for their evening swim, and now, damn, there she was, skipping across Absecon Inlet.

"Julie, no!" He ran to the shore and waded into the shallows. A show-off he could handle, even a prodigy. "Don't *do* that." But not this crap.

She stopped. The water sparkled in the fading sunlight. Murray squinted across the bay. What a marvelous little package she was, standing there with the retreating tide lapping at her shins.

She asked, "What's wrong?"

"We *swim* here, Julie, we don't *walk.*"

"Why not?" she demanded in an indignant whine.

"It's not nice! Swim, Julie! Swim!"

She dove off the bay's surface and into its depths. Within seconds she reached the shallows, toddling toward him on the weedy bottom. A bit on the chunky side, he realized. Julie was a fast girl with a cookie.

Perhaps he'd imagined it all. Perhaps the aberration lay not in Julie but in the water—an extra infusion of salt, causing super-buoyancy. Still, considering the stakes, considering the baby bank aborters and the Mount of Skulls, even the suggestion of water-walking was intolerable.

"Don't *ever* do that again!"

"I'm sorry," she said, smiling softly. "I'll be good, Pop," his daughter promised.

At dinner that night he told Georgina about the episode.

"I believe there was a lot of salt in the bay this morning," he hastened to add.

"Don't kid yourself, Mur. We're experiencing a major incarnation here. Water-walking? Really? Sensational!" Georgina sucked a pasta strand through the *O* of her lips. "Let's do the Philly Zoo tomorrow."

"I'm not a zoo person." Murray shook the Parmesan cheese, the clumps rattling around like pebbles in a maraca.

"Why? You afraid she'll levitate the elephants?"

"I'm not a zoo person, Georgina."

But the zoo went perfectly. Murray identified all the animals for Julie, naming them like Adam, and as she repeated each name in her reedy voice he realized he hadn't known it was possible to love anyone this much, no one had informed him. A regular girl, he told himself. A fast developer, sure. A water-walker, possibly. But at bottom just a regular little girl.

Later, they went to Fairmount Park for a picnic supper of hot dogs and Georgina's health salad. "Look at us," said his friend as evening seeped across the grass, bringing fireflies and cricket songs. "The all-American family. Who'd ever know it's a hermit, a bastard, a dyke, and a deity? Who'd even—?"

Astonishment cut Georgina off. Julie had tuned in the fire-flies, organizing them into constellations. "Go over there," she said, and the insects made a loop-the-loop. "Twist," and they formed long gossamer strands, braiding themselves into an air-borne tapestry.

Murray's bowels tightened. Phoebe squealed with delight: a two-year-old female Montgomery Clift, laughing merrily.

"Well, would you look at *that*!" Georgina squeezed her roll, launching a hunk of wiener into the air. "Absolutely cosmic! Wow!"

"They're only lightning bugs." Murray whimpered like a beaten dog. "I should make her stop."

Julie taught the insects to synchronize their flashes, then grouped them into letters: A, B, C, D...

"Stop? Why?"

"Exactly the sort of thing her enemies are watching for."

The organic billboard floated through the night, flashing, HI, POP, HI, POP.

Georgina scowled. "This reminds me. Er, I don't want to pre-sume, but..." She grew uncharacteristically shy. "You sure you're educating Julie properly?"

"Huh?"

"Well, it seems only logical to me that Jesus Christ's sister should be brought up Catholic."

"What?"

"Catholic. It served me well enough in my early years. I'll probably enroll Phoebe in a catechism class."

Murray snorted. "She's *not* Jesus' sister."

"That remains to be seen. Anyway, Julie would probably do best being brought up Catholic. Either that or Protestant—I'm not prejudiced, though it's a duller religion. Get her in touch with her roots, know what I mean? Put up a Christmas tree. Hide Easter eggs. Kids need roots."

"Easter eggs?"

"I'm just trying to be logical. I don't mean to offend you."

COKE IS IT, the fireflies said.

Offended? Yes, he was. And yet, the next day on his lunch hour, he undertook to explore the terra incognita called Jesus, venturing across town to the Truth and Light Bookstore on Ohio Avenue. God's putative progeny, he felt, he feared, could tell him something about his Julie.

"May I help you?" asked the clerk, a wispy, elderly woman who reminded Murray of pressed flowers. "Are you one of those Jews?"

"One of what Jews?"

"Reverend Milk says that, as the Second Coming gets nearer" —the woman unleashed an iridescent smile—"all you people will start converting to Christianity."

"That remains to be seen." Above Murray's head a painting loomed, a mob of pilgrims swarming over a cross-shaped bridge and sweeping toward a golden, mountainous, fortresslike city captioned *The New Jerusalem.* "Listen, should I buy an entire Bible, or can I purchase the Jesus material separately?"

"The entire Bible *is* Jesus."

"Not the Torah, no."

"Oh, yes."

Jesus was everywhere. Jesus books, Jesus tracts, Jesus posters, Jesus place mats, coffee mugs, board games, T-shirts, phonograph records, videocassettes. Murray pulled a New Testament from the shelf.

"A King James translation?" The clerk flashed *The Good News for Modern Man.* "You'll have an easier time with this one."

King James. Last month, at Herb Melchior's yard sale, Murray had unearthed a biography of England's most literary monarch since Alfred the Great. King James I of England was solid ground, a place to get one's footing before the leap into Jesus. "No, I'll take James. How much?"

"For someone like yourself, a convert and everything—free."

"I'm not a convert."

"To tell you the truth, we're going out of business. Landlord won't renew our lease. Know what Resorts International is giving him for this place? Eight hundred thousand dollars. Can you believe it?"

That night Murray plumbed the Gospels. He did not belong here—it felt like going through somebody else's laundry, like driving somebody else's car—yet he persisted, turning up one disquieting moment after another.

He came upon a parthenogenetic birth.

An episode of water-walking.

The Mount of Skulls.

He found an attempt on the infant's life: *And Herod sent forth and slew all the children that were in Bethlehem and all the coasts thereof, from two years old and under.*

Murray closed his King James. This paradoxical personality whose life was synonymous with his mission, this passive-aggressive prophet who'd gotten himself tortured to death before his thirty-third birthday, this Jew who, despite his subsequent rematerialization, never saw his poor bewildered parents again—was Julie really this man's half sister?

No, no, Georgina and the New Testament aside, the whole notion was preposterous.

And, indeed, for many months afterward, nothing remotely supernatural happened in southeastern New Jersey.

Like most members of his species, Spinoza the cat was boastful of his hunting prowess—aren't you proud of me, isn't it great being on top of a food chain?—but whereas inland cats stalked mice and squirrels, Spinoza specialized in the bounty of the sea. "What's *that*?" demanded Julie, age four, as Spinoza dashed into the cottage one frigid February afternoon, a half-dead something in his jaws.

"A crab," Murray explained. Spinoza carried the carcass to the fireplace as if intending to roast it and dropped it upside down on the hearth. "It's dead."

"But I *like* the crab."

Pinning the crab's corpse under his paw, Spinoza chewed on a leg. "Get away!" Murray shouted, and the cat, spooked, shaped himself into an oblong of fur and scurried off, leaving the inverted corpse to warm by the fire.

Fist crammed with crayons, Julie ran to the hearth. "I don't *want* it to be dead."

"I'm sorry, honey."

She poked the crab's belly with her yellow crayon.

"Leave it the hell alone," ordered Murray.

Now she applied the green. "Poor Mr. Crab." Now the red.

"Leave it alone!"

A crab leg twitched like a thistle in the wind. Giggling, Julie tickled the creature with her purple crayon. Soon all eight legs were in motion, rowing back and forth.

"That's *wrong*, Julie! Stop it!"

But the crab had regained the earth. It stuck out a great claw and levered itself upright. Instinctively, Murray turned. Spinoza was cranking himself down like a catapult's arm, making ready to pounce. Murray scooped up the cat and held him wriggling and hissing against his sweater.

With uncanny speed the crab scuttled forward and, as Julie opened the door, jumped onto the front porch, Spinoza howling all the while, enraged by this sudden reversal of the natural order.

"Julie, I'm mad at you! I'm really *mad*."

The parade—crab, little girl, man with cat—marched down the jetty. After ascending the highest rock, the crab pushed off with all eight legs and dove into the bay.

"Don't ever do that again!" Murray yelled. Spinoza wrested free and, running to the water, began pacing the shore and meowing maniacally. "You hear me?" *And Herod sent forth and slew all the children . . .* What a hateful face Julie wore, all pleased and beaming, cocksure, catproud. "Not *ever*!"

She approached, and he hit her.

They recoiled simultaneously. He'd never done such a thing before, smacking her cheek like that. Her skin reddened, the blotch growing like spilled tomato juice.

Silence. Then: a high, jagged scream. "You hit me! You hit me!"

"No more of this—this *stuff*, Julie. No more water-walking,

no more firefly alphabets, none of it. They're just waiting for you
to do things like this, they're just *waiting*."

"Why'd you hit me?" Her tears ran in all directions, detoured
by her nose.

"They'll take you away."

"Who will?"

"*They* will."

"Take me away?" Julie rubbed her cheek as if nursing a tooth-
ache. *"Take me away?"*

He moved forward, offering whatever of himself she might
choose to smack. She pounded on his chest, and the transition to
hugging happened quickly, like a change of figures in a waltz.

"Things have to stay dead?" she asked, her voice muffled by
his sweater.

"Uh-huh."

"Other children have mommies."

The thumpings of her heart massaged him. *"I'm* your
mommy."

"*God* is my mommy."

"That's a very strange thing to say, Julie."

"She *is*." Julie's turquoise eyes glistened with tears.

"Did Aunt Georgina tell you that?"

"No."

"Georgina told you, right?"

"*No.*"

"How do you know God's your mommy?"

"I *know* it."

Murray held his daughter at arm's length. "Does God . . . er,
visit you?"

"She doesn't even whisper to me. I listen, but she doesn't
talk. It's not fair."

God didn't talk. The best news he'd heard since Garbriel
Frostig announced his embryo. "Look, Julie, it's good she
doesn't talk. God asks her children to do crazy things. It's good
she doesn't whisper. Understand?"

"I guess."

"Really?"

"Uh-huh. Where'd the crab go? Is he looking for his friends?"

A profound weariness pressed upon Murray. "Yes. Right. His
friends. It's *good* God doesn't whisper."

"I got it, Pop."

Exhaustion—and what else moved through him as they stood silently together on the jetty? A justifiable self-pity, he decided. Other fathers worried about getting their girls off drugs. Out of jail. Into Princeton. But Murray Jacob Katz alone had to keep his daughter from ending up on that infamous hill where all those who could fix dead crabs were eventually sent.

CHAPTER 3

♦   ♦   ♦

In the beginning your mother created the heavens and the earth. "Let the waters under the heavens be gathered together unto one place," your mother had said.

Deeper, still deeper, you spiral toward the bay floor, baptizing yourself in the great gathered sea called the Atlantic, heading for your underwater cave and its secret petting zoo. Bubbles tickle your cheeks. Currents comb your hair. Joyously you take a big bite of oxygen from Absecon Inlet—the one miracle you've managed to talk Pop into letting you keep.

"What if I fall in the bay with a rock tied to me?" you asked him. "Can I breathe the water?"

Your father frowned so fiercely his eyebrows met. "Well, I suppose you'd have to. However, Julie, it's *very* unlikely you'd ever fall in the bay with a rock tied to you."

"If I can breathe water instead of drowning, can I sometimes do it for *fun*? Oh, please, Pop, I need to see what's down there."

For an entire minute he said nothing. Then: "Would it be like holding your breath?"

"Sure. Just like holding my breath."

"Well . . ."

So you won. You could give yourself gills. As for your other powers, bringing crabs to life and such, Pop remained unbending: you must never use them. The rule is a part of you, slap-carved on your cheek just as the Jewish God had etched the Law on stone.

"There's a deaf class in our school. Fourteen deaf kids."

"That's unfortunate."

"I won't fix them."

"Good."

"I won't even *think* about fixing them. Not Ronnie Trimble either, who's always in this wheelchair."

You touch bottom. Cool sand gushes between your toes. A gloomy eel, thick and rubbery like a live sausage, bumps your stomach, nipping at the Care Bear bathing suit Pop got you for your birthday.

You loved turning ten, except your mother didn't send anything, not even a lousy card. Phoebe gave you a sweater with cats prowling all over it. Aunt Georgina showed up with a bunch of neat stuff from the Smile Shop: a squirting carnation, sunglasses with windshield wipers on the lenses, a hat outfitted with a can holder and a plastic straw so you could drink a Coke while riding your bike.

Twisting your body like a seal, you swim into the cave. You hate being chunky—your shape resembles a zucchini and you want to be a carrot. Phoebe is a carrot.

Your petting zoo creeps and wriggles over, eager for strokes and tickles. Casually you tune in their soft thoughts. The flounder is hungry. The starfish wants to have babies. The lobster is frightened in some strange lobstery way.

—Hi, Julie, broadcasts Amanda the sponge.

—We shouldn't talk, you reply.

—Why?

—It's like doing a miracle.

—Talking with a sponge isn't exactly stopping the sun, Amanda notes.

—We shouldn't talk.

You glide away, deeper and deeper into the chocolate-frosting darkness.

A year ago, you and Pop sat together on the couch, flipping through a book of famous paintings. In your favorite, "The Birth of Venus," a woman with long hair the color of Tastykake Pumpkin Pie filling stood on a giant scallop shell. You decided this was how your mother would arrive. Here on the bottom of Absecon Inlet, a giant scallop shell would open and God would climb out, swimming to the surface and asking people, "Do you know where my little girl lives? Julie Katz?" "Oh, yes, she's waiting for you. Go to the lighthouse on Brigantine Point." Every night before you fall asleep, the same scene passes behind your eyelids: God appearing at the cottage doorway in a white dress, soaked, dripping, her hair tied back with ribbons of seaweed. "Julie?" "Mom?" "Julie!" "Mom!" Then your mother and father get married, and you all live together in your lighthouse above the petting zoo.

Whiteness flashes on the cave floor. You reach down, poke it with your fingertips. Something hard, buried. You brush the sand away. The more you uncover, you hope, the more there will be to uncover, until at last the scallop's shell is revealed, and it will open, and out will come...

But no. Not a door to heaven but a naked white face, the kind people bring out at Halloween. An eyeless stare, a lipless grin. You keep digging. It's all here, every spooky bone. You shiver. Maybe this is a sailor from one of those wrecks Pop is always talking about, somebody who went down with the *William Rose* or the *Lucy II*. You squeeze his hand—so rough and hard, like coral. You squeeze tighter. Tighter...

Things have to stay dead. They're waiting for you to do miracles. If you do miracles, they'll take you away.

Returning is always tricky. You can't swim straight up. If the lifeguard spots a little kid out that deep, he'll go nuts. Instead you cruise along the floor, watching till you see the swimmers' legs dangling down like the roots of water lilies.

Rising, you break the surface and feel the bright, pounding air on your face. Tourists swarm along the Boardwalk, hopping from casino to casino. At the bottom of the bay, the sun is like somebody else's mother watching over you—quiet, gentle, never strict—but up here it's hot and fierce, the way some people think of God. What good is it having God for a mother if she never sends you a birthday card? Why has God stuck you in this place, this filthy old Atlantic City where the grownups spend all their time playing games? It isn't fair. Phoebe has a mother. Everybody does.

You squint at the dazzling sun and wonder whether, at that moment, God is peering over the edge of heaven and noticing how terrifically her kid can swim.

*　*　*

Before they could graduate fourth grade, Julie and her classmates all had to write essays entitled "My Best Friend." The problem, of course, was how to talk about Phoebe without landing them both in trouble. "The thing I most enjoy about having Phoebe Sparks for a best friend," Julie began, "is that she's a lot of fun to be with."

Thanks to Phoebe, Julie was growing up skilled at throwing rocks through the widows of Atlantic City's vacant hotels and sneaking into the swimming pools of its inhabited ones. Within a single month, Phoebe had taught Julie how to smoke cigarettes, spray graffiti on boxcars, fly alphabet kites that spelled out dirty words, and stand on a railroad bridge and launch an arc of pee into the air just like a boy.

"My best friend and I like to sell Girl Scout cookies together," Julie continued her essay.

The props that figured in so much of their mischief came from Smitty's Smile Shop. It was a rare evening when Aunt Georgina, who knew how a mother should behave, did not bring home a joy buzzer, fart spray, or something equally fine. "Half orphans like us, we're always spoiled," Phoebe noted as Julie beheld her treasures, which Phoebe kept in a saddlebag slung over the wooden stallion they'd stolen from the wrecked merry-go-round on Steel Pier.

"What do you mean, spoiled?"

"We get what we want. That's because our parents know they should've married somebody."

"You ever think your father will show up, Phoebe? You know, come walking through the front door one night in time for dinner?"

"I think it all the time. He's a marine biologist, Mom says. Very smart and brilliant." Phoebe dredged up a string of firecrackers. "It's weird, I never saw his picture or anything, but I can still imagine him standing here in his marine uniform, looking through his microscope."

"Know what I think?" Julie fished out the rubber turd they liked to stick in slot-machine payoff boxes. *The machine's pooping!* they would scream, which always drew a crowd. "I think *your* mother and *my* father should get married."

Phoebe freed a firecracker from the pack and stuck it in her mouth like a Marlboro. "Can't ever happen."

"Why not?"

"You're too young to understand."

"I'm older than you."

"You wouldn't get it," said Phoebe, puffing on her fire-cracker.

"Hopscotch and jump rope are a few of the many games my best friend Phoebe and I play together," Julie wrote.

Two days before her tenth birthday, Phoebe decided to throw herself "an early party, just you and me, Katz," at the abandoned Deauville Hotel, whose crumbling remains adjoined the slick new casino called Dante's.

The sunken door on St. James Avenue was only slightly ajar, but skinny Phoebe had no trouble slipping around it. Once inside, she gave the door a hard kick, making a gap so wide both Julie and her A & P grocery bag fit through easily.

The basement was dark and soggy. It smelled like a diaper pail. Phoebe led the way up a groaning staircase to a restaurant called Aku-Aku. Broken glass speckled the floor; grubby white cloths covered the tables; dust lay everywhere like newly fallen snow. Phoebe clunked her mother's army backpack on the nearest table and pulled out six aluminum cans yoked together with plastic. Julie's stomach flip-flopped. This wasn't Coke.

"Where'd you get those?" Julie asked. Beer. Budweiser.

"Free." Phoebe pulled up a dusty chair and sat. "When you're a thief, stuff is free." The mural across the room showed a frowning stone idol rising amid a cluster of palm trees on a South Seas island. Blue waters lapped against sands as clean and white as artificial sweetener. "Let's go there sometime." Phoebe peeled off two Buds. "We can't spend our whole lives in this yucko city." She ripped open her beer, jamming the circular tab onto her little finger like a ring.

"Good idea," said Julie. The idol's eyes were crescent-shaped, like half-moons on the doors of two adjacent outhouses. Its thick lips were puckered in a perfect circle.

Phoebe guzzled half the can. "Bud's the best, Katz, and that's the truth. Bud's the best." Burping with satisfaction, she dragged her wrist across her foamy smile.

Julie opened her A & P grocery bag and drew out the rest of their feast—a box of pretzels, a bag of chocolate-chip cookies, a big bottle of Diet coke, and four waxily wrapped packages of Tastykake Krumpets.

"Excellent selections. Truly excellent." Phoebe polished off her beer in three greedy gulps. "Hey, know how I'm feeling right now? Know how? I'm feeling how it feels to be drunk. Try some, kid. Come in here with me."

Julie pulled the tab from her Bud and took a mouthful. She shuddered. Ants in spiked heels danced on her tongue. Wincing, she swallowed. "Yech."

"This is the life, eh?" Phoebe laughed like a roomful of morons and tore open her second Bud. "Hey, now that I'm drunk, I can tell you just how weird I think you are, how totally and completely weird. You're weird, Katz."

"Weird? *I'm* weird. You're the one who pees off bridges."

"Last night I heard our parents talking about your godhead. What's your godhead?"

"I don't know." She didn't, though it probably had something to do with her mother.

"Sure you do. Tell me. No secrets."

"I think it's what makes a girl a virgin."

"Really?"

"Yeah."

The Tastykake Krumpets came three to a package: three wondrous bricks of sponge cake mortared together with butterscotch icing. Phoebe ate an entire set in one stupendous bite, washing them down with beer. "Bud's *so* good," she said weakly, limping toward the wall like somebody walking barefoot on a hot sidewalk. "Let's save those other Krumpets for later."

"Happy birthday, Phoebe."

"Thanks, Katz. I have an announcement to make. Guess what?"

"What?"

"I'm going to be sick." A dopey smile crossed Phoebe's face, and she threw up on the South Seas mural.

Julie jumped to her feet. The stone idol wore a beard of puke. "Gosh, Phoebe—you okay?" The restaurant already smelled so bad that Phoebe's vomit made no difference.

"The beer's too damn warm, that's the problem." Phoebe pulled a tattered cloth from the nearest table and wiped her mouth. "Never drink beer when it's warm. Now you know."

"Now I know."

Julie wanted to go home, but Phoebe insisted the party had barely begun. Together they explored the Deauville's upper floors, wandering the rubble-strewn hallways, swallowing dust, inhaling mildew. They shouted "Asshole!" and "Pissface!" into the elevator shafts, giggling at the dirty echoes.

"Let's split up," said Phoebe. Standing on one thin brown leg, leaning toward the empty shaft, she looked like a pair of scissors. "You take the high road."

"Huh? Why?"

"More of an adventure that way. Whoever finds the neatest stuff gets to eat the other Krumpets."

"The Krumpets? I thought you were feeling sick."

"Nothing like a good barf to make a person hungry."

"What *sort* of stuff?"

"I don't know. Something real neat. Meet me in the lobby in half an hour. Bring something neat."

The rooms were all the same. Glass fragments. Ratty carpets. Bare mattresses, their springs breaking through the stuffing like a complex fracture or some other gross example from the Girl Scouts' first-aid handbook. The hotel, Julie decided, was like one of Pop's wrecked ships, *William Rose* or *Lucy II*, tossed up on shore. Maybe she'd been wrong about God's arrival. It could happen as easily on land as underwater. God might even appear in a hotel room—a spray of divine light rushing from a shower nozzle, shaping itself into a mother.

Julie visited the bathrooms, testing them. All the showers were dead. Whenever she flushed a toilet, a great moan arose, as if the Deauville could no longer perform even the simplest functions without pain.

Room 319. She looked in the bathroom mirror. Her eyes were as turquoise as Somers Bay; her dark hair was long and wild like the fur on the Wererat of Transylvania suit Aunt Georgina had made Phoebe for Halloween. (Phoebe always went trick-or-treating in the casinos, bringing home scads of quarters.) Her chin was chubby, her forehead bore a thin scar, and her nose, while nicely shaped, turned up slightly, as if she'd been punched by an elf. Her best feature was her skin, which had the smooth brownish gloss of a caramel apple.

She left 319 and went to the gym—at least, that's what it must have been. Sunbeams slanted through the glass ceiling, igniting the dust specks that swarmed around the parallel bars and broken trapeze. Rings hung down like nooses. Across the room, beyond a shattered wall, lay an empty swimming pool, big as a dinosaur's grave.

Near the deep end, a man sat on a plastic lounge chair, the kind people brought to the beach.

"Hello." His friendly voice bounced all over the room. He wore a red terrycloth bathrobe and an equally red swimming suit. Black-lensed sunglasses masked his eyes. "Welcome to my casino." One hand gripped a glass of iced tea, the other a book. "Don't be afraid."

"You must be lost, mister." If he came toward her, she could easily get away: there was a whole swimming pool between them. "The casino's next door."

"That's the *old* Dante's. We're expanding. Once we knock this hotel down, we'll have the biggest damn operation on the Boardwalk." The man's tongue shot into his tea and curled around an ice cube, drawing it into his mouth. "It's not easy running a casino, child, so many details—separate accounts for mobsters, bogus fill slips, falsified markers. Silly to pay more taxes than we have to, eh?" He snapped the book shut and pulled a small silver box from his bathrobe pocket. "You may call me Andrew Wyvern. My other names are legion. You're Julie Katz, aren't you?"

"How'd you know?"

"From going to and fro in the earth, and walking up and down in it. Come here, sweetheart. I have something special for you."

"I don't think I should."

"It's a message. From your mother."

"My mother?"

"God's one of my best friends. Read Job."

A delicious warmth rushed over Julie, as if all her petting zoo creatures were rubbing against her. Her mother! He knew her mother! "What message?"

"Come here. I'll tell you."

Julie climbed into the shallow end. Rotten wrestling mats filled the pool; cracks and fungus wove through the tiles. She scurried up the far ladder. Mr. Wyvern had a queer sweet smell, like oranges soaked in honey. "What does she look like?" Julie asked. "Is she pretty?"

"Oh, yes, very pretty." He drummed his large, popcornlike knuckles against the book. Strange title: *Malleus Maleficarum*. "She's just the way you imagine her."

"Yellow hair? Real tall?"

"You got it." Mr. Wyvern flipped open the silver box. One side was filled with cigarettes, the other was a mirror.

"You shouldn't smoke," said Julie.

"You're right. Disgusting habit." He rubbed the warts on his knuckles. "It stunts my growths." Sunlight shot across the mirror, and then a peppery mist appeared, like static on a television screen. The mist parted, and there stood a boy in a bathing suit, looking lost and frightened. "Study this boy's face. One day you'll meet him."

"I'll meet him? When?"

"Soon enough."

The boy in the mirror blinked rapidly. "What's his name?"

"Timothy. Notice anything strange about him?"

"His eyes..."

"Yes, Julie. Totally blind. The doctors couldn't cure him. But *you* could."

"Pop says no miracles."

"Yes, I know, and your father's very smart. However, in this one case, we must make an exception. 'Ask Julie to cure Timothy'—your mother's exact words."

"My mother said that?" It seemed as if the beer were back, scuttling along her tongue and into her throat. "But they'll take me away."

"Not after just one miracle—no."

"You sure?"

"Your mother's best friend wouldn't lie to you." Mr. Wyvern smiled. His teeth looked like shiny new pennies. "One more thing. Don't tell your father about our little meeting. You know how frantic he can get." The cigarette case clacked shut. "Don't forget —the boy's name is Timothy. Watch for him. Our special secret."

And then he was gone.

Julie blinked. Gone. The man, his book, tea, cigarette case— replaced by a wispy white cloud drifting above the lounge chair.

"Mr. Wyvern?" Maybe she'd been dreaming. "Mr. Wyvern?" A soft wind, nothing more.

Julie dashed across the gym and down the stairs, her heart pounding like a basketball being dribbled.

Phoebe was in the lobby, tossing bricks at the chandelier.

"This amazing thing just happened! I met somebody who

knows my mom!" Her friend, Julie noticed, had a bundle of fat red sticks tucked under her arm. "Hey, what're *those*?"

"What do you think? Dynamite, Katz, as in *kaboom*. It's all over the place. They must be planning to zap this building tomorrow."

"Dante's Casino is taking over," Julie explained. "You'd better return them."

"Return them? You crazy?" Phoebe slipped the dynamite into the army backpack. "So, how about it? Do I win the Krumpets? You find any neat stuff?"

"Not really." A ghost. A magic cigarette case. A message from heaven. "No."

"*Who* knows your mom?"

Julie shrugged. "Nobody special. He smells like oranges."

"Look, I'll give you one of the Krumpets anyway. Maybe we'll even try some more beer."

"Because of Phoebe, I got my first taste of pink lemonade," Julie concluded her fourth-grade essay. "All in all, a person couldn't ask for a better best friend than Phoebe Sparks."

Andrew Wyvern baits his hook with a *Lumbricus latus*, the twenty-four-foot worm hell's surgeons routinely implant in the intestines of the damned, and tosses his line off Steel Pier. Halfway across Absecon Inlet, the Atlantic caresses his schooner, lifting it up and down on its hawser like a mother rocking her baby. The line tenses, the bobber goes under. Wyvern yanks on the rod, savoring the lovely pizzicato of the hook tearing through the fish's cheek.

But he is not happy. Everywhere he looks, Christianity is in decline. It no longer burns Giordano Bruno for saying the earth moves past the sun, or Michael Servetus for saying blood moves through the lungs. The slaughter of the Aztecs is a mute memory, the fight against smallpox inoculation a vanished dream, the *Index Librorum Prohibitorum* a forgotten joke, the *Malleus Maleficarum* out of print. From pole to pole, Christians are feeding the hungry and clothing the naked. Just last week, Wyvern heard a Baptist minister say it was wrong to kill.

True, the sect called Revelationism holds some promise, but the devil doesn't trust it. "Revelationism," he tells the snagged fish, "is a flash in the pantheon." No, there must be a new religion, a faith as apocalyptic as Christianity, fierce as Islam, repressive as Hinduism, smug as Buddhism. There must be a church of Julie Katz.

With a sudden tug Wyvern pulls his catch from the water—a hammerhead shark, seaweed trailing from its mouth like dental floss. The walleyed monster thuds onto the pier and flops around as if being pan-broiled.

Unfortunately, God's daughter is not by nature a proselytizer. Indeed, if her meddling father gets his way, she'll simply live out her life, never going public. So the plan must be clever, each separate trap—Timothy Milk's ruined eyes, Beverly Fisk's purple gown, Bix Constantine's supermarket tabloid—deployed with cunning and finesse, lest Wyvern's fondly imagined church remain mired in the future like a *Lumbricus* inhabiting a sinner's gut.

Glowing with hope, burning with dreams, the devil pets the shark, enjoying its sandpaper flesh against his palm. Too bad he's a vegetarian. Shark meat, he has heard, is delicious.

Before becoming a center for gluttony, drinking, and carousing, a place for courting venereal disease and sitting at green felt tables despairing that your next card may put you over twenty-one, Atlantic City was famous as a health spa, a kind of saltwater Lourdes, and in the summer of Julie's eleventh year it seemed the place had grown nostalgic for its virtuous past. The sun gave off a lubricious warmth that seeped into the gamblers' bones and made them sleep soundly through the night. Salt-laced breezes wafted into its beneficiaries' noses and throats, healing inflamed tonsils and curing sinusitis.

Every morning after breakfast, Julie and Phoebe would pedal down to Absecon Beach, their bike baskets jammed with plastic buckets and aluminum lunch boxes, and spend the day constructing elaborate sand castles, complete with battlements made of oyster shells, moats guarded by killer scallops, and secret chambers where fiddler crabs scuttled about like outer-space creatures plotting court intrigues on a distant planet. Such enterprise did not represent a return to innocence. The point, always, was for Queen Zenobia and the Green Enchantress—such were Julie's and Phoebe's secret identities—to blow the castles up. Not crudely, not abruptly; this was not a job for Phoebe's dynamite. Each castle must fall in stages, piece by piece, spire by spire, as if under siege from an army of lobsters equipped with

nineteenth-century artillery. Aunt Georgina supplied the necessary technology—the firecrackers, sky rockets, Roman candles,
and cherry bombs, unsold items from the illegal fireworks inven-
tory that made the Fourth of July as important to Smitty's Smile
Shop as Christmas was to a toy store.

"Hey, Katz, it's a chimpanzee! An actual goddamn chimpanzee!"

Julie targeted a buzz bomb to sail over the west rampart of
Castle Boadicea—Aunt Georgina had suggested they name their
constructions after great women warriors—and hit the main
tower. "Chimpanzee? Where?"

But already Phoebe was off, running toward the decaying remains of Central Pier.

An old black woman in a nurse's uniform lay snoozing on a
deck chair, her crinkled body shaded by a red beach umbrella to
which a chimpanzee—Phoebe was right, an actual goddamn
chimpanzee—was tied by a leather leash. Were the chimp to
panic, Julie realized, it would pull the umbrella down like Samson wrecking the Temple of Dagon. (You're Jewish, Pop told her
whenever they finished reading a Bible story. You should know
these things.) Arriving on the scene, Phoebe let the chimp sniff
her butt and legs, then sniffed him in the same places. She
turned to the chimp's companion, a kid about their age sitting
exactly where the shadow of the umbrella met the sunstruck
sand: his white body seemed split, half dark, half light. Fuzzy
smiles appeared on his face as he talked with Phoebe and
pressed his hands into the wet sand. He was blind.

Julie's intestines kinked up. Blind as Samson. Blind as a rock.
Blind as the boy in Andrew Wyvern's mirror.

Now Phoebe was heading back, chimp following, blind boy
in tow like a water skier.

"We can't play with the monkey," Phoebe explained, reaching
the castle. The chimp smelled like used socks. His fur was matted, his eyes wet and yellow. "He's on duty," said Phoebe. "He's
a seeing-eye monkey. This kid comes with him."

The sand inside Julie's bathing suit nipped her rear like fleas.
No miracles, Pop kept saying. They'd take her away.

"An *ape*, not a monkey," the boy insisted. His hair was the
color of boiled carrots. Freckles spattered his round face. Sunken
and forever twitching, his eyes were like newborn gerbils living
in his head. "A chimpanzee."

Cure him, Mr. Wyvern had said. Your mother wants you to Your mother whose best friend would never lie to you . . .

"Sorry," said Phoebe. "Julie, this is Arnold."

"Arnold?" said Julie. "I thought it was Timothy." Not the right blind boy? She was off the hook?

"*I'm* Timothy," he said. "My *chimp's* Arnold."

The ape stank. The sun was sickeningly hot.

"How'd you know his name was Timothy?" asked Phoebe.

"Yeah—how?" asked Timothy.

"Lucky guess."

"We're about to blow up a castle," Phoebe announced proudly. "Roman candles, cherry bombs."

"Wish I could see fireworks," said Timothy. "They sound so strange, all fat and mad."

No miracles. Her mother wanted Timothy to see. They'd take her away. Her mother wanted . . . if Timothy got his new eyes, would her mother finally show up? Descend from heaven on a shining cloud, her arms jammed with strange and wonderful birthday presents for Julie from every planet in the universe?

Julie glanced toward Central Pier. The nurse still slept.

A miracle, Julie knew, took more than thinking. You needed objects. *Stuff.* To resurrect a dead crab, you poked him with your crayons. To cure the blind . . .

She removed a plug of sand from the main tower and, spitting on it, pushed it against the boy's left eyelid. Arnold squealed. Timothy drew back. "Hold still!" The boy froze. A soft buzz traveled out of her fingertips and looped around the dead eye.

"What're you doing?" Phoebe asked.

"Fixing him." Her pulse doubled, her palms grew damp. "I think." She pried another plug of sand out of Castle Boadicea and started on the right eye. "Hold still!"

"You're *what*?" said Phoebe.

Julie stepped back, studying the boy as if she'd just finished molding him out of Play-Doh. He brushed the wet sand away, running his fingertips over his eyelids. His hair burned with reflected sunlight. He blinked.

"I can do things sometimes," said Julie.

"What's going on?" Timothy shivered in the August heat.

"Do things?" Phoebe snickered.

Timothy's eyelids fluttered like hummingbird wings.

"What's going on?" he repeated, teeth chattering.

Arnold, frightened, forced himself between the girls, his fur warm and twitchy against Julie's bare legs. The boy's milky gaze traveled back and forth: girl, ape, girl. Nothing showed in his face, not a crumb of understanding. Girl, ape, girl. I've failed, thought Julie. Girl, ape, girl. For better or worse, I've—

"Which one of you's Arnold?"

"Huh?" said Phoebe.

"Who's Arnold?" Timothy thrust his index finger toward Phoebe. "You're not, are you? You're a *girl*, right?"

"Damn straight," said Phoebe, dancing crazily like a windup bear from her mom's store. "God, Julie, you did it! You actually did it! God!" She faced Timothy and tapped his seeing-eye chimp on the head. "Here's what a monkey looks like, kiddo. God!"

"Ape."

Julie took a large swallow of sea air. Between her thighs she felt an odd pleasurable quaking.

Phoebe kept dancing. "This is amazing stuff, Katz! We can make money with this! How the hell'd you *do* it?"

"I have powers," said Julie.

"Powers?" said Phoebe. "From where?"

"God."

"Could I get some?"

"I'm God's daughter."

"What?"

"Her daughter."

"God's? God's? I always knew you were nuts, but . . . *God's?*"

"God's."

Timothy moved his palm along the plane of the Atlantic. "It's so *flat*. I thought it was round." He spun toward Julie and made a quick, cymbal-crashing gesture. "*You* fixed me, didn't you?"

A sudden nausea came, hard and steady, like a gambler pumping a slot machine. No more miracles. They'd take her away. "Let me tell you something, Timothy." She grabbed his bare, sweaty shoulders. "You blab this to anyone, I'll make you blind again."

The boy stumbled backward. "Don't! Please!"

"Say you'll never blab!"

"I'll never blab!"

"Say it again!"

"I'll never blab! Never, never, never!"

Julie whirled around. She had cured him! She wasn't Queen Zenobia, she was God's daughter! The pleasurable throb returned: warm, wondrous shocks fluttering upward from her vagina. For all her darkness, Phoebe seemed suddenly pale. Yes, friend, God's daughter isn't somebody to mess with. Trip up God's daughter, and your body becomes a sack of blisters.

"Hey, you can count on me," Phoebe said weakly. "It's all locked in my head and the key's gone down the toilet."

"Good."

Julie took a matchbook from her lunch box, lit the main fuse. She faced her miracle. He'd pulled the front of his bathing trunks away and was staring into the space where his legs met. "I had to see what it looked like," he said, letting the trunks snap against his belly.

Castle Boadicea exploded like a peacock going nuclear, sparks and flames everywhere, a beautiful sight, perfect. The main tower, implanted with firecrackers, rose two inches into the sky before collapsing. The moat, mined with Saran-wrapped cherry bombs, overspilled its banks in great waves of foam.

Phoebe whooped and cheered.

Arnold ran around in circles, issuing high, nervous, birdish chirps.

Timothy cried, "Oh, wow!"

The nurse woke up and screamed.

"Time to leave, buddy," said Julie, hooking her finger under Phoebe's shoulder strap.

"Wow!" said Timothy.

"What *else* can you do?" Phoebe trembled with wonderment. "Can you make people happy?"

Dragging Arnold by his leash, Timothy ran toward Central Pier, clear-eyed and on a straight course. "Mrs. Foster, Mrs. Foster, I've got something to tell you!"

Again the nurse screamed.

"Mrs. Foster!"

Julie took off, Phoebe chuffing behind. Faster and faster they ran, pell-mell across the beach, kicking up sand clouds, and now came the battered steps, now the Boardwalk, now their bikes, Julie's footfalls echoing all the while through her bones, beating against the low chant playing over and over in her head, *never again, never again, never again.*

CHAPTER 4

◆　　◆　　◆

Forked tongue lashing, fangs spurting poison, a dark serpent of despair slithered through the Reverend Billy Milk as he strode down the Boardwalk. Futility, futility, all was futility and God's shattering silence. Seven, that rhythmic digit from Revelation, seven long years since Billy had been in regular communication with heaven: the seraphs' voices telling him that he and he alone had been elected to bring Jesus back, the white-robed hosts marching through his skull on their way to set Babylon aflame—the whole vast internal spectacle having culminated in 1984 with proof positive that the seraphs and hosts were indeed messages from Billy's Lord, not fancies from his brain.

He'd been taking a shower. Mrs. Foster, normally so cautious and prim, pulled the plastic curtain aside, so nothing more substantial than steam now clothed Billy's sinful flesh. "He's got eyes!" she screamed.

"Eyes? Who?"

"Timothy! Two eyes!"

"What do you mean?"

"Eyes!"

Naked, Billy ran from the bathroom. It was true. Chairs, tables, spoons, the family Bible, his mother's picture on the mantel, his father's soapy skin—the sweet blue-eyed boy saw it all.

"Timothy! What happened?"

"They gave me eyes!"

Eyes! His son had eyes! A boy with eyes could join Little League, see a circus, behold his father in the pulpit; he could skate and ski and ride a ten-speed bike. "Who did?"

"The angels! The angels gave me eyes!"

But then had come the terrible hiatus, God's maddening aphasia, seven years without a single sign, no corroborations from on high. Billy's theological instincts told him Atlantic City was indeed Babylon, yet on every visit his phantom eye had remained opaque as the devil's sweat.

He tried other cities: Miami with its drug caliphs, San Francisco with its sodomites, New York with its depraved teens murdering each other for sport. Futility, futility, all was futility. Why wouldn't God disclose his purpose? Had Timothy's sight been gained at the cost of Billy's vision?

ALL HOPE EMBRACE, YE WHO ENTER IN, exhorted the flashing neon slogan running across the entrance to Dante's. Inhaling deeply, Billy walked through the hotel lobby and into the throbbing casino. One-armed bandits and video-poker consoles lined the velvet walls of the upper circle. A huge disc labeled WHEEL OF WEALTH spun noisily, clicking off integers and hope. Convulsing bells, cascading coins, cigarette smoke sinuating through the air and wringing tears from Billy's good eye—how could this not be Babylon?

He descended. In the second circle, smiling dealers in blood-red tuxedoes presided over blackjack. Lower still, croupiers with shamrocks on their lapels supervised the craps tables. At last Billy reached the central pit, where a great roulette wheel held a mob of overdressed gamblers in its thrall. Everyone seemed so completely at home here, as if privy to facts about the casino—where the fuse boxes were, how much the water bill ran, what sections of carpet were due for replacement—that Billy would never grasp.

New Jerusalem. New Jersey. Surely this was the proper site for God's city. He'd even done the math. The Garden State and the State of Israel each comprised the exact same number of square miles—7,892, depending on how you drew Israel's borders.

The ball made its choice; the roulette wheel stopped. Dispassionately the gamblers toted up their gains, their losses, setting out fresh stacks of chips like suburban matrons serving Ritz crackers.

And then it happened. After years of dormancy, Billy's eye kicked in.

A disembodied hand rose from the whirring wheel and floated toward him like the soul of an aborted fetus. Wriggling a pale, pulpy finger, it directed him out of the pit, up through the circles, and straight to the corner of St. James and Pacific, where a street lamp poured its icy light upon a newspaper dispenser.

Billy slipped two quarters into the slot and removed a copy of *Good Times*, a periodical printed on brown, withered paper. A young woman leered at him, her flesh a lurid orange, as if her photo had been shot from an early sixties color TV. "Trish," the caption ran. Her negligee was made of Saran Wrap. "Phone 239–9999."

And upon her forehead was a name written, Mystery, Babylon the Great, the Mother of Harlots and Abominations of the Earth.

A sign! At long last, a sign! For if the Great Whore of Chapter Seventeen had indeed surfaced in Atlantic City, was this not the very Babylon God wanted razed? Billy scanned the possibilities. Babs with the metallic underwear and electric red hair. Gina of the "edible pajamas," her eyebrows trailing upward like jet-fighter exhaust. Jenny, as black and comely as the Shulamite in the Song of Songs. Beverly, with her lush blond hair, her heavy lips, her purple and red . . . *and the woman was arrayed in purple and scarlet* . . . her purple and scarlet nightgown!

The hand led Billy to a phone booth and punched up Beverly's number.

"Hello?" A wet, simmering voice.

"I admire your picture," Billy told her.

"What's your name?"

"Billy."

"Shall we make an appointment, Billy?"

"Tonight if possible."

"I can squeeze you in about midnight—and I'll bet you're fun to squeeze in, aren't you? Such a sexy voice you've got. It's like you're tickling me."

Billy gasped, nearly hung up, but somehow forced himself to say, "I especially like that purple nightgown. I don't suppose . . ."

"You want me to wear it?"

"Please."

"Sure, honey."

"There's something else, Beverly. I'm a minister of the Lord. This will be unusual for me, a kind of experiment."

"I know all about it, Reverend. You folks do more experimenting than Princeton's entire physics department."

He arranged to meet her at the First Ocean City Church of Saint John's Vision, for only there could he learn whether Beverly was truly the Mother of Abominations. When he drove up, she was standing on the great marble steps, her body encased in a trench coat, the shoulder crimped by her handbag strap. "Never done a church before," she said as Billy, wincing, approached. Her photo had been too kind, lying about the wrinkles, the eyelashes like rats' whiskers. "A crypt once, and a Ferris wheel, but never this." She drew a lock of blond hair into her mouth and sucked on it. "I like your eyepatch. Kinky."

Guiding Beverly into the anteroom, he flicked on the lights and pointed to the sad, stark painting—the Savior crucified, skulls heaped at his feet in a poignant parody of the gifts brought by the magi. "You know who that is?"

"Sure, Reverend." The whore slithered out of her trench coat, and suddenly there she was, arrayed in purple and scarlet. "I wore what you wanted."

"I appreciate that. Tell me who it is."

"Will this be American Express, MasterCharge, or Visa?"

"Visa." Billy slid the credit card from his wallet. "Who is it?"

"It's Jesus." Taking the card, Beverly drew out a leather case like the one in which Billy kept his cufflinks. "You want the standard package, or are we feeling—?"

"The standard. Do you know why he's on that cross?"

"Uh-huh. Eighty-five dollars, okay?"

"Okay." Billy led her into the silent nave. "Believe in him, sister." He threw the chandelier switch. Light descended. "His blood can redeem you."

"Right." Beverly marched down the aisle: the Antichrist's own bride, Billy thought. "So, what's your preference?" she asked. "The floor? A pew?" She opened her leather case, revealing five narrow bottles, each of their respective liquids a different shade of blue. "I think the altar has certain possibilities." Approaching the front pew, she arranged the bottles in a ring as if they were birthday candles and proceeded to uncap them. "Give me your finger."

"Huh?"

"Finger, honey." She pulled a needle and a thin glass tube from the case. "Don't worry, it won't hurt. I'm a pro." Her competence was indeed dazzling. An assured jab, and a bright straw of Billy's blood rushed into the glass tube. Carefully she released three drops into each bottle. "Don't be offended, Reverend." Sealing the first bottle, she held it to the chandelier light. "With all the experiments you people've been doing, I can't be too cautious." Second bottle, third, fourth..."Okay, Reverend, no condom needed—unless, of course, that's part of the experiment."

So far in Billy's life, lust had been merely a temptation, but now this particular sin was taking on geometric properties, shaping itself into a proof, hardening into a sign. For who but the Whore of Babylon would act this way, pulling off her purple and scarlet nightgown and stretching out on the altar, her breasts rising toward heaven like inverted chalices? And yet the proof wouldn't be whole until he'd followed her beckoning fingers and enacted the vileness she demanded, for who but the Mother of Abominations would force a man of God to lie with her? Gritting his teeth, he let her unfasten his belt, unzip his fly, and slide his pants and boxer shorts halfway to his knees. "Will you receive Jesus Christ?" he asked.

"Sure. Whatever you've got."

"You will?"

"Definitely."

Whereupon their actions began glowing with salvation, her sweet smell becoming incense, her rippling white form a church, her soft loins a newborn lamb. They kissed, connected. The altar seemed to drop away, angel-borne. So many ways to christen a person, so many substances! With the Jordan, as John had done. With the Holy Ghost, as Jesus had done...

A glorious measure of baptismal liquid rushed out of Billy, making Beverly's redemption peak. Cooing and laughing, she slid away.

"I'd like to buy it," said Billy.

"Buy it?" Perched Eve-naked on the front pew, Beverly fitted his Visa card onto her little machine.

"Your nightgown."

"Let me think. Fifty bucks, okay?" Tongue tucked in the corner of her mouth, she rammed the platen across the card, printing his address on the receipt. "That brings the total to one thirty-five. Sign here, honey."

He signed. Gladly. What a night of victory for Christ—the Whore of Babylon unmasked and redeemed, the city's true name revealed, Billy's mission confirmed. But a fearsome task lay ahead, he realized; somehow he must take his flock, at the moment more concerned with tax shelters and orthodontist bills than the Second Coming, and turn them into soldiers.

Timothy. It all came down to Timothy. Because of that astounding miracle, eyes where there'd been no eyes, Billy knew his will was God's, knew he would find a way to make his church accept the eschatological necessity of incinerating the city. Yes, Dorothy Melton, with your ridiculous feather hat, you've been elected to the Savior's army. And you, Albert Dupree, though you can barely keep your bowling ball out of the gutter, one day soon you'll splash God's wrath on Babylon. As for you, Wayne Ackerman, king of the insurance agents—yes, brother, the year 2000 will find you building the New Jerusalem, that great waterless port through which Jesus will again enter the earth.

"Have a nice night," said Beverly, gliding into her trench coat. She packed up her chemistry set, marched back down the aisle, and set off for the Babylon called Atlantic City.

Open-eyed, clothed only in the cool waters of Absecon Inlet, you begin your descent, down, down to the petting zoo of your childhood. Casually you tune in the colloquies of the cod as they pass in silvery constellations, the cabals of the jellyfish as they flap like sinister umbrellas, but you don't attend their thoughts for long—weightier matters crowd your mind. The precise nature of your divinity. The fourth-century Council of Nicaea. Sex.

It is 1991, and the world has little use for seventeen-year-old virgins.

According to one of your father's books, the year 325 A.D. found the Roman emperor Constantine convening a council in the Asian city of Nicaea, his goal being to settle a feud then raging throughout Christendom. In crude terms: was Jesus God's subordinate offspring, as Arius of Alexandria believed, or was he God himself, as Archdeacon Athanasius asserted? After their initial investigations, you discovered, the Council leaned toward the obvious: offspring. The epithet "son of God" appeared throughout the Gospels, along with the even humbler "son of Man." In the second chapter of Acts, the disciple Peter called Jesus "a man approved of God." In Matthew's nineteenth chapter, when somebody committed the faux pas of calling Jesus "Good Master," Jesus admonished, "Why callest thou me good? There is none good but one, that is, God."

But wait. There's a problem. The instant you bring a subdeity on the scene, you've blurred the line between your precious Judaic monotheism and Roman paganism. You've stepped backward. Thus did the council forever fix Jesus as "very God" through whom "all things were made." The Nicene Creed was recited in churches even in 1991.

Like Jesus before you, you know you're not God. A deity, yes, but hardly cocreator of the universe. If you stood outside Brigantine Mall chanting "Let there be light," a few neon tubes might blink on inside K mart, but heaven would gain no stars. God's children did not do galaxies. They did not invent species, stop time, or eliminate evil with a snap of their divine fingers. Jesus cured lepers, you often note, Jesus did not cure leprosy. Your powers have bounds, your obligations limits.

A cuttlefish drifts by, its tentacles undulating in sleepy, antique rhythms.

People are always asking, does God exist? Of course she does. The real question: what is she like? What sort of God stuffs her only daughter into a bell jar like so much pickled herring and dumps her on the earth with no clues to her mission? What sort of God continues to ignore that same daughter even after she cures a blind boy exactly as instructed? Seven whole years since the Timothy miracle, and while nobody has taken you away, no mothers have shown up either.

You will never forget the night you confessed. "Three summers ago I did something really bad. I gave a kid eyes."

"You *what*?" your father moaned, his jaw dropping open.

"God wanted me to, I thought."

"*She* made you do it? Has *she* been talking to you?"

"It was just an idea I got. Please don't slap me."

He did not slap you. He said, firmly, "We'll get this out of your system once and for all," and hustled you into the Saab.

"Get what out of my system?"

"You'll see." He drove you over the bridge into Atlantic City.

"Where are we going?"

"You'll find out."

"*Where?*"

"To visit my friend from the fire station."

Pop's fire station buddies, you knew, used to draw out his blood for your ectogenesis machine. "Mr. Balthazar? Mr. Caspar?"

"Herb Melchior. So how did it feel, fixing that boy?"

I think I had an orgasm, you wanted to say. "Pretty good."

"I thought I could trust you."

"You *can* trust me."

He pulled into the parking lot at Atlantic City Memorial Hospital. Mr. Melchior, you remembered, had lung cancer.

Pop was calmer now. "We'll leave if you want."

You were supposed to say yes, let's leave, but his remark about trust had really pissed you. "No."

The two of you rode the elevator six flights to the cancer ward. You marched past the nurses' station, entered the hellish corridor. Trench warfare, you decided, the view behind the lines —orderlies bustling about, victims gasping on gurneys, IV bottles drooping like disembodied organs. Pain prospered everywhere, seeping through the walls, darkening the air like swarms of hornets. "Why me?" a young, spindly black man asked quite distinctly as his mother guided him toward the visitors' lounge. "Why can't I get warm?" He tightened his bathrobe around his tubular chest.

"Pop, this is mean."

"I know. I love you." He led you to Room 618. "Ready to start?"

You steadied yourself on the open jamb. Beyond, two cancer-ridden men trembled atop their beds.

"As long as we're here, we can also try Herb's roommate," said Pop. "Hodgkin's disease." Heart stuttering, stomach quaking, you took a small step backward. "And then, of course, there's Room Six Nineteen. And Six Twenty. And Six Twenty-one. On Saturday we'll drive to Philadelphia—lots of hospitals. Next week we'll do New York."

"New York?" You were adrift on an iceberg, rudderless, freezing.

"Then Washington, Baltimore, Cleveland, Atlanta. You didn't make the world, Julie. It's not your responsibility to clean it up."

Another reverse step. "But—"

Seizing your hand, Pop guided you into the visitors' lounge.

The black man's mother had swathed him in a blanket; together they shivered and wept. "Honey, you've got a choice." Your father and you flopped down on the death-scented Naugahyde. Hairless patients stared at the walls. "Take the high road, and you'll be trapped and miserable." On the television, a game show contestant won a trip to Spain. "Take the low, and you'll have a life."

"How can it be wrong to cure people?"

White anger shot across Pop's face. "All right, all *right*," he growled, voice rising. "If you're going to be stubborn...!" From his wallet he removed a newspaper clipping, yellow and brittle like a slice of stale cheese. "Listen, Julie, I don't want to worry you, it might not mean anything—but look, the minute I carried you out of that clinic, somebody blew the place up."

BABY BANK ABORTED, ran the headline. "Huh? Bombed it?" Bile climbed into your throat. "You mean, they wanted to...?"

"Probably just a coincidence."

"Who'd want to kill me?"

"Nobody. All I'm saying is, we can't be too cautious. If God expected you to show yourself, she'd come out and say so."

That was years ago, eighth grade—since which time your divinity has remained wholly under control, your urge toward intervention completely in check.

Baby bank aborted. Bombed. Blown off the face of the earth like Castle Boadicea.

Reveling in your one permitted miracle, you draw a large helping of oxygen from the bay. As a gill owner, you'll never experience the great, glorious breath a pearl diver takes on surfacing, but you're determined to know the rest of it, everything bone and tissue offer. If your Catholic boyfriend is right, God subscribes to a spare, unequivocal ethic: body bad, soul good; flesh false, spirit true. And so in defiance you've become a flesh lover. You've become a woman of the world. Not a hedonist like Phoebe, but an epicure: it is always in homage to flesh that you devour pepperoni pizza, drink Diet Coke, admit Roger Worth's tongue to your mouth, and savor your own briny smell while playing basketball for the Brigantine High Tigerettes. Take that, Mother. So there, Mother.

Flesh is the best revenge.

As you swim into the cave, a small cloud of blood drifts from between your thighs, quickly stoppered by water pressure. You will give credit where due. The body in which God has marooned you is the real thing, all functions intact.

Your petting zoo is defunct. Starfish, flounder, crab, lobster—all gone. Only Amanda the sponge remains, sitting in a clump of seaweed like a melancholy pumice. Thanks to Mr. Parker's biology class, you know she is a *Microciona prolifera*, common to estuaries along the North American coast.

—Where's everybody gone? you ask.

—Dead, Amanda replies. Sickness, old age, pollution. I alone have escaped. Immortality, it's my sole claim to fame. Hack me apart, and each piece regenerates.

—I'm probably immortal too.

—You don't look it, Julie.

—God wants me to live forever.

—Perhaps, broadcasts the sponge.

—She does.

—Maybe.

Using your feet like hoes, you furrow the sandy floor, upending stones, overturning shells, uncovering...*there*, beside your heel, the skeleton you first spotted at age ten. Tornadoes of sand swirl upward as, with a sudden karate chop, you behead it.

You snug the skull against your chest and float toward the filtered sunlight. How you love having a body, even a blobby one; you love your caramel skin, opulent hair, slightly asymmetrical breasts, throbbing gills. Too bad, Mother. Menstrual blood encircling you like an aura, you bid Amanda good-bye, push off from the bay bottom, and ascend through a hundred feet of salt water.

Fresh water gushed from the shower nozzle, washing away the sweat of the game but not its humiliation. Julie had played well, sinking all her free throws and chalking up fifteen points, six rebounds, and seven assists. She had stolen the ball four times. Useless. The Lucky Dogs of Atlantic City High had walked all over the Brigantine Tigerettes, 69 to 51.

She shut off the water and crept out of the shower, the most miserable point guard in the entire division.

Eerie silence reigned in the locker room. At Brigantine High, defeats were not discussed. Toweling off, she rehearsed what she intended to say to Phoebe. "Yes, of *course* I can score any-time, sink the damn ball from midcourt if I want. Don't tell me what to do with my life, Sparks."

"I'm *not* telling you what to do with your life," Phoebe insisted the next day. "I'm simply saying you're an outside shooter—you wouldn't have to get physical, nobody'd suspect anything supernatural." They wove through the clattering cafeteria, found a table, slammed down their trays. "If the point spread stays under twelve at the Saint Basil's game, I'll walk away with sixty dollars. Naturally I'll go halves with you."

Surveying the food, Julie winced. Why did she have to work so hard at maintaining a half-decent figure while Phoebe lived on sugar and never gained a pound or grew a zit? "I'm not throwing a game just so you can make thirty dollars."

"You throw a game when you lose it, not when you *win* it." Phoebe shoved lemon meringue pie into her mouth. "Hey, you think it's easy being your friend, Katz? You think I'm at peace about it? I mean, here you come ripping into the world like Grant took Richmond, and you've got these damn powers, and some sort of God exists, and I have to keep *quiet*. It's driving me absolutely nuts. Mom too."

"Be patient. My mission's not worked out yet."

"I *am* patient." Phoebe devoured a doughnut. "Hey, did I ever ask you for help with my shitty grades? When my cousin got knocked up, did I ask you to fix it?"

Julie's face grew hot. "There're *lots* of things you never asked me to do." She pointed across the cafeteria to Catherine Tyboch, her stocky body suspended on crutches. "You never asked me to make Tyboch walk. You never asked me to cure Lizzie's anorexia."

"I was getting to them."

"I'm sure you were."

"Let's face it, buddy, running up and down a basketball court isn't exactly fulfilling your potential."

Vengefully Julie forked a hunk of Phoebe's pie and ate it. "There's a room in my house you've never seen."

"Where you and Roger hump? Hope you take precautions. Like Mom says, 'His bird in your hand is worth two in your bush.'"

Phoebe's genius for sex did not surprise Julie. Phoebe's face

was gorgeous, her shape lithe, her dark skin creamy and iridescent. Typically, God had given better flesh to Phoebe than to her
own daughter. "Roger and I don't do that. He worships me."

Phoebe giggled. "Worships the water you walk on." She ate a
brownie the color of her skin. "Really, can't you do better than
Roger? I mean, isn't he sort of boring, isn't he sort of a prude?
You're smart, friendly, got nice boobers, and score twelve points
a game. Not like me with my F in math and these acorns for tits.
Why waste yourself on Roger?"

"He's a good Catholic. I need that. It helps me."

"Helps you to love your mother?"

"Helps me to stop hating her."

"You shouldn't hate your mother, Katz."

"I hate her."

"What room?"

Her temple, Julie called it. Once it was the Angel's Eye guest
room, now the place that kept her sane. The project had begun
modestly, nothing but a few tragic stories clipped from *Time* and
the *Atlantic City Press* and pasted in a scrapbook. But soon it
spread to the walls, then to the ceiling and floor, until all six
inside surfaces positively dripped with humanity's suffering,
with earthquakes, droughts, floods, fires, diseases, deformities,
addictions, car crashes, train wrecks, race riots, massacres, ther-
monuclear bomb tests.

Was all this really *essential*? Pop had wanted to know.

It would keep her off the high road, Julie had explained.

He never questioned the project again.

"Impressive," said Phoebe, surveying the collages on the afternoon following the Lucky Dogs game, "but what's the point?"

Julie approached the altar, a former card table on which two
brass candlesticks, thick and ornate as clarinets, flanked the
sailor's skull she'd recently taken from the bay. "Right before
bed, I spend twenty minutes in this place. Then I can sleep."

"You mean you simply sit here, staring at everybody's pain?
All you do is *look* at it?"

"Uh-huh. Just like God."

"That's sick."

Julie lifted the skull, holding it as if about to make a free
throw. "My mother could've saved this sailor. She didn't."

"Maybe she has her reasons."

"Maybe I have mine." Julie stretched out her arm, extended her index finger. Slowly she turned, three hundred and sixty degrees, then another rotation, another ... "Look, Phoebe, it never stops. Round and round—forever!"

"You got pollution?" Phoebe caressed the scabby door, pausing atop a photo of a dozen fifty-five-gallon drums sitting in a landfill like unexploded bombs, oozing pink poison. "Oh, I see ..."

"I mean, where do I even *begin*?"

"Great place to do drugs." Phoebe's laugh was high and uneasy, like the yip of a dog barking on command. "There's *plenty* of it, I'll give you that."

"A girl could spend every waking minute performing miracles ..."

"And not scratch the surface," mused Phoebe. "Shit, here's a tough one." She punched a *People* magazine clipping. A four-year-old boy with spina bifida had undergone sixteen separate operations and then died. "I've been giving you a hard time lately."

"Uh-huh."

"Sorry, Katz."

"You should be."

"Sometimes I get jealous of you. That's stupid, isn't it?"

"My life's no picnic." Julie slumped to the floor, eyes locked on an Ethiopian infant's bloated belly and matchstick legs. "Remember when we snuck into that hotel? I don't want there to be famines or poverty, Phoebe, just beer and Tastykake and you."

"Oh, my poor little goddess." Dropping, Phoebe gave Julie a magnificent kiss, wet and tasty as a slice of watermelon, right on the lips. "You're under a curse, aren't you? You're all torn apart."

Phoebe, dear Phoebe: she understood. "I can't win," Julie moaned. "If only I could be just one way, caterpillar or butterfly, one or the other. My mother never says a word to me. I know I'm supposed to have some amazingly beautiful and earth-shaking purpose, but God won't talk. She won't say if there's a heaven, or whether I'll die, or *anything*."

"You'll always love me, won't you?" The second kiss was even juicier than the first. "Wherever you go, you'll take me with you?"

"Always," said Julie, thinking intently about her friend's lips.

* * *

No local theater was showing the double bill Roger wanted to
see, *Ten Thousand Psychotics* followed by *The Garden of Unearthly
Delights*, so they went all the way to the Route 52 Cinema in
Somers Point. It was an unusually passionate Roger who sat next
to Julie, comforting her during the zombie attacks, feeling her up
during the sex scenes. "He made me promise not to tell," Phoebe
had revealed earlier that day, "but I will anyway, that's what
friends are for. Sin no longer exists for Roger. God, Satan, hell—
gone with the tooth fairy. In short, if you're ready to become a
girl with a past, he's ready to give you one."

Phoebe's date for the evening, Lucius Bogenrief, had the
complexion of strawberry yogurt and the smell and general contours of a submarine sandwich, but he also had *Ramblin' Girl*, his
family's Winnebago, a kind of terrestrial yacht complete with
kitchenette, bar, and private bedroom. As the four of them ambled into the lobby after the show, Lucius drew out his keys and
ceremoniously presented them to Phoebe. "Your pilot for this
evening is Captain Sparks."

"Some people will give anything for a properly done blow-
job," Phoebe explained, winking. "The whole sixty-nine
yards, eh?"

Roger cringed and pretended to study the poster for *Ten
Thousand Psychotics*. Julie felt ice in her gills. Phoebe driving? The
point of the evening was to experience sex, not to die.

They piled into the Winnebago, Lucius taking the passenger
seat, Phoebe grasping the steering wheel as she might the handlebar on a roller coaster. Nuzzling like newborn puppies, Julie
and Roger slipped behind the kitchenette table. "It's like a club-
house," she noted excitedly.

"I used to have a treehouse," said Roger. "It blew out of the
tree."

Julie did not really understand Roger's interest in her, unless
his Catholic instincts told him who she was. He ran the student
council, edited the school paper, and looked remarkably like the
portrait of an extremely handsome Jesus hanging in Phoebe's old
catechism class. His only defect—as Phoebe would have it, his
only virtue—was his fascination with the grotesque, particularly
monster movies and Stephen King novels, enthusiasms Julie at-
tributed to the way the pre-Vatican II hell, so gaudy and voluptuous in its horrors, had captured his childhood imagination.

Phoebe lifted the microphone from the dashboard. "This is your captain speaking." Her amplified voice rattled around the van like a marble in a vase. "The party begins at midnight."

"Party," echoed Roger, sounding half thrilled, half terrified. "Great."

Predictably, *Ramblin' Girl* brought out the worst in Phoebe. "Christ!" Julie screamed as the Winnebago rocketed away from the Route 52 Cinema. "Not so fast!"

They plunged down Shore Road as if Phoebe had a large bet riding on her getting a speeding ticket. New Jersey rushed by— its shabby farms, grubby refineries, garish billboards exhorting you to win big at Caesar's and the Golden Nugget. The Winnebago rattled like a treehouse in a hurricane.

"Was anybody *in* the treehouse?" Julie asked.

"I was," said Roger. "It's a miracle I survived."

That explained a lot, Julie figured. Nothing like a brush with death to make somebody a good Catholic.

"Ah, hah!" shouted Phoebe, swerving into the parking lot of Somers Point High School. It didn't matter that none of them went here; they were all in the vast travel club called adolescence, and the parking lot was theirs, as friendly and inviting as a country inn. Phoebe guided *Ramblin' Girl* toward an unlighted area, killed the motor. Julie laughed, kissed Roger's cheek. Mangy basketball nets, twisted bicycle racks, gallowslike lamps —yes, they belonged.

Lucius and Phoebe joined them in the kitchenette, pulling bottles from the liquor cabinet. The labels fascinated Julie—Cutty Sark, Dewar's, Beefeater—each logo dense with staid print and Anglo-Saxon dignity, as if alcohol were really a type of literary criticism and not a leading cause of traffic fatalities and brain rot. Phoebe mixed the drinks, starting with her own rum and Coke, then doing Lucius's vodka and tonic. Julie's affection for liquor hadn't increased one jot since she and Phoebe had guzzled beer in the doomed Deauville, but she agreed to try a "Black Russian," which definitely sounded like something her mother wouldn't want her to have.

"Might I trouble you for one of those?" Roger asked cautiously.

"Sure," said Phoebe.

"Saw you on the court last Tuesday." Lucius served Julie her Black Russian. "You looked good."

"Julie always looks good," said Roger, smiling stupidly.

"Sixty-four to thirty-one, that sucks," said Julie, sipping. Sweet, sinful, exquisite.

"Julie can get a basket whenever she wants." Phoebe swizzled Roger's drink with the crazed competence of the mad scientist in *Ten Thousand Psychotics*. "She's tuned in on the cosmos."

Lucius opened the bedroom door, its back panel decorated with *Playboy* centerfolds. Julie pondered a certain Miss March. What an incalculable debt she owed whichever playmate had inspired the donation that was her gateway to flesh. Still, Miss March seemed pathetic. Why did males find breasts erotic, why did these mongrel solids drive them crazy? Yes, there were far too many unwanted pregnancies around Brigantine High, but certainly her mother shared some of the blame, wiring up guys' penises like that.

"Don't worry." Lucius winked lewdly. "Around here we knock first."

Roger led her into the little boudoir and set their Black Russians on the nightstand. Lucius closed the door. Julie and Roger jumped simultaneously. What a couple of overbred dogs we are, she thought, what a pair of skittish virgins.

The Winnebago's engine snorted to life. "Hey, what're you doing?" Julie called.

"What's going on?" shouted Roger.

Phoebe's voice zagged out of the bedroom loudspeaker. "This is your captain speaking." The van chattered and rolled. "Next stop, a deserted and romantic section of Dune Island."

Steadying their drinks, Roger called, "Do me a favor, Phoebe." Always so polite. "Go slowly."

"Do her a favor, Roger," came Phoebe's amplified reply. "Go slowly."

"You shouldn't be driving," said Julie.

"Should I help you ravish Roger instead?"

Julie wasn't sure how much of her dizziness traced to the Winnebago's movement, how much to the Black Russian. She drew a deep breath, sipped her drink. A private bedroom with a pornographic door. Well, well. A mattress jutting from the wall, white sheets wrapped around it, tight as drumheads. Well, well, well. Did she really want Roger inside her, pushing and stabbing? Would her chunky body suffice to make it work?

He didn't wait for Dune Island. Like a soldier ducking machine-gun fire, he hit the mattress, pulling her down with him. His fingers were everywhere at once, massaging her blouse, tugging at her jeans.

Julie drew away.

"Sorry," said Roger. His favorite word.

"Ground rules. We need some—"

"We'll use this." Roger pulled a condom from his corduroys, flashing it like a press pass. "If that's all right."

"I meant our relationship." Beyond curiosity, beyond her need to provoke God, the night had to be what Aunt Georgina would call cosmic. "Do you love me, Roger?"

"Of course."

"Truly?"

"I truly love you, Julie. It doesn't bother me a bit you're Jewish."

"Say it again."

"Say I love you?"

"Yeah."

"I love you."

Good. They weren't just satisfying their respective longings for defiance and ejaculation. This was devotion, ecstasy, mutual worship. "Attention, passengers," crackled Phoebe. "Unfasten your seat belts and everything else you can get your hands on."

Julie helped him remove her blouse and bra. Her heart seemed to have doubled in size. Would it be wonderful? Gross? What was she doing here? "I want to go to the stars," she'd told Phoebe that afternoon. "First time out," Phoebe had replied, "you won't get past the asteroid belt." The Winnebago's rumblings wove through her. Her jeans and loafers melted away, so that only her underpants stood between herself and spiting God. We didn't invent this preposterous stuff, she thought as she popped the button on Roger's corduroys. The two of them were innocent. Everyone was innocent. The universe was a place of blameless urges and morally neutral hydraulics.

"Shit!"

Phoebe.

The Winnebago listed like a ship in a typhoon, pitching them off the mattress.

"Fuck!"

Lucius.

The remainder of their Black Russians splashed onto the carpet, ice cubes rolling like dice. The door burst open and Phoebe swung in, her hand locked on the knob, her dark face bleached to the color of tobacco. "Help!"

"Get out of here!" Julie snarled.

"Aren't you driving?" Roger asked.

"Emergency!" shouted Phoebe. "Oh, God, I'm so *sorry!*"

Julie extricated herself from the fleshy pile and, throwing on her blouse and jeans, followed Phoebe into the cab.

Solid mud greeted her view. Across the windshield, against the side windows: mud, a worm's cosmos.

"She drove off the fucking bridge!" Lucius stood on the passenger seat, palms against the roof, feeling for leaks. "I can't believe it!" Tears glistened on his zits. "Phoebe's such an asshole!"

Again the Winnebago tilted, hurling the three of them against the passenger door. Silt oozed from the air vents. Buried alive. Sinking. The week before, twenty-five thousand Colombians had died in a mud floe, children suffocated, adults both righteous and wicked strangled by the impartial earth. Only that was merely news, another clipping for Julie's temple.

"What's the commotion?" Roger stumbled into the cab, hitching up his corduroys.

A urine stain bloomed on Lucius's crotch. "We're going to die!"

"Do it, Katz!" Like a sailor closing hatches on a submarine, Phoebe threw the vent levers to *off*.

"Do what?" said Lucius.

"This girl has powers!" said Pheobe. "She's God's favorite daughter!"

"God's what?" said Roger.

"She'll save us—won't you, Julie?"

"Of course she will!" moaned Lucius.

"Of course she will!" gasped Phoebe.

Julie rolled her eyes heavenward. Of course she'd abandon her principles? Of course she'd be a hypocrite, rescuing Phoebe and the others while all the Herb Melchiors died of lung cancer? Of course she'd be self-centered, raising up *Ramblin' Girl* while the surrounding planet bled?

No! She was better than that! "Mother," she rasped. The Winnebago descended. "Mother, it's in *your* hands."

"My God, I am heartily sorry for having offended thee," Roger recited, dropping to his knees, "and I detest all my sins because I dread the loss of heaven and the pains of hell, but most of all—"

"Mother!" Julie's voice made a hot breeze in her throat. "Mother, you owe me this!"

Phoebe seized Julie's arm. "No time to get religious on us—do it!"

"Mother, this is your last chance!"

"Do it!" screamed Lucius.

"Do it!" urged Roger.

Do it? Julie hauled herself behind the steering wheel, pressing her palms against the rubbery plastic. "Mother, I'm warning you!" She whipped the wheel hard. "Mother!"

And there was light.

Everywhere, light, enveloping the van as if the mud had transmuted into molten gold. The wheel became a halo, the gear shift a flaming sword, the speedometer a comet. "Mother, is that you? *You?*" A time-twisted universe suffused the cab. Ceramic fragments congealed into teapots, blossoms imploded into buds, clocks spun north to west . . . and, like a mammoth breaking free of a tar pit, the Winnebago struggled upward through the tiers of gunk and silt. "Mother!" Oh, yes, no question, the Primal Hermaphrodite had arrived, peeling away New Jersey's gravity like a farmer shucking corn. "Thank you, Mother! I love you, Mother!" Within a minute, *Ramblin' Girl* had cleared the trees and was hovering above the bridge like a helicopter.

"Unbelievable!" gasped Lucius.

"Jesus!" shouted Roger.

"Warm," said Phoebe.

The Winnebago became a domain of unfathomable gentleness: yolks left their shells and tumbled unbroken into frying pans; sleeping babies were lowered undisturbed into cribs. With a subtle bump, the van landed on the bridge and rolled to a halt. Hysterical cheers filled the cab, kissing Julie's eardrums.

"Unfuckinbelievable!"

"Mother of God!"

"Warmer."

Shivering with epiphany, Julie turned the ignition key, and in a cunning little coda to the miracle the mud-packed engine started up. "Where to?" she asked, smiling hugely.

"The beach." Phoebe beamed with wonderment and pride. God's daughter's best friend. "Go left here."

"Folks, I have no idea what just happened"—Lucius eyed his soggy crotch—"but I know I'll be spending the rest of my life thinking about it." He touched Julie's elbow tentatively, as if expecting an electric shock. "I don't suppose you could, er..."

"What?"

"Get the van cleaned up?"

"Nope."

"I just thought—"

"No way."

The coarse whisper of surf filled the night as Julie drove onto the sand and parked. Rolling down the driver's window, she let the mud flop onto her jeans. Her blood was on fire, an internal oil spill, smoking, burning. Curing some stupid blind kid was nothing compared with finally finding your mother.

"I'd like some fresh air." Phoebe smothered Lucius with the kind of grand, sensual kiss she'd given Julie in her temple. "You would too, Lucius."

"You nearly got us killed, Phoebe," Lucius grunted. "It'll take days to wash this mud off. *Days.*"

"She *did* get us killed," gasped Roger. "And then Julie..."

Quickly Lucius and Phoebe assembled their orgy—condoms, six-pack, beach blanket—and, jumping from the Winnebago, ran across the sand. The April night swallowed them. So they felt it too, Julie realized, the erotic thrill of near oblivion fused with the kick of epiphany. And Roger over there, sitting dumbfounded on the barstool, was he likewise aroused? She lurched out of the driver's seat and dove into him, wedging herself between his legs. She was desirable, gorgeous, a deity whose mother cared!

Roger pushed her away.

"Huh?"

"God's daughter," he replied, sweat marring his beautiful goy-Jesus face. "Phoebe said—"

"I thought you wanted to—"

"I can't do *that* with God's daughter!"

And suddenly she smelled it. A piercing stench, the acrid molecules of his adoration. The evening, she realized, had ended. Very well. Fine. She could lose it some other time—this was the night God got in touch!

She stumbled to the bedroom, snatched up her bra and loafers, and returned through the fumes of reverence.

"I thought the Church might call me back," Roger panted, tear ducts spasming with revelation, "but never this way, oh, no, never *this* way..." His awe was a mass of snakes, slithering over her body, driving her out of the van. "An amazing lady, the Church. Just amazing."

She opened the passenger door, and, jumping onto the beach, began reassembling herself, bra, blouse, loafers.

The night was cool and moonless. Tree frogs chirped like a thousand preschoolers testing their bicycle bells. Joyously she ran to the sea, its edge lathery with foam and horseshoe crab semen.

"Hello, child."

"Huh?"

"I said hello."

The sweet, spherical odor of fresh oranges reached Julie's nostrils, and suddenly she was a ten-year-old stumbling upon a supernatural stranger in the Deauville Hotel.

"Mr. Wyvern, the most wonderful thing just happened! God saved me!"

Her mother's friend stepped from behind a trembling cluster of cat-o'-nine-tails. He held a kerosene lantern aloft, its glow spreading into the channel, revealing a black brooding schooner afloat near Dune Island. "Ah, you remember me," he said, each word a staccato pluck of his tongue. "Good." A frock coat flowed down from his trim shoulders. The flame reddened his eyes and gilded his beard. "God?" He snorted like an asthmatic pig. "Did you say God? I'm sorry, Julie, but God had nothing to do with it. *I'm* the one who saved you."

"You?" Julie's throat grew suddenly dry. Her knees buckled, her intestines tightened. "No, *God* did. My *mother* did."

"It was I. Sorry."

"No!" Her collapse was instantaneous: one moment she stood, the next she lay sprawled in the wet sand, crying as hard as when Pop had slapped her for reviving the crab. "Noooo!"

"I couldn't very well let you spend your prime years at the bottom of a salt marsh waiting for you-know-who. Sheer insanity, that."

"You're *lying*. It was God."

"Nope."

Taking her hand, Wyvern pulled her upright and guided her to a clump of spartina grass. He flicked a tear from her cheek.

Julie stomped the ground, as if the whole planet were a disgusting bug, *stomp*, *squish*. No doubt it was all true, no doubt she mattered more to the devil than to her own mother. "You *are* the devil, aren't you?"

Wyvern made a quick bow. "Thanks to my efforts, Atlantic City will run in the black forever."

"You said you were my mother's friend."

" 'Now there was a day when the sons of God came before the Lord,' " he quoted, " 'and Satan also came among them.' A better age, Julie. Gone forever."

She sniffed the mucus back into her nose. "I've been good, I've been bad—*nothing* gets her attention. What am I supposed to do, sacrifice a goat?"

"Perhaps you should start a religion. You know—reveal your mother to the world."

"How can I reveal her when I don't know what she's like?"

"Use your imagination. Everybody else does."

Julie pulled off her left loafer, emptied the sand. "Be honest, Mr. Wyvern—God doesn't talk to *you* either. Curing that Timothy kid was *your* idea."

"True, true," the devil confessed.

"You . . . swindler."

"I've been called worse." Wyvern lifted back his frock coat and removed his silver cigarette case. "We're on our own, aren't we, child? Two lost soul-catchers. A couple of ad-libbers."

"Why'd you want Timothy cured?"

Wyvern flipped open the cigarette case, holding it before Julie's teary eyes. "Virtue is of great interest to me. I was curious to see what would happen. Look . . ." Inside the mirror, a shadowy figure stood on a pulpit and boomed a sermon to a packed church. "Timothy's father. You wouldn't like him. Major fanatic. Confuses migraine headaches with God." The preacher stalked up and down the aisle, showing his congregation what looked like a purple nightgown. "For years he worried that his visions might simply be in his mind, but then his son got those two new eyes, and now he's really *inspired*. Believe me, this man will do something wicked one day."

"How wicked?"

"Entirely wicked."

"And my miracle, it . . . ?"

"Inspired him."

"I'll never cure anybody again."

"Good for you." The devil grinned. His golden teeth glittered in the lantern light.

"I'm going to have a life. Marriage, children, career, all of it."

"Of course you will. Such a heritage, sired by a good smart Jew out of God. Got a college picked out?"

"Princeton."

"If I can ever help, just ask."

"I'm fine."

"No problems? No questions? Need a recommendation?" Wyvern closed his cigarette case. "I can tell you why the universe is composed of matter and not antimatter. I can tell you why the electron has its particular charge. I can tell you—"

"There is *one* thing."

"Shoot."

"My mother . . ."

Wyvern began retracting the wick. The flame grew translucent.

And so did he.

"It always comes down to her, doesn't it?"

"Why doesn't she care about people?" The spring air dried Julie's tears. "Why all the diseases and earthquakes?"

With a final twist of the knob, Wyvern's body became a gaseous haze. The dead lantern hit the beach, dug into the sand. "The Colombian mud floes?"

"Yeah. The Colombian mud floes."

"Actually, the answer's quite simple." Two red eyes floated in the mist.

"Really? Tell me. Why does God allow evil?"

The red eyes vanished, leaving only the lantern and the night. "Because power corrupts," said Wyvern's disembodied voice. "And absolute power corrupts absolutely."

CHAPTER 5

•   •   •

Princeton University rejected God's daughter, but she did receive acceptances from Wesleyan, Antioch, and the University of Pennsylvania, plus notification that Vassar had placed her on its waiting list.

Although Julie favored Penn—Ivy League, big city, close to home—her father was still making ends meet by donating to the resurrected and relocated Preservation Institute, and the idea of pursuing the lofty agenda of college while he whacked off down the hall gave her considerable pause. Her quandary ended the instant Penn's financial assistance office promised her a full-tuition scholarship coupled to a job at the university's bookstore. She would become, like her father, a shelver of books. One week after her birthday, she and Murray loaded the Saab with the collected detritus of her ill-defined life—her basketball, CD player, curling iron, all of it—and crossed the grim and matted Delaware into Philadelphia.

College, by damn. Abandoned by her mother, saddled with divinity, but she'd gotten all the way to college.

By Halloween her gills were throbbing with desires at once romantic and lewd. Howard Lieberman, he called himself—her immediate supervisor at the bookstore as well as a biology major stationed at the Preservation Institute, where he collected sperm samples from macaques. He put her in charge of the science texts. *Basic Physics, Principles of Geology, Primate Psychology, Physical*

Anthropology, Introduction to Astronomy. "It should be called 'astrology,' of course, the study of stars," Howard explained as he showed Julie the stockroom. With his small tight lips, wire-rimmed glasses, and Kropotkin shirt, he looked like Tom Courtney as the young revolutionary Pasha Antipov in Julie's favorite movie, *Doctor Zhivago.* Roger Worth had been nice, stupefyingly nice, but here was a man with a whiff of danger about him, a man who peered over precipices. "Unfortunately, 'astrology' got snatched up by the horoscope crowd, so we're stuck with 'astronomy,' the arrangement of stars."

"I'm really interested in this stuff." Julie rubbed a carton labeled ELEMENTARY PARTICLES.

"Physics?"

"Physics, biology, stars, everything."

Howard said, "Good for you. These days most people prefer to impoverish their minds with mysticism." Such a sensual person, intense as a violin, serious as a cat. "You're a rare woman, Julie."

"My mother's a mechanical engineer," she said.

Howard drew out his Osmiroid pen and inscribed a list on a stray scrap of computer paper. "Here are some courses you should audit." It was the first time Julie had ever seen anybody write in calligraphy; the list looked like Scripture. "I think they'll excite you."

Which they did. Julie may have snuck into Quantum Mechanics 101, Astrophysics 300, and Problems in Macroevolution to please Howard, but she stayed in each class for the sake of her soul.

What Julie found through science was not so much an atheist universe as one from which God, after the act of creation, had reluctantly but necessarily excluded herself. The universe was stuff. Energy, particles, time, gravity, electromagnetism, space: stuff all. So how could a being of spirit enter a wholly physical domain? She couldn't. The God of physics was obliged to inhabit only the unknown, the universe beyond the universe, a place the human mind would never reach before everything expired in heat-death and whimpering hydrogen. The God of physics might smuggle an occasional egg or spermatozoan into the Milky Way, but not her incorporeal essence. She could bring forth children, but never herself.

Science even explained the evident actuality of supernatural dimensions—of heaven, limbo, purgatory, and the fiery fran-

chises of Andrew Wyvern. The so-called Copenhagen interpretation of quantum mechanics practically demanded a belief in inaccessible alternative realities. "A myriad contradictory worlds,"
lectured Professor Jerome Delacato, "forever splitting off from
each other like branches on a tree, so that, somewhere out there,
I am presently giving a lecture explaining how the many-worlds
hypothesis cannot possibly be true."

For all this, Julie's rage remained. As she sat in ivy-speckled
College Hall, writing down Delacato's wild theories, her flesh
quivered with disgust. A mother ought to get in touch. Even if
the rift between them were as wide as the cosmos, God should
still try to heal it.

"The observable universe is ten billion light-years in size, correct?" she asked Howard. "Or, as Dirac observed, ten followed
by forty zeros times as large as a subatomic particle. But look, the
ratio of the gravitational force between a proton and an electron
is *also* ten followed by forty zeros. That implies a designer, I
think. Maybe even a caring, personal God."

He examined her with a mix of irritation and pity. He sucked
his lips inward. "No, it simply means the cosmos happens to be
that size right now."

"I have strong reason to believe God exists." Julie suppressed
a smirk. Her sexy, perfect boss didn't know everything.

"Look, Julie, these matters are best discussed over food and
drink. These matters are best discussed in restaurants. You like
Greek food?"

"I love it." She couldn't stand Greek food. "I go crazy over it."

So they became a couple. It was dumb and lovely. Boyfriend, girlfriend, holding hands. Off to the movies, the Rodin
Museum, the Franklin Institute, the Academy of Music. An
atheist Jewish biologist—Pop was sure to approve, no boy-
meets-girl jokes of the sort he'd made the time she brought
Roger Worth home.

Explaining the universe in Greek restaurants, Howard exuded a boundless passion. "What most people don't realize is
that something unprecedented has entered the world. Bang—
science—and suddenly a proposition is true because it's *true*,
Julie, not because its adherents have the biggest churches or the
grandest inquisitors or the most weeks on *The New York Times*
bestseller list." His eyes paced their sockets like caged animals.

"Earth orbits the sun. Microbes cause disease. The kidney is a filter. The heart is a pump." His voice built to a crescendo, making heads turn. "At long last, Julie, we can *know* things!"

They took a chance on the Southwark Experimental Theater and, after two hours of watching mediocre actors talk to household appliances, retreated to Howard's apartment, a space as disheveled as he. His posters of Einstein, Darwin, and Galileo were crookedly mounted on dispirited loops of masking tape. His clothes lay everywhere in amorphous piles. Rings of dried coffee pocked the top of his computer monitor.

"Want a beer?"

"Coffee," said Julie. "And I'm hungry, to tell you the truth."

"I've got a microwave pizza."

"My favorite."

They picnicked on the floor, amid widowed socks and back issues of *Scientific American.*

This time, Julie knew, she would make it work. "Howard, did the universe have a beginning?" she asked, fondling his hand.

"I believe so." He leaned over and pressed his lips against hers—nothing like Phoebe's masterful kisses, but sufficient to get things rolling. "I'm no steady-stater."

"Didn't think you were." She opened her mouth. Their tongues connected like two randy eels.

"The common misconception is that the big bang occurred at a point inside space, like an explosion here on earth." Howard giggled lustily. "Rather, it filled the whole of space, it *was* space."

She stretched out on the floor, carrying him down with her, still feasting on his tongue. His erection poked her thigh. "There's a condom in my purse."

He reached inside a nearby running shoe, pulling out a set of Trojans strung together like lollipops. "Don't bother."

Buttons, zippers, buckles, catches, and hooks melted under their eager fingers. "I've never done this before," Julie confessed as the surrounding chaos gobbled up their clothes. "Not entirely."

Howard's quick scientific fingers and nimble truth-telling tongue were everywhere, probing her tissues, prodding her bones, molding lovely flowing shapes within her. The mesh of black hair on his chest looked like Andromeda. "After the bang, space kept expanding, like a balloon or a rubber sheet." He unwrapped his condom and unfurled it down his circumcised expansion, all the while touching her, bringing forth delicious vibrations.

"Rubber," Julie echoed, groaning.

"Note that the movement is both isotropic and homogeneous."

She shuddered, every blessed cell. Her bones glowed. Her spinal cord became a rope of hot gelatin lacing her vertebrae. Gritting her teeth in pleasure, she jammed her palms against the floor and floated away on her own liquid self.

"To wit, the known cosmos has no center." Howard climbed on top.

At last she touched shore. Her eyes sprang fully open, and she beheld Howard's rickety bookshelves. *The New Physics*, she read. P-h-y-s-i-c-s. A coil of radiant energy shot from the word, flooding into her skull like a sunbeam passing through glass. She closed her eyes. Her dendrites danced. Her synapses sparkled.

"No privileged vantage point," Howard elaborated. She guided the ballooning universe toward her, laughing as it pried her apart. "Thus, we must abandon"—he pressed ahead with steady, metronomic thrusts, writing calligraphic poems on her vaginal walls—"any idea of galaxies in flight."

Cell Biology! Analytic Chemistry! Geophysics! Phylogenesis! Comparative Anatomy! Electricity sang through Julie's blood, the surge of observable data, the erotic rush of experimentally verifiable knowledge. Could it be? Her coming had something to do with science? She'd been sent to preach a gospel of empirical truth?

"In the macropicture"—Howard panted like a German shepherd—"the stars float at rest, separating from each other only as space itself"—a low, primal wail—"*grows!*" He spasmed within her, and Julie pictured countless galaxies, printed on his condom, moving apart as the universe filled with his seed.

She asked, "Do you believe science has all the answers?"

"Huh?"

"Science. Does it have all the answers?"

"Everybody thinks he's being oh-so-deep when he says science doesn't have all the answers."

Done. All of it. Virginity gone, flesh ratified, mother spited, mission discovered—the gospel of empirical truth! Yes! Oh, yes!

"Science *does* have all the answers," said Howard, withdrawing. "The problem is that we don't have all the science."

* * *

"Breathe," Georgina told him.

Murray breathed. The pains persisted, screeching through his arms and chest, making jagged humps on the oscilloscope. How tightly woven was the world, he thought. The scope ran on coal-generated electricity; at some specific moment, then, a West Virginia miner had pried up the very bituminous lump now enabling whoever occupied the nurses' station to confirm Mr. Katz as still among the living.

"Hopeless," he moaned, squeezing the crunchy sheets. He was strung up like a marionette: catheter, IV tube, a tangle of wires pasted to his chest. His clogged heart bleeped at him. When the monitor's pulsings stopped, he wondered, would he notice the silence, or would he be dead by then? "Like father, like son."

"Horse manure." Georgina tugged a strand of her graying beatnik hair. He tried to read his future in her tics: the more nervous Georgina, the closer oblivion. "Just breathe. It's gotten me out of all sorts of jams." He channeled air through the back of his throat. The humps on the scope crested, the pains faded. "Julie's on her way."

Julie, he mused. Dear, burdened Julie. How nearly normal she seemed, how relatively sane. "We've done all right by her, haven't we?"

"Aces," said Georgina.

"She's still the kid down the street," said Murray. "Her enemies haven't a clue."

"Never thought we'd get through her childhood. She and Phoebe sowed a lot of oats."

"Do girls have oats?"

"Of course girls have oats. I had oats." Georgina flipped on the TV; a Revelationist preacher announced that thirty cases of diabetes were currently vanishing in Trenton. "I can't say it's been easy keeping quiet. I wake up every day wanting to scream out the whole thing. But I don't. I bite my tongue. That's how much I love you."

The last, lingering pain died in Murray's chest. "You really love me? You aren't just being nice to me because my kid's connected to . . . whatever? The Primal Hermaphrodite."

"If I weren't a lesbo, Mur, I'd marry you."

"You would? You'd marry me?"

"Bet your ass."

"Will you do it anyway?" He changed channels: a tidal wave had just washed all of civilization from a Philippine island. "I mean it, Georgina. Let's get married. You wouldn't have to give up women. You could bring them home."

"Aw, that's sweet—but I'm afraid Phoebe's the only sexual generalist in the family." Navajo bracelets jangled on Georgina's wrist as she extended her index finger and traced the scribble on the scope. "Hey, look, if I ever get oriented the other way, you'll be the first guy I'll look up, promise. Meanwhile, it's better just to be friends, right?"

"I suppose."

"*Anybody* can get married, Mur. Friendship is the tough one."

His heart purred. Friendship was the tough one: true. Georgina drove him crazy at times—all her wild gypsy ideas about pyramid power and the souls of rainbows—yet she was the best thing in his life besides his daughter; he would never trade Georgina's friendship for a wife. "I hope *Julie* gets married," he said.

"You'll dance at her wedding."

He checked the scope—a perfectly placid sea, cardiac waves rising and falling. He smiled. Julie's wedding, exquisite thought. Would his grandchildren be free of godhead? Was divinity a recessive trait?

The curtain slid back and there she was, surely no more than seven pounds overweight, bearing a grand explosion of chrysanthemums. "Contraband," she said with forced cheer, setting the vase on the nightstand. "They don't allow these things in intensive care, foul up the air or something." As Julie's gaze strayed to the half-dozen suction cups leeching on his chest, her face grew so white her forehead scar almost vanished. "Hey, you're looking good." Her voice was fissured. She kissed his cheek. "How's it going?"

"I get tired now and then. An occasional pain."

Tears hung on Julie's eyelids, her large lips drooped sharply. "I know what you're thinking—this is how your father went." A tear fell. "They know a lot more about hearts these days. They really do. The heart is a pump."

"Give him a new one," said Georgina firmly.

Again Julie blanched. "Huh?"

"You heard me."

"Georgina," Julie whispered, turning the name into an ad monishment.

"I won't tell anybody—Girl Scout's honor."

"Georgina, you're asking..."

"A new one, kid. Forget about launching the age of cosmic harmony. Forget synergistic convergence. Just give your pop a new heart."

As Georgina backed out of intensive care, the television spoke of terrorists releasing hand grenades aboard a Greek cruise ship.

Georgina, you're asking too much, was what she'd wanted to say, Murray guessed. He stared at her forehead, the scar emerging as her color returned. He didn't doubt that Julie could cure him, nor that he wanted her to: the idea of oblivion filled him with an anger so intense his saliva boiled. How dare oblivion come and blot out his thoughts, his daughter, his best friend, his books?

But no. It *was* asking too much. She must stay off the high road. Once she started intervening, it would never stop—a new heart, a second new heart, an AIDS victim delivered, a cyclone forestalled, a mud slide retracted, a revolution resolved, and soon her enemies would be at her doorstep.

"Hey, if I confess to you," he asked, "does that make this my deathbed?"

"No way."

"I never told anybody, but...I met Phoebe's father once."

"Where is he?"

"He's dead."

Julie grimaced. "Dead?"

"He was in the old Preservation Institute when it blew up. Marcus Bass. He convinced me to steal you—your machine."

"Phoebe keeps imagining she'll find him."

"She won't."

"Should I tell her?"

"No point. Poor guy had four kids. Boys. I sent 'em baseball cards sometimes." Oh, how he'd love to see Marcus Bass again —see him, hug him, thank him for making him realize he needed an embryo. "Honey, has God ever told you what happens after death?"

"You're not going to die." Julie curled her fingers into tight lumpy balls. "You have to finish *Hermeneutics of the Ordinary.*"

"But has she ever told you?"

"My mother's outside the universe, Pop—the God of physics, I'm sure of it." Absently Julie spun the TV dial. The Road Runner *beep-beeped* across the screen. "We both know what we're thinking, huh? Georgina said—"

"I hate that Road Runner thing." He glowered at the TV. "Ants in his feathers." The God of physics? Julie's mother a mere equation, the fuse that had touched off the big bang? That explained a lot, he figured. "The answer's *no*. I'll get out of this the hard way."

She brushed his wired chest. "If I just made a few new cells..."

"Think it through. You can fix up my heart for now, but how will you take the stress and the fat away—fix up the whole world? Hearts aside, maybe it'll be a brain aneurysm next time, or kidney failure, or Alzheimer's."

"I can't let you *die*."

A spectacular nurse entered, a kind of Miss November with clothes on—aggressively busty, fine slutty lips—and deposited a pill on his tongue. "Visiting hours are over."

"My kid," he said, drinking down the pill. How dare oblivion come and blot out the world's nurses?

"Good for you." The nurse offered Julie a sunshine smile. "Those flowers can't stay."

Again Julie kissed his cheek. "All right, Pop. You win."

A smooth vascular tide rolled across the scope. He felt a nap coming on. "Go have a life."

"On the Boardwalk in Atlantic City," Phoebe Sparks sang as a nasty March wind propelled her past Steel Pier's dead merry-go-round, "we will walk in a dream." Her old Girl Scout canteen rapped against her side like a child trying to get her attention. "On the Boardwalk in Atlantic City, life will be peaches and cream." Broken and decayed, the piers were like a seedy version of the Acropolis—relics rimming the city, remnants of an earlier, nobler, more eminent age. They were also, Phoebe had learned, good places to spend one's lunch hour: plenty of privacy.

She uncapped the canteen, raised the spout to her lips. Mom didn't mind an occasional beer, but serious liquor was out. There were times, though, when only Bacardi rum could make the world feel right, rum the wonder drug.

A man was fishing off the end of the pier.

Licking Bacardi from her lips, Phoebe recapped the canteen. "Catch anything?"

He turned. A Caucasian. Not her father, then. It was never her father. "Hooked a barracuda last week, but they aren't biting today." The fisherman was bearded and handsome, his muscular torso filling a red turtleneck sweater. "How are you, Miss Sparks?"

"You know me?"

The stranger grinned. His teeth were bright, bent, and slimy, like pearls made by a depraved oyster. "I was in the Deauville Hotel when you found that dynamite. Julie and I talked."

"You're that friend of her mother's?"

"Andrew's the name. Wyvern." He reeled in his barren hook, began disassembling his rod. "I'll be frank with you. I'm worried about poor old Julie."

"She's not a happy camper," Phoebe agreed. She didn't like this Andrew Wyvern. He had the sleazy air of a casino pit boss. "Divinity's no joke, I gather. You always feel like you're not doing enough."

"Phoebe, sweetheart, I have something important to tell you."

Phoebe tapped her Girl Scout canteen. "Want a drink? It's rum."

"Never touch it. Did you know you have a crucial role to play in Julie's life?"

"She's never been very big on listening to me."

Wyvern picked up his fishing gear and, grinning luminously, started toward the Boardwalk. "You're intending to give her some newspaper clippings," he prophesied abruptly. "For Hanukkah. For her temple."

"Yeah. And on her birthday too." Against her better judgment, she followed Wyvern to the carousel. "How'd you figure that out?"

"Lucky guess."

Lucky guesses, no doubt, came easily to Katz's mother's friends.

"Certainly you mean well. You aim to tell her she's not obliged to end the world's pain, there's just too much of it. Fine." Wyvern climbed atop a splintery, termite-infested lion. He smelled of honeyed oranges and guile. A pit boss? No, somebody even worse, Phoebe sensed. "But the thing could backfire," he warned. "If we're not careful, she'll become obsessed, bent on repairing every little leak in the planet. Once she's on that course, she'll go mad."

"I used to believe that. Not anymore. Fact is, I *want* her damn temple to backfire, I *want* her to feel obliged." Phoebe mounted a moldering unicorn held together with nails, bolts, and fiberglass patches. "Katz should be out helping people—curing diseases, making food appear in Ethiopia, ending the civil war in Turkey. She should be out...beating the devil." The devil? Yes, it was he, surely. Phoebe uncapped the canteen, gulped; the magic fluid fortified her, a moat of rum surrounding her heart. A sensible girl would dismount and run now, she realized. She jammed her boots deeper into the stirrups. Sensible girls never got to rag the devil.

"Julie can't be bothered with earthly ephemera," Wyvern persisted. "Her mission is much higher."

"There's this blind kid who's not blind anymore."

"Julie was sent to start a religion. It's the only way she'll know peace."

"Your friend God's never told her that."

"Heaven communicates indirectly—through people like you and me."

"And we should tell Katz to start a religion?"

"Exactly."

"What sort of religion?"

"A big one. Apocalyptic. Like, say, Christianity."

"Know what I think, Mr. Wyvern?" Phoebe slid off her unicorn and, shielded by inebriation, staggered back onto the pier. "I think you're so full of shit you've got roses growing out your ass."

The devil's lips quivered like angry slugs. "If you knew who I am, you wouldn't—"

"I *do* know who you are."

Wyvern squeezed the lion's reins until his hand went white. Slowly, relentlessly, like a crumbling corpse twitching to life in one of Roger Worth's zombie movies, the carousel began to turn. Faster now. And faster still, spewing out dark, palpable winds like a spinning jenny making thread. "You're a poor friend to Julie!" Wyvern called from the core of the tornado. Music slashed the air, a screeching rendition of "The Washington Post March" played on the carousel's steam organ.

"Screw you, mister!" The winds tugged Phoebe's wiry hair. Caught in the gusts, paper trash scudded along the pier like tumbleweeds in a ghost town.

"A *terrible* friend!" Twenty-four wooden animals, back from the grave, galloping in homage to the glory that was Steel Pier, the grandeur that was Atlantic City. Flies and locusts flew from the stampede like bullets. A squadron of bats zoomed out, each with a human face—men, women, children, their flesh sucked dry, drained of hope. "Julie deserves better!"

"Screw you and the pig you buggered for breakfast!"

Slowly, like a child's top succumbing to gravity, the carousel ground to a halt. Wyvern was gone, his lion riderless.

The devil. The actual, goddamn devil.

Alone on the pier, Phoebe gasped and shivered and, after taking a bracing swallow of Girl Scout rum, quietly resolved that —one day—somehow—she would make Julie Katz fulfill her potential.

"The heart is a pump," Julie wrote in her diary the day after she and Howard Lieberman broke up, "weak and fickle as any other machine, and sometimes an embolism of indifference stops affection's flow."

The affair had ended as abruptly as it had begun. They were in his apartment, eating breakfast in bed—they'd been shacking up since April—when suddenly Howard was babbling about their presumed upcoming trip to the Galapagos Islands, laying out his plans as if that were the place she most wanted to visit.

"Why would I want to go *there*?" Julie asked, daubing cream cheese on a bagel.

"Why? Why? It's the Jerusalem of Biology, that's why." Howard slid her nightgown upward and kissed her belly button, the tough nutlike stub that had once plugged her into God. "It's the Holy City of Natural Science. At Galapagos, the mind frees itself from the illusion of divine guidance."

"Gets pretty hot, I hear."

"So does Philadelphia." Suspicious, he reclothed her navel.

"Rains a lot too."

"Julie, what are you *saying*?"

"I'm saying I don't want to go to the Galapagos Islands with you." She bit into her bagel. "I'm saying I don't . . . want to."

At which point Howard had flown into a rage, accusing her

of everything from laziness to vampirism. She'd exploited him, he asserted. Pretended to care while sinking her fangs into his intellect, drinking his mind. "Know what you said right before I asked you out? You said you believed in God."

"I *do* believe in God. I'm sorry, Howard, but I couldn't take a whole summer of hearing you whine about creationism."

"I *made* you, dammit. I taught you how to think."

"To think your thoughts."

"Without me, you'd be just another scientifically illiterate *girl*."

Whereupon Julie had risen from the bed, pushed her cheese-coated bagel against Howard's forehead—it stuck like the mark of a buffoonish Cain—and, after throwing on her clothes, fled the apartment and marched down Spruce Street to the University Museum, where she spent the afternoon contemplating embalmed Egyptians.

Men.

The next day she hauled her junk out of Howard's place and returned to Angel's Eye, home now to Phoebe and Georgina, whose landlord, a Revelationist, had booted them out of their Ventnor Heights apartment upon sensing the pluralism of their sexual inclinations. Good old Phoebe, good old Georgina. What formidable nurses they made, Georgina especially, forever mixing up bizarre potions to strengthen Pop's heart, forever feeding him the robust vegetables she'd somehow coaxed from the sandy soil.

Julie bought a diary, writing in it obsessively, hopeful that by projecting her mind, movielike, onto the creamy paper, she might glimpse who she was.

Her temple proved the ideal writer's den, a monk's cell complete with Smile Shop candles. Odd how Phoebe was always updating the place. Odder still how the images no longer soothed Julie reliably. It seemed as if her conscience were becoming raw and friable; her superego felt ready to bleed. As each new apartheid victim or traffic fatality appeared, she grew ever more certain that Phoebe wanted the images to cut both ways: Katz, you have nothing to do with this; Katz, you have everything to do with this.

"God didn't send me to perform a lot of flashy tricks," Julie insisted to her diary. "If Phoebe can't see that, too bad. Besides, she drinks too much."

Indeed, there was simply no point in taking Phoebe seriously these days. They now occupied two entirely different planes: Julie the Ivy Leaguer and nascent prophet of empiricism, Phoebe the high-school dropout and joke-shop clerk. What did Phoebe know of the Chandrasekhar limit? Of Planck's constant, Seyfert galaxies, Hilbert spaces? Poor girl. She should get out of South Jersey and learn about the universe. Perhaps, as Howard had tutored Julie, she should now tutor Phoebe, infusing her with the thrill of cosmogenesis.

Howard. Ah, yes, Howard. "In his relentless crusade, Howard missed something," Julie wrote. "Quantum mechanics and general relativity do not explain the universe, they *portray* it, as did Aristotle's crystalline spheres and Newton's clockwork planets." She reread the paragraph. Howard *missed*, she'd written, not *misses*. So: it was truly over, she'd exiled him to the past tense. Fine. Good riddance. "Howard took the model for the reality," she continued, "the metaphor for the meat. An authentic cosmic explorer, I believe, gleans a tacit moral from $\Delta\chi\Delta\rho \geq h/4\pi$, Heisenberg's famous uncertainty relation. At the heart of all truth lies a radiant cloud of unknowing, a glorious nugget of doubt, a shining core of impermanence."

Pop entered. Each day he seemed to get a bit smaller, a bit more stooped. Life followed the statisticians' famous bell-shaped curve: you grew, you peaked, you ungrew. His outlook, too, was shrinking. He'd simply drifted in, brought by the wind.

"Whatever form my ministry takes," Julie wrote, "I shall forge only a covenant of uncertainty. I shall declare only a kingdom of impermanence." She shut her diary violently, as if crushing a stray spider in its leaves.

"I'm lighting the beacon," said Pop, cinching the sash of his awful tartan robe. "Exercise is good for cardiac patients."

"Which is it?" she inquired through locked teeth. With age, his eccentricities had become decidedly less charming. "*Lucy II?*"

"*William Rose*, I think. Is this July?"

"You know it is, Pop."

"If it's July, it must be *William Rose*."

"Take your Inderal yet?"

"Uh-huh."

"Your Lanoxin? Quinidine?"

"Sure, sure. And some kiwi juice from Georgina."

He shuffled off.

"The tragedy of my species," Julie wrote, "is that it does not live in its own time. *Homo sapiens* is locked on history's rearview mirror, never the road ahead, bent on catching some presumed lost paradise, some alleged golden..."

She paused. Pop was climbing to the beacon. Exercise was good for cardiac patients, but...a hundred and twenty-six stairs?

"The human race is destroying itself with nostalgia," Julie wrote.

The pen fell from her hand. A hundred and twenty-six stairs. She left without closing her diary.

Above all, Pop's stare: frozen, upside down, twice normal size. Julie hadn't seen a gaze so extreme since that Timothy kid got his eyes. He lay on the third loop of the staircase, hands pressed against his chest as if trying to massage his own frozen heart back to life.

She ran.

Girl Scout camp, 1985. Take the cardiopulmonary resuscitation class, earn the merit badge. She slammed his chest, exhaled into his lungs. Such a grotesquely detailed corpse he made—the black hair flourishing in his nostrils, the gaping pores of his cheeks. *Slam, slam, slam, breath. Slam, slam, slam, breath.* When she was eleven, he'd started bringing home snapshots from Photorama, and they would set them out on the kitchen table. The women with emotional problems, those who photographed dismembered mannequins or teddy bears buried neck deep in mud, were automatically disqualified, ditto those candidates whose developed film revealed lovers, husbands, or hordes of offspring. *Slam, slam, slam, breath.* "How about her, Julie?" "Kind of grumpy-looking." "Here's a pretty one." "Nah." *Slam, slam, slam, breath.* Nothing came of it. Of the dozen or so women they found appealing, not one had been willing to commit to Pop. *Slam, slam, slam, breath.* And yet he was so sincere about it, so well meaning: yes, he'd wanted a companion for himself, but mostly he'd wanted a stepmother for his child.

Gradually her instincts, her maternal heritage, claimed her. Resting her palm atop his sternum, she made his heart go *thump*. And why not? Nobody would see her intervene, no baby bank aborters would ever know. *Thump* again. And *thump*. And—

Think it through, he'd told her. True resurrection was no childhood game, no simple matter of goading a dead crab with your crayons. Repair the heart, obviously. And by now his central nervous system was gone, blood-starved, a jumble of unraveled synapses, a stew of desiccated dendrites. Fix all that too.

Then what? Clean all the crust out of the veins and arteries? Yes, only it just started up again, didn't it? Pop was right: at some point you had to remake the world, at some point you had to be God.

And yet—she must try. *Thump*. And *thump*. And *thump* and suddenly something came into being, a creation half Pop, half not, a palsied parody of life, blinking fitfully.

"Ga-ga-ga-ga," her creation rasped.

"Pop? Yes, Pop? What?"

"Ga-ga-ga-go. *Go*."

"Go? Go where?"

"A l-life."

"Life?"

"G-go h-have . . ."

A shrill, watery whistle shot from her father's mouth, as if he had the Steel Pier steam organ for lungs. And then, for the second time that evening, he died.

"Pop! Pop!"

No pulse. No breath.

"Pop!"

Pupils fixed and dilated.

So instead of resurrection, instead of Lazarus II, there was merely this tearful climb to the beacon room. *Go have a life*. Very well—she would. She hadn't been sent to contradict death; rebirth was not her business. She would eschew the rearview mirror, lock on the road ahead, live in her own time.

The matches, she knew, were in a tin box under the lamp. Raising the lens, she wound the clockwork motor. Enough kerosene? He always kept the tank full, didn't he?

She struck a match, twisted the knob. The central wick rose like a cobra from a basket, meeting the little flame and catching. "Hello there, *William Rose*," she gasped, the words falling from her lips like rotten teeth. "This time . . . you'll . . . make it." She restored the lens. The lead piston descended, squeezing kerosene into the wick chamber.

Somewhere beyond the blur of her tears, the beacon glowed brightly, she was sure of it.

And now came her penance, the agony that all who fail their

fathers must endure. *Did you see our lamp, old ship?* Reaching out blindly with her right hand, she wrapped it tightly around the hot mantle. Impossible pain—uncanny, unprecedented pain—yet she held on till she smelled burnt flesh, screaming till she felt her throat might rip. *Did you find your way home?* Weeping, she pulled her smoking, blistered, martyred palm away. *Did you?*

By some miracle she got through the rest of the day and its obscene details. Calling the undertaker. Calling the undertaker a second time when he failed to show up. (He had confused Brigantine Point with Brigantine Quay.) Hauling herself down to Atlantic City Memorial, where they greased and bandaged her hand, put her on antibiotics, and admonished her to avoid kerosene lamps. The notification list was not long—Phoebe, Georgina, and, from the fire station, Freddie Caspar and Rodney Balthazar, Herb Melchior having died six years earlier of lung cancer.

"The dumb bunny wanted to marry me," Georgina sobbed over the phone. "Sounds like the premise of a bad TV show, huh? That's right, Bernie, this aging bookworm and his dyke friend move in together. He doesn't expect her to give up women, though secretly he's jealous, and they've got these two kids, and . . . you mean you just let him *die*? You didn't *do* anything?"

"I tried."

"Try again! Run over to the fucking funeral parlor this very minute and raise him up! This very minute!"

"He wouldn't want it."

"*I* want it. *You* want it."

Julie's stomach became a well of ice water. Her burned palm itched ferociously. "I'm supposed to have a life, Georgina—that was his big goal."

For an entire minute Georgina grieved, so much weeping that Julie imagined tears dripping from the receiver and splashing onto the phone-booth floor.

"Listen, Julie, we've got to do this right. I think we're supposed to rip our clothes, and then we sit on these little stools till next Monday. Hey, I'd be happy to do that, honey. For him, I'd put my ass to sleep for a week."

"I don't think that's for Pop."

"We've got to do *something*. How are you, baby?"

"Lonely. An orphan."

In the end they simply had him cremated. The small, solemn procession—Julie, Phoebe, Georgina—carried the urn across the lighthouse lawn and down the length of the jetty. After Julie said Kaddish, Georgina took out a peanut-butter jar filled with a second set of ashes, specially prepared by incinerating Pop's copy of *The Adventures of Huckleberry Finn.* Phoebe opened the urn and dumped in the contents of the jar, mixing everything together with a kitchen knife, merging Murray Katz with his favorite book.

"I always liked him," Phoebe said, closing the urn and passing it to Julie. "He was the kind of dad I'd have wanted for myself, even if he thought I was a bad influence on you."

"You *were* a bad influence on me." With her burned hand Julie uncapped the urn, glancing briefly at the dark ethereal flecks of her father. "Oh, Pop..."

Phoebe and Georgina melted into the dusk, leaving Julie alone with the monotonous and unfeeling surf. Was it a proper funeral? Had the un-Jewish procedure of cremation offended him? "Too late now," she muttered as she tore her black dress—tore it, and tore it again, and again, until she stood naked on the rocks. She snugged the urn under her breasts and climbed into the sea.

In the beginning was the Word. And the Word was made flesh, and dwelt among us.

Her gills throbbed, wringing oxygen from the bay. Endless gallons, but they couldn't dilute her acid tears or wash away her guilt. Two decades jacketed in flesh, during which time she hadn't done the vast damaged planet one atom of good.

She touched bottom and quickly buried the urn. *The Adventures of Huckleberry Katz.*

In the beginning was the Word, but now God's vocabulary was growing. The first Word was an English noun, *savior*, but the second would be a French verb, *savoir*, to know: at long last, Julie, Howard used to tell her, we can *know* things. Three more years of college, and then she'd buy a word processor (no, Word processor) and publish her covenant of uncertainty, declare her kingdom of impermanence, topple the empire of nostalgia—teach the truth of the heart. The heart was a pump? Yes, true enough, provided one meant: at the present moment in history, pump is the best metaphor we have for what a heart is.

She tamped down the grave with her foot, raising dust devils of sand.

And the kidney was a filter. Earth orbited the sun. Microbes caused disease. Yes! The time of her ministry was at hand. She would take neither the high road nor the low, but a byway of her own devising; she would beam her message onto every television screen in creation, etch it onto every phonograph record, smear it across every printed page. In the beginning was the Word, and in the end there would be a million words, ten million words, a hundred million words, all authored by the only begotten daughter of God herself.

PART TWO

· · ·

Atlantic City Messiah

CHAPTER 6

♦   ♦   ♦

Bix Constantine—morose, fat, and frank—had always seen the world as it was and not as people wished it would be.

While still a preschooler, he pondered the ways children's books depicted the relationship between humans and farm animals, soon sensing the disparity between these cheery visions and the proteinaceous facts appearing nightly on his plate. Shortly after he started first grade, Bix's mother told him dewdrops were elf tears, and he told her she was full of dog-doo. That evening his father spanked him, and Bix always suspected his real crime was not his surliness but his refusal to love a lie.

With adolescence his vision enlarged. God? Santa Claus for grownups. Love? A euphemism for resignation. Marriage? The first symptom of death.

On the morning of July 13, 1996, Bix Constantine discovered something even worse than walking to work through the dense sleaze of Atlantic City's Boardwalk: doing so knowing you're about to be fired. Nobody knew why the *Midnight Moon* was losing the great supermarket-tabloid race. Not Bix, not his staff, not Tony Biacco, the former Mafia chieftain who owned the paper. "Folks, we're going to have to pull the plug," Tony had been saying at least once a week for the past two years. Plug-pulling was a familiar motif around the *Midnight Moon*. COMA WIFE WAKES AFTER HUBBY PULLS PLUG. Also, MANIAC STALKS COMA

WARD PULLING PLUGS. And "DON'T PULL MY PLUG!" COMA GIRL TELLS
MOM THROUGH PSYCHIC.

Bix ambled past the Tropicana and bought a cup of coffee
from a vendor outside the Golden Nugget, its threshold pillared
and glittery like a fundamentalist's heaven. *Tonight: Neil Sedaka*,
screamed the billboards. *Next Week: Vic Damone and Diahann Car-
roll.* Who could possibly care?

When he was ten, his father had dragged him to a celebration
here. The Casino Gaming Referendum had just passed, and the
Boardwalk was overrun by chorus girls and brass bands. Clowns
bustled up and down the piers, giving out balloons. "It's not
going to succeed," little Bix had told his father. "The mob will
move in and ruin it," he'd elaborated. His father had scowled.
"The mob moves in and ruins everything. Don't you ever *read*,
Dad?"

Slurping Styrofoam-flavored coffee, Bix listed onto Sovereign
Avenue. A derelict was piled up at the Arctic intersection,
shrouded in wine vapors. Graffiti coated the city. The stray dogs
had it on their flanks.

Why was the *Moon* dying? Weren't its extraterrestrials every
bit as perverted as the *World Bugle*'s, its abominable snowmen as
randy as the *National Comet*'s? Had not Bix's surrealistic surgical
procedures, pregnant great-grandmothers, Siamese quadruplets,
and celebrities' ghosts set new standards for the entire industry?
Yes, yes, yes, and yes—and yet the stark fact remained that
Tony had arranged an emergency lunch for the entire staff, a
perfect occasion to solicit their resignations.

Arriving at 1475 Arctic Avenue, he approached the open elevator shaft—the car lay inert and broken at the bottom like a
sunken ship—and tossed his coffee cup into the square chasm.
Hauling his bulk up the moldering staircase, he disembarked on
the third floor, where Madge Bronston, the paper's chronically
smiling receptionist, told him "a pigheaded young woman" had
just invaded his office.

"I think she's here about a job," Madge explained.

"Good. I could use one."

"I tried kicking her out, believe me. A stubborn gal."

As Bix opened his monogrammed door, his visitor—chunky,
caramel skin, early twenties—spun away from his mounted collection of UFO photos, flashing him a grin of considerable sensu-

ality. "I've always wanted to visit Pluto," she said in a South Jersey accent. "Mars sounds dull, Saturn's a lot of gas, but Pluto..." Her hand came toward him like a fluttering bird, and without meaning to he reached out and captured it. "I'm Julie Katz. You must be Mr. Constantine."

"Uh-huh."

Her white sundress dazzled him, and her lips were of the succulent sort that inspired Muslims to veil their women. Glancing higher, Bix encountered a cute upturned nose, turquoise eyes, and a crop of unruly black hair.

So this was how it began: the pangs of libido, and then would come the first date, the courtship, the disingenuous nuptial vows, the snot-clogged children, the reciprocal illusion of permanence, the extramarital affairs (most of them his, but she would doubtless get in a few retaliatory screws), and, inevitably, the divorce. "I'm afraid this operation's headed for the sewer, Miss Katz." Bix strode to his King Coffee machine, which by some miracle Madge had remembered to turn on, and filled his inscribed mug: *I have come to the conclusion that one can be of no use to another person—Paul Cezanne.* "There's no job here for you."

The intruder tapped a flying saucer with her long, mitershaped fingernail. "You a believer?"

"The door's over this way, young lady."

"Tell me if you're a believer. Do UFOs exist?"

He swallowed coffee, quite possibly the only decent thing in the world. "Ten thousand encounters to date, and still nobody's walked away with a single alien cootie or paper clip. You don't *want* to work for us. We're the most heavily censored paper this side of *Pravda*." True enough, Bix thought. Even more than Soviet journalism, irrationality and mawkishness had to follow a party line. The man who died on the operating table and was subsequently revived could speak only of light and angels, and if it were gray or frightening you wouldn't be reading about it in the checkout line. "Time to go."

She marched forward and presented him with a manila envelope. Coarse white tissue covered her right palm like a wad of chewing gum. "Read this."

"I'm a busy man."

"My column—the preamble, actually. I can't give advice till I've stated my principles."

"We *have* an advice column."

"Mine'll be different—a kind of covenant. I want to rescue the masses from nostalgia, and yours is one of the few papers they read."

"Not enough masses."

"I could always take my message to *Scientific American* or *The Skeptical Inquirer*, but why preach to the converted?" That lascivious smile again. "My brother Jesus made a big mistake. He didn't leave any writings behind."

"Your brother *who*?"

"Jesus Christ. Half brother, technically."

"Jesus' sister, eh?" Bix drained his coffee. Jesus' sister: that, at least, was a new one. "On Mary's side?"

"God's." She gave his shoulder a patronizing squeeze. "It's hard to accept. I barely do myself."

Bix had spent most of his adult life dealing with self-appointed saints and saviors. With faith healers, fortune tellers, crystal gazers, spirit channelers. With people who took their vacations on Venus and their sabbaticals on the astral plane. Now came a woman with the grandest claim of all, yet she bore about as much resemblance to the average visionary as an interim report did to an orgasm.

He said, "Maybe if you changed my coffee into gin . . ."

"You're an agnostic, Mr. Constantine?"

"Used to be." Bix refilled his mug. "Then one day—you want to hear about it?"

"My favorite subject."

"One day I picked up my cousin's new baby and realized how at any moment this pathetic, innocent creature might die in a car crash or get leukemia, and in that moment of revelation, my Road to Damascus, I went the whole way to atheism."

Of all things: she laughed. A spontaneous display of amused assent. "Hey, if I weren't divine," she said, "*I'd* probably be an atheist too." In a gesture he found both erotic and endearing, Julie Katz wrapped her hands around his coffee mug and, leaving it in his grasp, lifted the rim to her abundant lips and sipped. "It's certainly the more logical choice."

I'm in love, Bix thought. He opened the manila envelope and lifted out a one-page letter stapled to a black-and-white photo of its author.

Dear *Moon* Readers:

God exists! Oh, yes! I have proof! Imagine!

"What proof?" you ask. Picture a female reproductive cell, rocketing through time and space from the regions beyond reality, passing through the walls of a crystalline womb, and coming to rest in a Jewish celibate's sperm donation. Thus did I enter the world. Yes: I am she. God's daughter. Water-breather, kin to Jesus, confessor to Satan, confidant of fish and fireflies. Proof!

Now: the bad news. Like all deities, I am a product of my era. I live in my own time, in this case the bewildering and uncertain twentieth century. Sorry. I wish I could comfort you with pretty promises of healing and immortality. I cannot. But God exists! Think of it!

Are you in pain? I understand. Does death frighten you? Tell me about it. Has your marriage or career brought disappointments you never anticipated? You are not alone. I look forward to receiving your cards and letters, along with whatever mementos you feel might help me to comprehend your suffering. Together we shall topple the empire of nostalgia!

> Love,
> Sheila, Daughter of God

"Well? What do you think?"

What did Bix think? He thought Julie Katz had dug up the basement of the *Moon* building and found a chest of Spanish doubloons. This wasn't ESP or the Loch Ness monster or the boy who filled the bathtub with piranha thinking them goldfish until they ate Gramps—this was genuine lunacy, this was playing to win. The ailing tabloid would either rise on Julie Katz's dementia or she would bury it forever.

"We don't need this bit about nostalgia," he said.

"Yes we do. Humanity must stop living in the past."

"Why'd you sign it 'Sheila'?"

"I require anonymity. I'm expected to have a life."

"This put-down of healing and immortality should go. Our readers are into those things."

"The Age of Miracles is over."

"The Age of Reason is also over. This is the Age of Nonsense. We have a policy."

"I don't care about your stupid policy."

"Hey, honey, do you want an editor or not?"

"Do you want a column or not?" She pushed back her hair, uncovering a thin, S-shaped scar. "I imagine the World Bugle would be interested."

"Look, it doesn't really matter what I think. Mr. Biacco has final say on any new feature."

Predictably, she declined his request for her phone number, promising instead to call on Tuesday. His eyes remained rooted on her as she brushed past Madge Bronston and started down the hall, and seconds later he was bent over the Moon's persnickety Xerox machine, rapidly reproducing her letter. That lush mouth, that luxurious hair. Why were the mad so singularly sensual?

Tony kicked off the lunch meeting exactly as Bix knew he would, noting that "a corpse's corpuscles have better circulation than we do." But today he went further. The time, Tony asserted, had truly, finally, irrevocably come to pull the plug.

"Let's try this first." Bix opened his briefcase. Within a minute each rat aboard the sinking ship called Midnight Moon was reading a copy of Julie Katz's letter.

"A schizophrenic, right?" concluded Patty Roth, the circulation director.

"Hard to say," said Bix.

"A paranoid schizophrenic, sounds like."

"Crazy or not, I say give her a chance." He had to see her again, Bix realized. Had to. "Look at it this way. The Bugle's got that happy fascist Orton March and his outrageous editorials, the Comet seems to know exactly which movie stars' penises people want to read about, but the Moon and only the Moon will have the living, breathing words of God's other child."

"Okay, okay, but she's not up to speed yet," said Tony. "I assume you'll cut this crap about our bewildering century?"

"That was my first instinct. I'm beginning to think it gives her a certain authenticity."

"It's not us. It's not the *Moon.*" Tony combed his graying hair with his withered fingers. "I want her to reveal what heaven's like, okay, Bix? Then have her try a few low-key predictions."

"Maybe she should help people explore their past lives," said Patty.

"And give tips for winning the lottery," said Tony.

"I doubt she'll go for it," said Bix.

"Hey, now that the concept's nailed down, why do we need this girl at all?" asked Mike Alonzo, the paper's science editor (DEAD ASTRONAUTS BUILD CITY ON VENUS). "Why not just have Kendra McCandless write it?"

Kendra's very name made Bix grimace. Kendra McCandless, the paper's free-lance astrologer, astral tripper, ecstasy monger, and goofball. "Nah, with Kendra all you get's a lot of secrets-of-the-universe stuff. Transcendence as usual. With Julie Katz you get . . . I don't now. Something else."

"The divine spark?" sneered Mike.

"She's ambiguous. Delphic. It might just work."

"We can offer three hundred per column," said Tony. "You think she'll sign for that?"

"Don't know."

"Title. We need a title."

"Hadn't thought about it. 'Dear Sheila'?"

"Doesn't goose me. Paul?"

"'Letters to Sheila'?" suggested Paul Quattrone, the paper's financial reporter (TOP PSYCHICS PREDICT MARKET UPTURN).

"'Sheila's Corner'?" offered Sally Ormsby, the film critic (NEW ELVIS FLICK RECOVERED FROM UFO CRASH).

"'Notes from the Netherworld'?" ventured Lou Pincus, the sports editor (DEVIL CULT USES HUMAN HEAD FOR HOCKEY PUCK).

"'Advice from the Afterlife'?" hazarded Vicki Maldonado, whose beat was burned children and the Bermuda Triangle.

"Hold on," said Tony. "This is hardball, people. This is Jesus Christ's sister. We'll be printing the stuff *everybody* wants to know."

"Brainstorm, Tony?" asked Patty.

"Forty days and forty nights."

"Give it to us."

"The girl's column will be called—now get this—'Heaven Help You.'"

Heaven Help You

DEAR SHEILA: My brother-in-law is writing this letter for me, because three weeks ago I was in a terrible car accident and broke my neck. Now I'm one of those quadriplegics, which makes me of positively no use to my wife or anybody else. You said to send a memento, so I'm enclosing a snapshot of me windsurfing on Cape Cod last summer.

Here's my question, Sheila. What's the very best way for me to kill myself?—BROKEN IN MASSACHUSETTS

DEAR BROKEN: In pressing your photograph to my heart, I have come to believe your future is much brighter than you imagine. You are definitely among the seventy percent of quads who can have normal genital intercouse. Beyond this inspiring fact, science and technology offer many resources for individuals in your situation: reading machines, robot appliances, computerized typewriters, electric wheelchairs.

If you ultimately decide suicide is your only option, I urge you to do it right, as a bungled attempt can be both painful and a real mess for your survivors to clean up. Try contacting the National Hemlock Society, which helps the terminally ill out of the world. But please don't kill yourself, Broken. Staying alive is the best revenge.

DEAR SHEILA: Accompanying this letter is a peanut-butter jar filled with our daughter's tears. Meggie is fourteen, sleeps poorly, and won't get out of bed, not to mention her bad grades, almost no appetite, and usually she can't stop crying. Is this growing pains or what?—WORRIED, MISSISSIPPI

DEAR WORRIED: I have drunk your daughter's tears, and a single diagnosis keeps ringing through my head. I believe Meggie suffers from clinical depression, which actually strikes children as often as it does adults.

What to do? Psychotherapy is one route. Get Meggie to confront her unconscious demons, and there's a chance her symptoms will vanish.

If Meggie were my child, I would take her to a hospital specializing in affective disorders. The doctor will probably prescribe amitriptyline or some other antidepressant. With the help of love and pharmaceutical intervention, your daughter has a good shot at recovery.

DEAR SHEILA: If anybody thinks they've got problems, I'd like to mention my six no-good children, also my husband Jack (not his actual name), who hits me though not all the time, normally by punching, and with his feet, and to prove it my back and worse places have got these bruises, and if you think he's any sort of father to these kids you're dead wrong, and I never get a minute's peace, besides which he's always drunk and lately he's been using his belt. I do love him, though.

Anyway, Jack has made me pregnant again because we're not allowed to believe in birth control, and I want to be dead. If I get an abortion, will I burn in hell? Forever? My parents are good Catholics, so they'll kill me if I do this. The thing I'm sending is the diaphragm I should have worn all along, because I thought if you touched it, Sheila, then maybe this baby I don't want would go away.—MISERABLE IN CHEYENNE

DEAR MISERABLE: As you might imagine, I am very torn on the abortion question. Freedom of choice? Let's remember that our choices normally begin in the bedroom, not the abortion clinic. Let's remember all those prime candidates for abortion who, reprieved at the last minute, went on to lead extraordinary and valuable lives.

On the other hand, pro-lifers have far fewer angels on their side than they suppose. The Bible teaches nothing about abortion. And have you ever heard of Saint Augustine? This famous theologian told us not to equate abortion with murder, the fetus in his view being much less aware than a baby. Thomas Aquinas, another major Catholic, allowed abortions until the sixth week for males and three months for females, the points at which they allegedly acquire souls. And I'm grievously troubled to see the pro-lifers shedding their crocodile tears over dead fetuses while thousands of *wanted* children die every day from causes no less preventable than abortion.

Like so much of this century, Miserable, your dilemma is fraught with ambiguity. You'll have to let your conscience be your guide.

DEAR SHEILA: I want you to know about our nine-year-old son, Randy, who succumbed to acute lymphoblastic leukemia last March after a valiant fight lasting many months. From the enclosed Pedro Guerroro card—Randy's hobby was collecting baseball cards—I'm sure you'll pick up his emanations and sense what a glorious little boy he was.

At first our grief was shattering, but then we realized Randy's illness was part of God's loving plan for us. Randy is now our angel and guide, preparing a place for us in heaven. When we walk with the Lord, the darkest tragedy becomes a gift, doesn't it, Sheila?—RENEWED IN BISMARCK

DEAR RENEWED: It's wonderful you've conquered your grief, and Randy's spiritual beauty positively gushes from that Pedro Guerroro card, but I can't help suggesting that a God who communicates with us through leukemia is at best deranged.

In my view, it's time we stopped having lower standards for God than we do for the postal service. Suppose the doctors had cured your son. Then *that* would have proved my mother's infinite goodness too, wouldn't it? Follow my reasoning? Heads, God wins. Tails, God wins.

"To be perfectly frank," Bix told Julie over the phone after she'd been at it for three months, "this isn't quite the column we had in mind."

"No?"

"It's got to be more *spiritual*. Tony wants Sheila to tell people how they can tap their hidden psychic powers and tune in the rhythms of the cosmos."

"But that's just what everybody's *expecting*."

"I know."

"It's bullshit." She wished she hadn't called him. "It's Georgina Sparks bullshit."

"It sells papers. Look, friend, you're not exactly a runaway smash. A one-point-two percent rise in circulation, that's all. And no more talk about God being deranged, okay? Those people lost a *son*, for Christ's sake."

The operator said, "Please deposit thirty cents for the next three minutes."

"I came to wake up the world," said Julie. Time to install a home phone, she decided. She had a job; she could afford it. "Not coo it to sleep."

"We just want you to work harder on the spiritual end," said Bix. "Is that asking so much?"

"I'll see what I can do. Bye."

"Promise?"

"Promise."

"How about dinner next week? A lobster dinner, then

we'll go hear Vic Damone at the Tropicana."

"This is my ministry happening now, boss. It's not a time for personal pleasure. Bye."

Click.

A ministry! Three hundred a week and a ministry! True, the launching of "Heaven Help You" had been marred by editorial tamperings. As someone who profoundly doubted the accessibility of heaven, Julie resented the title—almost as much as she resented the halo they airbrushed onto her photo. Equally distressing was the lurid kick-off story, GOD'S DAUGHTER LANDS IN AMERICA, its inaccurate text illustrated with an equally inaccurate sketch of the ectogenesis machine (miscaptioned *echogenesis machine*). But: a ministry, a ministry, three hundred a week and a ministry!

With each letter she received, each wretch she helped, Julie felt a measure of remorse leach through her flesh and vanish. This was exactly the right vocation for her, the glorious middle road, modest enough to confound her enemies, grand enough to assuage her godhead. Indeed, when Phoebe asked to move into Julie's temple—it was twice the size of her own bedroom —Julie immediately said "of course," for she had no more need of temples, no more convulsions of conscience, no more free-floating guilt. "Tear down the clippings if you want."

"I'll leave that job to you," said Phoebe.

"Uncover the window, at least."

"I like the darkness."

Dark Phoebe, Phoebe the troglodyte. Predictably, instead of stripping the temple bare, Phoebe continued to upgrade it, carrying it into the third dimension: a diorama of a jetliner crashing, a dollhouse consumed by paper flames, a plaster volcano spewing cotton fumes on an HO-scale plastic village, the cluster of nuclear-tipped missiles she'd created by gluing cardboard stabilizers to her stolen dynamite from the Deauville. "Why bother?" asked Julie one December afternoon as Phoebe scissored a baby's corpse from *Time.* The cover story concerned the recent epidemic of child abuse.

"Because you still need this place. You haven't figured out what it's really saying."

"Like hell I need it." Julie followed Phoebe into the temple.

"I have a ministry now. I'm out in the world."

"An advice column isn't a ministry. A word processor isn't the world." Phoebe slapped rubber cement on the clipping and centered it above her bed. "*This* is the world—parents wrecking their own babies."

"Last week I printed the number of the national child-abuse hotline," Julie noted.

"You and Ann Landers."

An occasional word of support from your best friend—was that too much to expect? Praise for a well-written paragraph or for an astute suggestion—did it never occur to Phoebe to offer any? "That quadriplegic wrote back, you know. He said I gave him the will to live."

"You gave him a stone."

"More than he got from my mother."

"These poor women write to you wanting to know about abortion, and you lecture them on Saint Augustine."

"Abortion isn't just emotional."

"Their husbands are beating them."

"In each case I mail out the address of the nearest shelter for battered women."

"You should be *driving* them to the nearest shelter for battered women." The centerpiece of Phoebe's dresser was a portable liquor cabinet containing miniature bottles, the kind given out on airplanes; they seemed to Julie like toys —today's the day the teddy bears have their cocktail party. Approaching, Phoebe snatched up a Bacardi rum. "Look, I know we've been through all this," she said. "The world's pain is endless, this room doesn't even begin to tell the story. But still..." She emptied the bottle into a Smile Shop DAMN I'M GOOD mug. "A column is really the best you can do? You, who could part the Red Sea and patch up the ozone layer, and instead you're content to be just another tabloid rabbi?" She consumed the rum in three rapid sips. "If *I* had your talents, honey..."

Obviously Phoebe hadn't been reading "Heaven Help You" closely, or she would have understood that divine intervention and instant cures belonged in the past. "My mother wants us to live in our own time. When a species fixates on the supernatural, it ceases to mature."

Phoebe opened a second Bacardi, swilling it straight from the tiny bottle. "How do you know that's what God wants? How do you fucking *know*?"

Phoebe's rebuke filled Julie with an odd amalgam of confusion and anger. All right, sure, maybe she couldn't say for a fact that God was smiling on the Covenant of Uncertainty. But Phoebe had no right to harass her like this. "I have a strong intuition about it." Shivering with dismay, Julie picked up the altar skull, working her thumbs into the eye sockets. "Believe me, if I start doing miracles, the wheels of progress will slip a thousand years."

Like a furtive urchin stealing an apple from a fruit stand, Phoebe palmed a third Bacardi. "Hey, you're right, Katz, you *don't* need this temple anymore. You've got a much better rationalization now."

Julie felt her brain shake like a plum pudding. "I'll chalk that stupid remark up to rum."

"Maybe I'm not living in my own time, but *you're* not living in your own skin." Phoebe polished off the third bottle. "And I'm not drunk."

"After that much liquor, you should be."

Phoebe winked spitefully. "Yeah, but tomorrow I'll be sober, Katz"—she wobbled out of the room—"and you'll still be the deity who doesn't help people."

"Get off my back, Phoebe. You're not me, so just *get off!*"

In Julie's fibrillating mind the altar skull acquired eyeballs. Its stare was unyielding, accusing. Had it owned a tongue, she felt, it would have spoken, saying, Phoebe's right, you know.

I doubt that.

She's right. "Heaven Help You" isn't the answer.

It's the best I can do.

It's a cop-out.

Maybe.

Remote-control miracles, Sheila—that's the way to go. Intervention-at-a-distance—try it. You wouldn't have to expose yourself.

I wasn't sent to do tricks.

Try it.

No.

Try it.

* * *

DEAR SHEILA: Look at these snapshots and you'll see why nobody's willing to take my picture, not even my older sister, so
instead I used one of those instant-photo booths at the amusement park.

It all began when my experiment blew up last year in chemistry class. Sure, my dad is suing the crap out of the school system, but that doesn't keep my face from looking like a horror
movie, does it? It wouldn't be so bad if I were an old lady, but
I'm seventeen, and when boys look at me I can tell they want to
puke. Anyway, I'm hoping if you meditate on these snapshots,
Sheila, the doctors will do a really good job next month with my
operation.—HIDEOUS, ILLINOIS

DEAR HIDEOUS: Take heart. Reconstructive surgery is one of the
most exciting frontiers of modern medicine. You can receive
state-of-the-art treatment at the new DeGrazzio Institute in Chicago.

Also, yes, I've meditated on your snapshots, and I believe
your admittedly distressing face will start looking better soon. If
you know what's good for you, you'll never mention getting this
reply, which is going directly to you and not my editor.

DEAR SHEILA: I'm a proud man who hates writing to you, only
I've been unemployed for three years, and the welfare checks
hardly cover our food and rent. Forget Christmas for the kids. I
don't need to tell you a spot welder with rheumatoid arthritis
and gout hasn't got much of a future.

This probably sounds crazy, but if Emma and I had a truly
large refrigerator we could save a lot of money buying our food
in bulk and freezing it, so here's an advertisement for a big Westinghouse monster that would be just perfect. Can you suggest
any way we might afford a fine refrigerator like this?—WOLVES AT
DOOR

DEAR WOLVES: For political reasons, I'm not allowing the *Midnight Moon* to publish this reply.

A set of catalogues from legitimate correspondence schools is
on its way. You should consider such growing fields as public
accounting, data processing, and Xerox machine repair.

This too: I'm returning the advertisement. Tape it to your
present refrigerator and concentrate on it every day. Keep the
results strictly confidential or, believe me, you'll be sorry.

DEAR SHEILA: It wouldn't surprise me to learn I'm the loneliest person in the world. After my dead husband Larry passed away, things went nowhere but downhill. Aren't there any men in Indiana who could appreciate a peppy little wife who's only fifty-four and can cook to beat the band? The thing I'm enclosing is a Triple-A map of our county, because maybe you'll jab your finger on it and, presto, there'll be the location of somebody who'll love me.—SOUTH BEND WIDOW

DEAR WIDOW: I'm not releasing this reply to the *Moon*, and if you ever divulge the contents you'll be in trouble.

Go to Parkview Terrace Apartments, Building G, Number 32. Alex Filippone is a sixty-year-old motorcycle salesman, never married. He's enthusiastic about Cole Porter, duplicate bridge, and the Indiana Pacers basketball team. I strongly suspect you two will hit it off.

Because Ruined in Newark or Anguished in Camden might be waiting to abduct Sheila and force her to perform miracles, Julie never picked up her mail at the *Moon*. She likewise refused to have it forwarded to Angel's Eye: the postman might be a follower. Instead she received her letters under conditions suggesting a cocaine transaction, donning dark glasses and meeting her editor inside the moist, dismal, abandoned aquarium on Central Pier.

"Want to see a movie tonight?" Bix asked, lurching out of the shadows, the canvas mailbag teetering on his shoulder. Each week, his infatuation grew more annoying and adolescent: the brushed tit, the patted butt, the raunchy valentines he planted in her mail.

"I already told you—I don't date these days."

"One crummy movie."

"No."

Julie upended the bag and, guided by the return addresses, divided the envelopes into two stacks: regular readers versus beneficiaries of her remote-control miracles. Barely ten percent of the letters Sheila got could be accurately termed hate mail—the people who wrote calling her a communist, a humanist, the Whore of Babylon, the Whore of Reason, the Antichrist, or the devil incarnate. Her gender had proven particularly galling—an Oklahoma City man once sent her a cigar box containing a dog's penis ("The Bible says God is male, so you're going to need this")—though by far the largest subcategory of hate mail came from those who resented Sheila's policy of no visits. *Dear Sheila: My (wife, husband, girlfriend, boyfriend, child) is (sick, addicted, insane, suicidal, dying). Please come over right away.* Sheila's form letter was curt, but it did the job. *Dear Grieving: If I start making house calls, I won't have time for anything else.*

She nabbed an envelope from the first pile, slit it. "Look, Bix, this sexually molested teen in Albany says that, thanks to me, she finally got the courage to run away . . . and here's Reconciled in Duluth saying that, because of 'Heaven Help You,' he now accepts being a dwarf. Maybe you don't take me seriously, maybe Phoebe doesn't, but *these* people do."

"I've never taken anybody more seriously in my life. This is Bix Constantine talking, the Voltaire of Ventnor Heights, and you've got the bastard sending valentines."

"That last one was so *sweet*. I'd never seen porcupines humping before." She ripped apart a cushy envelope, and a blindingly red, home-knitted scarf fell out. Her greatest fan, that ninety-year-old grandmother in Topeka, had come through again.

"Valentines are a big step for me." Bix rested his plump hand on her shoulder, where it remained like an affectionate parrot. "Listen, friend, Tony's getting really itchy about the circulation figures. Let's tear a couple of lobsters apart next Saturday and talk about some ways to boost your appeal."

She removed the presumptuous hand. His fulsome demeanor did nothing for her, though she conceded his eternal nihilism had a certain glamor, his steadfast fatalism a definite panache. "I don't eat seafood. When I was a kid, my friends were flounders and starfish."

"Order steak then. The *Moon's* treat." Bix knocked on a deserted fish tank, producing a glassy *bong*. "Dante's lobby at eight. Okay?"

"Dinner, Bix. Just dinner. Not the first act of a *shtup*."

"Sure." He slung the gutted mailbag over his arm. "Who knows—you might even have a good time."

As her boss waddled down the pier, Julie opened the letter from the unemployed spot welder.

"Dear Sheila: The Westinghouse refrigerator arrived on Sunday morning. There it was, standing on the back porch like a hobo looking for a handout. At first we weren't bothered it came with no guarantee, but then we plugged it in and this weird sort of green fog came pouring out the bottom, and before we knew it our wallpaper was peeling away and our houseplants had all died, and then Emma and I both threw up for about six hours straight, plus getting the runs, and we ended up taking the thing down to the dump. Anyway, if somebody else asks you for a refrigerator, Sheila, we suggest you give them a different kind."

Huh? Green fog? A phantom fist squeezed Julie's windpipe. She opened the next letter.

"Dear Sheila: No doubt you meant well in fixing me up with Alex Filippone, because he really seemed like a nice man. He brought me flowers and took me to shows, and all of a sudden we were married. The trouble began when he put on the diapers and insisted I spank him with a broken canoe paddle like the bad little boy he was, because I couldn't bring myself to do that, no way, and the next thing I know he's run off with most of my savings, so here I am, lonely as ever, except without any money."

Diapers? Canoe paddle? What the hell? She grew prickly with dread. No more high road, she vowed. Never again. Never.

"Dear Sheila: Obviously you worked hard at improving my face, and many parts of it truly look better now. So why am I here at the DeGrazzio Institute? Well, I suspect you got distracted when it came to my nose, Sheila, because now I have two of them, and I needn't tell you an extra nose is not necessarily a great improvement over a burned face. I'm sure you did your best, and the surgery will probably go fine, but I wish . . ."

Julie moaned. She wept. She rammed her fist against the nearest fish tank, which seemed suddenly populated with *Moon* creatures. With ravenous piranha and Loch Ness monsters, with embryonic aliens and aquatic Bigfoots—with tears and transplanted hearts and a thousand redundant noses.

CHAPTER 7

◆ ◆ ◆

No known bone, no discrete organ, no identifiable passage for blood was home to Billy Milk's pain. His uncertainty, like God, was everywhere at once. If only it would coalesce, as the Father had done to become the Son's sinless tissues, so that Billy might touch some specific part of himself and, pressing the swollen doubt, make it stop hurting.

He entered the First Ocean City Church of Saint John's Vision and methodically lined up seven candlesticks along the altar like a windbreak of golden trees. He rubbed his eyepatch. Had he truly been elected to bring down the Babylon called Atlantic City? The signs were right—his boy given sight, the Great Whore unveiled—and yet, for all the times Billy had demonstrated Timothy's new eyes in church, for all his public displays of the Whore's gown, his flock had remained largely unmoved. Whereas Revelation 7:4 explicitly called for 144,000, the crusade so far numbered only two hundred and nine.

Take it easy, Billy counseled himself as he lit the candles. God did not want soldiers who rushed in blindly; heaven must recruit at its own pace. Crusades were serious business, after all, matters of blood and fire, of severed heads hoisted aloft on spears to peer over medieval Antioch's walls at Christless Turks until the skin dissolved and only the skulls remained, still staring. Wait. Have patience.

He knelt before the altar, kissing the cool sweet marble.

The sanctuary door opened and in strode Timothy, eyes glowing a brilliant blue, a stack of tabloid newspapers tucked under his arm. Dear Timothy, so handsome and sturdy in his white, three-piece, all-cotton suit, the best a father might ever hope to reap from the line of gullible Eve and disobedient Adam. "Something you should see here, Dad." Timothy flopped the tabloids on the altar. BABY GIRL BORN PREGNANT, a headline proclaimed beneath the banner of the *Midnight Moon*.

"Timothy, we don't read this sort of material. Certainly not in here."

"Just look." Timothy opened an issue to an advice column, "Heaven Help You." The letters, Billy noted, all addressed someone named Sheila.

Rarely had the pastor beheld blasphemies such as now assaulted his existing eye. This Sheila counseled suicide. She called God deranged. Timothy opened a second *Moon* (ELVIS CURED MY CANCER). Sheila was still at it, encouraging divorce, sanctioning abortions...

"Pretty ugly, huh?" Timothy reached for a third tabloid. "Know where this paper's published?"

Billy stayed his son's hand. "In hell?" Together they laughed. It was good to joke around, father and son. The Lord enjoyed a certain amount of humor.

"Next town over. Atlantic City."

Atlantic City. *Atlantic City!* Billy's good eye expanded like an unchecked tumor. His skin bubbled, his heart seethed, and, slowly, steadily, he felt doubt's worm wither and die. Where was it written that the beast of Chapter Thirteen must be male? Might not female flesh prove an apt disguise for Satan's avatar? "Antichrist," he muttered. An obscene entity took shape in his eye socket. "Antichrist!" he shouted. There she was, *there,* she with the scaly skin, the brambly hair, the eyeballs in her breasts instead of nipples. "The devil's spawn and mistress!" He rapped on the altar, making the flames quiver like frightened sinners. Atlantic City was home to the beast herself—here, surely, was a staff for goading his flock to battle! *Deus vult,* they'd shout as they incinerated Babylon, stronghold of the Antichrist, *Deus vult,* the cry of Pope Urban II's crusaders—God wills it. *"Now* we'll get our army!" Billy led his son through the cloakroom to the church kitchen. *"Now* they'll cancel their ridiculous vacations!" Even the initials fit: Anti-Christ, Atlantic City.

Their descent into the basement was a dance of joy.

"*Deus vult*, right, Dad?"

"*Deus vult*, son."

Billy guided his boy to the New Jersey road map on the bulletin board. *Happy Motoring*, it said. *Exxon Corporation.*

Burning a city wasn't easy, their arson expert, Ted Rifkin, had warned. "Hit all those deserted tenements hard so you tie up the fire department, and you've got half a chance of pulling it off." But Billy had demanded a different plan. "This is an attack on Babylon, Ted, not on deserted tenements." Naturally they would strike a few—Billy had nothing against strategy. The main army, however, must go against the twelve casinos that would eventually become the twelve gates to the New Jerusalem. The Savior's soldiers must cleanse the world of the Golden Nugget, that beam in God's eye. Bring down the Atlantis, that fat affront to the Spirit. Burn the Sands, the Tropicana, the Claridge, Caesar's...

"Tell me about the First Crusade," Billy commanded his son. "Tell me about Dorylaeum."

"A great victory," Timothy replied, his voice edged with fervor. Many young men returned from college the duller for it, their brains blunted by unscriptural knowledge, but not Timothy. "Prince Bohemund splits his army—infantry in one camp, cavalry in the other." Timothy's hand chopped the air, splitting the Frankish forces. "At first the day seems lost. Qilij-Arslan's arrows rain down, the infantry panics—dropping their weapons, falling back to their tents. A disaster. But then, suddenly, Bohemund's cavalry rides out of nowhere, crushing the astonished bowmen!"

A letter-perfect account. Scholarly yet passionate. "We, too, shall divide our forces." Billy drove his bamboo pointer toward the Atlantic City inset. "Leaving the marina, the armada will cruise north and land a thousand believers before the Golden Nugget." He moved the pointer landward. "Meanwhile, having gathered in Absecon, the infantry under your command will march down the boulevard and harrow the bayside casinos."

"Burning as we go?" Timothy pronounced *burning* with prayerful zeal.

"Burning," Billy echoed, the word tearing at his throat like a thorn. "Only fire can scour Babylon and purify the path of Christ's return."

Breathlessly Timothy walled in Atlantic City with his cupped hands. "Dorylaeum wasn't the end." Licking his finger, he ran a line of spittle down the Boardwalk, from the Nugget to Resorts International. "When the crusaders finally reached Jerusalem, the streets became canals of blood."

"Sometimes God gives hard orders," Billy explained, guiding his son back to the kitchen. "Sometimes he asks his hosts to put on breastplates of iron." Shoulder to shoulder, they marched into the pulpit.

A tidal wave of love washed through Billy as, lifting the stack of *Midnight Moon*s from the altar, he faced his congregation. How he loved Susan Cleary sitting there in her fern-filled hat and flowered dress. How he loved Ralph and Betty Bowersox as they admonished their five children to be quiet.

"Do they look like hosts?" Billy whispered. "I want them to look like hosts."

"They look *exactly* like hosts," said Billy's bright-eyed son.

ALL HOPE EMBRACE, YE WHO ENTER IN, demanded the sign over the casino entrance, the red words made gray by Julie's sunglasses. Together they ascended the carpeted stairs—Bix in his ivory white polyester suit and artist's-palette tie, Julie in Aunt Georgina's old senior-prom dress—and strode into the sumptuous restaurant called Gluttony Forgiven.

What a horrible ordeal, that second set of letters, like reaching into a sock full of razor blades. The lesson was clear, she felt. Intervention-at-a-distance was impossible. Signals got crossed, distortions accumulated. Effective miracle-working meant breaching walls, laying on hands, conjoining flesh to flesh—all those showy, retrograde gestures the Covenant of Uncertainty did not permit.

At least she'd tried. No one could say she hadn't tried.

After the rolls arrived, Bix handed her a rumpled piece of *Moon* stationery ("All the News They Don't Want You to Know") containing a brief, cryptic list.

1. Prayers
2. Anecdotes
3. Photo offer

"Prayers?" Julie wailed. "What do you mean?"

"I thought Sheila might include a brief prayer every now and then. Our receptionist knows a couple of good ones. She's a Baptist."

"Have you lost your mind?"

"Most people are worse off than you, Julie. Give them something to hang on to."

Julie slapped margarine on a kaiser roll. She needed her column—*needed* it.

But: keep the thing at any cost? Compromise the Covenant of Uncertainty? Bend the mandate she'd received from God on the night she and Howard Lieberman seduced each other? (It was a true revelation, she'd decided; it wasn't just the orgasm talking.) "Prayers have no place in a kingdom of impermanence, Bix. Neither do 'anecdotes,' whatever that means."

"It wouldn't hurt if occasionally Sheila ran an inspirational story. You know, how her crippled nephew learned to knit award-winning sweaters with a needle strapped to his chin. How her cousin fell out of his hot-air balloon to certain doom, but then he called on the Lord and—"

"You've got to be kidding."

"I'm trying to save your ass, Julie. Now this last item—photo offer. The idea is that any reader who drops us a postcard gets an autographed picture of Sheila. Tony figures we can use the Xerox machine."

"Why are you treating me like this? You think I want a bunch of yahoos and fanatics hanging me on their walls? I don't."

"Mule."

"What did you say?"

"I said *mule.* I said *stubborn jackass.*"

Slowly, silently, Julie dunked her napkin into her water goblet and began cleaning her sunglasses. "Planning to fire me?"

"I certainly should." Bix acquired the pained look of a baby drinking beer. "The catch, as you may have guessed, is that I'm in love with you."

"I doubt that."

"I'm in love with you."

Evidently Georgina had been no less skinny a teenager than she was an adult; the prom dress squeezed Julie like a corset. In love, he'd said. He didn't just love her, he was *in* love, that disarming preposition, at once a confession and a trap.

Without quite knowing why, she blew him a kiss. He smiled softly, receiving her phantom lips. A bulbous nose, she mused, and his eyes sat too far apart, but he was also rather swarthy; a rugged old barn, weathered by the world's hypocrisies. "Dear walrus," she whispered. Howard Lieberman had never spoken of love. Roger Worth had used the word only because it was the password to her pants. But Bix, the sweetheart, seemed to mean it. "I'm touched. Truly touched." She launched a second kiss. "Love's an uncertain phenomenon, of course."

"I thought you'd say something like that."

"An enigma."

"Right. Sure."

"Indeterminate."

"Let's drop it, Julie."

"Impermanent."

"Here's our soup."

After dinner they strolled along the ocean. "Constantine Pictures presents, *Atlantic City: Metropolis in Transition*," Bix announced grandly. A teenage couple wandered by, hand-in-hand, exuding grim giggles. "Some come to play baccarat in the casinos, others to play pregnancy roulette under the Boardwalk." She followed him into Ocean One Mall, where he soon discovered an everything-for-a dollar store. He maneuvered through the bins, grabbing tacky novelties for his photography staff to turn into proofs. " 'Archaeologists Unearth Space Fetus!' " Bix enthused, picking up a rubber skull. Julie threw her head back and laughed. " 'Jesus' Own Baby Blanket?' " Bix persisted, waving a white silk scarf. " 'Ten Top Bishops Say *Yes!*' "

She perused his spherical stomach. His fatness, she decided, boasted a rare candor: there is indeed too much of me, but that's the way I am, take it or . . .

Take it. "And I love you," she said.

"Huh?"

She did? She did. Oh, yes, God of physics, our mother who art in the Dirac sea, she did. "You heard me."

"No shit?"

From that point on, their relationship could be charted as an upward progression through Dante's.

The level above Gluttony Forgiven featured a small, intimate, sinfully expensive restaurant called To Each His Own, and throughout the spring Saturday night meant overpriced spaghetti followed by the blackjack tables. Higher still, surmounting To Each His Own, were several strata of fine hotel suites—champagne vending machines, sunken bathtubs right in the room—and by early July they'd become regular guests, graduating each week to the next successive bed. Bix's attractiveness was one of the great biological mysteries, like the curing of warts through hypnosis or the presence of fully formed spirochetes on myxotricha. His aptitude for sex was meager, he had no appreciation for science, and he required an entire bottle of tanning oil for a single afternoon at the beach.

He made her happy. Perhaps some variation on general relativity was at work here, his bulk capturing anyone passing within his field. More probably his appeal lay in his sheer acceptance of her. Whereas Howard had ended up demanding Julie's assent to his worldview and Roger had ended up worshiping her, she could not imagine Bix doing either. Around him she felt *safe*, and with each passing day his swarthiness seemed sexier, his girth narrower, his pessimism more courageous.

Ever upward. The top level of Dante's was a posh conglomeration of saunas, pools, and gymnastic equipment servicing a community of penthouses intended for high rollers and mobsters. The weekend Julie and Bix spent there—they'd saved up their salaries for months—was also the weekend Bix revealed the latest circulation figures.

"I got the news this morning," he said, French-kissing her. "We leveled off in May."

Julie bit both their tongues. "And ...?"

"And we dropped two-point-one percent in June," Bix confessed. "I'm afraid Tony's talking about pulling your plug."

Dropped two-point-one. Julie felt as if something vital—her plug, her soul—had just been yanked out. "Can you appease him?"

"If we don't pick up fifty thousand new readers by Labor Day, well..."

"Fifty thousand? How likely is that to happen?"

"How likely is hell to go condo?"

"Fifty thousand?"

"Uh-huh."

"Fight for me, sweetheart."

"Fight? With what? What ammunition are you giving me?"

"Just fight. I need this column, Bix. Fight."

* * *

That the lighthouse was witnessing an endless parade of Phoebe and Georgina's girlfriends both Sapphic and Platonic, that it was becoming a kind of exclusive club—WELCOME TO ANGEL'S EYE, NO BOYS ALLOWED—did not bother Julie. Wholly feminine worlds had many virtues. You never wanted for a tampon. Copies of *Ms.* and bottles of hand lotion appeared as if by magic. The Super Bowl came and went unwatched, with some Angel's Eye residents not even certain which particular sport it consecrated.

Predominant among the live-in guests was Phoebe's lover Melanie Markson, an unpublished writer of children's books and the only woman Julie knew to whom the word *portly* applied: Phoebe and Melanie, the Laurel and Hardy of Atlantic City, tootling around the casinos like retired veterans of a hundred lesbian two-reelers.

"I've been going over your father's book," Melanie told Julie the morning after Bix had disclosed the disheartening truth about the *Moon*'s circulation, "that *Hermeneutics of the Ordinary* thing. Brilliant stuff. I no longer see snapshots just on the surface."

Julie had recently read one of Melanie's own manuscripts, a fable about a puppy who committed justifiable patricide. Julie was impressed, though she understood why it hadn't sold. "Wish Pop could hear you say that."

"Too bad he never finished it. It might have been publishable."

"He wasn't good at finishing things. Maybe you've noticed only half the rooms around here have doors."

"You never talk about your mother," said Melanie.

"Neither do you."

"My mother died right after I was born."

"And mine," said Julie, "died right after I was conceived."

"Huh?"

"A long story, Melanie. Some other time."

And then one day Melanie hit the jackpot, selling a series of five children's books for a thirty-thousand-dollar advance, with a movie option from the Disney empire for twice that much. She celebrated by getting herself a fancy new computer and her beloved Phoebe a portable video rig. Bad choice, that camcorder. No child banging on a toy drum had ever been as irritating as Phoebe running around the cottage like a muckraking stringer for Cable News Network.

"Shut that thing off!"

But Phoebe always kept the tape running, the lens gawking. "This'll be hot stuff someday, Katz. The Dead Sea Cassettes!"

"Leave me alone!" Julie tried elbowing Phoebe out of the kitchen.

"Take it easy—I'm getting the practice I need." Phoebe squinted into the viewfinder. "You think I plan to spend the rest of my life selling saltwater taffy and whoopie cushions? Bullshit. Soon I'll be starting my own company. I've got this amazingly brilliant idea—nonpornographic adult videos. Cinéma-vérité love, how sex *really* looks. A sure winner."

"Don't count on it." Julie slapped a tunafish sandwich together.

"You know your problem, Katz? You don't have enough faith in people." Phoebe zoomed in. "And now we have—taa-daa— our resident deity eating tuna on rye!" The camera lurched closer, breathing down Julie's neck as she drank milk. "*Milk*, great, very symbolic. Take another swallow. Next comes—could it be? Yes, she's actually placing the glass in the dishwasher; she's not leaving it on the table for her friend Phoebe to deal with. We've seen a real miracle today, folks. Next she'll be feeding the hungry and clothing the naked and booting the devil's butt."

At least Phoebe's obnoxious hobby was keeping her busy. At least she wasn't spending all her time drinking.

Julie had broached the issue subtly, or so she thought, taping her column on substance abuse to the temple door with a 3x5 card saying, "If you ever want to talk about this, I'd be open to it." The next day the clipping reappeared on Julie's computer. "If you ever want to mind your own business," ran Phoebe's note, "I'd be open to it."

Every Friday afternoon, Julie and Melanie would attempt to cleanse the cottage completely. A morbid game, this business of searching out Phoebe's little liquor bottles and flushing away their contents, a kind of perverse and mandatory Easter egg hunt conducted for the rabbit's feces. At Angel's Eye the damn things might turn up anywhere—the washing machine, the toilet tank, a hollowed-out dictionary. Once, when Melanie was checking the oil in her Honda, her eye wandered to the plastic container of windshield cleaning fluid. On intuition she uncapped it, dipping in her finger. Rum. A few days later, while commemorating the wreck of *Lucy II*, Julie noticed a curious purple cast to the flame. The beacon was running on gin.

Intervene? wondered Julie. Kick her habit? The obvious option, of course: a half-hour of pressing her fingers against Phoebe's forehead, driving out the desire. But that way Phoebe would never learn to stand on her own two feet. That way Phoebe would never grow up. As with the rest of Phoebe's species, Julie must not let her become dependent upon supernatural solutions, trading one addiction for another.

Baby bank aborted.

Blown to bits.

She had a thousand enemies, each waiting for her to start acting like God.

For all of Julie's valiant efforts, for all the rum and gin she poured down the sink, Aunt Georgina remained dissatisfied. Georgina the whiner, the worrier. She called Julie selfish and solipsistic. She accused her of cowardice and denial, of treating symptoms instead of causes—of failing her best friend. How long, Julie wondered, before Georgina's misplaced resentment came boiling over? How long before a major showdown?

It happened at breakfast. Sunday, 11:05 A.M.

"Cure her," snapped her aunt. "You understand, Julie? I can't take this anymore." She nodded toward the bathroom, where Phoebe was loudly purging herself of the previous night's binge. "Maybe your father didn't want any interventions, but *I* do."

Julie whipped up the French toast batter. Cure her. Intervene. It sounded so simple, so righteous, but Georgina couldn't begin to grasp the historical and cosmological implications. "Humanity —and this includes Phoebe—will never learn self-reliance if it's got me to bail it out."

"Come off it."

Phoebe's retching reverberated through the cottage, a sound like a canvas tent being torn in half.

"Know what we should do?" said Julie. "We should go to some Al-Anon meetings, you and me." She set a slice of bread afloat on the batter; a raft of whole wheat. "They're for people whose kids and spouses drink too much."

"I don't want a meeting, Julie, I want a miracle."

Julie laid the sopping bread on the griddle. "Look, she functions, doesn't she? Keeps the books straight as an arrow, doesn't bawl out the customers, never smashes up the car..."

"Fix her." Georgina pushed a slice of bread into the batter like a sadist drowning a kitten. "Just fucking fix her."

"You think it's easy for me to say no? I *love* Phoebe, damn it—but we must consider the greater good."

"What greater good? Phoebe's killing herself."

"If you can't see my logic, Georgina, there's no point in our talking."

"Even *you* can't see your logic, shithead."

"I don't think name-calling is necessary."

"Shithead. Asshole. Turd."

Sliding the spatula along the griddle, Julie pried up the half-cooked bread and flung it across the kitchen as if firing a catapult. "I have *enemies*, Georgina! They're out to get me!" She backed away from the stove. "Eat this crap yourself—I've lost my appetite."

"Same here, you little snake, which is exactly what you are, Julie Katz, a slimy, selfish snake."

Gills gasping with frustration, ears hot with Georgina's anger, Julie ran from the kitchen, dashed across the jetty, and dove into the soft and understanding bay.

Bix said, "I'm sorry." His face resembled a meteor, ashen, craggy, cold.

"Sorry?" said Julie. Now what? He was dropping her for some pert little Princeton philosophy major?

"We're twenty thousand readers shy, and that's that. Tony wants a pet-care column instead. Mike Alonzo will write it."

"Pet care? You're not serious." A hundred-degree tear rolled from Julie's right eye. She pressed a crisp Gluttony Forgiven napkin to her nose and blew. "You should've fought for me. Pet care?"

"I did fight for you."

"I'll bet."

"I did."

So it was over. The Covenant of Uncertainty had become fish wrap and hamster litter, there was nothing left for her but confusion and guilt, nothing but Georgina's misguided anger and God's malicious indifference. "Be honest, Bix, you never believed in my ministry." The tear reached her lips, and she licked. Battery acid. "You pretended to care because you had the hots for me."

Bix crushed a roll in his fist, the crumbs spurting between his fingers. "Dammit, Julie, I've been running interference for you ever since you walked into my office. The entire staff thinks you're crazy, you know."

"What about you? Do you think I'm crazy?"

"Sometimes. Yes. This whole God's daughter mystique— why do you push it so hard? You don't have to pretend around *me*. I'm not one of your stupid readers."

"I'm not pretending."

"*Prove* that you're God's daughter. My standards aren't high —take the wart off my ass, fly, anything."

"I don't do proofs, sweetheart. Not for traitors."

Bix pulverized another roll. "You little fraud."

One word, *fraud*, that was all it took, and Julie was on her feet, sprinting out of the restaurant and down the stairs to the casino floor. Traitor, traitor. *I did fight for you:* oh, sure, Bix. Sure. Traitorous bastard.

Such clockless worlds, these casinos. It always seemed like the same hour at Dante's, Caesar's, or the Nugget, always the same day—three-thirty on a Sunday afternoon, Julie decided.

Her ministry mattered. Why couldn't Tony Biacco see that? "Heaven Help You" had forestalled dozens of suicides, divorces, wife batterings, and child beatings. Last week, a compulsive gambler had written to say that, thanks to Sheila, he'd finally kicked the blackjack habit.

Blackjack: a fine game, Julie mused, sidling toward a remote and unpatronized table. She put on her sunglasses—the dealer might be a Sheila fan—and bought a hundred dollars in chips. At least she wouldn't have to disguise herself much longer; soon Sheila's photo would fade from the communal memory. The dealer, a grim, slender woman who handled the cards with the professional ennui of a whore unzipping flies, glanced nervously toward the Wheel of Wealth, as if being watched, tested.

Ah, sweet mammon. Luck, or God, was with Julie, tripling her investment in ten minutes. No matter what she did—splits, doubles, insurance bets—she came out on top. She might have a failed ministry, a traitorous lover, an hysterical aunt, and a rummy friend, but tonight she'd get rich.

Darkness slid across the table, human in shape, thick and palpable as spilled ink. "Vanish," a man said. The grim woman departed, the shadow stayed. "You picked the right table—this is where the big winners play." The dealer's voice conjured a vanished elegance, European artistocrats listening to Mozart. Julie didn't look up. A dealer was a dealer.

She placed four ten-dollar chips on the table, twice her usual bet. Slap, an ace of hearts for the player, slap, a ten of spades for the dealer. Tony wanted pet advice. Dear Dr. Doolittle: My canary has stopped singing. Why?—Worried In Milwaukee.

Dear Worried: Because it can't stand you.

"I've been thinking about your question," said the dealer.

Julie fixed on her ace. The pip, a large red heart, seemed to move. To vibrate. Throb. Lub-dub. She blinked. Lub-dub. A beating heart? Was her mind becoming unhinged?

She faced the dealer. On neither of his previous visitations had she appreciated how handsome Andrew Wyvern was. High cheeks, obsidian eyes, strong sculpted lips. His beard, gray and soft, seemed a thing more of fur than whiskers: a werewolf in bloom, shaved everywhere but his jaw. "What question?" she asked as the scent of honeyed oranges drifted into her nostrils.

"About God." Slap, slap. A three of diamonds for the player, a down card for Wyvern. "You wanted to know why she allows evil." His tuxedo gleamed like black marble. Julie beckoned: hit me. Slap, a ten of clubs, making her ace count low. She beckoned. Slap, a jack of diamonds, twenty-four, bust. The devil collected her bet. "I noted that power corrupts," he said, whisking away her cards, "but there's more to it." Julie bet fifty dollars. Slap, slap. A king of clubs for her, a nine of spades for Wyvern. "Everybody thinks if he were God, he would do a better job. Such vanity. The math alone would stop most of us."

"You're saying God gets overwhelmed?"

"Exactly." Slap, a six of diamonds for Julie.

"Liar. You don't know any more about God than I do."

Slap, the dealer's down card. "Very well—but just as my deceptions are obvious to you, then so are my descents into integrity. 'Come sailing in my schooner tonight—no harm will befall you,' says the devil. 'He's telling the truth,' notes Julie Katz."

"Schooner?" It would be crazy to accept a card now, but she did. Slap, a queen of spades. Bust. "Tonight?"

"A crusade is coming." As Wyvern gestured over her king of clubs, the flesh melted from both its heads, leaving only skulls and eyeballs. "You must intervene."

"I intervene all the time." Her king's eyes blinked. "Read my column."

"Your column's dead, Julie—didn't they tell you? It's all holy water over the damned."

"True, true," she moaned. As her king drew his sword from behind his crown, the adjacent queen cringed, trapped by the geometry of her universe, armed with only a flower.

"I greatly admired 'Heaven Help You'—read it every week." Wyvern collected her bet. "Once I even wrote to you. I was that shy Lutheran minister in Denver whose congregation misunderstood him." The devil pointed to Julie's cards. "Still, there are situations in which the sword is mightier than the pen." The king slashed, making the queen's upper head tip back like the lid of a cigarette lighter. Blood leaked from the wedge; the flower turned black and fell from the queen's hand. "Tomorrow a thousand such deaths could occur. Ten thousand. Did you know that when the eleventh-century crusaders took Jerusalem, they ran through the city disemboweling the citizens, hoping to find swallowed coins?"

"I wasn't there." Julie bet sixty dollars.

"You should've been." Wyvern pushed her bet aside. "A short voyage down the coast, that's all. I'll have you home before dawn."

"I'm not responsible for this crusade you're talking about."

"Then what *are* you responsible for?"

"Hard to say."

"*Pain.*"

"What?"

"My schooner is called *Pain.*"

The queen's upper head rolled onto the green felt. Laughing a small depraved laugh, the king slashed again, neatly decapitating the queen's lower self.

"Impressive ship," said Julie as the devil led her along Steel Pier, its rusted remains stretching into the Atlantic like the back of a decaying sea serpent. *Pain*, a huge three-master with sails suggesting a bat's wrinkled and membranous wings, lay moored to the dock by a live python.

"I'm a man of wealth and taste." Wyvern gestured proudly toward the hull. "Newly painted with the bile of ten thousand unbaptized children. Her spars are made from the bones of massacred Armenians. Her ropes are woven from the hair of Salem's witches. Her jib is Jewish skin. People give me all my best ideas, Julie. Like you, I can never count on your mother for inspiration. Bubonic plague is as creative as she ever got."

He helped her onto the foredeck, where dark, stooped figures scurried about like beetles responding to the loss of their rock. "Say hello to Anthrax," he urged, indicating the cockpit with a quick nod. The helmsman was fat, bristled, and plated, like something resulting from the love of a boar for an armadillo.

"Hello." She felt schizoid, half her psyche planted in South Jersey, half in whatever quantum alternative objectified the devil and his brood.

Anthrax smiled at her and tipped an imaginary hat.

Foul breezes arose as the demons cast off. "From my angels," Wyvern explained. "They spread their buttocks, and the rectal zephyrs fill our sails."

Pain headed south, cruising past the casino-hotels—bright Bally's, lurid Caesar's, the mighty Atlantis, the epic Golden Nugget. The moon hung over the city like a white cork.

Gradually Julie's anxiety yielded to an odd inner buoyancy. She laughed. A swift boat, a major ocean—a person could just pick up and go, couldn't she? Anywhere. Sunny Spain, exotic Thailand, Howard Lieberman's beloved Galapagos Islands, that South Seas paradise she and Phoebe had seen in the Deauville.

"You were barking up the wrong tree," Wyvern informed her. As the schooner blew into Great Egg Harbor, Anthrax kicked the anchor—evidently some species of sea urchin. Dragging its chain behind it, the great pulsing ball of spikes crawled across the deck and flopped over the side. "You wanted the masses to embrace reason and science. It will never happen. They can't join in—there's no point of entry for them."

"Science is beautiful," said Julie.

"You think I don't know that?" Wyvern opened the cockpit locker and, drawing out a brass telescope, eased the instrument against Julie's eye. "Some of my favorite things are scientific—nuclear bombs, Zyklon B, eugenics." He showed her how to focus. "The problem is, only a few people get to be scientists. You see the dilemma? Given the choice between a truth they can appreciate and a lie they can live, most people will take you-know-what."

A blur hedged with moonlight. Then, as Julie turned the focus knob: a solemn mob of well over two thousand men and women, dressed in bleached flak jackets and earnestly clutching red plastic gasoline jugs and battery-powered Black and Decker hedge trimmers. "The dark side of the American spirit," said Wyvern. "Specifically, a Revelationist marina. The parking lot." Julie shifted the scope, settling on a half-dozen pickup trucks, each bearing a large enamel bathtub. Two elaborately muscled men, hands sheathed in thick black rubber, approached the nearest tub, lifted out an enormous tuna—yes, good God, a sleek, wriggling, gasping tuna—and carried it over to a bowl-shaped barbecue grill. "Why a fish?" Wyvern anticipated. "Most venerable of Christian symbols. Fuse the initials of *Iesos Christos Theou Yios Soter*, and you get *Ichthys*, Greek for fish."

Shift, focus. A tall, middle-aged man—balding, smooth-shaven, one eye molten, the other covered with leather—stabbed the fish with a scaling knife. The blade ran a true course from trunk to anal fin, a letter *V* in its wake. Thick maroon blood dripped through the grate and, filling the barbecue grill, splashed over the sides. Shift, focus. A young redheaded man set a gold shaving basin beneath the grill and opened the flue, thus releasing a column of liquid Jesus. "'And they have washed their robes,'" Wyvern quoted, "'and made them white in the blood of the Lamb.'" Cupping his hands, the young man reached into the overflowing basin and drew out a full measure. His mouth flew open to release a fevered prayer. "Death to the Antichrist!" said Wyvern, dubbing in the young man's voice as he smashed the fleshy ladle against his chest. The folds of his flak jacket channeled the blood, giving him an external circulatory system.

"Death to the Antichrist!" echoed the congregation.

"Antichrist?" said Julie. "What do they mean?"

The devil pulled his cigarette case from his overcoat and flipped back the lid, catching moonlight in the mirror. "These people have a full schedule tomorrow, a prophecy to fulfill—the fall of Babylon. Ever read the Bible?"

"Babylon? In Mesopotamia?"

"New Jersey."

Shift, focus. The congregation passed the basin around as if it were a collection plate, each crusader retaining it long enough to smear himself with Jesus. "Damn," she hissed.

"They're planning to burn it," said the devil.

"The marina?"

"Atlantic City." Wyvern removed a cigarette, eyeing it with a mixture of revulsion and desire. "I really *must* stop smoking."

"That's crazy."

"Smoking?"

"Burning Atlantic City."

"Precisely."

"You're lying."

"Not at the moment."

"Burn a whole city? Why?"

"To trigger the Parousia, of course, Christ's inevitable return." As Wyvern snapped his fingers, a small flame rose from his thumb. "First they'll tie up the fire department with a diversionary attack on Baltic Avenue, then they'll strike the casinos." He lit the cigarette, blew out his thumb. "Some of them aren't convinced a holocaust is necessary, but their pastor, Billy Milk—the one with the eyepatch—he's the most interesting thing in their lives, so they give him the benefit of the doubt. A remarkable man. With enemies like Billy Milk, the devil doesn't need friends."

Shift, focus. A Coast Guard cutter lay at the end of the wharf. Julie's heart bounded like a happy puppy. Oh, glorious, blessed Coast Guard, such brave men, always prepared to prevent crusades. How authoritative the seven uniformed officers looked as, armed with semiautomatic rifles, they disembarked and started down the wharf.

Hands glistening with the by-products of sacrifice, Reverend Milk marched out to greet them, a mob of Revelationists close behind, somberly gripping their gasoline jugs and their Black and Decker hedge trimmers.

Wyvern puffed on his cigarette. "'And I heard a great voice saying: Go your ways, and pour out the vials of the wrath of God upon the earth.'"

The Revelationists and the officers exchanged loud, intemperate shouts. Thank God for those guns, Julie thought. This was law, order: the United States Coast Guard.

The gas jugs moved in precise crimson arcs. Nobody got off a shot. One instant the officers were berating Milk's mob, the next they were saturated, the next they were men made of fire, flailing about like marionettes operated by epileptics.

"'And power was given unto him to scorch men with fire.'"

Julie's scream trailed into a long, sustained moan. The poignant thing was the victims' disorientation, the way they sought to save themselves by jumping into the ocean but could instead only stagger blindly around the pier, spewing gray smoke, shedding red embers, randomly firing their rifles.

Shift, focus. The pilot house. A pale, baby-faced captain held the microphone of his ship-to-shore radio, his lips frozen like a tetanus victim's. Not one word left his mouth.

Now came the avenging angels, turning on their hedge trimmers and hauling the pilot on deck.

"'Behold the Son of Man,'" the devil quoted as the Revelationists fell upon the pilot, trimming him brutally, clipping him to death, "'and in his hand a sharp sickle.'"

Julie wept caustic tears. The officers collapsed on the dock, smoldering sacks of cooked flesh.

Wyvern stroked her burned palm. "'Because of your abominations I shall do with you what I have never yet done. Therefore fathers will eat their sons'—this is God talking, Julie—'and sons will eat their fathers, and any of you who survive I shall scatter to the winds." The devil sighed with admiration. "Oh, but I wish *I'd* said that."

"Get me out of here."

"You're not going to intervene?" The cutter was aflame now, glowing brilliantly above the harbor and in reflection below it.

"I...I..." The snake on her forehead shuddered and writhed. "Have to...think about it..."

"Think? Think? How can you *think*? Everybody wants you to intervene. Even God wants you to intervene."

"You said I'd be back before dawn."

"I expected better of you, Julie."

"Take me home."

"A bargain is a bargain." Wyvern shrugged. "Just remember this: I'll always be around when you need me, which is more than you can say for your mother."

The flaming Coast Guard officers clung to Julie's eyes like flashbulb afterimages as she stepped from *Pain*'s dinghy and climbed to the top of the jetty. Dawn seeped across the sky, molding shapes from the gloom—pine trees, lighthouse tower, cottage. In the temple a lamp burned, glowing through the pain-papered windows. Phoebe, most likely, drinking or adding exhibits or both.

Julie faced west. University of Pennsylvania: her father's sperm samples, sitting in their frosty test tubes.

"They're on the march, Pop!" she screamed.

She hoped he was in heaven. She hoped it had a library.

"Some interventions can't be *helped*!"

Surely he could see that.

In the bathroom, Julie stripped off Georgina's prom dress and turned on the shower. The Revelationists had performed their ablutions, now it was her turn; a person must fight purity with purity. The flaming officers were everywhere. Their bones filled the soap dish. Their skin hung from the curtain rod, their blood poured from the nozzle.

She washed, threw on Melanie's peach kimono, and entered the temple. Phoebe sat beside the altar, cutting an oil spill from *Mother Jones*. "Hi, Katz. Up early, aren't we?"

"Never went to bed." In a single spasm Julie snatched away the *Mother Jones* and ripped it in half. "You're about to get what you always wanted."

"A woman of action?" Phoebe asked uncertainly.

"The high road," said Julie, nodding.

"I thought you didn't want us looking to heaven for answers."

"They dress in blood, Phoebe. They *kill* people."

"Who?"

"Billy Milk's arsonists."

"Arsonists? There goes the neighborhood." Phoebe lit the altar candles. "You mean you've finally outgrown this place?"

"I suppose."

"Time to start living in your own skin? Time to start beating the devil?"

"That's one way to put it."

Phoebe's sweeping gesture encompassed the entire room. "So it's all obsolete, huh?"

"Obsolete. Right. Help me."

They hugged, and then it began, their violent excavation, suffering ripped from the walls in great ragged sheets like lizard skins, layer after layer of war refugees, flood victims, AIDS patients, earthquake casualties. They dismantled the flaming dollhouse. Destroyed the lava-smothered village. Threw the crashed jetliner into the wastebasket. Back to the walls; within a half hour they'd reached the original stratum—its floes and famines, epidemics and revolutions, jihads and foreclosures, chemical dumps and despair.

"Big day coming up, huh?" Phoebe peeled away a Nicaraguan adolescent whose arms were made of rubber and steel.

"Yeah, and you're going to wait it out, buddy." Julie pulled down a ten-year-old heroin addict. "I'm serious—follow me with your damn camera and I'll throw it in the ocean."

"Sure, Katz," said Phoebe with a skewed smile. Only the altar remained untouched—its anonymous sailor's skull, its cluster of dynamite disguised as nuclear missiles, its burning, penis-shaped candles from the Smile Shop. "Anything you say."

"Don't you dare cross me."

"You crazy? Mess with the wrath of Katz? Me?"

Julie fed the apprentice junkie to a candle flame. The paper ignited, becoming a bright orange blossom, then a swarm of ashes floating around the purified temple like black moths.

The wrath of Katz. She liked the sound of that.

CHAPTER 8

◆　　◆　　◆

Although Bix Constantine disbelieved in hell as intensely as he did in heaven, he knew what the place would be like. Hell, for Bix, was jealousy. It was failed journalists seeing their enemies receive Pulitzer Prizes. It was compulsive gamblers seeing jackpots gush from adjacent players' slot machines and sex-starved young men seeing their friends piled high with naked cheerleaders.

Bad enough that Julie had left Dante's with a dealer, one of those smooth, intellectual types with graying hair and an aura of smug fitness, but now things were getting even worse. The bastard had a yacht, a seagoing penthouse no doubt, moored to the ruins of Steel Pier, the word *Pain* spread across its transom. How carefully he'd tracked them—through the lobby, across the Boardwalk, down the wharf—at last finding a vantage point behind a wooden zebra on the moribund carousel. The outrages never stopped: when her lustful companion extended his hand, Julie took it eagerly; when he waltzed into his cabin, she stayed by his side. Within minutes the yacht was under sail, cruising south toward Ocean City. Who was he? A disciple who'd lost his heart upon seeing her picture in the paper? One of her old college professors, moonlighting in the casinos—they'd always been hot for each other, and now they were finally free to go rolling in the nautical hay?

Bix slunk away like a scolded but unrepentant dog. Where was gratitude? He'd given this bizarre and unemployable woman a job... made her a quasi-celebrity... loved her. Traitor, she'd called him. Bullshit. God Almighty couldn't have defended that column, not the way she wrote it.

Eight-thirty P.M., with the sunlight fading fast, stars peeping through the clouds. On the Boardwalk the change of shifts occurred: spiffily dressed couples strode out of their hotels while sad, penniless daytrippers drifted woozily toward their shuttle buses; a second exodus comprised the cripples and blind beggars, whose infirmities elicited sufficient guilt and alms only in the accusatory gleam of day. Bix flipped open his wallet, cracked the seam. Fifty dollars. For acute jealousy, what was the anesthetic of choice? Lobster? Alcohol? Whores? Slot machines? He slipped into Resorts International and, obtaining two hundred quarters, watched submissively as the one-armed bandits bled them away, a hundred and fifty quarters, ninety, sixty, twenty, ten.

A small fortune gushed forth, jangling into the payoff box. Damn. He was too tired to feed that much back. Like a Wall Street milkmaid, he staggered to the change island carrying two enormous buckets, quarters slopping over the edges, and converted his jackpot to bills. Roulette would solve the problem, ah, yes, Fortuna's wheel. "Here's three hundred," he grumbled to the croupier. "Six fat chips will do." The Mafia flunky counted Bix's wad, then fed it into a slot in the table, forcing it down with a lucite ramrod. Snapping up his six fifty-dollar chips, Bix placed them on ODD. The croupier spun the wheel, tossed the ball; it bounced among the grooves like a pebble skimming across a pond. The wheel stopped: 20. Even. Good. Bix left.

Dawn seeped through the city like the pale flashings of a million sickly fireflies. Sea gulls ruled the Boardwalk; the rich were back in their hotels. Bix walked south, scanning the ocean, gray and glassy in the pretide calm. Somewhere behind him, fire engines rolled, their sirens howling like tortured cats. No sign of *Pain*. He *had* fought for her, damn it, he *wasn't* a traitor.

A fearsome armada bore down on Absecon Beach.

Bix blinked. His chins fell. It was all ludicrously true: a long rank of cabin cruisers flying religious banners—saints praying, lambs nailed to crosses—and heading for the southern casinos. Revelationists, the crucified sheep announced. The flag on the lead boat showed Jesus beheading a winged serpent. Bix attempted to laugh, failed. With their dark windows and death-white hulls, the yachts were imperially unfunny.

Pale figures scurried about the decks tossing over large bundles that, smacking the water, abruptly transmuted into motorized rafts. The Revelationists climbed in. Ten rafts. Twenty, fifty,
a hundred. Two hundred rafts, dotting the smooth ocean like a
vast herd of migrating sea lions. Within minutes the first wave of
invaders arrived, leaping into the shallows, their bodies
wrapped in white flak jackets mottled with dark blotches, their
hands locked tightly around red plastic jugs and battery-powered Black and Decker hedge trimmers.

A tall, balding Revelationist wearing an eyepatch dashed up
the ramp. "Down with Babylon!" he screamed, brandishing his
hedge trimmer, its blade like the snout of a sawfish. "Down with
Babylon!" his flock echoed. Like demented picknickers carrying
an inexhaustible supply of lemonade, the invaders bore their
plastic jugs across the beach and onto the Boardwalk, all the
while waving their hedge trimmers in wild circles over their
heads. "Down with Babylon!"

And Bix thought: Down with Babylon? Huh? Babylon?

As the Revelationists charged the Golden Nugget, Bix melted
into their ranks, feeling oddly immune. Their utter oblivious-
ness, that was it. These crusaders had a divine mandate, a holy
mission that shone from their eyes like sunlight glancing off
snow; they would never stoop to murder a mere bystander.

Marching past the liveried doormen, the army stormed into the
lobby and entered the casino, a tide of zeal flowing boldly between
two guards and depositing Bix in the nearest slot-machine aisle.
Did their jugs contain quarters? The Revelationists intended to
play the slots till Christ came back? "Spill it," the one-eyed shepherd said in a gravelly whisper, addressing a stout, fortyish female
crusader whose flak jacket was unbuttoned sufficiently to reveal a
small silver lamb nailed to a cross. "Pour out God's wrath."

The woman did not move.

"Spill it."

She remained immobile: Lot's wife, locked in salt.

Zonked as usual by the noise and the lights, the gamblers
took no note of the incursion.

"'And the angel poured his vial upon the seat of the beast,'"
the shepherd quoted in the patient tone of a teacher prompting a
fourth-grader in a Columbus Day pageant. "Pour it out, Gladys."

Nothing from Gladys.

With a bold sweep of his arm, the shepherd snatched

Gladys's jug and, uncapping it, splashed a clear fluid onto the carpet. The smell clawed Bix's nostrils. Gasoline. Gasoline? *Gasoline?* A chain reaction of curiosity rolled across the casino. Pit bosses looked up, the slots stopped tolling, the gamblers' chatter faded. God in heaven—gasoline!

Other vials popped open, additional wrath spilled out. Hydrocarbon fumes spread through the Nugget like the fartings of a thousand Exxon supertankers.

A counteroffensive converged, a ragtag squad of guards and Mafia strongmen. The Revelationists dispersed, soaking the blackjack aisles, baccarat bays, and video-poker stalls. Like a farmer slopping his hogs, one crusader emptied his jug into the trough of a craps table.

The shepherd pulled a cigarette lighter from his jacket. "'And the angel poured his vial into the air'!"

"Stop!" shouted a pit boss, charging forward with a drawn pistol. Someone turned on a hedge trimmer and ran it along the pit boss's abdomen, zipping him open. The pit boss tried to cry out, succeeded only in gurgling. His pistol hit the saturated carpet; blood spurted from his belly like agitated beer. He screamed silently, wetly; he screamed blood.

Keep going, Bix told himself as he staggered toward the lobby, don't look back.

A fiery roar. A choral shriek.

He looked back. The inferno surged through the casino in great waves, as if an ocean of flames had risen from its bed to engulf the helpless Nugget. So many combustibles: rugs, curtains, felt, currency, playing cards—players. A burning young man embraced a slot machine as he might a lover. An old Pakistani woman, convulsed with terror, flames fanning from her back like a peacock's plume, flared even brighter as she tried to douse herself with a pitcher of martinis.

In the lobby, a summer shower descended as the sprinkler system cut in. Smoke flowed everywhere, nicking Bix's eyes. Their mission evidently accomplished, the crusaders poured out of the casino, smiling, laughing, kicking over urns. Blindly Bix charged, coughing violently, each spasm jolting him like an electric shock as he opened the main door.

Air. Sunlight. A sea breeze. The Boardwalk strollers regarded him without interest, as if his panic signaled nothing more than a night of heavy losses. But now came the fire, bursting through the building, blowing out its windows, clambering up its face. And now came the crusaders, their hedge trimmers emitting coarse insectile buzzes. The tourists scattered like infantrymen caught in a strafing—to little avail, for the Revelationists were suddenly upon them, trimming lethally, screaming "Down with Babylon!" Heat whipped Bix's face, sweat soaked his summer suit. The Golden Nugget shed people like a tree losing fruit in a storm. Panicked vacationers, many aflame, jumped from the hotel tower to the casino roof and from there to the ground, where they climbed over the Boardwalk rail and hurled themselves into the cool unburnable sea.

The army split. Three separate raiding parties charged up the Boardwalk, hedge trimmers poised, wrath at the ready. Hastily Bix performed a mental triage. The Tropicana: fated to fall. The Atlantis: it hadn't a chance. Next came Harrah's at Trump Plaza, then Caesar's Palace. Harrah's was probably doomed, but it would take them five minutes to reach Caesar's.

He ran, Bix the unfit blob, chuffing past pizza parlors, fortune-telling booths, and Smitty's Smile Shop. He must have seen Julius Caesar's kitschy statue a hundred times before, but only now did he notice the fear beneath its imperial gaze; or perhaps the fear was new, the natural terror of a pagan emperor beholding hundreds of Christians gone berserk. "Everybody out!" Bix screamed, charging into the casino. "You're in danger!"

The blackjack players turned toward him. The slot addicts looked up from their machines.

"There's a crazy army coming! You must get out!"

The gamblers smiled indulgently and went back to their fun.

Flames bloodied the horizon as Julie drove her Datsun across Brigantine Bridge and headed into the besieged city. Fire engines jammed Baltic Avenue, red lights flashing in stroboscopic bursts. The tenements blazed brightly, an epic disaster tying up the combined Atlantic City and Ocean City fire departments just as Wyvern had foretold. The street was a mass of glistery puddles and tangled black hoses. Ladders rose from the red trucks, angling into the stricken buildings like flying buttresses. Tridents of flame and coils of smoke shot from doorways and windows. Firefighters in rubber masks and oxygen tanks lumbered about like scuba divers from hell. In the center of the chaos, the paramedic Freddie Caspar, last survivor of Pop's poker club—Rodney Balthazar had shot himself during Passover—gave CPR to a supine woman.

She continued down South Carolina. Eyes swimming in tears, handkerchiefs pressed against their faces, a wave of terrified tourists swept past. A blowsy woman wearing Bermuda shorts and a Bally's sweatshirt stood at the Atlantic Avenue intersection holding huge wads of charred money in her fists, the jackpot of a lifetime, now ash. A bewildered young man in a motorized wheelchair made crazed figure eights in Harrah's parking lot like a child driving a bumper car.

Stuff. Miracles always needed stuff. She pulled over by Dante's, got out. At least she was dressed for the heat: denim cutoffs, a Smile Shop T-shirt (START A MOVEMENT—EAT A PRUNE). The smoke was like a disease air gets, spreading outward, penetrating everywhere. Her eyes smarted, her chest heaved, her throat felt like a sack of needles. God had it so much easier. Julie's fleshless mother could intervene all day and never once gag or weep.

Charging up the Boardwalk ramp, she started through the swarming cinders. Everything from the Nugget to the Sands was lost, a writhing cloud of jet-black smoke laced with flames. Only the district east of Tennessee—the Showboat, Resorts International, Dante's—remained untouched, as if Wyvern had dispatched a fallen guardian angel to protect his personal casino, his earthly pied-à-terre.

Stuff. She had to find her stuff.

The massacre was all the devil had promised. Human firebrands tumbled from the collapsing casinos. Others succumbed to the hedge trimmers—a harvest of gamblers, reaped by God's sickles, bundled by God's wrath. New Jersey, thought Julie, fighting incredulity and nausea, New Jersey, the Garden State.

She faced the sea. Tourists rushed into the tide, hoping to soothe their burns. Other survivors carried their loved ones' corpses to the beach, setting them on the sand so they might mourn uninterrupted before more judgment arrived. Directly ahead, the truncated hulk of Central Pier shimmered in the August sun. And suddenly there it was, rising above the wharf, reaching for the clouds. Her *stuff*.

"Julie!"

A fat man waddled out of the smoke, ripping away his white

cotton shirt as if to free himself from the heat's insistent grip. Soot streaked his ballooning flesh. His sweat shone like fresh varnish.

"I can't believe it," Bix rasped. "These fanatics with their gasoline, and people are dying, and I went to Caesar's and nobody even *listened*. How come you never told me about him?"

"Who?"

"The yachtsman. Did he hump you?"

Anger stunned her. Atlantic City burning, her anonymity on the line, and the traitor dared to be jealous. "I'm Jesus Christ's sister!" She spat the words in his face. "Of *course* the devil's going to be interested in me!"

"Don't start on that—not now!"

"Get out. Go east along Pacific, it's clear all the way to the inlet."

She headed toward the pier—toward her stuff—and the foolish walrus followed: through the crumbling archway, around the huge plaster mermaid, past the ceramic sea horses heralding the abandoned aquarium.

"Listen, Julie, you've got to stop this daughter of God shit! You're going to get hurt!"

"Leave me alone!"

She broke into the sunlight, her gaze lifting along the steel spire to the doughnut-shaped observatory. According to Pop's book on amusement parks, Frederick A. Picard had dubbed his creation the Space Tower, but Julie did not have to leave her planet today, merely gain a divine perspective. Her gills shivered. She vibrated with godhead. Oh, yes, she was ready! Reverend Milk's army might have its gas, its trimmers, its strategy, its righteousness, but Julie Katz had her genes.

Although the counterweight had long since vanished, she had no trouble bringing the observatory under her control. No shepherd's staff required, no flamboyant gestures—a mere nod cracked the rust and set the cabin in motion.

"What in hell—?" Bix's wet face glowed with astonishment.

She grinned. "You bet, baby doll. Your eyes don't lie." Metallic squeals filled the air as the observatory slid down the tower.

"Are *you* doing that?" gasped the traitor, staring dumbfounded at the anomaly.

"I am God and gravity and quantum mechanics. I am the girl from the ectogenesis machine."

"You're making it happen?" His eyes quavered like poached eggs, his bare chest trembled. "Don't do this to me, Julie, I won't allow it! You can't have powers!"

"I have powers, sweetheart."

"Stop it, Julie!" Bix shook his fist as if strangling a snake. "The universe has to make *some* kind of sense! Don't *do* this to me!"

She ran to the grounded observatory, leaving him alone on the pier, quaking with mystified outrage. The interior was chaos —rotting cushions, a million splinters of glass. No matter, she wouldn't be entering anyway. Intervention on this scale must happen in the open. The Red Sea had split by day, Jesus had raised Lazarus before a crowd.

She climbed to the roof and stomped her foot. As the observatory began rising, slowly, steadily, it seemed at first that the tower was moving instead, like a gargantuan hypodermic needle plunging through New Jersey to draw the planet's blood. Higher she ascended, and higher. She became her stomach, the rest of her flesh a mere vestige, orbiting around last night's gourmet spaghetti. The hot smoky air whizzed across her face. Sea gulls drifted by, ash-speckled.

Her life lay before her. To the south, Longport, site of her conception. To the north, Brigantine Point and Angel's Eye. She picked out Absecon Inlet, her elementary school, the *Moon* offices, the swamp near Dune Island where the Winnebago sank.

The southern half of Atlantic City was now one vast firestorm—a burning, outsized Monopoly board. Even as she watched, spores of flame blew across the passage and took root in Chelsea Heights and Ventnor. With luck, she could still save Margate and Longport, not to mention the upper horn of the city, from the inlet to the bayside casinos.

The sun publicized her advent, wrapping the tower in ribbons of light, cloaking her body in golden robes. Already the traumatized survivors on the beach had spotted her. A forest sprouted: raised arms, pointing fingers. Who could she be? Who was that strange, luminous woman in the sky?

The ocean was hers, a spectacular legacy, mother to daughter, *Here you are, Julie, take it, my wet masterpiece.* "Bring on the waves!" she screamed as a crowd collected at the base of the tower. The ocean trembled and seethed. "Waves!" Burning thimbles encased her fingertips. "Waves!"

"Waves!" echoed the dazed multitudes below.

And there were waves. Julie conducted the Atlantic like a symphony. Her hands moved and the water obeyed, swelling majestically, eager for commands. Godhead rose in her loins. "Waves!" she cried. It was all gushing out now, her bottled-up divinity, pouring from her nose as blood, her nipples as milk, her gills as lymph, her vagina as the slippery fluids of sex. *And, lo, Sheila took the high road.* Her phantom fingers seized the largest wave, sculpting it into a great phallic spout, and now the spout arched toward shore, sweeping the Revelationists off the Boardwalk. *And she did flush the fevered hosts into the back streets.* "Waves!" Gasoline jugs floated away, hedge trimmers sank in the divine flood. Julie's brain sparkled and spasmed as on the night Howard took her virginity. The high road, the high road!

As she lifted her hands toward the sun, the ocean yielded up great cords of water—long tubular rivers that Julie proceeded to tie around the casinos like rope. She wrapped the Tropicana. She trussed the Atlantis. Harrah's. Caesar's. Strangled, the fires died. *And the casinos were extinguished, and Sheila saw that it was good.*

She fixed on the city—flaming Chelsea Heights, smoldering Ventnor. Under divine mandate, a second spout emerged and reached toward the holocaust. Like a butcher slicing a sausage, Julie cut the spout into cylinders, deploying them upright in a circle from Albany Avenue to the West Canal. The liquid dikes shone like mountains of silver, quivered like mesas of gelatin. Eels and flounders leapt from the vertical tide. *Thus spake Sheila.*

The crowd shouted: "Mary!"

They cried: "Ave Maria!" and "Queen of heaven!"

The watery ramparts fell, smothering the inferno in a mesh of overlapping tides.

Just like that. *Finis.*

"Hail Mary!" "Ave Maria!" "She's come!"

Finis? Julie squinted toward Venice Park. Fresh troops: Milk's army had an entire second column. Down Absecon Boulevard they marched, over five hundred crusaders bound for the bayside casinos, their white flak jackets glowing in the morning sun.

Bring on the column, she thought. Bring on a dozen. Bring on Pharoah's chariots and Rommel's Panzers and the Strategic Air Command's warheads.

I am she.

*   *   *

It is she, Billy thought as he waded across the swollen and unholy river Atlantic Avenue had become. Sheila of the *Midnight Moon*, the beast herself, the very Antichrist, chewing her way out of the Dragon's putrid egg.

A gas jug drifted past. Billy reached into the cold flood, retrieved it. Empty, drained of wrath, and to such little effect. Why wasn't the fall of Babylon going better, why this damnable intervention? The initial assault had been sheer perfection, the Golden Nugget catching fire like straw, whereupon the inferno had grown increasingly mighty, engulfing everything from the Tropicana to the Sands. And when God willed that the tourists be cut down, Billy's army had acquitted itself bravely, turning on their hedge trimmers and slicing with all the piety of Christ's soldiers taking Jerusalem in 1099.

But now came this woman, this Dragon's spawn, dousing the flames, sealing up the only portal by which Jesus might return.

Billy faced the Boardwalk. Dante's, intact. Resorts International, untouched. The mighty Showboat, not a scratch.

Dorylaeum, he thought. At Dorylaeum, too, the day had seemed lost... until the second half of the army arrived, the troops of Lorraine and Provence, overcoming the enemy's numerical advantage with better horses and tougher armor. It was all up to Timothy. Even now the boy was probably attacking the bayside casinos, throwing Jehovah's incandescent sweat on Harrah's and Trump Castle, rekindling the holocaust that would drive out the beast forever.

Drenched head to toe, burly Joshua Tuckerman waded toward Billy, the wet sleeves of his lumberjack shirt hanging from his arms like Spanish moss. Each of the Savior's soldiers had a different reason for joining the crusade, each had his own unique and inspiring story to tell. In Joshua's case, he'd decided to enlist upon learning he was dying of pancreatic cancer. "I was supposed to do Dante's," Joshua gasped. "All this water. I don't understand."

"Steady, brother," Billy commanded. "Timothy will soon be here." His eyepatch trembled. "The flames that were quenched shall rise again!"

"Really? Your boy has that much gas?"

Together they headed north on Tennessee, slogging past the black stinking remnants of the Baltic Avenue apartments. The water seemed lower. Lower? Could it be? Did his corporeal eye deceive him? No, the flood was receding, the sea slipping back into place. It had all been foretold, Billy realized. Revelation 12:15. *And the Serpent cast out of his mouth water as a flood . . .* But all ends well, oh, yes, brothers and sisters, the flood absorbed in 12:17, Babylon thrown down in 14:8, the beast imprisoned in 19:20.

Strange—no smoke on the western horizon, not a wisp. Had Ernie Winslow of Venice Park Texaco failed to open up two hours early as promised? Was Timothy unable to fill his vials? Billy broke into a run.

Trump Castle loomed up, gloating in its wholeness, no sign of fire anywhere. Beyond he saw Harrah's, corrupt and complete.

Defeat lay on Timothy's freckled face like a death mask as he led his five hundred away from the bayside casinos. Gamblers and whoremongers motored down the boulevard, bisecting the column with their mocking Ferraris and cruel Porsches. What monstrous delight they took in honking at Timothy and the retreating troops, what obscene pleasure suffused their cries of "Hey, Holy Joe!" and "Look out, God-freaks!" How quickly their smugness would vanish when they saw the city's other side—the gutted casinos, collapsed Boardwalk, bleeding idolators!

Father and son met at the McKinley Avenue intersection. "The gas station—was that the problem?" Billy asked.

The boy seemed confused. "Huh?"

"The place was closed? You couldn't fill up?"

"No, Dad." Timothy's hedge trimmer was gone. His jug hung from his hand like a penitent's weight. "Plenty of gas. No problem."

"What then?"

"Between Venice Park and the island . . ." The boy stooped sharply, as if balancing the Dragon's egg on his shoulders. "Somewhere in there, the gasoline . . . well, the gas . . ." Like Christ offering a thirsty stranger a gourd of water, Timothy gave Billy the jug. "Take a sip, Dad."

"No, Timothy. It's God's wrath."

"Drink."

Billy opened the jug, poured a small measure into the cap—odd color, no hydrocarbon smell—and tested the fluid with his tongue.

Bland. Smooth.

White.

The Savior had once changed water into wine. And Sheila had . . .

"What is it?" Billy demanded.

"Milk," said his son.

"Milk?"

"Skim, I think."

"You know what we'd better do, Reverend?" said Joshua Tuckerman. "We'd better get back to the beach before all heck breaks loose."

What kind of deity am I, wondered Julie as, dizzy with exhaustion, rapturous with power, she swayed back and forth on the observatory roof. A deity of love, or of wrath? Love was wonderful, but with wrath you could do special effects. Part of her wanted to channel the floodwaters against this crazed and ridiculous army, drowning them like the rats they were, washing that *trayfnyak* Milk into the sea. But ultimately a person must seek her better self. Somehow her brother had stayed the course without once bloodying his hands, a rare feat for a prophet, and she would do the same, letting Milk's brigands go, no, *helping* them go. She objectified her decision on her forearm, sweeping the sweat away with her thumb. As above, so below; the flood fell, giving Milk's shattered hosts a dry path to the beach.

Not until the retreat was well under way, with the first scraggly knot of crusaders piled into their rafts and fighting past the surf, did temptation return, beating through Julie's flesh. Break them, smash them, crush them, an eye for a Mosaic eye. What a spectacle she could stage for the wretches on the beach, what a climax, raising up the Revelationists' yachts a thousand feet, dropping them from the sky like stricken airplanes.

No. Not today. Another time perhaps. Pressing her palms toward the ocean, she bid the observatory descend. *And upon the noon hour Sheila rested.*

As Julie climbed onto the pier, cries of recognition battered her aching flesh. "Hey, the *Moon* lady!" "Like in her picture!" "It's her!" "Sheila!" Dazed, she moved down the ramp, the crowd parting like water before the prow of a ship. By the time she touched the sand they had coalesced into a single creature, adulation personified, awe given flesh.

Viewed from the tower, the misery on the shore had seemed

ordered, comprehensible. But down here all was chaos, stunned gamblers milling around, corpses strewn about like beached fish. Her brain buzzed, her eyes glazed over. Slowly she stumbled forward, safe inside the bubble of her divinity. The groans of hedge-trimmer victims mingled randomly with the weeping of orphaned children. Flesh quivered everywhere, scorched muscles, bleeding gobbets. She tripped over an adolescent boy, his upper leg a charred log.

Was she still supposed to help this pathetic species? Did her obligations encompass the whole damn beach, move into the city with its heaps of the burned and maimed, then across the state, and finally . . . everywhere? She had no ultimate salvation for these people, no means of curing their mortality and melding them with God, but she did have her two bare hands; she could throw herself into a healing frenzy, sewing torn tissue with her fingertips, soothing burns with her spittle, knitting bones with her laser stare . . .

And then it came, the same odor Roger Worth had exuded the night the Winnebago flew, the stench of worship, razoring into her brain. Gasping, she doubled over and hit the sand. Pop was so right. Take the high road and she'd be shackled forever, a slave to adoration and praise.

Phoebe. Phoebe, who had ignited her self-confidence, taught her to take risks. Phoebe: sitting in the cleansed temple, waiting to be freed from the imprisoning spell of Bacardi rum. But for Phoebe, would she have even dared move against Milk's army? She surveyed the expectant multitudes. There would always be expectant multitudes, always. The fight that mattered lay back at Angel's Eye.

Cries of "No!" and "Please!" hovered in Julie's ears like malicious wasps as she hobbled across the sand and tumbled into the surf. The Atlantic slid over her, and the shouts grew muffled and unreal. Damn them. Wasn't it enough that she'd put out the fire? How many lives had she saved by doing that? Five thousand? Ten? Ever deepening, the sea pressed against her skull, ending the din, and she set her course for Angel's Eye, alone with her wrath and the soft steady flapping of her gills.

CHAPTER 9

◆　　　◆　　　◆

Eyes jellied with seawater, body tattooed with goose bumps, Julie ran along the jetty. The rescue of her best friend—what better denouement to her great intervention? Bring on the bottles, she'd smash every one, she'd pulverize them and build castles from the sand. Bring on the Bacardi bat, the Gordon's boar, the Courvoisier Napoleon, the Beefeater. Give her Old Grand-Dad, Jack Daniel's, Jim Beam, Johnny Walker, the whole besotted crew. "Phoebe!" she yelled, barging through the front door. No answer. "Phoebe! Phoebe!" Pop's books soaked up her shouts.

She stumbled into the kitchen, the frigid Atlantic guttering down her arms, puddling on the linoleum. Empty. "Phoebe?" The laundry room: only the washer, the drying rack, the cobwebbed remains of her crib. "Phoebe?" She peeked into the temple. Aunt Georgina sat on her daughter's bed, staring at the bare walls like a schizophrenic. "Hi."

"Oh . . . *you*." Georgina pulled her narrow, hatchetlike face into a sneer. "Our local incarnation." On her lap lay a piece of computer paper, embroidered with sprocket holes. "I've been hearing fire engines all morning."

"Some arsonists attacked the city, but I stopped them. Where's Phoebe? I came to cure her."

"I figured as much." Georgina thrust the paper into Julie's dripping fingers. "This was on the kitchen table."

Phoebe's unmistakable handwriting, all loops and tangles.

DEAR SHEILA: My friend and housemate, who happens to be God's daughter, has just come out of the closet. She believes I drink too much, and any day now she's probably going to start messing with my metabolism. Should I leave a note behind, Sheila, or simply let her find me gone?—WONDERING IN ATLANTIC CITY

"Gone?" Julie grimaced. Her gills trembled.

"Cleared out half her clothes. See for yourself."

"Damn." Julie glanced toward the altar. No missile complex, no dynamite; she'd even taken *that*. Dear Wondering: Wait.

Georgina cinched the belt on her karate suit. "Why'd you tell her you were going public? Don't you know alcoholics fear recovery more than death? Phoebe must've *panicked*."

"Hey, I did you a big favor today." As Julie sat on the edge of the bed, Georgina rose reciprocally, like a seesaw partner. "I saved your shop. When your aunt's shop's on fire, you do something."

"Phoebe's *life* was on fire for the last six years, and you didn't do squat."

"Miracles were never my business. I was born to reveal—"

"The plain truth, Julie Katz"—Georgina slid the karate belt from her waist—"is that nobody knows why the hell you were born, least of all you." She wrapped the belt around her arm like a phylactery strap. "When you cracked out of that ecto-thing, I thought a golden age was dawning. I thought you'd have some great wisdom for us. Now I see what a pig you are. Phoebe's got the right idea—split. Without your father around, this place is death."

Julie's scar pulsated indignantly. "I'm death? That's what you think? Death? If *I* had you for a mother, Georgina, *I'd* probably be a lush now too."

Regret spasmed in Julie. Too late: the words were spoken, unretractable as a baby spilled from a glass womb.

Saying nothing, Georgina marched stiffly out of the temple. Five seconds later the front door slammed explosively, as if Queen Zenobia and the Green Enchantress had just blown up another sand castle.

In the beacon room of Angel's Eye, Andrew Wyvern pulls the soaking wick from the lamp and jams it into his mouth. Slowly he swallows, enjoying the tang of the kerosene on his tongue, the feel of the wet threads slithering down his esophagus.

It hasn't taken much to gain the attention of the city's cardiacs, kidney patients, cancer casualties, welfare cases, lunatics, sociopaths, and bums. "Sheila of the *Moon* has revealed herself!" Wyvern had declared upon entering each hospital and flophouse, and instantly they were his, fixed in his hairy palm. "Follow me!" And they did, right to the beach, where he deftly merged them with Milk's victims, thus fashioning his final trap: a congregation of despair, hungry for hope.

The rest went quickly—telling the multitudes he knew where Atlantic City's savior lived, herding them across the bridge, deploying them around the lighthouse. His plan was at its peak. After years of careful calculation, he has finally made his enemy go public, finally made her sow the seeds of a church.

The devil laughs as the wick crawls into his bowels. *Church*, such a lovely sound, *church*, like the gasp of an Arab child impaled on a Frankish sword at the siege of Jerusalem. Before long Revelationism and its ilk will fade, but not to worry, for Julie Katz's church—ah, that word again, more delicious than kerosene—her church has taken root.

The next twenty-four hours will be crucial. If things go awry, the fragile bud will fade: his enemy will slip back into obscurity or, worse, continue mucking around with reality—help for the crusade casualties, a cure for Alzheimer's, an end to African droughts, a safe and potent insecticide, God knew what.

Instead she must exit the earth. Abruptly. Unequivocally. Memorably.

Like Jesus.

A spirited afternoon breeze blew through the bedroom window, cooling Julie's sopping and exhausted flesh. Sleep took her to the Galapagos Islands. Hand in hand, she and Howard Lieberman toured the evolutionary showcase—its monster tortoises, dragonlike lizards, psychedelic birds. Howard became Bix. A shovel appeared. Her lover dug into the beach, as if looking for buried treasure. A brilliant light geysered up. Sheila, he shouted, this is wonderful. Sheila, come see. Sheila!

"Sheila!"

Bix?

"Sheila! Sheila! Sheila!"

Many voices, a mob. Not in the dream—outside it. New Jersey, Brigantine Point, here.

"Sheila!"

She slipped into Melanie's peach kimono and climbed the hundred and twenty-six steps to the beacon room, her nom de plume falling upon her like a succession of blows. Moving past the dormant lamp, she noticed the wick was missing: a Wyvern lamp, she decided, beaming darkness into the world.

She stepped onto the walkway.

"Sheila! Sheila!"

Vibrating like conglomerated bees, the crowd surrounded the lighthouse and overran the jetty. It was as if her temple had suddenly returned to haunt her, a museum of pain converging from all directions. Wheelchairs, crutches, and dialysis machines punctuated the swarming flesh. Stretchers lay on the grass like grave mounds, their occupants strung to IV bottles hanging from aluminum poles. Disease prospered. Blindness thrived. Burned and mutilated corpses proliferated—Milk's victims, she surmised—yet, curiously, not one of them touched the lawn, each lying instead across the arms of a parent or lover, as if resurrection were contingent upon the body literally being handed over to the divine Sheila.

"Save us!"

"We're yours!"

"Sheila!"

Julie cringed. Here, she realized, were the villains of her life, the ones who perpetuated the empire of nostalgia. Their needs were a thousand scalpels slicing her flesh, chopping her into relics—you take the holy spleen, I want the sacred brain. Damn them. She extended her arms, scissoring them as if marionettes dangled from her fingers. The clamor tapered off. "You must live in your own time!"

"I tried that!" screamed a gaunt young man, his writhing body bound to a wheelchair by leather straps.

The crowd seemed infinite. She imagined it stretching northward along the coast—the entire Eastern Seaboard lined up, waiting for deliverance. Nobody could be expected to deal with all this, nobody. "You must look to the future!"

"Screw the future!" called a potbellied man carrying a preadolescent girl, her body wracked by cystic fibrosis.

"Sheila!"

"Please!"

"Help!"

A siege. That was the only word. Julie thought of the rainy Saturday afternoon they'd watched Roger Worth's videocassette of *Night of the Living Dead*. Bar the door, board the windows, the zombies are coming. The living dead? No, these were the dead living, she decided. They'd never known the tomb, and yet they were inert, sapped, stunned by the innumerable failings of flesh.

Bar the door board the windows—forget it, that wouldn't do, the crisis demanded extreme measures.

Fixing on the lawn, Julie removed the grass with her stare, shearing it away like a nurse depilating a neurosurgery patient. The dead living drew back, awed, expectant. Seized by Julie's mind, the spit rumbled and shook. Earth upheaved, sand billowed, rocks shot from the ground like reverse-motion meteorites. The dead living scattered. Every deity is an island, Julie concluded as Angel's Eye split off from the mainland. Like mother, like daughter: detached, distant, incommunicado.

The Atlantic gushed into the gap. With three emphatic hand claps she transmuted the surrounding sea into acid as easily as she'd turned the Revelationists' gasoline into milk. No ordinary acid, not hydrochloric, not sulfuric—the stomach juices of the primordial goat, smoking and swirling, potent enough to gnaw the bottom off any invading vessel, the very stuff a deity might use to etch a tidal basin into a planet or carve a mountain range from a continental plate. Water to acid. Child's play, elementary alchemy.

Julie backed into the beacon room.

Her loneliness had fiber and weight. She could have determined its boiling point, measured its specific gravity. Aunt Georgina hated her; Phoebe had split; Bix was a traitor; Melanie was in Hollywood getting rich; Pop lay divided between a bunch of icy test tubes and a jar on the ocean floor. Alone.

A deep, low hiss issued from the wickless lamp. A voice rattled in its brass belly. "Let me make you an offer."

"What?"

"An offer."

"Who's there?"

"An old acquaintance." The lamp's inhabitant, a lewd red snake with poison sacs for cheeks, crawled out of the wick slot. The creature smelled of honeyed oranges. "The mob owns you, child. Your secret's out. You can't put yourself back in the bottle."

"I've lost a great deal," Julie confessed to the snake. "My ministry, my friends..."

"In twenty-four hours, *Pain* departs." Andrew Wyvern slithered down the lamp and sinuated across the floor. "Join the voyage, child. Better to be a citizen in hell than a slave in New Jersey."

Julie frowned, crinkling her scar. Join the voyage? Leave the comprehended cosmos? She pondered the possibility. "Hell is a long way off, Mr. Wyvern."

"Believe me, a person with your background would receive the best treatment there, first-class accommodations. Hell has some of the finest cooks and wine-makers who ever lived. Our masseurs know the lost chords of flesh."

Freedom...but no, no, for whatever reasons, her mother had planted her in Atlantic City. "I can't."

"Naturally you'd get in right away. No waiting list for you."

"You have a waiting list?"

"Of course we have a waiting list. Don't believe everything you hear about hell. Next time you run into some anti-hell propaganda, consider the source."

"You inflict eternal punishment on people," Julie countered.

"Merely because it's our job. And remember, we persecute only the guilty, which puts us one up on most other institutions." The serpent hissed like a dynamite fuse. "Twenty-four hours, Julie. The trains don't run after that. Come with us. There's nothing more you can do here."

It was crazy to give credence to the devil. "You mean—I've fulfilled my purpose?"

"You published the covenant. Put out the fire. Curtain."

"Be honest, Mr. Wyvern. I needn't break with the known universe to have a life. I could go to...I don't know. California."

"In California they'd track you down instantly. For eleven months your picture was in every issue of the *Moon*."

"I could change my face."

"But not your genes. As long as you're on the earth, your divinity will keep leaking out. Sooner or later, all masks fall off, and *then*—"

A fiery drama spouted from the wickless lamp. In the center lay a small, doll-like simulacrum of Julie, nailed to a wooden cross. The doll screamed like a boiling teakettle. Shadowy homunculi stood at its feet, cheering. Cheap trick, Julie thought. Silly, unconvincing... "Shut it off!" Pinprick spots of blood fell from the doll's wounds. *"Off!"*

The lurid puppet show vanished.

Her arteries vibrated like plucked harp strings. For the first time ever, she felt herself heir to Pop's heart, that vulnerable pump, so easily damaged. God had demanded propitiation deaths before, and would probably do so again.

Unless she escaped...

"Do it, Julie. Save yourself." The serpent smiled, showing fangs like fish hooks. "I promise you safe passage. One simple condition."

"Your conditions are never simple."

"You must give the crowd something to remember you by. Make a grand exit—you owe them that."

"I could try the Galapagos Islands."

"Galapagos, Madagascar, Bali, Tahiti, Sri Lanka—wherever you go, you'll spend your life looking over your shoulder. There's pizza in hell, Julie. Movies, physics monographs, ice cream—everything you care about." The snake slithered back into the lamp. "Remember, child, a grand exit."

I should've done this years ago, Phoebe thought as the Greyhound coach plunged from the West Side's blinding daylight into the cool, grimy shadows of the Port Authority Bus Terminal. Atlantic City was nothing, an R-rated Disneyland full of losers and whores. At last she'd reached the real thing—Manhattan Island, Gotham, Big Apple, El Dorado with subways. No more waiting forever for a good movie to reach town. No more dealing with tourists and weirdos at the Smile Shop.

She'd miss Mom, of course, and she was sorry she wouldn't be there when Melanie got back from Hollywood. But her so-called friend Katz had left her no choice. Phoebe wasn't about to let anybody mess with her metabolism, no way. A drinking hobby wasn't the same as alcoholism—in New York, at least, that truth would be understood.

The bus pulled into its stall, groaning and belching like a colicky rhinoceros. Okay, so Manhattan wasn't the South Seas island she and Katz had seen in the Deauville. Still, she belonged here. Shouldering her Smile Shop tote bag (WHEN THE GOING GETS

TOUGH, THE TOUGH GO SHOPPING), she staggered down the aisle
and stepped off the coach. New York, population nine million,
and twenty more had just blown in from South Jersey. She sidled
toward the luggage bay, where the passengers waited like
mourners around a grave. As usual, she felt detached from such
people, outside. Knowing Katz did that to you. A God existed:
Phoebe had proof. The devil was loose in Atlantic City: Phoebe
had ridden a merry-go-round with him. But what was the final
sum? Did Julie Katz matter more than anything, or barely matter
at all?

The bus driver appeared, popped the hatch, and began
dragging out the luggage. The most important item in Phoebe's
suitcase wasn't her liquor cabinet or dynamite but her camcorder. Cinéma-vérité sex—how could she lose? Staged forni-
cation was such a bore. What people wanted, the focus of their
primal curiosity, was the genuine article—an actual police-
woman boffing her husband, an authentic delivery boy doing
it with his girlfriend; every step of the process, each probe and
clutch and caress.

As the passengers paired themselves with their suitcases, a
trim, thirtyish black man came toward Phoebe, a fedora snugged
down past his eyebrows, gold rings stacked on his fingers. "New
in town?" he asked, grinning spectacularly. "I'm Cecil." He
tipped his fedora and thrust his hands into his lavender three-
piece suit. "Got a place to stay?"

Phoebe retrieved her suitcase. "You look like somebody I
knew once. You a marine biologist by any chance?"

"A what?"

"Marine biologist."

"Not exactly, though there's definitely a biological side to
what I do."

"You never donated to the Preservation Institute?"

"What's that, a religion?"

"Forget it."

The stranger picked up her suitcase. "You've got gorgeous
eyes, sister. I could start you at three hundred a week. Escort
profession. Come home with me, babes."

Frost formed in Phoebe's heart. Escort profession—hah. "I
have a career, thank you." She yanked the suitcase away from the
pimp. "I'm in the entertainment business."

"Me too." The pimp winked lasciviously.

"Video's my trade. Buzz off."

"I just wanted to—"

"I said buzz off."

She entered the Port Authority, rode the escalator up one flight, and waded into the dense screeching streets where she planned to make her fortune.

But first she needed a drink.

Between the din of the media and the crowd's unceasing voice— a polyphonic howl such as wolves might make disgorging broken glass—Julie could not sleep. Throughout the night, newspaper people and TV crews kept arriving, and by dawn they were camped out all over the lawn, occupying it like a hostile army. *Atlantic City Press* reporters bellowed across the acid moat using bullhorns, demanding to interview the woman who'd saved their town. Video cameras leered at Angel's Eye from out of cherry pickers. A helicopter labeled WACX-Radio buzzed the tower, its rotor so unnerving that Julie had no choice but to cloak her home in a dense mantle of mist.

She sought to distract herself with television, but there were so many Sheila stories it was like looking in a mirror. On Channel 9 a statuesque woman swathed in blond hair stood on the edge of the freshly carved moat, surrounded by the dead living, a tower of fog in the background. "Who's inside the cloud?" she asked the camera. "A magician, some say. The Virgin Mary, others claim." A microphone hovered near the reporter's lips like an all-day sucker. "But no rumor is more persistent than the one that brought these people to Brigantine Point. For them, Atlantic City's mysterious benefactor is none other than Sheila, daughter of God." The reporter winked. "Tracy Swenson, Channel 11 Action News, Brigantine."

At dusk Julie removed the fog, peeling it away like a label from one of Phoebe's rum bottles. *Pain* cruised the horizon like a shark patrolling its feeding ground.

Dress right, Julie told herself. Melanie's kimono would not befit the memorable exit on which her safe passage was predicated. She put on Melanie's suede boots, crammed herself into Georgina's prom dress. Nor could she leave her face untouched —a few minutes with Georgina's makeup, and her eyes widened, her scar vanished, her lips became rose petals.

She stepped onto the walkway. A thousand eager stares

drilled into her heart. Cheers pounded her flesh. Climbing atop the railing, she balanced on the metal bar like an aerialist. She flung her arms apart, enshrouded herself with light—a full-body halo pulsing outward from her head and trunk like a rainbow on fire—and jumped.

At first it seemed the crowd's astonished whoops were buoying her up, but no, this was her heritage at work, whizzing her across the darkening sky like a sentient comet. "Look!" "She's flying!" "Sheila!" "Stay!" "Mary!" "Flying!" "Sheila!" She looped the loop. She spiraled around the lighthouse as if decorating a maypole, then zoomed over the bay toward the waiting schooner. The cool air frizzed her hair, billowed her dress, caressed her naked arms. Flying was better than swimming beneath Absecon Inlet. Flying was better than sex.

She landed in the crow's nest, startling a drowsy vulture and breaking one of its eggs. The damp, sinewy rigging squeaked and groaned as, hand under hand, she climbed down. To freedom. To safety. To a reality no baby bank aborter or crusade victim could ever invade. Clouds of unknowing and shadows of quantum doubt rolled in from the north, enveloping the schooner like black veils, catching on her spars, clinging to her masts.

Julie stepped onto the foredeck. Three coal-eyed angels looked up from their labors—they were fixing a hole in a flesh-sail, suturing it closed with needle and thread—and applauded. Anthrax, stationed in the cockpit, placed a clawed hand to his lips and blew her a kiss.

Resolutely she marched through Wyvern's oak-paneled cabin and into the salon beyond, her pace slowed by the gummy yolk on her boots. The devil stood by the settee. "Welcome aboard," he said, brushing her arm. A red carnation hung on the lapel of his white dinner jacket like a brilliant wound.

"I made the right decision," Julie asserted, voice quavering.

"Nobody with our talents can abide the earth for long," Wyvern corroborated. "Such a vale of unrealistic expectations. The bastards just grind you."

She glanced at the table, swathed in immaculate linen. A bottle of champagne poked from an ice bucket like the periscope of an Arctic submarine.

Two place settings. "Who's coming to dinner?" she asked.

"You are. Lentil soup and bean curds. Hope you don't mind —I'm a vegetarian."

"Oh?"

"It's irresistible—the screams of the carrots as I dice them, the agonized beets convulsing in my mouth. Hungry?"

"Famished."

"The voyage will pass quickly. There's much to talk about and more to see. I look forward to your companionship, Julie. Please call me Andrew." He offered a succinct, gentlemanly bow. "Yours is the first stateroom on the left. My angels have laid out an evening gown. That prom dress is all wrong—white is your color."

She followed Wyvern onto the foredeck. "Raise anchor!" he called in a soaring, bell-like voice. Julie looked toward the lighthouse. Would she ever miss it? She wished she'd brought a souvenir—a Smile Shop T-shirt, Pop's manuscript, her "Heaven Help You" scrapbook.

Slowly *Pain*'s anchor crawled over the transom, salt water rolling off its spikes, seaweed swaying from its chain. Issuing a series of liquid grunts, the creature curled up by the windlass, closed its rat-red eyes, and went to sleep.

"Dinner's at eight," said the devil.

Pain surged under Julie's feet. The sails expanded like huge puffy cheeks. Wyvern's angels must have been eating ambrosia, their intestinal winds were so heady and sweet. The city's ruined silhouette receded—dark skeletal girders that had once framed the Golden Nugget, the Tropicana, the Atlantis...

A white gown, Wyvern had said. He was going to dress her in white. She hadn't felt this good in a long, long time.

CHAPTER 10

◆   ◆   ◆

Wave-tossed, angel-powered, His Satanic Majesty's ship *Pain* blew across the Atlantic, the Pacific, and from there to the gloomy and indeterminate seas beyond. Julie stayed below, away from the spray that scratched her eyeballs, the air that filled her lungs like raw cotton.

The devil knew how to live. *Pain's* cabins were air-conditioned. Its library was a cornucopia of gilded volumes redolent of oiled leather and wisdom: *The City of God, Summa Theologica, Das Kapital*—all Satan's favorites. Every night at eight, Anthrax brought her a dinner menu, and Julie would check off pepperoni pizza or, on alternate evenings, something more sophisticated: stuffed lambchops, breast of peacock. Once she ordered the "musical entertainment," subsequently dining to a violin concert performed by twenty dead preschoolers whose plane had exploded during a demonstration tour of the Suzuki method.

"Happy?" the devil asked. His metamorphosis was simultaneously startling and banal. Horns poked blatantly from his forehead. Overlapping scales covered his body like slate tiles. His nose had doubled in size, its nostrils wide and gaping like the bores of a shotgun.

"Happy," said Julie emphatically. She stared through a porthole into the fibrous mist. Nausea pressed its rude thumb against her stomach. "You bet your tail I'm happy." Tail: true

His coccyx, no longer a mere vestige, was growing an inch every day.

Happy? What she really felt was disconnected, standing here in a white evening gown and conversing with Satan himself in the galley of a hellbound schooner. Hard to believe she'd once been a Girl Scout, played point guard for the Brigantine High Tigerettes, or had a love affair with the *Midnight Moon*'s managing editor.

"I should have shipped with you long ago," she told the devil.

The glutinous days accumulated, congealing into weeks, lumping into months. Bricks of black lustrous coal filled the sky, at first hovering individually, then fusing into an endless arch. Yet night did not descend, for the vault reflected the glow of a thousand burning islands, bathing *Pain*'s course in a rosy and perpetual dusk.

Good intentions, Julie learned, were among the more innocuous commodities paving the road to hell. The sea lanes threading the archipelago were dark sewery channels choked with dead tuna, while the islands themselves suggested humpback whales stitched together by Victor Frankenstein. The predictability of Wyvern's operation depressed her: one hears from earliest childhood that in hell the convicted dead receive atrocious punishments, and that was exactly what each island offered. Training her binoculars on a plateau, she saw over a dozen naked men chained Prometheuslike to huge rocks; crazed panthers ripped open their bellies, hauling their soppy intestines down the slopes like kittens unraveling yarn. On the shores of the adjacent island, a long line of sinners stood buried up to their necks, their exposed heads resting atop the sand like beachballs; shell-crackers fixed in their claws, ravenous lobsters crawled out of the surf, breached the skulls, and, buttering the exposed brains, feasted. On other islands Julie beheld the damned drawn and quartered. Skinned alive. Broken on racks, impaled on stakes, drilled to pieces by hornets. And always the pain was infinite, always the victim would find his mangled flesh restored and the torment beginning again. Contrary to Dante Alighieri's inspiration, hell's motto was not, ALL HOPE ABANDON, YE WHO ENTER IN but merely, SO WHAT DID YOU EXPECT?

Intervene? Save them? Whenever the idea reared its head,

she had only to recall the hydralike nature of eternal damnation: the moment one agony ended, another instantly bloomed; Julie's powers—abracadabra, your skull is whole, alakazam, your wound is mended—meant nothing here. Besides, as the devil had told her in the beacon room, these souls were guilty. On earth, saints suffered along with sinners; not so in hell. Wyvern's world might be endlessly gruesome and impossibly brutal, but it was strangely, uniquely just.

Just? So said the devil, so said the theologians, and yet the closer *Pain* got to her destination, the further she seemed to drift from reason. Day by day, the categories of iniquity grew ever more arbitrary and excessive. Julie could understand why there was an Island of Atheists. Ditto the Island of Adulterers, the Island of Occultists, the Island of Tax Dodgers. Depending on one's upbringing, the precincts reserved for Unitarians, Abortionists, Socialists, Nuclear Strategists, and Sexual Deviates made sense. But why the Island of Irish Catholics? The Island of Scotch Presbyterians? Christian Scientists, Methodists, Baptists?

"This offends me," she said, thrusting a navigational chart before Wyvern and pointing to the Island of Mormons.

The devil's tail, a kind of rubbery harpoon, looped upward. He grabbed the barbed end. "Throughout history, admission to hell has depended on but one criterion." He gave the Island of Mormons an affectionate pat. "You must belong to a group some other group believes is heading there."

"That's perverse."

"It's also the law. Doesn't matter if you're an embezzler, a slave trader, or Hermann Goering himself—you can elude my domain if nobody ever imagined you in it."

"How terribly unfair."

"Of course it's unfair. Who do you think's running the universe, Eleanor Roosevelt?" Wyvern kissed his tail, sucked on the barbs. "Quantum realities don't have checks and balances. There's no cosmic ACLU out there."

"You're lying."

"Not in this case. The truth's too delicious."

'I can't imagine a Methodist doing anything particularly damning. Why would—?"

"Like all Protestants, Methodists abandoned the True Church. Only through the Apostolic Succession can a person partake of Christ's continued spiritual presence on earth. This is basic stuff, Julie."

"Catholics, then. They remained faithful to—"

"Are you serious? With their Mariolatry, Trinity, purgatory, indulgences? How unbiblical can you get?"

"My father was a good man, and he—"

"The *Jews*? Give me a break, Julie. The *Jews*? They don't even accept God's son as their redeemer, much less practice Baptism of the Holy Spirit. Let's not even discuss the Jews."

"All right—I give up. Who got saved?"

Wyvern reached under one of his shoulder scales, lifting out an errant earwig. "Heaven's not a crowded place."

"So I gather. A million?"

"Cold."

"Fewer?"

"Uh-huh."

"Ten thousand?"

"Lower."

"One thousand?"

"Such an optimist." Wyvern snapped his fingers, crushing the earwig. "Four."

"Four?"

"There are four people in heaven." The devil's diaphanous eyelids began a snide descent. "Enoch and Elijah, for starters. I couldn't do anything about that—it's in Scripture. Then there's Saint Peter, of course. And, finally, Murray Katz."

"Pop? He was a Jew."

"Yes, but consider his connections. Of all beings in the cosmos, he alone was selected to gestate God's daughter."

Julie rolled up the obscene chart. Pop was saved, great, but how could so many others be lost? Her seasickness worsened, a thousand delinquent ants defacing her stomach walls with graffiti. "This is horribly depressing, Andrew. It robs earthly existence of all meaning."

"*Au contraire*, Julie. The fact of damnation *gives* earthly existence its meaning. Enjoy life while you've got it, right? Eat, drink, and be merry, for tomorrow you make a quantum leap."

"Gandhi?" she suggested weakly.

"A Hindu."

"Martin Luther King?"

"His sex life."

"Saint Paul?"

"The feminists wanted his ass."

"The Madonna?"

"A rock star."

"No, *the* Madonna."

"A Catholic."

"*Jesus?*"

"The last time I saw Jesus, he was working in some hospice in Buenos Aires. I think we should count Jesus as missing in action."

Friday, August 15, 1997. First the firebergs appeared, great hummocks of floating, flaming ice. Then the sea monsters surfaced, pulpy masses of gray flesh with tentacles and redundant eyes, their dorsal fins cutting into the sky like jibs as they accompanied *Pain* toward the central continent.

"Rough drafts," Wyvern explained, pointing across the wind-blown deck to their malformed and forsaken escorts. "No wonder your mother got it together in only six days—she'd already *made* her mistakes."

Initially the continent seemed to Julie nothing but a black, burning ingot glowing in the distance, but then it grew, showing sheer cliffs and incandescent hills. Dining on the sea monsters, Wyvern's angels acquired sufficient fuel to blow *Pain* into the harbor at fifty knots. Hell, by God. For better or worse, she'd gotten all the way to hell.

The anchor limped across the deck and hurled itself over the side.

The Port of Hell vibrated with activity, rumbled with hubbub, buzzed like an asylum for insane bees. It belched and bellowed and smoked. Dozens of barges and freighters crisscrossed the harbor, looping around marker buoys outfitted with pealing bells and clanging gongs, a carillon more suited, Julie felt, to a New England village on a Sunday morning than hell on a Friday afternoon. Vast loading cranes stood against the anthracite sky, their high steel towers bobbing like the necks of brontosaurs as they plucked semitrailers from moored ships.

"What are you importing?" Julie asked.

"What do you *think*?"

Even as Wyvern spoke, howls of despair—Catholic despair,

Protestant despair, Eastern Orthodox, Jewish, Buddhist, atheist
—shot from the semitrailers.

The central pier was a peninsula of black fissured granite
swarming with bat-winged angels, scaled fiends, and piggish
imps. "Hail Lucifer!" the sycophants shouted. A huge welcom-
ing party sailed forth, scores of demons packed into swan boats
and outrigger canoes. "Hosanna!" they cried, tossing bright yellow leis onto *Pain*'s foredeck. Cheers boomed across the harbor
as Wyvern saluted. Banners unfurled along the maze of wharfs.

WELCOME JULIE!

AVE KATZ!

HAIL DAUGHTER OF GOD!

"Think you could blow them a kiss or two?" asked Wyvern.
"They'd get off on it."

A coach clattered down the central pier, drawn by a team of
four white horses.

"I'm going to enjoy this place," said Julie, her voice toneless.
She blew three small, pinched kisses toward shore. Enjoy hell?
Could that be remotely true? Did any coordinates exist in or out
of reality that she could ever call home?

Anthrax rowed them to shore through a blizzard of confetti
and rose petals, and they climbed into the velvet-upholstered
coach. The driver, a demon whose physiognomy melded a wea-
sel's leer with a toad's complexion, cracked his whip above the
horses' heads.

And they were off, speeding over deserts of burning sulfur
and through forests whose trees were the fleshless hands of gigantic skeletons. They rattled across rainbows of rock arcing over
gorges filled with writhing piles of the damned. They circumvented vast lunarian craters formed, Wyvern asserted, by the
impact of falling angels.

Within the hour a marble palace swung into view, its slender
towers soaring into the smoky air like the masts of some fantastic
frigate. Pennants flew from the parapets, snapping in the hot
hadean breeze. A portcullis hung in the main gate like a leop-
ard's upper jaw.

"The foundation stones once pressed witches to death," Wyvern explained as the coach rolled into the courtyard. With a
ceremonial flourish, the driver opened the door and Wyvern
stepped out. "We wash the carpets with orphans' tears," said the

devil. "The mosaic floors are inlaid with the teeth of starved Ethiopians."

He extended his scaly arm. Julie jumped down, inhaling the foggy, clotted ambience of her new home, an odor suggesting cabbage cooked in molten asphalt.

"Visit me in the capital whenever you like," Wyvern said.

"Hell has a capital?"

"Of course hell has a capital. You think we're a bunch of anarchists? You think I'm not up to my ass in politics and bureaucracy? Thank God for computers—that's all I can say."

Hell was not perfect, but it was paradise compared with New Jersey. She had a life now. She was free. No more insults from Georgina. No more fights with Bix, hunts for Phoebe's liquor, or battered wretches crowding around her house. Her every wish became Anthrax's command. When she spoke fondly of diving into Absecon Inlet, the obliging demon constructed a swimming pool in the basement, heated by natural sulfur. When she mentioned her lack of a wardrobe, he loaded her closets with the previous year's fashions. "I used to enjoy movies," she told him, and immediately he located a 35mm projector plus a ceiling-high tower of Busby Berkeley musicals and Marx Brothers comedies.

The melancholy started slowly, subtly, like a cold spawned by a diffident virus. Where was Phoebe now? Hollywood, Julie speculated, nailing down her dreams of cinéma-vérité eroticism, snarfling up lines of cocaine from her desk on the Paramount lot. And Bix. She hoped he missed her—the *real* her, not the intervener who'd so confused and angered him the day Billy Milk's army came to town. Would they have eventually married? She suspected so; they meshed in so many ways, their skepticism, their chubbiness. She imagined herself pregnant with Bix's child, a sweet, round rationalist sprouting in her womb.

Feverish with longing, numb with boredom, Julie decided to explore.

On the central continent, she learned, everything was basic and direct: fire. Fire had it all. Fire, which strips away the derma, the nervous system's armor, leaving the victim clothed in pain. Climbing hell's ragged peaks in her silk blouse and peasant skirt, Julie witnessed angels tying prisoners to tree trunks and burning them alive. The next day, descending into hell's glowing canyons in her safari jacket and designer jeans, she saw the damned cooked in swamps of boiling diarrhea. Horribly, the multitudes never became more than the sum of their selves—particular women with personal hair styles, particular men of varying physiognomies, even particular fetuses, each with its own smell, an amalgam of pain and original sin. If only she could help them. But no, pointless—snap, your burns are temporarily healed, clap, your blisters are momentarily gone: so what? She had but two hands and one godhead—two hands and one godhead against the whole of perdition.

As far as Julie could discern, hell's major industry was iron smelting. Driven by the angels' whips, the naked men and women coalesced into teams. For some prisoners, damnation meant hollowing out hell's mountains with pickaxes and loading the ore into hopper cars. For others, it meant pushing the cars along narrow-gauge railroad tracks. For others, it meant feeding limestone and coke to the blast furnaces: limestone that seared the prisoners' skin, coke that ate their lungs. A final team drew slag and molten metal from the hearths, then carried the pig iron by wheelbarrow to a seething, swirling river and dumped it over the banks, whereupon it dissolved and began the slow but relentless process of soaking back into the continent, ready to be reclaimed, a perfect circle.

And always the heat, forcing water from the prisoners' flesh like a winepress squeezing grapes. In hell, people sliced their wrists and guzzled the blood, anything to feel wetness on their tongues. In hell, a father would shoot his firstborn for a jigger of piss.

On close inspection, the label worn by each damned soul proved to be a thick asbestos shingle secured about his neck by a gold chain. *March 23, 1998—7:48 P.M.*, said the shingle on a young Philippine woman who was perpetually scalded in five-hundred-degree chicken fat. On an old Swedish man clothed in white-hot barbed wire, *May 8, 1999—6:11 P.M.* On an Hispanic child rushing down an electrified sliding board, *April 11, 2049—10:35 P.M.* Death certificates? wondered Julie. At this moment I entered hell? No, all these dates still lay in the future, a truth that made the prisoners' idolatry—the way they would periodically lift the shingles to their blistered lips and kiss them—a total mystery. The future, she felt, was the last thing these people should worship.

Everybody damned? Could that really be? Only Enoch, Eli-

jah, Saint Peter, and Pop had gained the quantum reality called
heaven? In her most despondent moments Julie sensed it was all
absurdly true. Everybody damned—even Howard Lieberman
over there, pushing a wheelbarrow along the steamy banks of
the great pig-iron river.

She blinked. Yes. Him. Her old boyfriend, sheathed in sweat,
speckled with blisters, naked as when they'd last made love. He still
had his wire-rimmed glasses, his tight lips. "Howard?" His skin
was like an ancient linoleum floor, entire hunks broken away. A
corona of pain surrounded his entire being. "Howard Lieberman?"

Pausing, he lowered the wheelbarrow. "Julie? That really
you? Julie Katz?" His voice vibrated as though he were speaking
through an electric fan.

She nodded, brushing sulfur from her hoop skirt. "What
happened to you?"

"Shipwrecked," Howard moaned. Sparks danced around him
like flies encircling a carcass. "Coming home from the Galapagos
Islands." The sparks blew into his chest, bouncing off his asbestos shingle. *October 3, 1997—11:18 A.M.*, a date that according
to her watch was a mere forty-eight hours away.

"What's that tag, Howard?"

"You don't have one?" He sounded alarmed.

"I'm not dead."

"Really?"

Julie nodded. "Uh-huh."

"Is that why you have clothes on?"

"Well, yes."

"But why did you—?"

"I couldn't stand the earth."

"You came *voluntarily*?"

"There's something in my family history you don't know
about."

"How's that?"

"I'm tuned in on the cosmos, Howard. I'm one of your quantum aberrations."

He appeared on the point of responding to this assertion, but
instead said, "If you want to know about the tags, come back in
two days." Pressing the shingle to his lips, he kissed it fervently,
as if it were Newton's favorite prism or a toy magnet once owned
by Einstein.

"At 11:18?"

"Earlier. Takes an hour to get there."

"Where?"

"Back to work, sinner!" an angel screamed.

The lash uncoiled instantly, like a frog's tongue snaring a dragonfly. Howard's knees buckled; he pitched forward across his wheelbarrow. Again the angel struck, and again, the thong slitting Howard's back like Aunt Georgina opening a carton of joy buzzers. Sparks landed in his wounds, making his fresh blood sizzle.

Julie backed off, spun around. Come back in two days—a trap? It sounded like one. She'd come back, and Howard would ask her to employ the pull she evidently enjoyed here. He'd drop to his boiled knees, clasp his scarred hands together, and beg her to get him a reprieve.

She hurried home, screened *A Night at the Opera*, and swam twenty laps along the bottom of her pool. She had a life now, she told herself, far more so than in her Atlantic City days. An enviable situation, a hermit's cave with room service. She owed Howard Lieberman nothing.

Two days later she arrived at the pig-iron river in time to see her old boyfriend flash his shingle to the chief overseer, a pasty-faced angel with an AK-41 assault rifle slung over his shoulder. Possessed by a wild and primal expectation, Howard barely acknowledged her. The angel nodded, and Howard took off, skipping down a highway of sulfur, singing a medley of Beatles songs, his rendition of "Octopus's Garden" flowing seamlessly into his "Let It Be."

God alone knew what the years of hauling iron had done to Howard, how many cracks in his bones, how many aneurysms in his heart. Yet whenever he stumbled and fell, he immediately picked himself up and continued, limping eagerly across the death-shadowed valleys and burning hills. Nothing discouraged him, not hell's acid snow, bird-sized mosquitoes, or storm-trooper angels, on whom his shingle acted as a kind of amulet, charming them into letting him pass.

"You still think science has all the answers?" Julie asked, struggling to keep up. "You still think the problem is that we don't have all the science?"

"Of course I do," said Howard. "Look at this place, Julie—incomprehensible, absurd. *Obviously* we don't have all the science."

But for the absence of narrow-gauge railroad tracks, the cave might have been yet another hadean iron mine. A golden glow pulsed from its mouth, haloing the dozens of naked humans waiting to enter. Their collective stench burned Julie's nostrils as Howard took his place at the end of the line. She decided to pull rank; she abandoned Howard and walked straight to the entrance, where a fragile-looking Japanese man labeled 10:58 waited anxiously. "Next!" a male voice called from the gloom, and the Japanese man rushed into the cave as if he'd just snatched up the baton at a relay race. Julie looked at her watch. 10:58 on the dot. 10:59, a redheaded teenage boy, whose face was a mass of acne and sulfur burns, moved into place. Sixty seconds later, the Japanese man emerged, shingle gone, wearing the most contented smile Julie had ever seen.

She crossed the threshold.

The stone room was sparsely furnished—horizontal granite slab, kerosene lantern sitting on a stalagmite, canvas director's chair supporting a black-bearded, thirtyish man. A narrow stream, its waters bright and burbling, cut across the floor like a vein of silver ore. "Next!" the bearded man cried as Julie melted into the shadows. The boy named 10:59 collapsed on the slab, whereupon the bearded man performed a quick ritual, dipping a hollow gourd into the stream and sprinkling half the measure on the young prisoner's head.

"Excuse me."

"Yes?" The water-giver held the remaining measure to 10:59's desiccated lips.

"My name's Julie Katz."

"Ah, the famous Julie Katz," the water-giver said cryptically, locking his dark shining eyes on her. A strong Semitic nose, a wide intelligent brow—quite a handsome fellow, really, marred only by the garish holes in his ankles and wrists. "Your arrival is all we've been hearing about lately."

The noise of the slurping boy reverberated off the granite walls. "I thought you were in Buenos Aires," said Julie.

"Who told you that?" demanded God's son, removing 10:59's shingle and tossing it into the inky darkness.

"Satan."

"He lies." Jesus helped 10:59 off the slab, guided him toward the cave entrance. "Not always, but often." Her brother's leather sandals were scuffed, cracked, and, in the case of the left, strapless. Burn holes speckled his robe. "I'm dead. How could I be—where did you say?"

"Buenos Aires."

"Nope. Dead. Nailed to a cross." Jesus poked an index finger into his violated wrist. "So how'd they kill *you*?"

"I'm not dead." Why did everyone think her dead?

"Then what are you doing here?"

The snappishness in his voice was unwarranted, she felt. "I wasn't happy in Jersey. I couldn't figure out my purpose."

"And you thought hell would be nicer?" Bending by the stream, Jesus filled his ladle. "You call this foresight, girl? Next!"

Such a comedian, and she could do without the sexism. "I had no freedom up there. Everybody was out to get me. I'm not a girl."

A skinny, creased old man threw himself on the slab.

"Where's Buenos Aires anyway?" Jesus asked.

"Argentina."

"In Asia Minor?"

"South America."

"I'm very busy," said Jesus curtly, dousing the old man. Rude, she thought. He was definitely being rude. "Whatever brought you to hell," said her brother, "you won't find it in this sorry little room."

"Obviously not."

"Then leave, why don't you?"

"Do you know who I am?"

"Yes, my well-dressed little sister, I know who you are, and I have nothing to say to you." Jesus sighed—a low, long, symphonic sound compacting weariness and impatience. "Please go away, daughter of God."

Maybe she'd caught him on a bad day. Maybe he was really a warm and tender fellow. She doubted it. This man who had somehow abstracted himself from history, exempted his character from judgment, this man in whose name the world had built cathedrals and burned down cities, this man, her brother, was a *shmuck*.

Walking home through the sulfurous mist, she wondered where Jesus' operation stood in the general scheme of things. Was it wholly clandestine, a one-man resistance movement? No, the prisoners displayed their shingles publicly, didn't they? More likely her brother's charity was like the black market in Russia, a tolerated subversion, unofficially sanctioned.

She'd never been more grateful for her mansion—its resuscitating shower, Anthrax's expert cooking, her film collection. So Jesus was giving out water. So big deal. It reminded her of Pop turning on his lighthouse for ships that had already sunk. Pathetic.

But God's son wouldn't leave. Ladle in hand, he hovered within her, lodged in her thoughts as she napped by the hearth, fixed in her imagination as she ate pepperoni pizza. Retiring to her canopied bed, she spent the night thrashing atop her silk sheets and eiderdown mattress.

By morning he had won. Dashing into her cavernous kitchen, she yanked out all one hundred drawers and overturned them on the floor. The silvery clatter brought Anthrax running. "Sorry," she said, noting his bewildered face. "You thought I was a thief?"

Anthrax shook his head. "Hell is a low-crime district."

"Do we have a ladle?"

"A what?"

"Ladle—I just want a ladle," she replied sternly, kicking the glittery mountain of utensils. "Do we have a goddamn ladle or don't we?"

Anthrax opened a cabinet above the stove. What he drew out lacked the organic romance of Jesus' gourd—it was an aluminum cup with a black plastic handle, barely suitable for serving punch at a junior prom—but it would do. She ordered Anthrax to hire her a coach, and by noon she was back at the cave, pushing past the line of thirsty dead people, her jeans and sweatshirt coated with sulfur specks. A little girl with blond ringlets lay on the slab. Seated in his director's chair, Jesus looked up, his lustrous stare fusing with hers.

"Is this the right answer?" she asked, displaying the shabby ladle.

"You know it is," Jesus replied smoothly, patting the little girl's head and smiling.

Julie dipped the ladle into the stream, doused the child, and offered her a drink. She lapped it up eagerly, beaming a prodigious smile into Julie's face.

"Welcome," God's son told his sister.

CHAPTER 11

◆　　◆　　◆

Sister and brother, side by side, day after day, comforting the damned. It was like tending a garden, Julie decided, like watering flower beds of flesh. They divided the labor, Jesus cooling the bodies, Julie dispensing the drinks. He had the most wonderful hands, two featherless birds forever aloft on sleek, graceful wings. As he moved them, air whistled through the holes in his wrists.

"Tell me about yourself," he insisted.

She did. All of it. Her test-tube conception. Her temple of pain. Her orgasmic encounter with empirical truth. Pop's heart attacks. Her *Moon* column, her remote-control miracles, the burning of Atlantic City, Phoebe's desertion of Angel's Eye.

When she was done, Jesus simply looked at her in stupefaction, eyes wide as a lemur's, jaw hanging open like a hungry seal's.

"I'm glad you put out the fire," he said at last.

"It wasn't easy." Julie wanted to cry. How tawdry and small her story sounded, how bereft of grandeur—how noncosmic, as Aunt Georgina would say.

"And I'm most impressed with this science business. The courage to disprove your convictions, quite amazing."

"Historically unprecedented," she groaned, catching a tear in her ladle.

"It was a good message to preach. I'd even rank it near love. But..."

He fixed her with a stare so bright she had to close her eyes. "Yes?" she whispered hoarsely.

Splaying his fingers, Jesus ticked off his displeasures. "Giving your father that half-assed resurrection, doing those noncommittal interventions, running away from those people on the beach, rejecting the mob outside your lighthouse, abandoning your alcoholic friend—it's not what this family stands for, Julie, not for a minute. Next!"

Face speckled with sweat, an Asian woman entered the cave.

A twinge of belligerence moved along Julie's spine. "Okay, okay, but maybe *you* aren't exactly God either. Didn't you leave lots of cripples and lepers and blind beggars behind?"

"Not without regret."

"But you left them."

"Look, divinity's a confusing condition, no doubt about it. A curse." Those burning eyes again: Julie thought of ten-year-old Phoebe channeling sunlight through her magnifying glass, frying ants on the sidewalk. "But we can't use it as an *excuse*. We can't just paste a lot of gruesome news stories on our bedroom walls and wait it out."

She had never felt worse. Her gills gasped, her eyes swam. "I've been an idiot."

His demeanor took a sudden swing—accuser to comforter, supreme judge to angel of mercy. "What's done is done." He eased the Asian woman onto the slab, doused her. "I sometimes feel my life doesn't add up to much either."

The confession was so distracting Julie accidentally dropped her ladle. "You do?"

"Yes."

"I find that hard to believe."

"I reread the Gospels last night," Julie's dead brother explained as she refilled her ladle and held it to the prisoner's lips. "Not exactly my authorized biographies," he said. "Still, Mark gets the chronology right, and Matthew does a good job with the speeches. In John, of course, we have all that peculiar light-versus-dark imagery—a Gnostic influence, I suspect—and I don't care for the anti-Semitism. But even there, my essential ambition comes across." Jesus helped the Asian woman to her feet. "I wanted to be a Hebrew messiah, right? Drive out the Romans, restore the Davidic throne, found a nation of the spiritually transformed. The kingdom of God, I called it."

"Sometimes the kingdom of heaven," noted Julie, removing the woman's shingle.

"Paradise now, overseen by a benevolent Jewish monarchy." Drawing a Bible from his robe, Jesus turned to Matthew. "Anyway, there I was, a deity, a blood descendant of God's, and I *still* couldn't bring it off. 'Verily I say to you, this generation shall not pass till all these things be fulfilled.' Well, the generation passed, didn't it?" As the Asian woman left the cave, Jesus placed a perforated wrist on his heart, comforting himself. "I'm happy about what I taught, though, most of it. Next!"

"'If somebody asks for your tunic, give him your cloak as well,'" Julie quoted.

"Still sounds good to me."

A new customer entered, a man with a goiter the size of a cantaloupe. "Wait a minute." Julie eased the prisoner's aching flesh onto the slab. "Are you saying you don't know about your Church?"

"My what?" Jesus doused the goitrous man.

"Don't the damned ever mention your Church?"

"By the time I see them, they're too numb for conversation." Again Jesus cracked his Bible. "You mean this thing here in Acts, the Jerusalem Church? Is *that* still around?"

"No."

"I wouldn't think so, not after I stood everybody up. Peter, James, John—they all expected me to return posthaste. 'The end is at hand,' Peter says here. And John: 'Thereby we know it is the last time.' But the dead don't come back, do they? They don't leave hell."

"The Jerusalem Church faded away." Julie gave the goitrous man a drink, removed his shingle. "But there was another, a gentile Church."

"'I was sent only to the lost sheep of Israel.' That's in Matthew, I think. How could there be a gentile Church?"

"Paul..."

"Paul? Some terrific stuff about love, as I recall." Jesus flipped toward the back of his Bible. "Paul started a church?"

"You really don't know what happened up there?" Julie

dipped her ladle into the stream. "You don't know you became the center of Western civilization?"

"I did?"

"Uh-huh."

"You're kidding."

"There are Christians in every corner of the globe."

Jesus helped the goitrous man off the slab and escorted him out of the cave. "There are who?"

"Christians. The people who worship you. The ones who call you Christ."

"*Worship* me? Please . . ." Jesus scratched his forehead with his ladle. " 'Christ'—that's Greek, isn't it? An anointed one, a king. Next!"

"By 'Christ,' most people mean a savior. They mean God become flesh."

"Odd translation." As Jesus refilled his ladle, a woman entered whose hair was singed down to her scalp, giving her the appearance of a chemotherapy patient. "What *else* do Christics teach?"

"That, by following you, a person obtains remission from original sin. You don't *know* this?"

"Original sin? When did I ever talk about that?" Jesus wet the hairless woman. "Ethics was my big concern. Read the Bible." His birdish hands wove through the air, landing smoothly atop his King James version. "Original sin? Are you serious?"

"Your death atoned for Adam's guilt."

"Oh, come on," Jesus snickered. "That's paganism, Julie. You're talking Attis, Dionysus, Osiris—the sacrificial god whose suffering redeems his followers. Every town had one in those days. Where was Paul from?"

"Tarsus."

"I dropped by Tarsus once," said Jesus, leafing through the epistles. "The local god was Baal-Taraz, I believe." He pressed the open Bible against his chest like a poultice. "Good heavens, is *that* what I became? Another propitiation deity?"

"I hate to be the one telling you this." Julie ministered to the hairless woman.

"So the gentiles won the day? Is that why John's book talks about eternal life instead of the kingdom? Did Christicism become an eternal-life religion?"

"Accept Jesus as your personal redeemer," Julie corroborated, "and you'll be resuscitated after you die and taken up into the clouds."

"The clouds? No, 'Thy kingdom come on *earth*,' remember? And look at my parables, all those gritty metaphors—the kingdom is yeast, Julie, it's a mustard seed, a treasure in a field, a landowner hiring workers for his vineyard..."

"A pearl of great price," said the woman on the slab.

"Right. We're not talking clouds here." Jesus' beautiful hands soared, wrist holes singing. "I mean, how can you bring about utopia with one eye cocked on eternity?" His hands fell. "Oh, *now* I get it—that's how they accommodated my not returning, yes? They shifted the reunion to some netherworld."

"Evidently." Julie removed the bald sinner's shingle.

"What *chutzpah*."

"While we're at it," gasped the prisoner, "maybe you could settle a major controversy. Does the wafer literally turn into your flesh and bones?"

"Does the what do what?" said Jesus.

"The Eucharist," Julie explained. "The wafer becomes your body, the wine becomes your blood"—her voice trailed off: how, exactly, would he feel about the next step?—"and then, well..."

"And then?"

"And then we eat you," said the bald woman.

"You what?" said Jesus.

"Eat you."

"That's disgusting."

"No, the whole thing has a real, mysterious poetry," the bald woman hastened to add. "Through the Eucharist, we partake of your life and substance. Go to Mass sometime. You'll see."

"I think I'll pass on that one," said God's son. "Next!"

Lunch became Julie's favorite part of the day. She and her brother would close up the cave for an hour and, slipping past the dazed prisoners, retire atop a cliff overlooking hell's largest foundry.

Often they talked of science. "Teach me about evolution," Jesus would say. "About the benzene ring, black holes, Heisenberg's uncertainty relation." His curiosity was prodigious. Julie's account of a universe stretching far beyond the prophets' visions, the epic tapestry of clustered galaxies, the inspiring violence of pulsars throbbing and collapsed stars gulping down light, all of it migrating outward in the wake of the big bang—such theories captivated Jesus no less than the ambiguities raised by the Good Samaritan or the Barren Fig Tree.

"Of course," noted Julie after her lecture on gravity, "these models will be revised as more information comes to light, facts like my advent and the actuality of hell—but that's the beauty of science. It's self-correcting. It welcomes new data."

"If Einstein is right, then space is an endless rubbery cloak," Jesus enthused, fanning out his tattered robe. "Large masses indent it, causing passing objects to follow the natural depression."

Julie opened the picnic basket and handed her brother a chicken-salad sandwich. "Einstein said that, when science is operating at peak, you can hear God thinking."

"One day that smart Jew will show up here."

"God?"

"Einstein." Jesus pried the pickles out of his sandwich and tossed them over the cliff. "I want to meet her."

"God?"

"God."

God. So, the name had at last been evoked, the festering wound lanced, the family skeleton rattled.

"What can I say?" Jesus shrugged. "Obviously our progenitor is hard to figure. Maybe Einstein could hear God thinking, but *I* can't."

Once again it surged up, the full flood of her resentment, the rage of the abandoned child. "Put me in charge of the universe, and my first act will be to arrest my mother for criminal neglect."

"That's pretty harsh, Julie."

"Easy for you to say. God *cared* about you. You got gold, frankincense, and myrrh. I got whoopie cushions and latex dog vomit."

"But if we're really talking about the God of physics, some unknowable prime mover, we can hardly presume to judge her." Jesus consumed his sandwich in six equal bites. "Maybe God *wants* to intervene directly, only that would mean tearing apart timespace and destroying the physical universe. So she sends us instead."

"I figured that out back in college." Julie chomped into a half-moon of watermelon. "I'm still resentful. It doesn't matter *how* inaccessible my mother is, she shouldn't let this place exist."

"Hell is Wyvern's domain, not God's."

"*Let* her tear timespace apart! *Let* her!" Julie choked on her own scream. "Anything to end all this suffering!"

"The matter's being taken care of," said Jesus evenly.

"Huh?" The matter's being taken care of: so much eschatology in so few words. *"What?"*

"I said—"

"That blast furnace down there looks pretty sturdy to me."

Jesus' hands fluttered. "This water we're giving out... remember the marriage at Cana, when the water became wine?"

Julie pointed to an adolescent male wheeling pig iron out of the foundry. "It's really wine?"

"No, an anesthetic. My own recipe. From what you've told me about chemistry, I believe it's an opium derivative, akin to morphine."

"Morphine? We're giving them *morphine*?"

God's son bit the meaty cap off a banana. "It lodges in the prisoner's brain for weeks, delivering him to sweet oblivion—a real death this time, no resurrections in hell. Right before losing consciousness, he throws himself into the Lake of Fire and vaporizes."

"And Wyvern thinks it's just water?"

Jesus nodded. "It amuses him to see us wasting our time. 'Putting band-aids on eviscerations,' he calls it."

"No wonder they look so happy when they leave. You should've *told* me."

"When you believed it was water, did you doubt it was worth dispensing?"

"Are you kidding? 'Let's go to hell and have our skin burned off, because, by damn, we'll all get a free glass of water!' Of *course* I doubted."

"But you kept coming. Day after day."

"I kept coming," Julie snorted.

"How irrational."

"They were hot."

"Correct."

"Thirsty."

"Exactly."

"Rejected."

Jesus' beard blossomed into a grin. "Rabbi Hillel couldn't have put it better." He leaned forward and lovingly massaged Julie's back. "I'll make a Jew of you yet, daughter of God," he whispered, placing a soft kiss on her cheek.

Julie Katz would never say the fifteen years she spent in hell giving designer morphine to the damned were the best of her life, but they did boast a beatific simplicity and a ritual purposefulness that would, she believed, eventually occasion the fondest of memories. She felt the flesh aging on her frame. Blue veins rose in her hands and thighs. Her hair acquired a silver streak, as if she'd survived an electrocution. Her teeth got looser, her gums softer, blood thicker, bones brittler.

Often, stretching out her arm to offer a prisoner morphine, she would imagine the ladle puncturing the quantum barrier like a knife slicing a veil, giving her access to the planet she'd forsaken. She longed for Bix's enigmatic affections—he wasn't a traitor, she realized; her own pigheadedness had doomed "Heaven Help You." And Phoebe. Dear, anguished Phoebe. Oh, Mother, let her be prospering. Let her be sober. Give her the Oscar for Best Cinéma-Vérité Erotic Film.

Without her dead brother at her side, distracting her from the moans of the damned and the pangs of her regrets, Julie would have gone mad. When happy, he sang psalms in his sonorous tenor voice. When tired or annoyed, he did not hesitate to call their malodorous clients skunks. He chided his own tendency toward bombast and sweeping generalizations. Jesus of Nazareth, Julie decided, was a *mensh*.

"Next!"

The man entered the cave pushing a wheelbarrow.

A small man: lighthouse keeper, Photorama clerk. Sweet Lord, his ashes had been reconstituted—sweet Lord, it was he!

Julie dropped her ladle. "Pop! Pop!"

"Julie?"

His barrow was the type the damned used for removing the endless excreta of the furnaces, though right now it held not pig iron but a person, a handsome black man with a rakish mustache. Quite essential, this barrow, for the passenger's entire body ended abruptly at his waist.

"Julie!" Murray lowered the barrow handles. Scar tissue stippled his rotund belly. His beard was singed and knotted. The brown, withered organ from which half her chromosomes had issued dangled like an overripe pear. "It's really you!"

They hugged for a full, silent minute. Laced with sucrose, a thousand tears flowed from her turquoise eyes. "The devil told me you were in heaven."

"He lies."

"Not always," said Jesus, "but often."

"Were you murdered, honey?" Murray asked in a coarse whisper. "Your enemies got you?"

"I'm not dead," said Julie.

"Not dead?"

"I thought I'd be happier here."

"You did?"

"Uh-huh."

"*Are* you happier?"

"I miss Phoebe. And this guy Bix. But in many ways, yeah, I'm happier."

She could tell he found this bizarre, though instead of protesting he offered only a quick diffident smile and placed a respectful hand on Jesus' shoulder. "Rabbi, it's a privilege meeting you. I read the Gospels once. Maybe you could answer a few questions. 'I came not to send peace, but a sword . . .'"

Jesus coughed. "We're a little tight for time."

"Oh, Pop, I'm sorry I didn't give you a real resurrection," said Julie. Taking her father's forearm, she felt the agony coursing through his flesh. "You should've let me bring you back."

He shrugged. "Maybe. I can't say. Life is confusing. Death is confusing. Everything is."

"I hope the cremation didn't offend you."

"It's all in the past." Murray tapped a blistered finger on the legless man's shoulder. "Julie, I'd like you to meet someone. Any idea who this is?"

"No."

"It's Phoebe's father. The sperm donor."

Leaning over the edge of the barrow, the torso extended a soft hand, and Julie shook it. "Marcus Bass," he said in rounded, bell-like tones.

She inhaled sharply. Phoebe's father! "I'm Julie." God, if only he and Phoebe might meet somehow—surely Marcus could talk her out of that next bottle of Bacardi, and the one after that.

"You first," said Pop, tilting Marcus toward the slab.

"No, man," said the torso. "You."

"You've been here much longer," Murray argued.

Marcus broke his friend's grip. "I insist."

As Murray climbed onto the slab, Jesus doused him with a full measure. Julie pressed her ladle against her father's lips, resting his head in the crook of her arm. He swallowed the sacred oblivion. For how many months had he nursed her a half-dozen times a day from a plastic bottle full of infant formula? Drink deep, she thought. Drink it all, Pop.

"Tell Marcus about his daughter," said Murray.

"Would I be proud of Phoebe?" Marcus asked.

"She tried to be my conscience," said Julie, removing Pop's shingle. His chest sparkled, coated with a soup of morphine, pus, and sweat. "A thankless job, I now realize. I loved her very much."

"Excuse me." Jesus pointed to the portion of Marcus that wasn't there. "You have a daughter?"

"There used to be more of me," said Marcus wistfully.

"Wyvern mutilated you?"

"No, man. Some crazy reverend."

"Billy Milk, as far as we can figure," said Murray.

Julie shivered like the charred victims to whom she ministered. Milk, Milk, would she never escape that bastard? She should've drowned him when she'd had the chance.

"I guess Phoebe's about...what, thirty-eight?" asked Marcus. "What does she do? Did she ever marry?"

"I think she went into the film business," said Julie. "She's the footloose sort."

"Wild, you mean? Spirited?"

Chuckling, Murray rose from the slab. "That's Phoebe all right. Always had a slingshot in her back pocket. Looked like a tail."

"I was that way," said Marcus. "Once I burned down my parents' garage. Building a moon rocket."

"I worry about her drinking," said Julie.

It'd just slipped out. Julie winced, gasped. Damn. Now the man would never enter nothingness in peace.

"She, uh, she"—a deep moan left Marcus, the low of a despairing ox—"drinks? Not a complete surprise, really. Her aunts were both alkies. The disease runs in families."

Together Jesus and Murray lifted the black man's top half and set it on the slab.

"Funny, I never met Phoebe"—Marcus smiled as the splash of morphine arrived—"but I still feel like she's my little girl." His face fell. "Does she drink a *lot*, Julie?"

"I wouldn't know. I've been here a long time. Phoebe was always proud of you. She knew all about your career."

"I just hope nobody sends her to a psychiatrist. That's one thing I learned from dealing with my sisters—sending an alcoholic to a shrink makes about as much sense as sending a heart patient to a poet." Marcus sandwiched Julie's scarred hand between his palms. "You were a good friend to her, weren't you?"

"I tried to be." She gave the man his morphine. "It's a shame I'm stuck down here."

"I thought you weren't dead."

"I'm afraid we're running behind schedule," sighed Jesus.

Furtively, deliberately, Julie whacked the ladle against her knee, sending a blast of pain through her whole being. She wasn't dead. Not remotely. Yet here she was...

"Say, I don't suppose Georgina has shown up yet," said Murray. "It'd be great to see her again. I was always sort of in love with her."

"I imagine she's still alive," said Julie. "Oh, Pop..." They came together in a sudden snap, human planets discovering each other, love's gravity. Her father's substance was thin and failing, yet it still managed, as always, to do the work of two parents' flesh. "I love you, Pop."

"My head's come loose," said Murray. Slowly their embrace dissolved. "Spinning like a dreidel. I love you, Julie."

"The drug," Jesus explained.

"Pain's fading," gasped Murray, eyes dancing in his circular face. "It's really fading. Incredible."

"They died," said Marcus as Murray deposited him in the barrow.

"Who?" said Julie.

"My sisters. Bottle killed 'em."

"Next!" said God's son.

"*Sholem aleichem*, Pop," Julie whispered.

"*Aleichem sholem*," he replied softly.

Murray lifted the wooden handles and started away, forming what she knew would be her final view of him, a picture she would cultivate until entropy knocked on the door: a small, hunched old Jew trundling toward a cave entrance, *shlepping* a wheelbarrow in which rode the remains of the man who'd convinced her now and forever that she didn't belong with the dead.

"You really have to go?" Jesus asked.

Julie, silent, let her gaze wander over the cliff toward the iron foundry. They were making their last lunch together as special as possible: pepperoni pizza, cold chicken, Blue Nun wine, knishes. "I guess I'll always be a New Jersey girl," she said at last, tearing a pizza slice free. "Now I see why Pop kept lighting the beacon. It's good to have a second chance. This time around I'll get it right. End hunger, reverse the greenhouse effect, restore the Brazilian rain forest, destroy nuclear arsenals—you'll see."

"You won't do any of those things," said Jesus calmly, popping a knish into his mouth.

"Yes, I will." She bit into the slice of pizza.

"Wyvern would never put up with it." Jesus jabbed the wine cork, twisting the handle on the steel screw. "Don't expect to leave here with your godhead intact."

"What are you talking about?"

A staccato burp issued from the bottle as Jesus yanked out the cork. "No more divinity, Julie."

A disc of pepperoni came free in her mouth, the spices gnawing her tongue. No more divinity? Godhead gone?

She felt torn, fractured, as if God's fingers were reaching into her soul, breaking it like an egg. True, she had never deduced what her powers were for, but they were still *hers*, and on those few times she had exercised them—the dead crab, Timothy's eyes, the deliverance of Atlantic City—the rapture had lingered for days. "I've always been a deity," she protested. "It's who I *am*."

"Then you'll stay, right? Please stay."

Stay, such a seductive word. But no. She wasn't dead. "It's who I am," she echoed, "but I can do better."

Jesus smiled, sniffing the impaled cork. "Spoken like my true sister. You're very precious to me."

"What do we use for glasses?"

Jesus pulled their scruffy ladles from the picnic basket.

"When you die, I'll get you a shingle with an early date." He filled the ladles with Blue Nun. "I won't have you in pain." Resting his palm against her cheek, he raised his wine in a toast. "L'chayim."

"L'chayim."

They clanked their ladles together and drank.

The city of Carcinoma was a byzantine metropolis strung along a chain of active volcanoes, a conglomeration of crooked ramparts and twisted spires, its innumerable government buildings so dark and amorphous they might have been clots of lava spewed from the craters. A full-scale eruption was in progress when the coach bearing Julie pulled through the main gate, its portals flanked by two titanic copies of the *Winged Victory*, their heads replaced by stone skulls. Sparks drifted through the central forum like fireflies; smoke blanketed the sky. Angels and demons stood on the cement pavement and marble stairways, jaws tilted upward, mouths open, catching hot cinders on their serpentine tongues: food from above, hadean manna.

Piloted by Anthrax, the coach rolled beyond the range of the eruption, gliding past street vendors displaying carts of vintage carrion, racing through a public garden whose plaques commemorated great moments in evil—the evolution of cholera, the Dred Scott decision, the slaughter of a hundred thousand Nanking civilians by the Japanese—and stopping before Wyvern's palace. Julie stepped out, placing her ratty sneaker on the ash-speckled plaza. Fenced by iron spears, the palace suggested a kind of upended labyrinth supporting priapic towers and voluptuous balconies. An apelike angel leaned out of the guardhouse and, recognizing Anthrax, informed him that Lord Wyvern was doing his Sunday gardening.

"Hello, Andrew," Julie called out as the demon directed her through a wooden trellis wrapped in vines resembling barbed wire. "I've come to visit."

"Julie! What a superb surprise!" The devil was merrily pruning a tree laden with wormy mangoes. He waved his secateurs. "Welcome to Eden. Yes, *the* Eden. After the fall, we had it shipped down here." Shooing Anthrax away, he fondled a fat tomato dangling from a spidery green plant. "To tell you the truth, I expected you much sooner."

"I've been happy in hell," Julie asserted. Breezes sinuated

through the garden like small tornadoes, making the mangoes sway. The grass beneath her feet twitched with the maneuvers of ant battalions. "I've been useful."

Wyvern guffawed, tipping his left horn in the general direction of Jesus' cave. "Fifteen years running some ludicrous lemonade stand—you call that useful? Your brother was always something of a masochist, but *you*, I thought you had better sense."

"I'm homesick. I want to go home."

The devil angled his tail toward hell's vault. "I won't abide any more deities running around up there. You people are such wild cards."

"Jesus told me your price." She folded her arms across her sweatshirt in a posture of defiance. "I'm prepared to give it up."

I'm not, she thought. It's me. A person needs her heritage.

"Are you certain?" asked Wyvern.

Screw heritage. Screw divinity. "Uh-huh."

"Look at the bright side—look at what you're getting." A huge grin bisected the devil's leathery, crimson face. "The earth, a full life, no more huddled masses cluttering up your driveway..."

"Take it. Take my divinity."

"It will hurt."

Coldness climbed up Julie's vertebrae, lodging against her neck like a guillotine blade. "I'm tough."

"Stand still." Wyvern's left paw was suddenly aglow, each scale winking like a jewel. "Don't move."

There followed an obscene rendition of Michelangelo's *Creation of Adam*, the devil reaching toward her, index finger erect. The hot claw touched her sweatshirt, burned through the cotton, and kept moving, splitting her flesh like a surgeon's knife.

I won't cry out, she vowed. Won't. Won't.

Wyvern leaned in close and kissed her, his lips leeching on her cheek, his breath clawing her eyes. "Love your enemies, right?" he said.

The volcanoes snorted like minotaurs. They roared like hadean blast furnaces.

Now came his other fingers, now his whole brown and bristled paw, moving through skin and gristle, unbuckling her ribs as if they were the halves of an overcoat, driving deeper and deeper into her chest, searching, probing, and she knew this was pain, *pain*, the endless ripping, slashing, chopping hell of it. Within and without she bled; she felt the horrid warmth. Her teeth crashed together, a bite to grind perdition's iron, red sparks flying from the friction, and still she kept silent, even when he continued to twist and dig as if his hand were a gravedigger's spade, her chest a plot of earth.

After an infinity he found the thing, found her godhead and exhumed it, plucking it from its fleshy tomb and bearing it into the light of day.

Her divinity was a bird. It was a white glistery dove, now trapped in Wyvern's paw. Blood crowned the bird's head, glutinous fluids flecked its feathers—a perfect dove, wholly biblical, complete with an olive branch trailing from its tawny beak.

With his free hand Wyvern massaged her wound, plucking murderous germs from the weeping wreckage, making fresh tissue grow in the cavity, rank upon rank of robust cells.

"W-why that?" Groaning, drenched in pain, Julie pointed to the olive branch. Nausea spread through her stomach like a hemorrhage.

Wyvern opened his mouth. Oily saliva spilled over his leathery gums. He spoke.

Nothing—for already a palpable darkness was flooding her brain, giving Wyvern's voice the harsh incoherence of wind, and she heard not his words but only old memories of his words. *Heal this blind boy. Save Atlantic City. Make a grand exit.* Heal a boy, save a city, fly to heaven: no, that was all over now, she realized —she would never again raise up crabs or give sight to the blind, no more cities delivered, no more flying, nothing but the fire in her chest and the oncoming night and her falling flesh, falling, falling—

PART THREE

$\bullet \qquad \bullet \qquad \bullet$

The Second Coming of Julie Katz

CHAPTER 12

◆　　　◆　　　◆

No ectogenesis machine this time. No immaculate glass birth canal, no steamy soap-scented laundry room, no soft crib with plastic geese circling overhead. Just nakedness and mud. Like worms determined to devour you, the mud seeks every opening, your nose, ears, mouth, vagina. The hot afternoon sun batters you, the mud sickens you, and, oh, how you want to rise. You cannot; even the thought of movement is exhausting. Pinned on your side, pasted to the world, you stare at the mud, naming the creatures that thrive amid the spartina grass and cat-o'-nine-tails: mosquito, gnat, garter snake, snapping turtle. God's mistakes? Satan's masterpieces? No, this is the modern age, 2012 in fact. Darwin's dice throws.

The sinister buzzing something you named *dragonfly* lands on the soft yellow object you termed *lily*. The veined, translucent wings stop beating. The dragonfly's intentions, you sense, are wicked. It will not pollinate the lily; it will rape the lily, rape it with all the ferocity of Wyvern ripping out the dove of your divinity.

You pour your strength into an upward surge, crying out as the effort echoes through your violated chest. Frosted with silt, chewing on your pain, you slog toward hard ground. A cornfield spreads before you, the frail stalks vibrant with sunlight, the ripe ears encapsulated like papooses. You run, the mud drying on your bare skin and flaking away. It's not the corn you want, but the straw man who guards it. Your plan originates in a Universal Studios horror movie Roger Worth once made you watch, a B-picture in which the Invisible Man, cast out of society, naked, shivering transparently, steals a scarecrow's clothing lest he die of exposure.

A preadolescent girl dresses the scarecrow, hitching up its pants with a strand of clothesline. Her T-shirt bears a deliriously happy clown and the inscription, CIRCUS OF JOY. She's freckled, skinny, and gawky; except for your nudity, this whole scene might be an old *Saturday Evening Post* cover. You throw an arm across your breasts, another across your pubis. The girl's mouth becomes an egg of astonishment, and you say, "What's the matter, kid—never saw the goddess Venus before?"

"You're from Venus?" she asks, impressed.

"Right." You notice that the girl clutches a small, bald, alabaster doll—a Pro-Life Talking Embryo, according to its christening dress.

"You're naked," says the girl.

You drop your arms. "This is my spacesuit."

"I'm a person," says the Pro-Life Talking Embryo. "I have thoughts and feelings."

From under her Circus of Joy T-shirt the girl retrieves a little silver crucifix attached to a gold chain, thrusting it forward as if trying to demoralize a vampire. "You a heretic?" She releases the crucifix and lets it dangle; instead of Jesus, a Revelationist lamb is nailed to the cross. "You'd better not be a heretic, lady. The hunters, they'll shoot you. Maybe worse."

"Let me live," says the embryo.

You wish you had your powers back so you could flatten this brat and her stupid doll with a snap of your fingers. Brushing her aside, you unbutton the scarecrow's plaid flannel shirt. Circus of Joy—what's that, the floor show at Caesar's? Good news, if true. You might be near Atlantic City.

"Hey, that's not *yours*," the brat whines.

You put on the shirt. Tattered and smelling like tainted bologna, it reaches all the way to your knees—the girl's father must be gigantic. "Where am I?"

"Tyler's Farm."

"In New Jersey?"

"Uh-huh." The girl gives her embryo a quick kiss on the fontanel. "The Believers' Republic of New Jersey."

You remove the pants. To steal a scarecrow's clothing, you realize, is to steal its flesh as well. New Jersey, hooray. Phoebe and Bix are near. Your chest pain tapers into a tolerable throb. "You mean state."

"Republic," the girl insists. "We've seceded."

"Seceded? That's crazy."

"The Jersey secession."

"*Seceded?* Like the Civil War?"

"I'll get Dad. If you're a heretic, he'll blow you away."

You form an instant image of Dad, a *Moon*-type Bigfoot with overalls and a shotgun. Lord, deliver us from the wrath of Dad. Swirling around, you rush madly through the labyrinthian cornfield. You're thirty-eight but you're fast, a former point guard for the Brigantine Tigerettes. Is Dad behind you already, getting you in his sights?

Heretic hunters, believers' republics, Jersey secession... *secession?* Mortality, you sense, will be thornier than you'd ever imagined.

Breaking free of the cornfield, you come to a major highway. Candy wrappers and discarded seed packets cling to the signpost: ROUTE 30. You cross the macadam and stick out your thumb. A river of trash—fliptop rings, empty motor oil cans, broken 7-Up bottles, outdated Republic of New Jersey license plates—fills the gully between road and shoulder. Automobiles whiz toward the ocean, ancient rusted hulks intermixed with more futuristic models sporting silver-plating and clear plastic domes. But of course: it's 2012, isn't it? While you were gone, the future arrived.

A pickup truck pulls over, its passenger door decorated with a smiling angel holding aloft a flaming sword. With your loose shirt and muddy face, you look like a victim of sexual assault, and you decide this will elicit either sympathy or a rapist who gauges you an easy mark. In your mind you rehearse a move Aunt Georgina taught you, a technique that leaves the attacker writhing on the ground clutching his testicles. But no, forget it—the driver, while male, is small, agitated, and cherubic. A tense Buddha, sportily dressed. "Heading for the city?" he asks quickly.

"Been out of the country," you reply, nodding. "Fifteen years. Is the Atlantic Ocean still down this way?"

The driver forces a chuckle.

You climb in. "What do you carry in this thing?"

"Sinners," the driver answers laconically, edging into the traffic. A small, silver, crucified lamb peers mournfully from beneath his blue blazer. "Been working for the Circus almost seven years now, hauling their sinners, and they *still* haven't given me a free pass. They simply don't appreciate their employees." He studies you with soft, teddy-bear eyes. "You're a real mess, ma'am. What happened? Run into some heretics?"

Remembering the farm girl's hostility, you put two and two together. To prosper in contemporary New Jersey, one must stand unequivocally against heresy. "Yes," you lie. "They beat me up."

"What devils. Should I take you to New Jerusalem Memorial?"

"Leave me at Huron." You recognize an old Tropicana billboard that now says, THE CIRCUS OF JOY PRESENTS: *THY SWORD SHALL COMFORT ME,* COMING APRIL 11TH. "I'll walk home."

"You should see a doctor, ma'am."

"I'm fine."

"Hey, I wouldn't normally tell a total stranger this, but seeing as how you've got a score to settle..." The driver winks mischievously. "We'll be dealing with a heretic tomorrow night—on our own, know what I mean? They just nabbed him in Somers Point. I heard it on the CB. Interested?"

"Sure," you say, smiling artificially. The dried mud is merciless, a million itches swarming across your skin.

"Come to the K mart parking lot. Seven-thirty—plenty of time to beat curfew. Ask for me, Nick Shiner. I'll get you admitted. Charlie Fielding's bringing the bricks."

"Bricks?"

"To throw."

You're not sure, but you believe Nick Shiner has just invited you to help stone somebody to death. "This brick business is new to me," you say as Route 30 dissolves into Absecon Boulevard.

"The thing about a heretic is, once you catch him, you'd better move quickly, or they'll take him away from you." The silver lamb jiggles atop Nick Shiner's chest as he gestures angrily toward the sky. "Shouldn't they come up with an occasional free pass for a guy who's spent seven years carting their lousy sinners around? Isn't that the *least* they should do?"

"The least."

"Watching the Circus on cable isn't the same as being there," Nick Shiner whines.

As night settles, your gaze drifts across the salt marsh. Sitting atop three tiered foundations, the metropolis looks like the upper stratum of an immense layer cake.

"Atlantic City's changed," you observe.

"New Jerusalem," Nick Shiner corrects you. "They finished it seven years ago. It's going to trigger the Second Coming"—he issues a weary sigh—"assuming we can process enough sinners."

"I don't suppose they do the Miss America Pageant there anymore."

"The what?"

"Miss America Pageant."

"This isn't America, ma'am."

Luminous marble ramparts burn through the darkness. Instead of recreating the Nugget, the Tropicana, the Sands, Caesar's, and the others separately, their owners have seemingly turned the whole city into one vast casino. The buildings are like garishly trimmed Christmas trees, huge conical structures dotted with silver floodlights and gold-tinted windows.

Before leaving you at the Huron intersection, Nick Shiner reminds you to come to the Somers Point K mart tomorrow night. "Don't keep your emotions bottled up. Toss some bricks. It'll do wonders."

You hike across the bridge and start down Harbor Beach Boulevard, its stately townhouses smothered in fog. Speckled with rivets, spiny with gun muzzles, a steel-plated car with a sword-wielding angel on the door sits beneath a street lamp. Two policemen are changing a front tire; with their efficient gestures and green body-armor, they seem like surgeons performing some surrealistic and unfathomable operation.

The earth is cooling. Insect jazz drifts toward you from the Bonita Tideway. At last you hear the breakers, the vast Atlantic hurling itself against the continent, and you feel better. You hurry to the 44th Street Pier, so somber under the fogbound moon, and, stripping off your stolen shirt, sprint to the end of the dock and dive in. Ah, this is truly your old planet, its vast and reliable sea, closing over you like a cold quilt, scrubbing away the Tylers' cranberry bog.

From habit, you inhale. Instantly your body convulses, offended by the briny poison you've offered it instead of air. So: Wyvern has truly mortalized you. Good or bad? Coughing and gagging, you struggle to the surface and scramble clumsily onto the dock. You lie on the wet planks, panting. Divinity gone, not enough left to summon a rain shower or cure a wart. Good or bad, good or bad? You pull on your shirt, rub yourself warm—studded with goose bumps, your skin feels like a raspberry—and head south along the beach. Am I ready for it? you wonder. Ready for a life without gills, no holy dove fluttering in my chest, no godhead throbbing in my bones? Am I ready for sheer flesh?

Streamers of fog encircled the moonlit shaft of Angel's Eye. Pop's lighthouse was like a redwood tree, Julie decided: rotund, eternal. An ironwork footbridge now coupled the mainland to the island she'd cleaved into being before her trip to hell. An Aunt Georgina project, no doubt—if you must erect a bridge, use iron, do it right. She scrambled up the rocks and, crossing the lawn, studied the windows for signs of life, but every room was as dark and dead as Billy Milk's right eye.

Moonlight beat soundlessly against the front door, revealing the comforting grain, the familiar knotholes. Such a regular feature of her life, this door, as rhythmic as the slash separating measures of music. You came home from school and there it was, the door. You returned from a date—the door. She pushed it open.

Angel's Eye had been gutted like a fish. Rugs, furniture, lamps—all gone. Nothing remained of the five thousand books that had ballasted her father's life, nothing save a single volume lying near the hearth where Spinoza the cat had once deposited a dead crab. She approached, fixing on the title. Something about eternity.

A beam of sharp white light shot from the kitchen, tearing into Julie's astonished eyes and nearly knocking her down. "Stop," slurred a male voice. "Stop right there." He sounded drunk. Shock and indignation crackled through Julie. How dare anyone tell her to stop—this was her father's house. She advanced resolutely, snatching up the book. *Is Your Spiritual Passport Stamped "Eternity"?* by the Reverend Billy Milk, Grandpastor, New Jerusalem Church of Saint John's Vision.

"Who's there?" Julie asked.

Clicks. Thunks.

"Who is it?"

Then: cold guttural reports, like popcorn cooking in a spittoon.

The first bullet caught the baggy elbow of Julie's scarecrow shirt, drilling a nickel-sized hole.

The second slit her cheek and snipped a tress from her hair.

She howled. She jumped. She stumbled backward and lurched into the laundry room. Her cheek felt like a second mouth in her face, chattering and cursing, spitting out blood. Her flesh quivered with outrage. This was invasion, it was rape, it was Wyvern's malevolent paw reaching into her soul.

Crib, mobile, washer, drying rack, shattered bell jar—all her primal visions, the jumbled pieces of her advent. The crib gave her the height she needed, putting the window in reach. She climbed onto the sill, wriggled through, and dropped into a clump of eel grass. Bullets. Good Christ—bullets. Holding her slashed cheek, she charged over the iron bridge onto Ocean Drive West, her dazed mind longing for that time when she could have hurled her enemies into the bay with a flick of her wrist and slapped their bullets out of the air like fireflies.

Lurching onto Sea Spray Road, she stopped dead and, like Orpheus taking his fateful glance, looked behind her. No one— no carapaced soldiers or Revelationist crazies, no Nick Shiner vigilantes. The streets were silent. The surf purred. Moving forward, she soothed herself with Phoebe's favorite song.

"On the Boardwalk in Atlantic City, we will walk in a dream. On the Boardwalk in Atlantic City, life will be peaches and cream..."

At the Sandy Drive intersection an upright sarcophagus loomed, a sparkling glass cylinder labeled NEW JERUSALEM TELEPHONE SYSTEM. As Julie approached, the tube split open like a breakfast egg and a cloying female voice spilled into her ear. "Enter, please."

She did. The tube healed itself.

"Jesus is coming—please state your calling card number."

"I want my friends! I don't want to be shot at! I want Phoebe and Bix and Aunt Georgina!"

"Please state your calling card number," said the disembodied woman.

The future, 2012. Forget wires, mouthpieces, headphones; simply talk. "I don't have a calling card number."

"Is this a collect call?"

"Right—collect. I need to reach Phoebe Sparks."

"In the Greater New Jerusalem area?"

Julie studied the fog for armed zealots. "Give it a try."

The voice had no Phoebe Sparks in its data bank. No Georgina Sparks, no Bix Constantine. Julie inquired after herself. Nothing. Numb with frustration, she asked about Melanie Markson, and, miraculously, a Melanie Markson lived in Longport. A pause, then: Melanie's dignified voice, asserting that of course she'd accept a collect call from Julie Katz.

"Hey, is that really you? *You?*" Melanie's normally staid enunciation was joyful, gasping. "I can't believe it. Sheila, you've come back!"

"I'm Julie—forget that Sheila stuff. What the hell's going on around here? I was just at Angel's Eye, and they tried to shoot me."

"They thought you were a heretic."

"Huh? Me?"

"To your disciples that place is holy ground, so the hunters use it as bait."

"My *what*? Disciples?"

"I'm definitely one of them, Sheila. You can count on me. I'm only a Revelationist on paper."

"The bastards stole my house!" Julie stomped her bare foot on the phone-booth floor. Her wounded cheek throbbed. Disciples? Holy ground? "I have to find Phoebe," she insisted, staring into the blackness. Pieces of fog hung in the night air like cataracts on an aging eye. "Phoebe needs me."

"'Fraid I lost touch with Phoebe years ago."

"Melanie, can I stay with you tonight? I'm a little disoriented."

"Stay with me? I'd be *honored*. Have you eaten? I'll broil you a steak. Where are you?"

"Brigantine."

"I'll pick you up. Curfew's not for another hour. Oh, Sheila, there's so much you can do for us, there's so amazingly much you can *do*."

* * *

Portly as ever, Melanie had through astute applications of makeup wholly defeated the last fifteen years. Her rotund features were youthful and vivid. "So here I am," she gushed, nervously ensnaring her fingers in her brightly dyed, pumpkin-colored hair, "talking to Sheila in my own living room." Julie could remember when Melanie used to call the cosmetics industry a boot stamping on women's faces everywhere. "Incredible," said Melanie. "Just incredible."

Smiling wearily, her stomach burbling with porterhouse steak, Julie stretched across the corpulent velvet couch. Melanie's BMW had been classy enough, but her Longport condominium was truly spectacular, a twelve-room extravaganza reminiscent of Julie's mansion below. "Looks like the Disney people are paying you pretty well."

"Not the Disney people," Melanie answered, face reddening under her makeup. "The Revelationists." She rose from her imported Sears and Roebuck ottoman and, gliding toward a wall of books, took down a stack of oblong volumes. "Sure, this isn't the stuff I *want* to be writing, but who can resist a thousand mammons for a week's work?"

Julie wrapped herself tighter in Melanie's white terrycloth bathrobe. The topmost book, *Ralph and Amy Get Baptized,* showed two adolescents immersed to their shoulders in a clear shimmering river. Underneath lay *Ralph and Amy Visit Heaven.* Julie flipped back the cover—the title characters scampering toward a mountainous, multiturreted city—and turned to page one.

> Imagine a meadow with grasses of silk,
> Imagine a river with waters of milk,
> Imagine a rainbow as big as the skies,
> Imagine a city where nobody dies...

"Most every kid in the country owns a set," Melanie explained. "Rather hefty royalties, I'll admit. Hey, listen, I'll chuck the whole career if you want. Just say the word. Yours is the church for me, Sheila—the only one." Contemptuously she squeezed the crucified lamb on her necklace. Her jowly face twitched with anxiety. "Okay, okay, maybe I'm not as devout as some, maybe I haven't been hearing your voice, maybe I let those Revelationist idiots baptize me and convince me not to sleep with women and everything, but believe me, I'm with you all the way."

"Church?" Julie tugged the gauze bandage on ner cheek. "I've got a whole *church*?"

"Honestly, I'm an Uncertaintist down to my toes. Sometimes I drive clear to Camden just to hear Father Paradox. Oh, yes."

Julie fixed on the dust jacket of *My First Book About Eternal Damnation:* a satanic hare leering at a frightened bunny. "Melanie, I'm confused. Right before leaving, I drove the Revelation-ists into the sea. And now they're—"

"You certainly did, Sheila, and they stayed away for months. *Months.* When they came back, they were a much subtler bunch —didn't burn anything, not one building. Eventually, of course, Milk got himself elected mayor, then—"

"Mayor? Milk's the mayor? But he's a maniac and a butcher."

Melanie grinned sheepishly, as if embarrassed by history's unlikely turns. "Within a year, just about every apocalyptist east of the Mississippi was living here. It became a wholly Revelation-ist state—the secession was something of a formality. For a while there was talk of an invasion from across the Delaware, but after Vietnam and Nicaragua I guess the Pentagon was pretty sick of ambiguous little wars. Fact is, the U.S. State Department likes the idea of a right-wing terrorist theocracy along America's eastern border. Keeps New York in line—they wish they'd thought of it themselves." Melanie acquired an uncanny expression, a kind of diffident Machiavellianism, the mien of a shy country parson accepting an invitation to rule the world. "Hey, I want to suggest something. Know what tomorrow is? It's the Sabbath—not the Jewish Sabbath, Milk's—it's the Sabbath, and I suggest we go to church. *Your* church."

Julie wrapped her palms around her coffee mug. A wonderful little stove, but the warmth failed to reach her heart. She had a church. It was like hearing: you have cancer. And yet, and yet . . . she must go. It was all a mistake, she'd tell these Uncertain-tists. I was tricked. Cut this heresy crap and get yourselves baptized.

"Your church needs you." Melanie gritted her teeth and smiled. "Nobody knows who'll be caught next."

"I'll go with you tomorrow, Melanie, happy to, but I can't stop these heretic hunters. I gave up my divinity."

"We're scared all the time, Sheila. We're . . . you *what*?"

"I'm not divine."

The smile vanished, the gritted teeth remained. "I don't understand."

"True, Melanie. No more powers." Good or bad? "It was the only way I could get home."

"I see," said Melanie icily. "Fine. But once you realize what's been going on around here, how trapped we are . . ."

"My old life is behind me."

"Your powers will come back. I know they will. Try, Sheila. You have to *try.*"

The traffic in Margate and Ventnor was lethargic and expensive, wave after wave of Revelationist clergy heading for work in their imported Cadillacs, Mercedes, and Lincolns. Slowly Melanie drove Julie past New Jerusalem's gem-studded walls; past pearly gates where ten years earlier had stood the Golden Nugget and the Tropicana; past a gleaming monorail train gliding soundlessly over the ramparts, hugging the groove like a caterpillar moving along a twig. They headed west. A thirty-story building labeled ROOMS AT THE INN loomed above the salt marsh. At the entrance to the New Jerusalem Expressway, churchgoers swarmed around a mammoth cathedral that looked like a spaceship designed to ferry Renaissance princes to Alpha Centauri. A mile down the highway, nestled between two vast oil refineries, a public garden called GETHSEMANE PARK glowed under the rising sun, waiting to receive Sunday strollers.

At the Pomona exit, the bones began.

Everywhere: bones. "God," Julie gasped. Bones. "Sweet Jesus."

The columns stretched for miles, an army of grim reapers dangling from power lines, telephone poles, lampposts, cattle fences, and billboards, lining both sides of the expressway like defoliated trees—skeleton after skeleton, grinning skull after grinning skull, but each bone blackened, soot-painted, as if the world had become its own photographic negative.

"This is news to you?" Melanie asked.

"It's . . . yes. News. God."

Crows perched on craniums and shoulder blades, pecking out marrow. Around each fleshless neck, a wooden plaque swayed like a price tag.

"Public executions," sighed Melanie. "Very popular."

"You mean they were burned *alive*?"

"Alive. In the Circus." Melanie's tone hovered between bitterness and resignation. "Always douse the fire before it reaches the bones," she lectured. "Otherwise you end up with a lot of ashes, and the message gets lost."

"The message?"

"Don't be a heretic. Don't sin."

Julie's heart felt uprooted, a wild muscle caroming around inside her chest. "Do Americans know about this? Does their government know? The United Nations? Somebody's got to *intervene.*"

"They know," said Melanie, nodding. "But there won't be any interventions, Sheila, not while Trenton's such a bulwark against socialism."

The skeletons glided by like the resurrected dead rushing toward their Judgment Day appointments with God. "Are they all my"—the word stuck in Julie's throat like a sliver of bone—"disciples?"

"About a third. The rest are murderers, homosexuals, zotz dealers, Jews, Catholics, and so on. Only Uncertaintists go to the stake willingly, though."

"*Willingly?*"

"Some of us do. Not many. You talk to us, and we go."

"I don't talk to you."

"We hear you, Sheila. Not me, I'm afraid, but some of us."

As Melanie eased into the slow lane, the skeletons' marathon became a more stately procession, and Julie could read the plaques. Below each victim's name—Donald Torr, Mary Benedict, James Ryan, Linda Rabinovich, a thousand names, two thousand—a single word explained his presence. *Heresy, Heresy, Adultery, Blasphemy*—the convictions fused into a terse poem— *Heresy, Perversion, Theft, Murder, Socialism, Coveting, Heresy, Heresy, Sodomy, False Witness, Heresy, Adultery, Zotz Dealing, Blasphemy, Heresy...*

At the Hammonton exit, Melanie pulled onto the shoulder and cut the engine. "Something you should see..."

"Hey, things are really over the edge these days," Julie protested. "I get it. Entirely demented. If I were still a deity, I'd put Milk out of business. I don't need—"

"You *do* need. Excuse me, Sheila, but you *do.*"

Squeezing her burned palm, pouring her outrage into the gummy tissue, Julie followed Melanie to a quartet of skeletons chained to an old Trump Castle billboard. Armored in green, a chubby police corporal approached, moving past the ranks of sinners like a wolf on the prowl, crows scattering before him.

"He wants to make sure we aren't stealing relics," Melanie muttered. "Your followers do that sometimes."

"Will he arrest us?"

"*Us?* We're just two old-fashioned gals on their way to a Revelationist service."

Thanks to Melanie, they looked the part. Melanie sported a dress suggesting an immense doily, Julie a maroon silk blouse and a white dirndle skirt splashed with yellow; silver lambs hung from their necks, and they both wore what Melanie called optimal makeup: enough to suggest they valued their femininity, not so much to suggest they enjoyed it.

Pointing his assault rifle downward in a conscious gesture of hospitality, the corporal greeted them in a slow, sandpaper voice. "Morning, ladies." He swept his arm across the black forest. "When Jesus comes, it'll be just like this, only a million times greater. Armageddon. Amazing."

Julie glanced at the nearest skeleton: a broad feminine pelvis, the gnawed bones sewn together with piano wire.

"Let's go, honey." Melanie poked Julie's shoulder as if operating a telegraph key. "We'll miss the sermon."

A hole formed in the pit of Julie's stomach, a tunnel plunging straight to hell

Bored, the corporal drifted out of hearing range, leaving Julie free to weep and bleed and die.

Aunt Georgina's plaque proclaimed two convictions. *Perversion:* no surprise. *Heresy:* why? Oh, God, oh, no, Georgina, no, no. Julie ran her finger along a blackened rib, revealing the whiteness beneath. Did you go out cursing them, old aunt? Did you spit in their faces? I know you did.

"I always liked her," said Melanie. "She was a real good mother to Phoebe."

"You should've warned me," Julie croaked.

"I'm sorry." Melanie glanced toward the retreating corporal. "We need you. You can see that now, right?"

"This isn't fair, Melanie!"

"I know. We need you."

"This isn't fucking *fair!*"

She tried reconstructing her honorary aunt atop the bones—

the sprightly hands, narrow laughing face, quick spidery walk. But a skeleton was a house, not a home; whatever relationship this matrix bore to the vanished events called Georgina, it was too obscure to matter.

"Phoebe know?"

Melanie shrugged. "Didn't see her in the Circus that day. She'd probably left Jersey years before."

Julie brushed her aunt's plaque. "Heresy, it says."

"They kept asking her to convert, and she kept saying she already had a religion—she said she worshiped the Spirit of Absolute Being. Once they even brought her to the sacred canal to try baptizing her. You know what she did?"

"What?"

"She peed in it. Georgina died well, Sheila. She didn't beg for mercy till the flames came."

The faith and funding by which Atlantic City had been upgraded to New Jerusalem had not yet reached Camden, which still retained the blasted, bombed-out look Julie remembered from routinely crossing its southern tip on her way to college. As they approached the Walt Whitman Bridge, she looked toward America. Brick walls, watchtowers, and high spirals of barbed wire flourished along the Jersey side of the Delaware, a metallic jungle, thick and bristling like the seedy Eden that Wyvern was cultivating below.

Declining the bridge, they took the Mickle Boulevard exit and looped east into the city's bleak, rubbled heart. Broken glass paved the streets. Dandelions sprouted everywhere, nature's shock troops, invading the empty lots, fracturing the sidewalks. Melanie pulled over, aligning her BMW between two parking meters with cracked visors and scoliotic shafts.

"Don't tell them who I am." Julie grabbed Melanie's lacy sleeve as they walked to the Front Street intersection. "I'll reveal myself when I'm ready." They stopped before an ancient saloon, the Irish Tavern, as tightly sealed as a crypt, with boarded-up windows and a cluster of padlocks on the door. *Cold Beer to Go*, said a shattered neon sign. Melanie opened the adjacent wooden gate and started into the trash-infested alley. "Promise you won't tell," Julie insisted.

"Promise," Melanie mumbled. She pounded on the side door,

a riveted metal slab, and called *"Moon* rising" in a high, urgent whisper.

Nervous eyes flickered in the diamond-shaped window, and seconds later the door opened to reveal a young woman in a billowy white dress hung with ribbons and frills. She was remarkably thin, a kind of inverse fertility doll, a totem fashioned to foster population control. *"Moon* rising."

Melanie tossed Julie an anxious glance. *"Moon* rising," Julie responded, stepping cautiously forward.

The thin woman led them through the murky saloon, its air stale, its furniture sheeted like corpses waiting to be autopsied. They descended the basement stairs, then the subbasement stairs, eventually landing in a cavernous room, a major intersection of Camden's sewer system, its curving brick walls crisscrossed by ducts and cables, a network that Julie imagined shunting away the city's undercurrents—its septic blood and unclean thoughts. A swift, malodorous creek gurgled across the floor, spanned by wooden planks on which the Uncertaintists had erected a half-dozen pews, several random chairs, and a lectern plus accompanying altar. Melanie slipped into an unoccupied pew near the back, Julie right behind. Brass candlesticks shaped like lighthouses paraded along the altar, capped by squat white candles. Behind the lectern, a banner proclaimed Heisenberg's uncertainty relation, $\Delta\chi\Delta\rho \geq h/4\pi\varsigma$. Two outsized paperback books rose from the rack before Julie, their white covers emblazoned with computer-generated Old English script. Passing over the *Hymnal*, Julie opened a *Word of Sheila*. Each page reproduced a "Heaven Help You" column. Her eye caught one of the few replies Aunt Georgina had liked—Sheila giving tax advice to a coven of witches in Palo Alto.

Oh, Georgina, Georgina, how could Georgina be dead?

The skinny Uncertaintist who'd greeted them glided toward the altar and, turning, addressed the heretics. "Number thirty-one." The congregation, a hundred spiffily dressed men and women, lurched forward like bus passengers reacting to a sudden stop, snatching up their hymnals.

"We'll share." Melanie shoved an open hymnal under Julie's nose. The performance proceeded a cappella, an austerity Julie alternately ascribed to purism and to the difficulties of getting an organ into Camden's sewers.

She came to place uncertainty
And science on our shelf.
She taught us to doubt everything
And seek her sacred self.

While every truth is putative
And every faith a lie,
We know she'll let us praise her name
And love her till we die.

By the time the refrain arrived—"Despite the fact belief's absurd, we'll follow you, just give the word"—Julie's entire body had become a wince, a posture she maintained during hymn seventeen, "Her Daughter's Growing Under Glass."

"Ahhhhh-mennnnn," the heretics sang, holding the note as they replaced their hymnals.

From the sewer pipe nearest the altar, a preacher emerged. "Father Paradox," Melanie explained.

The man was fat. His belly arrived like an advance guard, heralding the bulk to come, huge shoulders, a surplus chin. His white cassock had settled over his body like a tarpaulin dropped on a blimp. Dear mother in heaven, sweet brother in hell: him. Bearded now, older, bespectacled, but still unquestionably him.

"Fellow skeptics, logicians, doubters, questioners, relativists, rationalists, pragmatists, positivists, and enigmatists," Bix announced, "today we'll be talking about God."

As her former lover wrapped his stubby fingers around the lectern, Julie realized that its cylindrical contours and glassy surfaces were meant to represent an ectogenesis machine. Bix Constantine—in a pulpit? Her heart stuttered. Her brain seemed to spin in its skull.

"Column five, verse twenty," Bix boomed, flipping back the cover of an enormous *Word of Sheila*. Julie pulled the nearest *Sheila* from the rack. Column five, verse twenty was her answer to a young man in Toronto who'd wanted to find faith.

Bix cleared his throat, a noise suggesting a despondent garbage disposal. "Sheila writes, 'Over the centuries, four basic proofs of God's existence have emerged. To be perfectly frank, none of them works.'" Snapping his *Sheila* shut, he yanked off his bifocals and swept them across his flock like a maestro wielding a baton. "Does she speak the truth here? Is it impossible to verify God through sheer deduction? Proof one—the ontological. In Saint Anselm's words, 'God is that being than which nothing greater can be conceived.' Unfortunately, no evidence exists that, simply because the human mind can devise ideas of perfection, infinitude, and omnipotence, such qualities occupy an objective plane."

"Agreed!" the congregation called in unison.

Next Bix demolished the moral argument: if God were the source of humankind's ability to distinguish right from wrong, then believers would behave better than atheists, a postulate unsupported by history.

"Agreed!"

He ravaged the cosmological argument: one has no warrant to move from the innumerable causal connections within the universe to a comparable connection between the universe and some hypothetical transcendent entity.

"Agreed!"

He made hash of the teleological argument: from the mythic universe of the Greeks to Aristotle's crystalline spheres to the contemporary big-bang model, all pictures of reality are wholly human in design, and it is therefore presumptuous to ascribe any of them to God.

"Agreed!"

"As we all know," Bix concluded, "there is but one proof of God's existence, and that proof is she to whom we give our confused hearts and confounded minds." His voice rose powerfully and majestically, like a supersonic jet leaving a runway. "Sheila who revealed the God of physics and forged the Covenant of Uncertainty! Sheila who, against all logic and natural law, commanded the ocean, quenched the fire, and ascended!" He listed away from the lectern. "Thank you, bewildered brethren. Next week we'll discuss what Sheila meant by the empire of nostalgia."

With a sprightliness that defied his mass, Bix disappeared into the sewer pipe from which he'd come. The thin woman resumed the pulpit and instructed the congregation to sing the morning's final hymn, "And the Tropicana Went Out, Out, Out."

And Julie wondered: intervene?

No, pointless. To debate these fools would be to beat her head against a wall as palpable as the one encompassing their church.

So why was she rising? Why drawing in such a large breath?

"Hey, everyone!" Julie lurched into the aisle. "It's me. Sheila!" The Uncertaintists' amiable chatter faded. "Yes, it's really me— listen, folks, we've got to talk. I'm not divine anymore, but maybe I can help." A hundred quizzical faces met Julie's gaze. "To begin with, you must all get baptized before they catch you."

Jaws dropped. Frowns formed. Eyelids flapped in rhythmic curiosity: a congregation of owls.

"Sheila speaks to us," asserted a gaunt man in a ramshackle tuxedo.

"And tells you to become martyrs?" Julie asked.

"Sometimes."

"No, I don't! I absolutely *don't!*"

"Sheila cured my diabetes," asserted a peppy old woman, her skin as wrinkled as an elephant's.

"Got me off zotz," revealed a young man wearing a blue serge suit and a mildly bohemian beard.

"Who *says* you're Sheila?" demanded a pretty, thirtyish woman whose white gloves reached to her elbows.

"Sheila wears the sun," asserted the recovering zotz addict. "She's a living rainbow."

"Sheila flies," explained the gaunt man.

"She's young," added the white-gloved woman.

"You think God's children don't *age*? We age." Julie waved a *Sheila* over her head like an island castaway signaling an ocean liner. "I wrote this stuff fifteen years ago. I've been in hell ever since. For Christ's sake—"

"Sheila went to *heaven*," the elephant-skinned woman corrected her.

The zotz addict started up the aisle, drawing the rest of the congregation with him like a magnet luring paper clips.

"There's no profit in being burned!" Julie called after them. "Get baptized! Please!"

Within two minutes Julie and Melanie were alone in the nave.

"A brick wall." Julie threw her *Sheila* onto the floor.

"I guess they have minds of their own," said Melanie.

Approaching the pulpit, Julie steadied herself on the ersatz ectogenesis machine. Dear walrus. Sweet whale. Yes, he might be insane, he might have gone gaga over her stunt with the Atlantic, but there was also this: she had once loved him and probably still did.

"Wait here, Melanie."

Beyond the pulpit, the main pipe widened into a large, damp, algae-coated room. Julie sloshed forward through Camden's excretions. To her left, a half-dozen narrow tunnels diverged like roots, each reeking of slug turds and the oily festering Delaware. To her right lay an efficiency apartment lit by a kerosene lamp.

Father Paradox's asceticism was severe: army cot, cracked mirror, sterno stove, chemical commode. The one technological touch was an offset printing press wired into an overhead cable, blatantly looting New Jersey's electricity. Bix sat at a shabby metal desk basting the back of a "Heaven Help You" with rubber cement.

"Hello, Bix."

Blinking, he grabbed his bifocals like a surprised gunfighter drawing his six-shooter. "Yes?" he muttered, dropping the glasses in place. "What'd you say?"

"Bix—hi."

"I'm Father Paradox."

An ingenious device, bifocals, so Age-of-Reasonish. "It's me. Your old pal Julie Katz."

Bix readied the clipping for printing, affixing it to a piece of shirt cardboard. Cement flowed out in languid waves. "I knew a Miss Katz once. I was never her friend."

Could it be? He really didn't recognize her? "We dated," Julie pleaded. "Spent nights together at Dante's."

"I dated . . . a younger person."

"Of *course* I look older. You're no puppy yourself. You don't remember sending me valentines? You said you loved me."

"I love Sheila of the *Moon*."

"You used to *shtup* Sheila of the *Moon*. That was Sheila in your bed, Bix! Her—me!"

"No," he rasped. Repression, she decided: the unconscionable banished to the unconscious. "No," Bix repeated, firmer now, more snappish.

"Listen, sweetheart, tell your flock to stop this heresy nonsense. They have to become Revelationists."

"No they don't."

"Yes. Sheila's orders."

Bix pulled off the bifocals, as if blurring her image would also blur the anxiety she was causing him. "Sheila bid the sea rise up—and it did. It's impossible, but I *saw* it. Nothing makes sense anymore. The good news is that God exists. The bad news is that God exists."

"If we put our heads together, we can probably get out of this nutty republic. Philadelphia's only two miles away."

"Philadelphia?" Bix's smirk was incredulous, as if she'd just proposed a trip to Neptune.

"Yeah. Any of these pipes lead to the river?"

"They're stuffed with barbed wire."

"We'll cut it."

Bix hammered the clipping with his fist. "Time for you to go, Miss Katz."

Her tears caught her by surprise. "Oh, Bix, honey, they killed Georgina. She came to all my birthday parties, and they *burned* her."

"Leave!"

The tears rolled into her quavering mouth. Ordinary tears, profane tears, salt tears, no wrathful acids anymore, no supernatural sugars. We cry an ancient ocean, Howard Lieberman liked to point out. Powerful evidence for biological evolution, he used to explain.

Stumbling out of Father Paradox's apartment, she ran through the sewer pipe, past the pulpit, and straight into the dripping belly of her church.

CHAPTER 13

•   •   •

Like a wily predator, like a hawk or shark or lioness, the urge to contact her mother had struck Julie suddenly and from behind, and she was not happy about it. She wanted no more of this grotesque comedy of futile prayers and unreciprocated shouts, of busy signals and being put on hold, enough of this maternal neglect, the aloofness of the God of physics, the indifference of the differential equation. Yet here she was, leaning against a Longport street lamp and petitioning heaven for advice.

Can I save him, Mother? Is Bix savable? Answer me.

In the tea-leaf whorls of the Milky Way, Julie read his fate. Another year of preaching, two perhaps, but inevitably the heretic hunters or the vigilantes would find him, no old age for Bix, no quiet nights preparing sermons by the hearth. His own public burning was the closest he'd ever get to a hearth.

Beware the stars, Howard had always warned her. Babylonian astrology, Greek mythology, Aristotle's crystalline spheres—the stars had occasioned more pure bullshit than the rest of reality combined. And yet, midway between Orion and the Big Dipper, floating over Melanie's condo, she saw—thought she saw—a constellation meant for her eyes only, a tool of forged steel, waiting to cut her a path to America.

"I'm going to intervene," Julie declared, rushing into Melanie's book-lined study.

Seated at her computer, Melanie glanced up from the phos-
phorescent text of *Ralph and Amy Learn About Catholics* and
grinned. "I *knew* you'd help us. Will you start with the Holy
Palace?"

"I need wire cutters."

"Throw it down stone by stone?"

"Do you have any?"

Melanie's excited jowls collapsed. "Wire cutters?"

"Yeah."

"No." Melanie frowned darkly. "Why?"

"To get that preacher and me across the Delaware. He's my
friend."

"Black market might have wire cutters." Melanie's face became the quintessence of betrayal: the child seeing Santa's beard
fall off, the bride finding her husband in bed with the maid of
honor. "If you really need them."

"I need them."

On Melanie's cable-television monitor, *The Monday Night
Auto-da-Fé* unfolded. A man in a red dinner jacket and white top
hat escorted a teenage boy across a sandy field and chained him
to a wooden post. "It's a balmy night here in downtown New
Jerusalem," the offscreen commentator noted gaily, "with a
tangy wind rolling in from the sea."

A sudden smile lifted Melanie's pudgy cheeks. "Going to
America, are you?" She whisked an antique postcard off her
desk. "Look what came in today's mail."

Beneath the caption, GREETINGS FROM ATLANTIC CITY, three
photographs formed a triptych of frivolity: bathing beauties
romping through the surf, Rex the Wonder Dog riding his aqua-
plane, a high-diving horse in flight. Julie turned it over. American stamps. A Philadelphia postmark. "Melanie Markson," Julie
read aloud, "Longport, New Jersey." The handwriting was inflicted with a stammer. "Dear Melanie: How's it going? Could
you please—" Bars of black ink obscured the rest. "Yer Ever-
Lovin' Phoebe."

"Our mail goes through the government," Melanie explained.

Julie folded the postcard, bisecting the Wonder Dog as Billy
Milk had bisected Marcus Bass, and stuck it in the pocket of her
borrowed jeans. *Yer Ever-Lovin' Phoebe*. Phoebe! In Philadelphia!
"Want to come with us?"

"Don't think ill of me," Melanie begged, pecking the TV

screen with her glossy, perfect fingernail. "Hey, if you were your old self, a deity and everything, I'd be the first to sign up." As the man in the top hat pulled a black cloth bag over his young prisoner's face, the camera panned to a dozen harlequins gripping semiautomatic rifles. "May I give you some advice, Sheila? If you don't have those powers anymore, you're crazy to try crossing the Delaware, truly crazy. People get shot for things like that."

"I'll take my chances," said Julie.

"Twenty-five rounds per minute," the offscreen commentator was saying, "with a muzzle velocity of two thousand feet per second."

Andrew Wyvern spreads his wide, webbed, gelatinous wings and sails across hell's bustling port, swerving past a steel crane as it lifts a semitrailer full of new arrivals off the magnificent barge *John Mitchell* and sets it on the dock. He seriously considers returning to Carcinoma for a relaxing afternoon of inflicting aphids and Japanese beetles on his tomatoes, but instead lands on *Pain*'s foredeck.

"Where to?" asks Anthrax, saluting crisply.

A miniature cloud of depression congeals above the devil's head. "New Jersey. The Believers' Republic." Seeking relief, he counts his blessings. Venereal disease on the rise, pollution prospering, totalitarianism thriving, the Circus of Joy a perpetual sellout. Best of all, Julie Katz's church is a glorious success, a wellspring of meaningless martyrdom.

No good. His depression remains, black and hovering.

"Did I ever tell you what the universe is, Anthrax?"

"No, sir, you never did."

"The universe," says Wyvern, "is a Ph.D. thesis that God was unable to successfully defend."

Anthrax picks his nose, impaling a boll weevil on his claw. "Didn't you get enough of New Jersey last time? Couldn't we do the Middle East instead? I've never seen the pyramids."

"Are we cleared for sea?"

"Cleared for sea—yes, sir." Anthrax pops the skewered weevil into his mouth. "Take her out?"

"Take her out."

"Set course for North America?"

"Set course for North America."

"Why New Jersey?" asks Anthrax.

Wyvern grimaces so fiercely the cloud above his head spits rain. "Because the bitch still believes she has powers."

She thought: The heart is a pump.

A pump . . . and an augur.

No question. The closer the taxi got to the Irish Tavern, the louder Julie's heart became, pumping premonitions, broadcasting omens. "Pull over!" She secured the wire cutters under her belt like Queen Zenobia sheathing her sword and shoved a five-mammon bill toward the driver. "Keep the change!"

Melanie had underwritten the expedition generously, dressing Julie in a cowhide jacket and Eurocut slacks, paying for the black-market cutters—a formidable tool, reminiscent of Wyvern's secateurs, with rubber handles and serrated blades—and giving her a wallet filled with six hundred dollars in case she got to America and a hundred and fifty mammons in case she didn't.

Stomach acid fountained up Julie's esophagus as she ran across Front Street. Her veins throbbed with the crude rhythms of a dog scratching its fleas.

The approaching mob was single-minded, focused, its arms and legs all linked to one aim: abducting Father Paradox. Lurching away, Julie let them pass, over a dozen Revelationists giving up their lunch hours to vigilance. They whooped, whistled, catcalled, and cheered.

Bix wore Indian moccasins and a white bathrobe with a lighthouse on the breast. His naked eyes were sunken and bleary, desperate for their bifocals. Julie melted into the mob. The majority were slick-haired, business-suited men who, when not cleansing Camden of heresy, probably sold used cars and bargain carpets. The four women were equally well groomed—real-estate agents, Julie figured.

The vigilantes bore Bix to a vacant lot, a tract of shattered glass and broken brick, gutted automobiles hulking up from the rubble. Along the western edge rose the back wall of a hardware store, a pink stucco mass against which the vigilantes now pushed their captive. Bix's smile was gone. He sweated in the noon sun. Afraid? Who wouldn't be afraid? And yet at the core of his sorry posture, Julie felt, lay something else: disappointment. If I must die, at least let the Circus do it, not these amateurs. At least let me appear on *The Monday Night Auto-da-Fé*. At least let me adorn the New Jerusalem Expressway.

From among the mob's many brains, one now emerged to take charge, a cherubic man in a blue blazer. He was like a scaled-down version of Bix, soft, round, a kind of . . . tense Buddha? Quite so: Nick Shiner himself, the disgruntled trucker with whom she'd hitched a ride four days earlier.

"Father Paradox!" he screamed.

"I am Father Paradox," Bix admitted.

"Father Paradox—do you love the Church of the Revelation?"

Bix blinked spasmodically. He reached under his bathrobe and scratched his doughy chest, right beneath the lighthouse. "I love Sheila of the *Moon*," he said at last.

The crowd grumbled indignantly, yet to Julie his conviction seemed wonderfully tentative, his devotion to Sheila gloriously incomplete.

"Will you receive the teachings of Revelationism?" Nick Shiner persisted.

Bix seemed to think it over. "I shall receive the Kingdom of Impermanence," he said hesitantly.

Yes, his faith was shakable, she felt, his sanity savable. She *knew* it.

Nick Shiner plucked a fat chunk of brick from the ground. Inspired, his covigilantes bent down and, like peasants harvesting potatoes, equipped themselves—bricks, rocks, soda bottles, sections of lead pipe, bits of cinder block. To Julie the moment seemed arcane, forbidden. You saw such incidents in the movies, read about them in history books—you were never actually there for one.

"Tell us you accept the truth," demanded Nick Shiner, massaging his brick as if making a snowball.

Julie tightened her grip on the cutters. This murder would be worse than most, there being so much of him, all that superflous flesh to hew away, that extra span of skull to shatter.

"I accept the Covenant of Uncertainty," said Bix.

Legs powered by instinct, resolve flowing from she-knew-not-where, Julie marched to the pink wall. What was courage? Doing what comes unnaturally, Aunt Georgina used to say.

"Hey, you!" a vigilante called.

"Stop!"

"Get away!"

"Out!"

Reaching Bix's side, she kissed him. Smack, right on the lips, like those watermelon kisses Phoebe used to give her.

His muzzy eyes fixed on her. His mind seemed locked in ice, a glacier-sealed mammoth, but now a warmer epoch was coming, her Miocene lips. She kissed him again. How could she love this oversized nose, these dual chins, these sixty extra pounds? She did.

"Hey, I *know* you," Nick Shiner called from behind her.

Julie's heart hurled itself against her sternum: get out, they'll kill you, run.

"I gave you a ride last week," said Nick Shiner. "Come take a brick, lady. There's plenty of bricks."

Another kiss. Yes, this was surely the cure; her Miocene lips would suck the fog from his brain.

"We don't kiss these people, lady," said Nick Shiner. "Didn't they beat you up? Where does kissing figure in?"

Get out? Run? No, she was free now, no more infinite potential weighing her down. She faced Nick Shiner and, stooping, snatched up a wad of pebbles embedded in cement. The disproportion was at once terrible and comic. On one side: a Camden mob brimming with bricks, stones, glass, and metal. On the other: Julie Katz armed with nothing but her brother's best line. She debated which source to use. The King James? Revised Standard? New International? Douay? She settled on the version Max Von Sydow had spoken in one of Georgina's favorite movies, *The Greatest Story Ever Told.*

"'Let him among you who is without sin'"—Julie held the concrete glob at arm's length, proffering it—"'cast the first stone.'"

Nick Shiner said, "Huh?"

Julie raised her voice. "'Let him among you who is without sin cast the first stone.'"

"What?"

"Here, Shiner. Take it."

He scowled. Julie could almost hear the sputters of rusty neurons firing in his brain. She imagined a severely retarded adolescent, a boy wholly ignorant of the sexual act, who is one day shown *Playboy*. A response occurs, a fully realized hard-on.

So it was with Shiner, a response, an ethical erection. She'd tapped something basic here.

"Well?" Julie pressed her advantage. "Are you sinless?"

Shiner took a backward step. A small one, nothing to depend on for long, but still a backward step. "That's hardly the point, lady," he said resentfully. "The point is—"

"Sheila! Sheila!"

Julie spun around. Bix was gasping. His eyes were as wide as a lemur's.

"My sweet Sheila!" he cried. "My sweet Sheila of the *Moon*!"

"Not Sheila, darling." She seized Bix's hand. "Mere Julie."

"He called you Sheila!" Nick Shiner shouted accusingly. "He called you Sheila of the *Moon*!"

Julie screamed, "Let's go!"

"Go?" said Bix.

"We're crossing the Delaware!"

Shiner wailed, "He called you Sheila! You're *her*!"

Together they hobbled across the lot, Bix moaning as the sharp trash cut through his mocassins. Even before Julie and Bix reached Front Street, Shiner's gang was on the move, breathing down their necks as they entered the Irish Tavern and rushed into the sewers.

"Not Sheila?" said Bix.

"Julie. Your old pal Julie. No divinity. I gave it up."

Like Jesus' good line, the maze of tunnels bought them a reprieve. Vigilante footfalls echoed everywhere, but no bricks arrived, no bottles or cinder blocks. Leading now, Bix selected the route most likely to bring them to the river. Heat, moisture, and a primal stench fell upon Julie's senses; heat, moisture, stench, and . . . a glow? A glow, a comforting radiance, beckoning.

Their entwined fingers tightened. Like an expanding iris, the glow grew from pinprick to hole to gateway of light.

"Will you make it disappear?" Bix asked as they reached a plug of barbed wire the size of a forsythia bush.

"No powers, Bix. I meant it." Julie pulled out the cutters. "I use these instead."

She scissored madly. The barbs tore her Eurocut slacks, snagged her cowhide jacket, bit her thighs. She felt like a baby performing its own cesarean section, knifing its way into the world. The river loomed up. Swarming with gulls, a garbage scow rumbled south toward the ocean. Julie stretched into the daylight and surveyed the drop—ten feet, no more than twelve. A Philadelphia police cruiser glided noiselessly under the Benjamin Franklin Bridge.

"We've got to go in there!" Julie pointed to the languid currents, dark and bubbly like coagulated Pepsi.

"That's crazy." Bix drew up beside her.

A brick spiraled past Julie's brow. She turned. Raising their pitching arms, the vigilantes released a volley. Rocks ricocheted off the cylindrical walls. A half-full ketchup bottle sailed over the severed wires, exploding at Bix's feet like a blood bomb.

"Can't you, er, *part* it?"

"Ow!" A chunk of brick bounced off Julie's knee. "Shit!"

She closed her eyes, grabbed Bix's bathrobe sash, and jumped.

They embraced as they fell, holding fast to each other even as they smashed into the river. The Delaware snapped shut. Down, down they plunged, a baptism of sludge, the water growing ever colder, denser, fouler. Oh, glorious cesspool, she thought, wellspring of avant-garde diseases, laboratory for state-of-the-art carcinogens, surely no vigilantes would follow.

She arched her back and, rising, guided Bix to the surface.

The scow cruised toward them, its entourage of gulls hovering and screeching, pecking at the cargo like dilettante vultures. "There!" Julie sputtered. Whichever force had sent the scow, God or luck or Heisenbergian uncertainty, had thought of everything, including the mooring line trailing from the stern. "Grab on!"

A minute of frenzied splashing brought the rope in reach. Bix went first, scaling the hull with a fevered and wholly uncharacteristic dexterity. Together they flopped over the transom and tumbled into the blessed mush.

"Look, honey." Spitting out the Delaware, Julie pulled Melanie's wallet from her pocket. Burning nails lay imbedded in her kneecap. "Six hundred bucks." She slipped out a hundred-dollar bill, saturated but functional. "We won't starve."

Bix sneezed. "How about a pizza tonight?"

"My favorite." They crept toward each other, pushing through heaped refuse and thick walls of fetor. Meeting, they hugged passionately, bobbing up and down on a beach of coffee grounds. "Tomorrow we'll do the zoo."

"And the day after that we'll get married."

"Married?"

"My parents were married," said Bix. "I truly believe it made life less horrible for them."

She let herself relax, enjoying the pungent, vital moment, the sultry garbage, growling river, outraged gulls, domestic fantasies—a baby flashed through her mind, lolling groggily against her chest, milk leaking from its rosebud mouth—and above all the throb of the scow as it bore them toward the Philadelphia Naval Shipyard and freedom.

The Reverend Billy Milk—mayor of New Jerusalem, grandpastor of the Revelationist Church, executive producer of the Circus of Joy, and chairman of the New Jersey Inquisition—shuffled morosely onto the west balcony of the Holy Palace and surveyed the city below. In his good eye the sun blazed hotly, ricocheting off the shining walls and soaring towers, but as usual the truth lay in his phantom eye, by which account a satanic frost descended, sealing the twelve gates, freezing the sacred river, and killing the Tree of Life.

Disgrace, rasped the ocean. *Ignominy*, taunted the wind. Gas lines, bread lines, coal lines, powdered milk lines, and then, when you finally got to the head of a line, inflation. In Billy Milk's republic it took a sack of currency to buy a sack of flour. Disgrace, ignominy. The mining of Raritan Bay and the patrolling of the Hudson River were costing the Trenton junta eighty-five thousand mammons a day, a bill the American Congress was no longer willing to foot. Disgrace, ignominy, inflation, debt, and, worst of all, no Second Coming. Yes, the Circus was keeping people's minds off the shortages, but what did that matter when its purpose remained unrealized? Billy bit his inner cheeks, bringing the pain he deserved. Blood washed over his teeth. How many more sinners must the Circus process before the Parousia? How many more must the flames punish, the bullets chastise, the arrows devour, the swords consume?

Then there was his son. Archshepherd Timothy: devout, bright-eyed, God-fearing—and something else, something difficult to name. Zeal was a fine impulse, a godly emotion, but...

"Our Savior won't return unless his people have known suffering," Timothy insisted whenever he snuffed a candle with his palm. "An archshepherd cannot be a stranger to penance," he

would explain as he shoved hat pins under his fingernails or
loaded his boots with broken glass.

A tear rolled down Billy's gullied face. God takes your wife
and gives you a son. You do your best—the check to the diaper
service every second Friday, endless hours in the supermarket
buying Similac and Gerber Strained Sweet Potatoes and cali-
brated spoons for shunting Septra down his throat in hopes of
knocking out his latest ear infection, a thousand trips to play-
grounds and day-care centers and strange houses where Timothy is playing with some boy whose name you can't remember.
You single-handedly organize his fourth birthday party. Half the
children are blind like Timothy; they are wizards at pinning the
tail on the donkey. You organize his fifth birthday party: Come
As Your Favorite Bible Character. His sixth, seventh, eighth,
nearly a dozen birthday parties. You do all this, and your son's
closet ends up filled with whips, dangling into the darkness like
a normal man's belts and ties. Could such be the proper destiny
for a child to whom the angels had given eyes?

Billy's gaze drifted to the Tomás de Torquemada Memorial
Arena, a great bowl-shaped amphitheater jammed with tier
upon tier of enthralled spectators. Bestriding the western gate
was a fifty-foot marble statue of Saint John the Divine receiving
the Revelation, his left hand gripping a quill pen, his right holding aloft a scroll in which Billy's brilliant engineer—the grandson
of the man who did Giants Stadium—had embedded a bill-
board-sized television monitor. A matinee was in progress. On
the monitor, a man stood bound to a wooden post: a papist,
hence a papist's chastisement, the one inflicted on Saint Sebas-
tian. A dozen men in diamond-patterned harlequin tights loaded
their crossbows.

People were wrong about inquisitions, Billy felt. Look at the
word: an inquisition was merely a questioning process. The
court's purpose was leading lambs to the fold, not the slaughter;
torture and the Circus were persuasions of last resort. Even the
Spanish autos-da-fé, most debatable of Billy's inspirations, had
probably burned fewer than three thousand, a tittle compared
with the output of the same era's secular courts.

Turning from the Circus, Billy went to his desk and opened
the top file. His good eye raced past the plea (not guilty) and the
verdict (guilty), settling on the evidence. "The defendant, one
'Brother Zeta,' was apprehended while conducting Uncertaintist

services in an abandoned Hoboken subway," Harry Phelps, former Cape May orthodondist and current inquisitor general, had written.

Billy took up his fountain pen. The hand that now countersigned the execution order was white and withered, its veins like strands of blue twine. So many years stored in that hand, and what, really, had it accomplished? A believers' republic, a New Jerusalem—good enough. But God had made Billy a father, and he'd failed. God had appointed him gatekeeper for Jesus, and he'd failed.

Billy's commandant entered on the run, gasping, his smile testifying to good news. A fine specimen of believer, Peter Scortia, the kind of soldier who could have kept the Holy Land from infidel hands for a millennium. Hard to imagine he'd once managed Scortia's Jiffy Dry Cleaning in Teaneck.

Good news. Or possibly even . . . the *best* news, the very Second Coming? More likely the news concerned the stranger at Peter's side, a cherubic man dressed in brown corduroys and a blue blazer.

"He works for us," Peter explained. "Carries sinners out of the city. His name's Nick."

"Nick Shiner," said the cherub. "It's an honor, Reverend. Being here, I mean. Not the hauling."

Billy kept his monocular gaze locked on Peter. If you looked directly at people of Nick Shiner's station, they often ended up pressing their advantage, telling you their opinions about taxes and bread lines. "Is Mr. Shiner unhappy with his situation?"

"That's not why he came," said Peter.

"I wouldn't mind a couple of free passes on occasion," said the truck driver.

"He's seen someone," said Peter. "In Camden."

"I'm sure it's her," said Nick Shiner. "I remember how she looked from that picture they always ran with her advice. She's gotten older, but it's her."

"What is Mr. Shiner talking about?" Billy focused on the Distinguished Service Cross that Peter had received for flushing out a family of sodomites in East Orange.

"Sheila of the *Moon*," said Peter.

"Sheila of the *Moon*," said Nick Shiner.

Spontaneously Billy unleashed a dual stare—real eye, phantom eye—upon his visitor. "*Her?*"

"Her."

"In Camden?"

"She was kissing this fat man, and he pointed to her and shouted, 'Sheila of the *Moon*!' Then the two of them escaped to Philadelphia in a garbage scow."

"Garbage scow?"

"I figured there's a kind of message in that."

"And he really called her 'Sheila of the *Moon*'?"

"Right to her face."

Fire. Billy saw fire. He rubbed his eyepatch. Not the Circus's flames, not the inferno below, but a holy conflagration raging within his own skull, a psychic burning bush, its hot roots probing the soft meat of his brain. In the center: a face, her face, Sheila of the *Moon*, abomination-666; her gross and voluptuous limbs emerged, her breasts with eyeballs for nipples. All was clear now. The Antichrist ruled. Maybe she'd quit the earth as her followers believed, but today she was back, preventing the Parousia, blocking Jesus' return.

"Go to our *Midnight Moon* files," said Billy as he guided Peter Scortia to the balcony. Below: Act Three. The stake. "Clip her photo, brother. Before your brigade slips across the Delaware, make sure each man knows her face as well as he knows the Lord's Prayer."

"We'll find her, Reverend," Peter promised.

As the sinners smoldered on their stakes, applause swept through the arena, thousands of hands waving like summer wheat. An intense gladness swelled the grandpastor's heart. Sheila was in Philadelphia now, but soon she'd be back in Jersey —soon she'd be right here. Billy's inner vision showed all, the flames peeling away her flesh, revealing the worms beneath, and now the worms disintegrated, yielding to the thousand locusts clustered on her bones, beyond which, as the fire continued to undress her, he saw wasps, scorpions, and the foul, stinking ordure at her core.

"Give that man Shiner a lifetime pass to the Circus," Billy instructed his commandant.

CHAPTER 14

◆   ◆   ◆

Phoebe Sparks slammed her plastic Pluto the Dog cup onto the Formica tabletop and told the bartender to fill it up again. Reverse *God* and you got *Dog*, she thought; you got Pluto, Lord of the Underworld. What a surreal place hell must be if indeed ruled by a cartoon dog who was once the pet of a mouse.

For a six-foot-tall gorilla with garter snakes slithering from his eyes, the bartender operated most efficiently, filling half of Phoebe's cup with Bacardi rum, half with Diet Coke, using his hairy thumb as a swizzle stick. She tilted Pluto toward her lips and swallowed. Ah, blessed ichor, blood of the worst gods. As always, the stuff did wonders. Her kitchen walls stopped moving like windblown sheets on a clothesline. The gorilla, cunning shapeshifter, changed back into her refrigerator. The tombstones commemorating her abortions became what they were, red and green boxes of Girl Scout cookies.

Self-destruction had its etiquette. Emily Postmortem. No, forget it, she decided. What, exactly, could her suicide note say? "To Whom It May Concern: My life has never concerned anyone, therefore you aren't even reading this. My mother's disappeared. My father will never find me. Everybody in New York City hated me, so I came here, where everybody hates me too."

The pistol had turned up during a routine frisking. First rule of the hooker biz: never admit a customer until you've disarmed him. Take away his snubnose, blackjack, stiletto, hand grenade.

Leonard, he'd called himself, barely seventeen. He had a skin disease. While Leonard sat on the bed drinking her rum, Phoebe slipped the Smith & Wesson into her panty-hose drawer. Maybe it was the rum, maybe the lack of proximity to his revolver, but the poor leper couldn't get it hard. He hurried off in a fog of shame laced with Bacardi, leaving behind the Smith & Wesson and a thousand discs of dried flesh, pennies from hell.

Lepers. Christ. Still, free-lancing was better than franchising. Over the phone, Phoebe could usually screen legitimate customers from pimps, though occasionally one snuck past her guard, in which case she got out her Deauville Hotel dynamite. One glance at Phoebe holding a match in her hand and a nitroglycerin stick between her teeth—for the sake of effect, she'd replaced the electric detonators with gunpowder fuses—and the pimp knew here was a woman to avoid, a woman who, when you least expected it, might nuke your cock.

She fixed herself another diet rum and, taking a swallow, patted her stuffed friend, H. Rap Brown Bear. She ate a Do-si-do. Finished the rum. Scratched her left temple with the Smith & Wesson. Such an exquisite gun, she thought. Its muzzle smelled like Robbie the Robot's asshole.

Act, girl. Do it. Die. She coiled her tingling finger around the trigger. Each chamber was full, Atlantic City Roulette. Her hand vibrated as if she were operating a chain saw. Slowly she flexed her finger, tighter, still tighter: she might leave a note behind after all, written on the wall in blood and rubbery loops of brain.

A small, sharp explosion.

The bullet grazed her scalp and burrowed into her refrigerator.

Missed? *Missed?* How could anyone miss? The blood felt thick and warm, like a glob of egg fresh from a hen's toasty womb. No time to waste. This time the muzzle would go elsewhere, past the lips and across the teeth. For blowjobs, Phoebe always insisted on a condom, but this case was exceptional.

Finger on trigger. Gun in mouth, the oily metal teasing her taste buds. Flexing...

The phone rang.

Ah, the wondrous, beyond-the-grave powers of Alexander Graham Bell. The phone could interrupt intimate conversations, screws, shits, suicides, anything. Phoebe lifted the receiver. "We're out of business. Try humping your hand."

"Phoebe?" A woman's voice.

"Take two aspirin and call me in the afterlife."

"Is that you?"

"I can't come to the phone right now. I'm shooting myself. If that fails, there's always the dynamite."

"Phoebe, it's me! Julie!"

"Katz?" Phoebe wrapped the phone cord around her arm like a tourniquet. "Julie Katz?"

"Don't do anything! Don't hurt yourself!"

"Katz? Fifteen years? Katz?"

"Right."

"Fifteen goddamn years?"

"Fifteen. Give me your address. Where are you?"

"Simple funeral, please. No flowers. Only one band."

"You're in West Philly, right?"

"A rock band, not a brass band."

"West Philly, Phoebe?"

"South Forty-third Street."

"Where on South Forty-third Street? What number?"

"You really in town?"

"Yeah. What number?"

"What are you talking about?"

"Your street number!"

"Forty-third Street."

"No, the *number*!"

"Five twenty-two. Why? You want to get laid?"

"Listen, I'm sending Bix over. We're married. Stay on the line. You can live with us. Let's sing a song, Phoebe. 'On the Boardwalk in Atlantic City, we will walk in a dream.' Stay on the line, honey. Don't do anything."

"I'm going to pull the trigger, but I won't do anything else."

"'On the Boardwalk in Atlantic City, life will be peaches and—'"

"See you in hell."

Phoebe pumped two slugs into the phone, sending a spray of plastic and metal against the refrigerator, and lovingly licked the hot smoking muzzle.

522 South 43rd Street. A converted row house, one apartment per floor. On the mailboxes, faded illegible pencil scrawls adorned semidetached labels, as if the tenants had no ultimate

interest in receiving their mail. *No. 3—P. Sparks.* Julie grabbed the knob, a bulb of engraved brass worn smooth by a century of flesh. Why had the idiot hung up? Just once in her life, couldn't Phoebe do what she was told? The door opened. Julie charged up the steps, swerving past the second-floor banister, Bix puffing behind her.

But for Julie's flesh, but for her bladder, she would never have discovered the fateful phone number. The search for Phoebe, a frantic three-day marathon conducted out of a Kensington hotel, had taken them through every human catalogue in the Delaware Valley, through police files, coroner's reports, taxpayer lists, welfare rolls. They placed an ad in the *Philadelphia Daily News*: Phoebe, Get in Touch—Queen Zenobia, Box 356. Then, ten minutes after the Upper Darby Township Justice of the Peace pronounced her Bix's wife, Julie went to the ladies' room and saw, scratched in the gray paint, "For Professional Sex, Contact the Green Enchantress, 886-1064. All Genders Welcome."

Apartment 3 was locked. Julie pounded, no answer. But now came Bix, Father Paradox to the rescue, hurling his two hundred and twenty pounds against the door.

A tornado's wake: clothes in ragged heaps, newspapers and Bacardi bottles strewn about, a decrepit, unraveling teddy bear surrounded by Tastykake wrappers and boxes of Girl Scout cookies. Beyond, in the sallow kitchen, a figure in a mint bathrobe slouched at the table, crusted blood clinging to her forehead like a snail.

Julie charged. Oh, let me be divine again, Mother, I won't lose heart, I'll fix every neuron...

"Hi," slurred Phoebe, waving a revolver over her head. "You're gonna pay for that door, fatty." She gulped down the contents of a plastic Pluto cup.

"Jeee-ssus," wheezed Bix, snatching the gun away.

Alive. A mess, a sunken-eyed drunk, a whore, her hair a nest built by psychotic sparrows. But alive.

Julie reached out. The hug cure. Phoebe hiccuped. Food cascaded from her mouth, the steamy stinking remains of a thousand cakes and cookies, splashing into Julie's shocked palms, rolling through her startled fingers.

"Wasn't a nice greeting for my old buddy, was it? Shitty greeting. Remember when we dropped those dead fish on that Fourth of July parade?"

"We're bringing you home with us." Gritting her teeth, Julie marched to the kitchen sink, jammed with oily frying pans and scabby dishes. The slime in her hands was heavy and warm. "We've got a house on Baring," she explained, washing.

"You think I want to live with deities and pigs?" sneered Phoebe, stuffing cookies into her mouth. Trefoils, Do-si-dos, Thin Mints, Samoas. "Whatever else they say about me, I supported the Girl Scouts."

They pulled off her bathrobe and stuck her in the shower, holding her upright like two people trying to erect a Christmas tree. "Get him out of here," she moaned, flailing at Bix. "He wants to see me naked, he pays." The water grew pink as it hit her bleeding head. Her thinness frightened Julie; she had a ballet dancer's chest. "Better not mess with my metabolism, Katz. You mess with my metabolism, I'll punch you out."

"I'm not divine anymore. I'm just another *geshmatte* Jew."

"I'll bet."

After stuffing Phoebe in the only clean clothes they could find—black bicycle pants, a man's Hawaiian shirt—they flagged down a taxi and took her to the detox center at Madison Memorial, where a bony young paramedic named Gary, tall as a basketball center, sonogrammed her liver, pumped her full of vitamins, and locked her up in a ten-by-ten lucite chamber equipped with a closed-circuit television camera.

"She tried to shoot herself," Julie explained as Gary ushered them into the observation room. On the monitor, Phoebe punched and kicked the air like Saint Anthony beating back temptation.

"That's often the point when we see them," said the paramedic with a knowing nod. For all his height, he did not inspire Julie's confidence. The world was not set up to save its Phoebes.

"Get me out of here!" Phoebe's voice zagged out of the speaker.

"You find the gun?" asked Gary.

Julie nodded. "I think she's got dynamite hidden away somewhere."

"Dynamite? That's a new one."

"Bastards!" wailed Phoebe. "Gestapo fascists!"

"I want to *help* you!" Julie screamed into the microphone.

"You never helped anybody in your life!"

At last an M.D. appeared, a Dr. Rushforth, a tall, pompous

Englishman with enormous hands, strutting into the observation room on a cloud of noblesse oblige.

"Get your friend to stop drinking, and there's a fifty-fifty chance her liver'll bounce back," he prophesied, unfurling the sonogram printout.

Phoebe screamed, "Storm troopers!"

"Stop? *How?*" moaned Julie.

"Nazis!"

Rushforth knotted his sausagelike fingers. "She seeing a psychiatrist? We use Dr. Brophy. And encourage her to attend an Alcoholics Anonymous meeting. In this town you can find one every day."

"Fuckers!"

"You're not going to discharge her," Bix protested.

"We haven't *admitted* her, sir."

"Cocksuckers!"

"Admit her," Julie pleaded.

"We're not a treatment facility, Mrs. Constantine," said Rushforth. "Call Brophy tomorrow. And get her to A.A."

Julie winced, recalling Marcus Bass's opinion that sending an alcoholic to a shrink made about as much sense as sending a heart patient to a poet.

And so Phoebe was on their backs again, the addict as addiction. They carried her out of Madison Memorial and maneuvered her onto the Market Street subway.

"Dear Sheila, I'm a lousy whore!" she screamed over and over above the screeching and clacking of the train. Like Judeans avoiding a leper, the passengers moved as far away as possible. "I'm hungry! I just puked my guts out! Get me some fucking food!"

They took her to the Golden Wok in Chinatown, where, by threatening to rip off all her clothes, by threatening to "make a scene," she cowed them into buying her a bottle of plum wine. She drank it in ten minutes and, seizing a moo-shu-pork pancake, filled it with the contents of the nearest ash tray.

"Phoebe, no!"

But already she was stuffing the befouled pancake into her mouth. "Yum₁," she said, choking it down. Charred tobacco flecked her lips; her tongue curled around an orphan Marlboro filter. Phoebe the agnostic ash eater, the false penitent, going through the motions of contrition. "Yum, yum," she said, and promptly passed out.

Everyone was watching. A scene after all.

"Now what?" said Bix.

"I want to bring her home," said Julie. "I mean, I don't *want* to, but—"

"That's a crazy idea."

"I know. You have a better one?"

Considering the modest rent, their neo-Victorian house in Powelton Village—a bohemian enclave on the west bank of the Schuylkill, a world of brick sidewalks, dozy cats, and walk-in garages jammed with bearded young men welding hunks of squashed metal into art—was astonishingly large. Crumbling, true. Roach-ridden. But certainly a surfeit of space, including a relatively uninfested back parlor. They dumped Phoebe unconscious on the living-room couch and set about preparing for the worst, nailing bed slats over the parlor window, installing a dead bolt, and removing every object with which she might stab or strangle herself—sash cord, table lamp, radiator valve. A war was coming, Julie sensed. They must dig their trenches and gird up their loins.

"Should we call that psychiatrist?" Bix asked after Phoebe was imprisoned.

Julie threaded the key through a length of twine. "I think this is bigger than psychiatry, Bix." She suspended the key around her neck like a Saint Christopher medallion—like a millstone, an albatross, like Phoebe's weighty and confounding dementia. "I think this is war."

"Happy honeymoon," said Bix.

Had Julie not actually lived in Andrew Wyvern's domain, she might have called the subsequent six days hell. Grotesque, impossible, nerve-shattering, but not exactly, not quite hell. "Life imitates soap opera," she moaned. To enter the back parlor— here, Phoebe, eat some chicken; hey, kid, we have to empty the commode—was to invite a skirmish, Phoebe swooping down on you like a fascist angel, kicking your shins, uprooting your hair. A war. A war, complete with artillery fire, Phoebe's screams answered with her keepers' pathetic replies: Phoebe, settle down, Phoebe, get a grip on yourself. Like Eskimos naming the myriad varieties of snow, Julie and Bix catalogued her screams, each unique in pitch and rhythm. There was the scream that signified general despair, the scream that accompanied her pleas for beer and rum, the scream that underscored her demands for her Smith & Wesson. It was like living with a diurnal werewolf, a lycanthrope from the new spinning city in the sky called Space Platform Omega, world of eternal moonlight. They wanted a silver bullet, anything to put Phoebe the werewolf out of her misery, anything to get her out of their lives. They wanted to bash Phoebe's brains out with a silver-headed cane as Claude Rains had done to Lon Chaney in Roger Worth's favorite movie, *The Wolf Man*.

On the seventh day, Julie marched up to Phoebe's door, tugging on the key. "Phoebe?" The twine pressed against Julie's throat like a garrote. "Phoebe, you there?"

"Get me a drink."

"Phoebe, I've got something important to say."

"A beer. One damn Budweiser."

"This is important. I've seen your parents."

"Oh, sure. Right. Get me a six-pack."

"Your mom and dad—I've seen them."

Silence. Then, "My father? You saw my *father*? Christ—where?"

Hope, Julie concluded. A nibble from God. "I'll tell you... when you start going to Alcoholics Anonymous."

"Is Mom okay? Dad alive?"

"Promise you'll go to A.A."

"Assholes Anonymous," Phoebe wailed. "I tried it. Bunch of macho dorks bragging about their binges—forget it. Is Mom all right? Tell me that."

"Get your act together," said Julie, "and we'll talk about your parents."

"Two drinks a day—okay? What's my dad like? He in America?"

"Zero drinks a day."

"You're lying! You don't know where they are."

"Think it over."

Perhaps it was the week of mandatory sobriety she'd already suffered, perhaps the proposed bargain, but ten hours later Phoebe declared that she'd seen the light.

"I'm a new woman, Katz."

Julie said, "Tell me about it."

"Really. A new woman. Where are my parents?"

"Do you love me, Phoebe?"

"Of course I love you. Where are they?"

"Will you stay sober for me?"

"I'm a new woman. I'm no bum."

"Will you stay sober for twelve weeks?" Twelve weeks, Julie figured, and Phoebe would be home free. "Can you ride the wagon that long?"

"I told you—I'm no bum."

"Twelve weeks, okay?"

"Whatever you want."

Twelve weeks, and—what? The truth? Both your parents were murdered, Phoebe, too bad, kid? "In twelve weeks I'll tell you everything."

"Deal, buddy. Unlock the fucking door."

A new woman? Ambiguous. Uncertain. On the surface, things looked good. Phoebe returned to 522 South 43rd Street and prospered, supporting herself through a conglomeration of part-time jobs—McDonald's server, laundromat attendant, grocery bagger. She called Julie every day.

"Sobriety bites the big one, Katz." Phoebe's voice was wobbly but clear. "Sobriety sucks raw eggs."

"Can you hold out?"

"My hands shake. There's a Brillo pad in my mouth. Yeah, I can hold out. Pussycat. Watch me."

According to Bix, Phoebe's transformation was a sham, the deal she'd cut with Julie a farce. According to Bix, they were "walking on eggs." Julie disagreed; Bix didn't know Phoebe as she did. Bix had never peed off a railroad bridge with Phoebe or collaborated with her on bombarding a Fourth of July parade with dead fish. Julie and Phoebe's love would conquer all. It would conquer the Courvoisier Napoleon, shoot the Bacardi bat, run the Gordon's boar to earth; it would defeat Old Grand-Dad, Jack Daniel's, Jim Beam, Johnny Walker...

On Phoebe's birthday, Julie visited 522 South 43rd bearing a bottle of Welch's Nonalcoholic Sparkling White Grape Juice and a stout chocolate layer cake. *Happy Third Week of Recovery*, the compliant clerk at the Village Bakery had squirted onto the icing.

"Know what I *really* want for my birthday?" asked Phoebe, sipping the virginal champagne. Her face seemed deflated; her eyes looked like rusty ball bearings. "I want to pack up H. Rap Brown Bear and move in with my best friend."

"We've got roaches." Julie slashed open the cake with one of the stilettos Phoebe had confiscated during her career as a hooker.

"Yeah." Phoebe devoured *Recovery*. She was dressing in style these days—a green blouse made of the flashiest new silkoids, a gold earring dangling from her left lobe. "I miss 'em."

"We've got my husband."

"He doesn't like me, does he?"

"Bix likes you fine," said Julie. Bix could not stand Phoebe. Yet he would agree, Julie knew. The man was loosening up. "I'll take the boards off the window."

"Great." A new woman. Before, Phoebe would never have wanted the sun.

As spring wafted into Powelton Village, Julie came to realize that ministering was both harder and more satisfying than having a ministry. Saving a friend from rum easily eclipsed saving humankind from nostalgia, especially since the former ambition lay within the possible.

Not that this life could hold her forever. True, there were no overt signs of Revelationism in Philadelphia, no hints that anyone hunted heretics on the American side of the Delaware. Ostensibly the founder of Uncertaintism was as safe at 3411 Baring Avenue as anywhere. But a stark fact remained: Milk's ravenous theocracy was barely seventy miles away, so close that, lying beside her husband at night, Julie imagined she heard the squeal of Ned Shiner's pickup truck hauling dead sinners down the bone-lined expressway.

Bix was no less her patient than Phoebe. Just as her friend might return to the bottle, so might her husband slip into either his traditional nihilism or more recent religiosity. And yet, he seemed to be healing. "You have to understand," he explained one evening during a roach hunt in the kitchen. "Your performance on that Space Tower knocked me out. I was completely unprepared—the South Seas native getting the white man's head cold. Disaster."

"It's all behind us now." Julie removed her shoe, raising it like a hammer.

"Will we *ever* get this behind us? Haven't we been touched by some deep cosmic mystery?"

"I suppose so. Sure."

"I mean, you *did* have powers, you *were* a deity."

Slap, Julie sent a roach to hell. "Cosmic mysteries don't interest me much these days."

"It really helps talking with you, Julie. I think I'm becoming a normal person."

"Know what a normal person has, Bix? A normal person has a job."

Bix squashed a roach with a paper towel. "Job?"

"We could use the money, sweetheart. We could use the damn medical insurance."

Ever since the turn of the century, the Philadelphia Public Schools had been short of English teachers, and Bix the former *Midnight Moon* editor was a shoo-in. The only mandatory credential was American citizenship, a status that everyone caught up in the Jersey secession still technically retained. A week after applying, Bix was deputized to bring "language arts skills" to one hundred and twenty-three eleventh graders at William Penn Senior High School.

He was terrified. The eleventh graders bewildered him. "I never know what they're thinking," he told Julie. "There's too much going on at once. I can't keep track of it."

"Every teacher has that problem."

"They say I'm fat."

"You are fat. I'm proud of you. You've come a long way, Bix. Father Paradox to Mr. Chips."

Public education in America was not following a rigid curriculum that year, progressivism being on the upswing. As far as Bix could tell, only three standards held for everyone on the William Penn faculty: no blood on the floor, no sexual relations with the students, and leave all window shades half-drawn at the end of the day. It was an era of creativity and change, of innovation and relevance—Bix talked incessantly of something called "the curriculum of concerns"—and when Julie suggested he toss away the syllabus and have the students publish a newspaper instead, a rehabilitated and rationalistic *Midnight Moon*, his spherical face glowed. A newspaper! Sure-fire. Fabulous. Jack Ianelli would do the sports column. Rosie Gonzales would write the horoscopes

Julie could barely keep up with the transformation. The man who used to have difficulty loving his own mother had fallen for a bunch of adolescent zotzheads and thugs.

And Phoebe. Talk about idealism, talk about rebirth! Phoebe
now believed in everything—in resuscitated rain forests, lesbian
pride, saved whales, full bellies, empty missile silos. "I have
powers," she liked to say. "I have powers coming out my ears."
She bought a truck, converting it into a kind of traveling soup
kitchen. It consumed her life savings, the full fruit of her years
on the streets, but there it was, parked in the driveway of 3411
Baring Avenue—a used United Parcel van, repainted a bright
shamrock green. The Green Tureen, Phoebe dubbed her soup
kitchen. Love on wheels.

"You should see how these people live," she told Julie and
Bix. "Home is a packing crate, if that. Come with me on Sunday,
Katz. You too, Bix. Plywood City."

"A lumberyard?" asked Bix.

"These people sell their blood," said Phoebe. "They sell their
bodies. Will you come?"

"We'll come," said Julie brightly.

"We'll come," said Bix gloomily. Always this skepticism, this
devout disbelief in Phoebe's recovery. Walking on eggs, he kept
saying.

Plywood City: not a lumberyard, Julie learned that Sunday,
but a West Philly shantytown, its splintery suburbs sprawling for
half a mile between two sidings near 30th Street Station; it was as
if the Penn Central Railroad had erected a theme park, Poverty
Land, and this was the first exhibit. Phoebe drove the Green
Tureen as far into the yard as she could, parking beside a Chesapeake and Ohio refrigerator car, a traveling abattoir whose
hundred slaughtered haunches—Julie imagined them hanging
in the car like subway commuters—could have nourished the
shantytown for a year. Julie and Bix unloaded both serving carts,
outfitting them with charity. Fresh coffee, sugar, milk, oranges,
Hostess powdered doughnuts. Most importantly, Phoebe's
homemade soup, its broth packed with diced carrots and robust
lumps of chicken.

"What they *really* want," said Phoebe, "is for us to hold the
broth and lay on the beer."

"No doubt," said Bix.

"How about you?" asked Julie, uncertain whether Phoebe's
mentioning liquor was good or bad.

"A nice hot cup of Budweiser? I could go for that, sure."

Julie winced convulsively. "It'd kill you."

"Like a bullet," said Bix.

"Where are my parents?" said Phoebe.

"Five more weeks," said Julie. "Thirty-five days."

Phoebe tugged her gold earring so fiercely Julie expected the lobe to rip. "Where are they?"

"Five weeks."

"I must say, Katz, I liked you better divine."

"Thirty-five days."

"Right. Sure. You bet."

Phoebe shrugged and took off, cart rattling along the rocky ballast, soup slopping over the rim of her pot. The old Phoebe would be a handy person to have around now, Julie thought— the crazy, alky Phoebe, the one who would've jimmied open the Chesapeake and Ohio refrigerator car and passed out the meat, Santa's little redistributionist.

Side by side, Julie and Bix started into the town, pushing their cart through the planet's discards, through the olfactory cacophony of tobacco, cabbage, urine, feces, and beer. Zotzheads with three-day beards sat on fifty-five-gallon drums, staring into space, brains running on empty. Naked preadolescent boys with muddy feet urinated against the sides of their homes, painting the plywood with curlicues. A portable radio blared Gospel music. By Phoebe's account, the majority of Plywood City's inhabitants were refugees of one sort or another, people for whom cold, cruel homelessness was preferable to their colder and crueler domesticities: their abusive husbands, molesting parents, fleabag orphanages, hellish reformatories. The second largest category comprised the winos and zotzheads, forever in need of transportation to Madison Memorial for detox or to the West Philadelphia Free Clinic for general repairs. Then, of course, there were the itinerant mental cases, a manageable group provided they remembered to take the free chlorpromazine that Dr. Daniel Singer, an iconoclastic shrink from Penn, dispensed from the back of his station wagon, Dr. Singer's soup kitchen for psychotics.

Each in his own way, Julie sensed, the inhabitants of Plywood City hated their benefactors. Charity was not justice. Let Julie, Bix, and Phoebe give out food all day, fine, but come nightfall who had to stay in this cesspool and who got to return to Powelton Village? Nor was their resentment wholly unrequited, for Julie could not exactly say she loved these people, could not even say she liked them. Yet here she was, paying her brother homage: hell below, Plywood City above, morphine below, chicken soup above. Here she was, dipping her ladle into the soup, pouring the soup into plastic cups, passing the cups to a narrow Malaysian woman, a puffy, rheumic-eyed Pakistani man, a raffish Puerto Rican boy...

"I wish she went to A.A.," said Bix.

"Phoebe? She's staying sober."

"A.A.'s the thing, I hear."

"Not her style." Ladle into pot, soup into cup. "She's been dry seven weeks." Cup into the mistrustful hands of a crinkled old man with a gray tumbling beard, a rummy Ezekiel. "Our deal's working."

"Seven weeks," Bix echoed, sneering. "I've been looking into this business. You don't make deals with alcoholics, Julie. You maneuver them into rehab programs. Sometimes an alky'll go through three or four before she gets well."

"That's one approach, certainly."

"Seven weeks is zilch. It's borrowed time. The disease will foreclose, always does. I've been reading about it."

"Phoebe has lots of willpower."

"Willpower has nothing to do with it. She's feel things she's never felt before. She's got to find something bigger than herself."

"Like what? God?" Ladlie into pot. Soup into cup. "Forget it."

"Like A.A. Until then, honey, we're walking on eggs."

"You keep saying that."

"Really. Eggs. Crunch."

Julie's bowels tightened, a gastrointestinal Gordian knot, hard, insoluble. "Did I ever tell you what happens after death?"

"You're changing the subject. Eggs, Julie."

"Everybody's damned," she explained. Cup into a hag's leathery hands, a stringy-haired creature right out of the Brothers Grimm. "Earth is as good as it gets."

"You have any pepper?" asked the hag.

"Next time," said Bix.

"My ass," said the hag.

"I promise," said Bix.

Julie could practically feel the eggs underfoot. She could almost hear the crunch.

On the morning of July 24, 2012, Julie awoke possessed by a conclusion so sharp and certain it felt like the climax of a dream. Encircling her husband's bearish body with both arms, she told him the time had come for a new generation.

"Huh?"

Down in hell it had been a mere notion, back on the garbage scow a simple whim. But now... "I want a baby."

"A what?" Bix drew away, breaking her embrace.

"I want a baby happening inside me." She did. Oh, God of physics, yes. Let her mother procreate planets and black holes; her own ambitions would be sated by a fetus. "You know—one of those protoplasmic blobs that grows up to be an orthodontist or something."

"Got anybody in mind for the father?"

She untied the drawstring of Bix's pajamas. "Some of them become English teachers."

"Language arts."

"Language arts." Julie thought: A blob, a baby, a squalling organic ball chained to her leg, dragging her down. Scary. But Georgina had faced it. Her *father*, for Christ's sake, had faced it, all alone in his lighthouse, raising his problem child. "The clock's ticking, husband. Burn your condoms. Let's have a kid."

"Really?" Of all things, he seemed ready to cry. "Honestly?"

She kissed his lovely lower chin and slipped off her nightgown. "Honestly."

"I want to be a regular guy, Julie. I really do."

He had a fine erection, angled like a flagpole. She rolled toward him, all her lushness, her big arms and thick black hair and irresistible thighs. Her throat thickened. A regular guy, the father of her child. She felt like a beautiful planet, and now here was Bix, becoming her axis, south to north, and when she climaxed she indeed experienced the proper Newtonian rotation, a wild swing into her own miraculous flesh.

Almost forty: a perfectly safe age for a pregnancy, but she still resolved to get herself checked out. Her baby must have every advantage, the best preconceptual care. Studying the gynecological listings, she had trouble deciding between a classy-sounding Swede within walking distance and a Jew in Center City. If a girl: Rita. If a boy: Murray, little Murray Constantine-Katz.

She hiked over to 40th and Market and took the bus downtown.

Dr. Hyman Lefkowitz's clinic was the most fecund place Julie had ever seen, its hallways lined with photographs of drooling, toothless infants, its waiting room jammed with back issues of *Parenting*. Swollen and wobbly, expectant mothers came and went. They all seemed astonishingly beautiful: fecund Madonnas, knocked-up Aphrodites.

The nurse took a dozen sonograms of Julie's baby-making organs. Phoebe should have come, Julie decided. She imagined her friend extrapolating from this technology. You know what we've got here, Katz, we've got a whole new kind of smut, we've got a pornography of the internal.

"I'll be frank with you," said Dr. Lefkowitz as he ushered Julie into his office.

He held up a sonogram. Fear rushed into Julie's stomach like cold chicken soup.

She said, "Oh?"

"This news isn't good."

"Not good?" Uterine cancer—it had to be. A true pornography of the internal.

"Your ovaries . . ."

"What?"

"They aren't there." The doctor's thick glasses gave him Peter Lorre's popping eyes. "You don't have any."

"Not there? What do you mean *not there*? Everybody has ovaries."

"You don't. It's as if they'd been"—Lefkowitz's eyes came at her like headlights—"stolen."

And Julie thought: A bird. A luminous bird, ripped from its perch atop her heart, its beak clamped around an olive branch. An olive branch—or so it had seemed to her blurry vision when Wyvern had ablated her divinity.

Not an olive branch. Never was. Something else. Two moist, pulpy stalks, the fallopian tubes of God's only daughter. Wyvern . . . Satan . . . evil incarnate . . . deception made flesh.

Julie pleaded, "Can you fix me?" A photograph sat on Lefkowitz's desk, framed in K mart gold. The doctor. His buxom wife.

Three perfect, shining children; boy, girl, baby. She hated them all, the children especially, the baby most especially, so smugly present, so cockily there. "Can you do a transplant?"

"Sorry."

"Isn't this supposed to be the future? Isn't this 2012? I want a transplant."

Lefkowitz smiled wistfully. "Science doesn't have all the answers."

She thought: You mean we don't have all the science, asshole.

All the way home, the city tormented her. Pregnant women shadowed her like KGB moles. The number 31 bus reviled her with its ads for day-care centers and well-baby clinics. She alighted near the Sundance Nursery School. Toddlers roamed the sandboxes like cruel mocking dwarves; birds chirped everywhere, a million little birdshit factories. Reaching 3411 Baring, she dragged her sterile middle-aged body up the steps and stumbled into the living room. You'll be getting a full life, that malevolent angel had told her, that creature who held the patent on lies.

A scream sawed through the air like a violin note played by a maniac.

A Phoebe scream. Type one: despair.

Julie ran. No, God, wait, Mother, this is the day I find out I'm infertile, not the day Phoebe falls off the wagon.

Wrong. The window stood open, yet a dense malty cloud hung in the air, as if Phoebe had washed the walls with beer. On the vanity, five empty Budweiser bottles encircled H. Rap Brown Bear. Phoebe lay slumped in her chair, gripping the sixth. She was, as usual, well dressed: a clean white blouse, a madras skirt of the sort popular among the Powelton Village gypsies. A box of kitchen matches, half open, lay on the segment of skirt bridging her thighs.

Julie felt as betrayed as on the day Bix ordered her out of his sewer. "Phoebe, how *could* you, how *could* you?"

Phoebe quieted herself with a swallow of Bud. "Dead," she announced, voice thick and lumpy, eyes small and dull as pearl onions.

"How *could* you?"

"She's dead, isn't she?" Phoebe struck a kitchen match, alternately moaning and giggling. "You think Plywood City doesn't have any Jersey immigrants? You think they don't all know what happened to the poor old lesbo who ran the Smile Shop?"

Julie studied the evil bottles. Bud, Bud, Bud, Bud, Bud. "That's not all. Your *father's* dead too."

"My father? Dead?"

"I met him in hell."

"Dead? *Dead?* You shithead—for *this* you string me along? *This?* 'Wow, Phoebe, guess what, you're a goddamn orphan'?"

Julie grimaced, making her S-scar bulge. What was driving her, some sadistic urge, some mean-spirited wish to maximize her friend's pain? No, in the end Phoebe would profit from this news, provided it came embellished with a benign untruth. "Listen, your father wants revenge. Really. 'Tell Phoebe to get that bastard'—his last words to me."

"Revenge? Huh? *What* bastard?" Phoebe blew out the match.

"Your father died when Billy Milk bombed the Preservation Institute."

Phoebe struck another match. "Milk? Milk? I can't kill *Milk*. He's the fucking poobah grandpastor." The flame skittered down the stick and snuffed itself against her thumb. She pulled back her skirt, burying the matchbox in the folds.

"You *can* kill Milk."

"I can't even kill myself. Maybe this time, though." Phoebe struck a third match, inserting the flame between her dark thighs.

"Hey, you'll get burned."

A coarse hiss, a cobra's gasp—but not from Phoebe's throat. Lower, where the match was.

Julie rushed forward.

And suddenly she saw it. Jesus Christ. Jesus Christ in hell. She curled her fingers around the terrible stalk. Of all things, she thought of "Heaven Help You"—how she'd always counseled the despondent that, if they truly saw no other option, they should at least contact the National Hemlock Society and do it right. Hadn't Phoebe read that one? Certain prescription drugs were quick and efficient. A plastic bag cinched around your neck served well. But never this. Oh, God, never this.

Bix arrived just in time to see Julie yank the stick of dynamite out of her friend's vagina. Ah, leave it to Phoebe to expand her husband's horizons—even the Plywood City derelicts couldn't offer him anything quite so baroque. "No!" he screamed.

She had only to grab the sputtering fuse, the pain a small price...

No fuse. "Christ!"

She ran to the open window. A quick sky-hook from her old days on the courts and—

Midair, a thunderclap and a blinding blast, lashing against Julie's outstretched arm, turning the window into a tidal wave of pulverized wood and shattered glass.

She looked at Phoebe. Bix. The teddy bear. The corral of brown bottles. And then, before the nausea, the jetting blood, the unspeakable pain, Julie saw in an instant of brilliant stroboscopic clarity that she no longer had a right hand.

CHAPTER 15

◆   ◆   ◆

Designed by a pious and literal-minded architect, the new Seraph of Mercy Hospital on City Avenue looked, when viewed from the clouds, like an angel. An oval driveway sat poised above the administration building like a halo. A maternity ward occupied the hospital's midriff. The two main wards sloped gently away from the central block and, arcing sharply, simultaneously enclosed restful green parks and gave the seraph its wings.

Julie Katz and Phoebe Sparks ended up in opposite wings—in the amputee unit and the alcoholism clinic respectively. They communicated through get-well cards from the hospital's gift shop.

"Dear Sheila, I'm sorry," Phoebe scrawled beneath the printed doggerel accompanying Correggio's *Assumption of the Virgin*. "I'm so fucking sorry."

"You *should* be," Julie wrote back beneath Piero della Francesca's *The Discovery and Proving of the True Cross*. Her left-handed printing was childlike, chaotic.

"Dear Sheila, tell them to cut off my hand and sew it on you," Phoebe wrote beside Dürer's *The Four Horsemen of the Apocalypse*.

"Too late for that," Julie replied next to Signorelli's *The Damned Cast into Hell*.

"Dear Sheila, they have A.A. meetings here four times a day. I go every afternoon."

"Go four times a day."

"Bix said the same thing."

"Listen to him."

Bix. Dear Bix. But for Bix she'd be dead. The ride to Madison Memorial was lodged in Julie's brain like a fossil in granite: Phoebe pushing H. Rap Brown Bear against the faucet that was her best friend's wrist; the question mark of bone protruding from the stump; both women screaming uncontrollably. And throughout the nightmare—her husband at the wheel of the Tureen, moaning and weeping and shouting over and over that he loved her, he loved her.

"Feeling better?" Bix asked, setting a vase of pale, dispirited roses on the nightstand. For the third time that week, he'd snuck in before visiting hours.

"No," said Julie. Roses: quite touching, actually. Her husband was truly becoming normal.

"You don't like Seraph?" Bix had opposed the transfer to Seraph of Mercy—she's not Catholic, he kept telling the doctors at Madison, leave her here—but they insisted that only at Seraph would Julie receive what they called a holistic approach to limb loss. "They aren't treating you well?"

"I like it fine." The Madison doctors were indeed right about Seraph. It was nourishing and spiritual. Sun-drenched rooms, glowing portraits of saints, spry wimpled nuns waddling around like little organic churches, soothing the city's legless, footless, armless, handless. "It's not this place. It's not the hand."

"It's the ovaries, isn't it? I wish I could comfort you. I wish I knew how."

"Not one of your language arts skills, huh?" she said with more bitterness than she'd intended. She rubbed her nose with her bandaged stump. By some theories she was closer to transcendence now, less flesh dragging down her spirit, but instead she felt wholly corporeal, a broken piece of matter mourning its lost symmetry. "Nobody can comfort me. God couldn't comfort me. Have you ever wanted to be dead?"

"Don't talk like that. Please." Bix lifted her stump to his lips and kissed it. Julie hated her wound: its itch, its ooze, the stinking gauze. For the sake of a safe closure, the surgeon had sacrificed most of her wrist, debriding the ragged tissue, recessing ulna and radius, and tucking the skin inward, so that her suture looked like a smile on a drunken catfish. "I saw Phoebe this morning," her husband said. "She's becoming a real A.A. demon."

"After blowing off your best friend's hand, you start rethinking your priorities." Odd how she kept imagining the hand as an intact object, lying in the alley beside 3411 Baring like a prop from one of Roger Worth's horror movies, a Beast with Five Fingers, a Hand of Orlac, when in fact it had been mashed beyond recognition, the finger bones scattered like bits of clam shell strewn across Absecon Beach.

An elfin, lab-coated young man appeared in the doorway.

"Kevin from Prosthetics," he announced with fake glee. "How are we today, Mrs. Constantine?"

"My thumb hurts. The one back in West Philly."

Kevin gave her off-hours visitor a sharp, disgruntled stare.

"It's okay—I'm a patient here too." Bix pointed to his crotch. "Just had a new set installed."

"My husband." Julie gestured with her fishmouth suture. The hand she'd lost was no beauty, its palm a mass of scar tissue, but it'd been a hundred times more eloquent than this.

Kevin dragged forward a cart on which sat a gauntleted glove of rubber and steel. "*Voilà.*" He swirled his open palms above the device, as if attempting to levitate it. "Programmable. Voice-activated. User-controllable temperatures. Fluent in English, Spanish, French, Korean, and Japanese. Molly, wave."

The hand reared up on its gauntlet and, animated by the kind of blind striving Julie had previously observed only in penises, flexed its palm.

"How am I supposed to afford this shit?" Mentally, Julie gagged. Molly? *Molly*? Jesus.

"We're reviewing your husband's medical insurance," said Kevin. "Far as we can tell, Molly's all yours. Soon you'll know her like"—he issued a quick, snorty laugh—"the back of your hand." He parked the cart beside Julie's bed and gently slipped the gauntlet over her stump. The device felt soft and warm, an incubator in which tiny, wet-lipped creatures grew. "Go ahead—try her out."

What an unsatisfactory century, the twenty-first. A million high-tech hands, but not one robot ovary. She guided the ridiculous machine to within grabbing distance of the roses. "Get me a flower," she demanded.

Nothing.

"Say her name," Kevin urged.

"*Molly*, right?"

"Right."

"Molly, get me a flower."

A glass eye rose from the hand's dorsal side like a periscope from a submarine, swiveling slightly. The thumb and index finger parted, then closed around a rose stem.

A shudder crept through Julie's spine. A dance had just occured, but who had done the dancing? "Molly, drop it." Her new fingers parted, sending the rose floating into her lap.

"Just be careful nothing happens to her," Kevin admonished. "One to a customer, right? Get her insured, is my advice."

In the days that followed, Julie grew increasingly fond of Molly, as if the machine were a sponge or a starfish from her old underwater petting zoo. Indeed, at times Molly seemed the sole island of competence and warmth in an otherwise pointless universe—literal warmth, for the variable-temperature feature meant Molly could function as a kind of vibrating hot-water bottle, a ninety-degree caress ready to be applied anytime, anyplace.

Disembodied, the hand proved equally useful. Molly was a tireless servant, forever crawling around the hospital room in compliance with Julie's whims. "Molly, fetch me that *TV Guide*." "Molly, dial Phoebe's room." "Molly, rub my back." "Molly, turn the page."

Turn the page, for Julie was at it again, her old obsession, the mother quest, the God odyssey. But things were worse than ever. According to the pile of books and scientific journals Bix had smuggled in from the Philadelphia Free Library, the God of physics was not simply outside timespace, she was outside timespace's outsideness. In the April 2011 issue of *Nature*, for example, the renowned particle physicist Christopher Holmes, extrapolating from the new Theory of Imaginary Time, had postulated a universe having no boundary or edge, no beginning or end—a universe in which a Supreme Being would have nothing to do.

"Molly, get me that other one. The blue cover."

Carl Basmajian's *God and the Biologists*—for maybe she'd been conducting her search on too lofty a level. Maybe God lay manifest in the lily, the butterfly, or the subtly engineered optics of a baby's eyeball. By invoking the classic argument-from-design—

no watch without a watchmaker, no eye without an eyemaker—
Julie might lure her mother into reality after all.

She read Basmajian. The wonders of nature, she learned,
from wing of bee to sonar of bat to eyeball of baby, were not so
much perfect machines as adequate contraptions. If nature be-
spoke a mind, it was a confused and inchoate one, a mind inca-
pable of locating the optic nerve on the correct side of the retina,
a mind unable to accomplish much of anything without resort to
jerry-building and extinction.

"Molly, I want *Primordial Clay* over there."

Molly didn't move.

"Molly—*Primordial Clay*."

Something was wrong. A short-circuit, a busted silicon chip,
something—for instead of obeying, Molly marched across the
stiff white bedsheets, seized the pencil with which Julie did the
Philadelphia Inquirer crossword puzzle each morning, and, returning, began writing on the endpapers of *God and the Biologists*.

"Molly, I said to get *Primordial Clay*."

JULIE, ARE YOU THERE? the hand scribbled.

"Stop it, Molly."

I'M NOT MOLLY.

"What?"

The hand underlined: NOT MOLLY.

"Huh?" Not Molly? "Don't joke with me, Molly." But this was
no joke, Julie sensed, no fraud from some neo-Boardwalk chan-
neler quack. Not Molly. A spirit, then? The spirit of Murray
Katz? The spirit of primordial clay? Perhaps even . . . *her*, the big-
shot, the Spirit of Spirits?

"Mother?" Was it possible? At long last? *"Mother?"*

NO, SISTER, the hand wrote. SORRY.

"Jesus?"

JESUS, the hand wrote.

"Really? Jesus?"

EM EMI, the hand wrote.

Odd. For all the wonders Julie had experienced in her life,
calling into the air and being answered by a disembodied hand
still made her extremely queasy. "I miss you, brother," Julie
called. "I'm so depressed."

The hand underlined: SORRY.

"It's not your fault."

I WANT TO WARN YOU, the hand wrote.

"About what?"

PLYWOOD CITY.

"It's not safe?"

RIGHT.

"I should stop going?"

A DANGEROUS PLACE, Jesus wrote.

"I'd hate to stop going. They need me."

THEY NEED YOU, Jesus agreed.

"My chicken soup."

Jesus underlined: RIGHT. He circled: A DANGEROUS PLACE.

"So I shouldn't go?"

Jesus circled: THEY NEED YOU.

"I know. It's almost winter."

SOUP, BLANKETS, HEAT, Jesus wrote.

"It's dangerous, though? I'll stay away if you want."

Molly splayed her fingers. The pencil rolled down the end-papers of *God and the Biologists* and disappeared into the bed-sheets.

"Jesus?" Julie placed the pencil in Molly's grasp. "Answer me. Should I stay away?"

Nothing.

"Tell me what to do."

But the hand had stopped writing.

"Dear Sheila, I'm smitten," Phoebe wrote inside a Seraph of Mercy get-well card—Tintoretto's *Christ Before Pilate*—two days before she and Julie were scheduled to be released. "Irene Abbot, a homeless alky. It's love, Sheila."

"Now you have something to live for," Julie wrote back.

"I want her to move in. We have great news, Sheila. The kind of thing you announce to your oldest and dearest friend over a Chinese meal."

In her eccentric sentimentality, Phoebe selected the Golden Wok, the same restaurant to which they'd dragged her the night she almost shot herself. All during dinner, the litany of Alcoholics Anonymous—one day at a time, count your bless-ings, live and let live—rolled from Irene Abbot's thin lips with the regularity and fervor of one whose entire brain has become a warehouse for clichés. How could Phoebe have fallen for such a dull person, this pale, skinny, talkative lesbian who looked like a victim of leeches?

"The main thing to realize is that I've given myself over to a Higher Power," Irene told Julie as the fortune cookies arrived. "God got me off the bottle"—she tossed Phoebe a coy little smile—"with a little help from Phoebe Sparks and A.A."

"How nice," Julie grunted. God got Irene off the bottle. Maybe so, Mother. Good for you, Mother.

Phoebe said, "You should come to an A.A. meeting sometime, Julie. You'd learn a lot about life."

"I'm afraid I know more about life than I care to." Julie instructed Molly to seize her black dragon tea, then lifted the cup to her mouth. Her brother was a fine man, but his recent coyness—*a dangerous place, they need you*—was as irritating as it was uncharacteristic.

Not only could Seraph supply hands, they did exemplary work with lushes. Phoebe hadn't looked so healthy since she was ten. Her spiraled hair glowed; her dusky complexion had the tight expectancy of a trampoline. "People are completely honest at A.A.," she said. "'Hello, I'm Phoebe, and I'm an alcoholic.' No lies."

"I could've used an organization like that. 'Hello, I'm Julie, and I'm an incarnation.'"

"You're not very religious, are you?" said Irene.

"I'm more into gravity."

Phoebe snapped open a fortune cookie and drew out the paper slip. "It says, 'You're about to tell an old friend some great news.'"

"Does it really?" asked Irene.

"Headline stuff," said Phoebe. "Bigger than 'I Was Bigfoot's Surrogate Mother.'"

Julie chuckled without meaning to. "Bigger than 'Scientists Prove Aliens Wrote U.S. Constitution'?"

"Bigger. Me and Irene, we're getting...what's the word, sweetie?"

"Married," said Irene.

"Married," echoed Phoebe, winking as she tapped Julie's wedding band.

"You really love each other, don't you?" said Julie, forcing a smile.

"Is that okay?" asked Phoebe. "You're not jealous, are you?"

"I'm not jealous." Of course Julie was jealous. Who wouldn't be? For the first time in years, the real Phoebe was back, and Julie had to share her with a boor.

"I need this, Katz. You'll always be my best buddy, but in the end only a drunk can help a drunk."

"Marriage is just the half of it," said Irene. "We're hoping to have a baby."

"A baby," said Phoebe.

Julie clenched her teeth, her fist. Her dredged and damaged uterus spasmed with envy. "Which one of you's growing the *shlong*?"

"I had myself checked out," said Phoebe. "I'm fertile as a cheerleader. All we need is some pixie dust and—pow!" She brushed Julie's existing palm. "Listen, buddy, I know about your ovaries, really shitty, but this is going to be everybody's kid— mine, Irene's, Bix's, *yours*. We'll never tell her who the mother is."

Julie opened her cookie, retrieved her fortune. *You are careful and systematic in your business arrangements*. She must be happy for Phoebe. Must be. "It says, 'Your best friend is about to get pregnant, and you are very, very happy for her.'"

"Really?" asked Irene. "It says that?"

"Really?" asked Phoebe. "You're happy?"

"Of course I am." Julie felt a disembodied ache in her right thumb. She rubbed Molly's. "And the pixie dust? You have anyone in mind?"

"Uh-huh. Somebody I always admired."

"Who?"

"A good man. One of the best."

They could have waited a few nights, but patience had never been Phoebe's strong suit, so they went over to Penn right after dinner. Breaking into the Preservation Institute proved a mere matter of explaining the problem to Molly and watching the various locks crumble under her steel grip.

The three women scurried down a corridor suffused with sixty-watt gloom, its walls lined with three tiers of squat steel doors, until at last Julie found Pop's alias, *Four Thirty-two*, etched on a brass plate above the handle. She opened the door—a blast of cold air, like a corpse sneezing—and slid the frosted drawer forward. Test tubes jammed the rack, their identification tags stiff with ice. Evidently the Institute had gotten someone to pick through the rubble after the Longport explosion, excavating the sperm canisters, for the stockpile covered her father's entire career. He'd been a faithful subject, one shot per month for over twenty years.

History could be read here, as in the concentric rings of a tree stump. Pop had first contributed on March 14, 1965. The telling gap began in December of 1973 and ran through June of 1976, when the Institute had reopened at Penn. December: her month of conception, then. Julie did the arithmetic, December to her birthday: nine months. She'd been a full-term baby. When God went with flesh, there were no shortcuts.

"This would be our best bet." Julie lifted the most recent donation away, presenting it to Phoebe like a trophy.

"She's got your nose, Julie. I like her already."

"Nose?" said Irene.

Phoebe passed the sperm to her lover. "Here, sweetie. Let's go have ourselves a bookworm."

A DANGEROUS PLACE.

THEY NEED YOU.

And Julie thought: I'll go.

Although Phoebe hedged her bets by dividing the sample into two equal halves, she succeeded on the first application, a mere matter of using a Sanyo Improved Urine-Testing Kit to determine her precise day of ovulation, then applying Murray to herself with a turkey baster. Just like Georgina, Phoebe kept pointing out. Just like Mom.

"I wish you'd told me about this," said Bix upon learning Phoebe was pregnant. "I live here too, you know."

"This place needs a baby," said Julie.

"This place needs a roach fumigation and a shower that works. Babies are like kittens, Julie, they grow into something much more sinister. Can you imagine the amount of chaos a baby will bring to our lives, can you even *imagine*?"

"She'll be outnumbered. Four to one. We're all going to raise her."

"Not me."

"Once she arrives, you'll fall for her, I just know it. You'll take her to school, show your students what babies look like."

"Far too many of my students know what babies look like."

"Don't rain on this particular parade, Bix Constantine. Not on this one. Don't."

Humanity did not have all the science, but by 2012 it did have a simple way for a pregnant woman to learn her baby's sex within seven weeks of conception. Go to Dr. Lefkowitz's clinic, get your womb sonogrammed, and a minute later a technician named Bob announces the either/or result.

"It's a boy," Bob said.

"It's a boy!" Phoebe screamed, running deliriously through the house. "I've got a boy growing inside me!" she shouted to Julie, Irene, and Bix.

A boy. The news won Julie over completely. A boy, a nascent Murray Jacob Katz—oh, the wondrous stories she'd tell her little brother about his pop. "Can we call him Murray?"

"Little Murray, eh? Little Murray Sparks?" Phoebe rolled the syllables across her tongue, testing them. "Sure, honey. Absolutely. Little Murray."

A perfect warmth moved through Julie, clear to her steel fingertips. "And he'll really be as much mine as yours?"

"Girl Scout's honor. He'll love us all equally."

While nothing in her past history indicated that this middle-aged alcoholic, dynamite thief, and retired prostitute would take expectant motherhood seriously, that is exactly what Phoebe did. She followed Lefkowitz's advice religiously, giving up coffee, wolfing down vitamins, and daily inserting a kind of vaginal suppository known to prevent miscarriages. Although she planned to have the baby at home—"the natural way," as she put it, "like a goddamn cave woman," as Bix put it—she readily agreed that Bix and Irene should rush her off to Madison Memorial the minute things got too natural for her own good.

Phoebe's pregnancy filled the house like flower fragrance, penetrating every crack and wormhole, oiling the wainscoting with its sweet fecund ooze. Her face glowed like brown porcelain, her voice grew mellow, her small breasts swelled. Prodded by Georgina's pagan blood, she took to strolling naked through their azalea-choked conservatory, thrusting her abdomen toward the windows, letting Little Murray feel November's diamond sun.

And yet, beneath the earth mother's crust rumbled an earlier Phoebe, Julie felt—the louder, angrier, wilder one. "Something's eating you," Julie asserted during one of Phoebe's sun-worship sessions.

"True."

"Is it hard staying sober?"

"It's a bitch and a half staying sober." Phoebe patted Little Murray. "That's not it." Stretched and squeezed by the pregnancy, her navel had become as flat as the valve on a basketball. "My dad expects me to shoot Billy Milk."

"No, Phoebe. That was just something I made up."

"You made it up?"

"So you'd want to go on living."

"Oh." Phoebe sounded mildly disappointed. "Did you *really* meet Dad? Is he good-looking? Smart like me?"

Julie nodded. "Good-looking. Smart."

"Proud of his African blood?"

"Oh, yes. A terrific father, evidently. He had four sons."

"And a daughter. A daughter who should shoot Billy Milk."

"No, *I* said that. Not him. Me."

"I don't care who thought of it—it's a great idea either way. Milk even has Mom's bones, doesn't he? Know what I'd like to do, Katz? I'd like to slip over to Jersey right now, shoot the bastard, and bring those bones back home. Right now."

"Don't talk crazy, Phoebe. It's bad for the baby."

"The Sermon on the Mount—it never ends for you, does it? If somebody kicks your right buttock, turn the other cheek."

"Settle down, Phoebe."

"Once you've got somebody's bones, you can give her a funeral. A major production, with eulogies and flowers and all that shit. It wasn't easy raising me."

"I know. I was there."

"Ever notice what a great word 'revenge' is, Katz, how it throws your lips apart like you're about to blow a lion?" Phoebe threw her lips apart. "*Revenge*, honey. Let's go shoot Milk."

"Hey, you want a funeral? We'll do a funeral. Fine. But stop talking crazy."

"I want a funeral."

And so, the following Sunday, the four inhabitants of 3411 Baring gathered in the backyard beneath a sycamore tree, its leaves aglow with their incipient deaths: strawberry red, pumpkin orange. The funeral began with Phoebe addressing the ground, assuring Georgina her daughter was off the sauce for good, telling her a grandson was on the way. Irene said a few banalities to the effect that anyone who could raise so fine a person as Phoebe had surely found a favored room in God's many mansions. Bix, self-defrocked priest of Uncertaintism, speculated aloud that Georgina had fused with the Universal Wave Function, ashes to ashes, quarks to quarks.

"Amen," said Julie.

At last came the burial itself, Bix and Julie grabbing their spades, chopping a hole in the taut November earth, and depositing a yard-sale hope chest filled with a joy buzzer, a whoopie cushion, a swatch of latex dog vomit, and a fully functional pair of windup chattering teeth.

A dangerous place, the hand had said. But the planet kept circling, tilting, carrying Plywood City away from the sun, and now came December, the worst in memory, crashing into Philadelphia like a frigid meteor, dunning it with ice, snow, and record lows. The Green Tureen stayed on call around the clock, fighting the incipient winter with soup. To Milk's church, no doubt, Julie and her followers had always been avatars of Satan, and now they were indeed Lucifers, bringers of light, bearers of incandescence: Sterno heat, Coleman heat, off-brand heat, any source would do.

Just as Pop used to comb flea markets and thrift stores for books, so Julie now frequented such places in quest of used fur coats, second-hand blankets, castoff woolen mittens, hand-me-down ski caps, and recycled insulation, for the heat once brought needed to be preserved and nurtured. And if the coats, blankets, and mittens failed to appear in the bargain spots, then Julie would visit the retail stores, paying when she could, shoplifting when she couldn't—Julie Katz, the thermodynamic Robin Hood, robbing the warm to give to the cold.

"A dangerous place," Julie muttered to herself as she and Mohammed Chaudry nailed a swatch of Corning insulation to the north wall of his family's shanty. The stuff was pink, fluffy, and laden with glass, like some corrupt form of cotton candy.

In the far corner, Mohammed's eleven-month-old daughter issued a sound somewhere between a moan and a gasp. The baby's teeth chattered like the windup novelty they'd buried at Georgina's funeral; Julie could hear the tiny clicks.

"I shouldn't be here," she whispered, the words buried by the whacks of her claw hammer. She enjoyed the feel of the hammer, its unambiguous utility and steely balance. Her brother, too, knew his way around tools.

But this particular night, she realized, none of it would be enough. "Zero degrees exactly," said the sprightly young voice on Julie's portable radio. "The WPIX Weatherwatch Team predicts twenty below by dawn." A can of Sterno wouldn't protect the Chaudry baby tonight, nor would a garage-sale comforter or a flea-market snowsuit. Forget warm milk. Forget these feeble chunks of fiberglass.

Julie liked Mohammed Chaudry, refugee from the CIA's recent and wildly successful attempt to reinstate a shahdom in Iran. He made his way in the world collecting scrap metal and redeeming it for fifty cents a pound, the tin cans of wrath, except Mohammed wasn't Pa Joad, he wasn't the deserving poor. He stole. He thought the world was owned by Jews. He talked, half seriously, of assassinating the secretary of state. Mohammed's plausibility, that is what Julie liked about him, his lack of any uncommon virtues, and when she resolved that night to give him something more than Corning insulation, she saw it not as charity but as justice, not as his deserts but as his due.

Justice served, she headed into the snow-swept dawn toward the Green Tureen, the sepulchral boxcars to her right, the frozen shantytown to her left. Snowflakes mashed against her parka like soft-bodied insects. She yawned, long and hugely, her mouth filling with the miniature crystals. Next stop, the all-night Superfresh at 35th and Spring Garden. The Tureen was out of coffee, sugar, oranges, everything. She didn't want to go. She wanted to drive straight home and make furious love to her husband.

A sudden sound, reverberant, like a bowling ball colliding with steel pins. Julie turned. The massive metal door of a New York Central boxcar slid back, and even before the dark figures poured out she knew something ungodly had been set loose. And then, as the policemen charged through the storm, her heart, prophetic pump, drummed the full truth: Circus. "Get out of here!" she screamed into the cold blaze of their flashlights. "Leave me alone!"

There were over a dozen, decked out in globular riot helmets and green armor, a swarm of malevolent grasshoppers. Their captain, a tall, coarse-skinned man whose handlebar mustache flared from beneath his nose like antlers, marched forward wielding a Mauser military pistol. "The sacred river will burn you like acid," he declared, raising his visor, "and by that sign we shall know you."

"This is American soil," Julie snarled. "Let me see your passports."

"Brother Michael, show the woman our passports." The captain's syllables emerged as palpable clouds, words made flesh.

A stumpy, pimple-faced sergeant approached—Brother Michael, evidently—brandishing not passports but handcuffs.

He clamped one manacle around Julie's left wrist.

He whipped the other through empty air.

"Hey, she's only got one hand!" Brother Michael sounded bewildered and hurt. "Somebody stole her hand! Where's your hand?"

Quite true, no hand, no Molly. Molly of the hot circuits, Molly the oven with five fingers, now permanently installed in the Chaudrys' shanty. Not a loan, not even a gift. A sacrifice, rather, the penny from the pauper. She could hear Bix say: But Julie, it's not insured, we can't get another, why'd you give it away?

"Then chain her to yourself," ordered the captain.

Done. Tethered. Trapped. A dangerous place. The frigid metal gnawed Julie's left wrist.

The captain's Mauser prodded her to the end of the siding, past the Green Tureen, past a dark brooding chemical car sitting on the tracks like a shipment of liquid hate. "I have my rights!" Julie insisted. Beyond the bumper lay an unassuming Tastykake delivery truck, fleecy with snow. "Where're you taking me?" she demanded. The sergeant climbed into the passenger seat, pulling Julie in beside him. Suffocating clouds of sugar drifted into her nostrils. "I'm an American citizen!" The captain got behind the wheel. "Let me go!"

As the Tastykake truck pulled onto Market Street and headed toward the Delaware, Julie wept. From fear, naturally. From regret and anger. From self-pity, loneliness, uncertainty. But most of all from her sudden realization that her true fortune-cookie destiny read, *You will miss seeing your second brother come into the world.*

CHAPTER 16

♦ ♦ ♦

Zipping up his stark-white neoprene wetsuit, Billy Milk strode past the eternally fecund Tree of Life, scrambled down the bank, and waded into the River of Christ's Return, its bubbling currents rushing from the northern creeks straight through the city and onward to the sea. Exactly as the Book of Revelation required, the tree grew "on either side of the river," its mammoth trunk arcing across the canal like a footbridge, a miracle predicated on the existence of root systems at both ends. Among God's gifts to the year 2012 was the biotechnology required to fulfill Scripture.

Although the baptisms were less popular than the burnings, Billy's flock still attended faithfully. Over three hundred believers lined the riverbank while another hundred sat atop the tree trunk, their bright faces peering between boughs laden with golden apples. But was it sheer love of God that brought them here, wondered Billy, or did they come because, at least once during each such gathering, their grandpastor's phantom eye looked beneath the skin of a supposed convert to reveal the wormy guts of a closet Uncertaintist? "Heretic!" Billy would shout. "Let God and the Circus have their way with you!" Whereupon the crowd would go wild.

Most of them. There were always those who misinterpreted the New Jersey Inquisition, those who found it unloving or even unscriptural. Billy had learned to live with such judgments. Equally false readings had attended his attack on Atlantic City.

Reaching the sandbar, Billy mounted the submerged slope and turned. A full house, but no Timothy. Doubtless the archshepherd was still on his penance retreat, still sitting naked in the frozen muck under Brigantine Bridge. Billy's inner vision displayed his boy's ordeal, the ice sealing Timothy's eyes and lips, December's malign winds lashing his flesh. You raise a blind son. You tell him about Jesus, feed him oats and bran, tuck him in each evening, and, on the very day heaven heals his eyes, buy him a fifteen-speed bicycle with a horn and a saddlebag. And yet he ends up torturing himself like some sort of papist flagellant. It doesn't make sense.

So cold, the holy river—but then the Jordan was no sauna either, Billy realized. Shivering violently, the day's first convert approached, a black man, doubtless another Newark citizen who'd wearied of trying to reach the humanist fleshpots of Staten Island and had elected to receive his redeemer instead. Staten Island: God etched his messages everywhere, didn't he, not just in Scripture, not just on the Mosaic tablets. Take away the first *T* in Staten, take away the cross, and you got Saten, that is, Satan.

Billy placed one hand on the convert's shoulder, the other against the small of his back. Scripture was crystal clear about baptism. The whole body must go under, one, two, three—death, burial, resurrection—none of this fey papist business of sprinkling a person's head. "We descend with Christ in the likeness of his death." Billy bent the man, immersed him, held him under. "We're raised to walk in a new way of life." Billy brought the convert up, the bright waters rolling down his ebony face like tears of joy.

"Hallelujah!" shouted the convert, simultaneously coughing and laughing. No Satan Island for him.

The crowd echoed, "Hallelujah!"

Minute followed minute, conversion begat conversion, and suddenly Billy's commandant was before him, waist deep in the canal, a plump woman at his side. Jewish, Billy sensed. Fortyish, half homely, half voluptuous, brown skin, fungus-green eyes, a turban of dense black hair spilling from her scalp and across her forehead.

Billy asked, "Is this . . .?"

"I think so," Peter Scortia replied.

She lacked a hand. From the right sleeve of her parka a grinning suture emerged. A fitting irregularity, Billy thought, for everything about this woman was sinistral: left, demented, malevolent, wrong.

"Tell me your name," Billy demanded.

Teeth clacking like castanets, mouth slung at a contemptuous angle, the one-handed woman came forward. "Julie Katz. And you're Reverend Milk."

Odd: the waters were causing her no pain. The holy river should be scalding the Antichrist; it should be boiling the meat off her bones.

"Some call you Sheila of the *Moon*," Billy asserted.

"My pen name."

Odd: as thoroughly as Billy probed her frame, his phantom eye could find no locusts scuttling along her ribs, no scorpions in her heart.

He channeled the full force of God's will into his left eye, swelling its vessels, countering the woman's terrible gaze. "Do you know why you've been arrested?"

"Hard to say. There's something inevitable about it, don't you think? Jesus tried to warn me."

"Christ talks to you?"

"Sometimes. Yes. Brother to sister."

Billy took a loud swallow of air. "You believe you're the Lord Jesus' sister?"

"I believe it because it's true. I suppose that makes me a blasphemer?"

"I suppose it makes you something much worse, Sheila of the *Moon*." The interview was giving Billy no pleasure. For the first time in years, his phantom eye was tingling, an itch that couldn't be scratched. "It makes you—"

A sign! A stark unequivocal sign! Just as the Holy Spirit had visited the Savior's baptism in the form of a dove, so did a New Jersey sea gull now soar into view, its course sure, purpose certain. Billy's phantom eye grew hot, a molten marble seething in his head. How clearly God speaks, he thought as the gull released a large black-and-white pudding. How lucid the language of heaven.

The sign splatted against the woman's brow and crept down her cheek. "Damn," she said, wiping her face with her glove.

"Children of the Lamb—behold!" Billy addressed the Tree of Life. "The Antichrist's reign has ended! Spring will come to New Jerusalem, and with it our redeemer!"

Only: the waters hadn't burned her.

Except: he'd seen no locusts on her bones.

The tree erupted in cheers so thunderous a dozen golden apples fell into the canal.

Thank God for the courts, thought Billy, thank God for the Inquisition. The learned judges would answer the riddle once and for all. Sheila of the *Moon*: venially guilty or mortally guilty, simple atheist or very Antichrist, mere foul-mouthed Jew or eternal scourge of God?

It was one trial, Billy vowed, his son would not miss.

Satan is seasick. Leaning over *Pain's* starboard rail, he coughs into the watery border where the Straits of Dirac meet the Pacific Ocean.

The vomitus arrives in a great tide, as if from a horn of liquid plenty. Andrew Wyvern disgorges the eight tons of soybeans he pirated and swallowed before they could relieve the 1997 Sudanese famine. The devil regurgitates the river's worth of fresh-frozen plasma he's been keeping from Canada's hemophiliacs. He spews out a thousand vials of hijacked interferon originally intended for a Peking cancer clinic. He upchucks the mountain of nickels and dimes collected last Halloween by California schoolchildren on behalf of UNICEF.

"What ails you?" asks Anthrax, surveying the archipelago of puke.

"Katz," Wyvern mutters, mouth burning with beneficence. What uncanny umbilicus now binds him to his enemy, what infernal thread? That woman with her smarmy lines, *Let him among you who is without sin*... Her pretentious moves: holding the vigilantes at bay with a wad of pebbles, cradling her friend's vomit, seizing her friend's dynamite, giving out soup. Katz with her Corning insulation.

"What about her?"

"The bitch has been busy."

"But she got caught." Spawned by a leprous tongue, rolling

past rotten teeth, Anthrax's tones are nonetheless soothing. "Milk will put her in the Circus."

"Not necessarily. Not without some encouragement from us. How long till we're in Jersey?"

"A month. Relax, sir. She hasn't got a prayer."

"In my experience," Wyvern explains, drawing his hand across his seared and pulpy lips, "you can never rely on Christianity. I was positive they'd torture Galileo to death, absolutely certain. Remember my bet with Augustine?"

"You lost quite a lot as I recall."

"A trillion lira, Anthrax. A cool trillion."

The New Jersey National Dungeon was a kind of underground wasp's nest, a conglomeration of passageways and cells imprisoning its population less through stone than through confusion: the illogic of its twists, the perversity of its turns. Bars of psychic chaos bound the prisoners. Shackles of entropy held them fast.

It was, on balance, a modern place. It belonged to its century. Argon lighting, solar heating, centralized air conditioning. Crystal-eyed androids tore out the papists' fingernails. Computerized racks elongated the homosexuals' bodies. Fusion reactors heated the tongs that seared the Uncertaintists until they renounced their ignorance and begged admittance to the True Church. Only at the bottommost stratum, the level where they placed Julie Katz, did a certain medievalism prevail.

Every day her cell—Cell 19—seemed to shrink, its wet walls pressing closer and closer as if wired to the haunted brain of Edgar Allan Poe. She knew her companions by name. Bix Rat, that mobile ball of fur. Phoebe Rat, skinny and assertive, her nose ever twitching. And the runty one, wide-eyed, his pelt like a kitten's: according to Julie's calculations the birth had happened last week, Little Murry Sparks, barging out of Phoebe, squalling and gurgling.

Even as Julie drew into herself, she sensed her fame spreading throughout the republic. Hour after hour, Jersey's cable-television screens crackled with Sheila stories. For over four months, the good news had commanded the front page of the *New Jerusalem Times*. SHEILA CAPTURED...SHEILA IMPRISONED...TRIAL IMMINENT...SECOND COMING CERTAIN. Church bells pealed in celebration; Inquisition patrol boats fired their cannons in joy. TRIAL IMMINENT: an old story, Julie realized—Christ before Pilate, Joan before the French priests. Burn, heretic, burn. She dreamed each night of drowning in blood; she awoke drenched in sweat, her straw pallet smelling like Absecon Inlet. Her fear was like the cranberry bog in which she'd awakened after her depotheosis, a bed of stinking slime. She suffered headaches, stomachaches, spastic bowels.

Keys clattering like a slot machine paying off in the vanished Tropicana, Oliver Horrocks entered. Julie did not hate her jailor. She almost liked him. He was a former "Heaven Help You" reader whose Revelationism was much shakier than his employers suspected. He simply couldn't decide about Julie, on some days holding her responsible for all of Jersey's ills, from its bread lines to its failed Parousia, on other days smuggling her Tastykake Krumpets.

"Ugh," Oliver Horrocks said, noticing the convocation of rats. "Here we are, the cleanest city on earth, and . . . rats. They dug too deep, that's the problem. You put your dungeon this low, you get rats." He was a kind of male crone, bent and birdish, his thin face laced with blood vessels. "Whoever you are, you don't deserve rats. Let's go."

Julie's phantom thumb itched. "Go where?"

"Not supposed to tell you." He leaned toward her as if to keep the vermin from hearing and, brushing the sleeve of her zebra-striped pajamas, whispered, "I will say this. They'd rathei convert you than burn you. These aren't *bad* people I work for. Talk to them. They'll listen."

Together they ascended, following the corkscrew staircases, the raked tunnels, the wildly tilted passageways, every wall wrinkled and damp like an esophagus, at last breaking into the dazzling day.

Although Jesus had only once in his life asked why God had foresaken him, Julie now found herself voicing the question over and over, mumbling it as she and Horrocks walked gold-plated avenues jammed with merry children, whispering it as they crossed the sacred river, circumvented the Pool of Siloam, and passed a row of trim little boutiques. Immaculate streets, antiseptic sidewalks, pristine gutters: Billy Milk had done what the Mafia could not. His regime had scrubbed Atlantic City clean, lifted the old harlot's face, killed her fleas. In the spotless front window of the New Jerusalem Toy Store, a pretty teenage girl arranged a Pro-Life Talking Embryo, a Sodom and Gomorrah

Playset, and a display rack of Melanie Markson's books. Aι onε time, Julie realized, Smitty's Smile Shop had occupied this same location. It was as if the store had been reincarnated on a higher plane; no squirting carnations or pornographic salt shakers here, not a single whoopie cushion.

They crossed Parousia Plaza and entered a building resembling an immense cinder block, then followed a hallway hung with tapestries depicting what Julie took to be great moments in biblical jurisprudence. Elijah beheading the prophets of Baal... Gideon shredding the elders of Succoth... the children who mocked Elisha being torn apart by bears... Jael nailing Sisera's head to the ground with a tent peg.

The courtroom was a stark white cube reminiscent of the detox chamber where she'd brought Phoebe a year earlier. Along one wall, three urpastors in dark blue business suits sat behind a polished breccia bench. In the opposite corner, a dais supported a pair of leather chairs whose conservatively dressed occupants —gray three-piece suits, narrow black ties—were manifestly blood relations. Father and son, Julie mused, grandpastor and archshepherd, Pilate—she smiled feebly—and co-Pilate. The juxtaposition struck her as ghoulish. Ah, that pathetic little hop from youth to senility, so quick. Youth? No, beyond his boyish freckles and lustrous red curls, Billy Milk's offspring was not young. My age, she thought. Older. Older and, if not wiser, then certainly wearier, for the more she studied him, the more narcissistically wasted he seemed, the more an epicure of his own decay.

"You may begin," Billy Milk said, nodding toward the judges.

Love your enemies, her brother had reportedly taught. An impossible ambition, self-contradictory and insane. Julie felt but one emotion toward this man, this criminal who had slaughtered Boardwalk tourists and killed her Aunt Georgina: raw, unalloyed loathing.

"I am Urpastor Phelps," the middle judge announced in a paternal, almost kindly tone as he tidied up the dozens of news clippings cluttering the bench. He was athletic and handsome, tanned by the Jersey sun, bright blond hair sprouting from his head like a halo. "To my left, Urpastor Dupree. To my right, Urpastor Martin. Please stand before us, Sheila of the *Moon*."

"My name is Julie Katz."

Urpastor Dupree asked, "But are you the author of these advice columns, this 'Heaven Help You' series?" His round, ruddy face was so pocked by acne it might have been sculpted from a sponge.

They'd rather convert you than burn you, her jailor had insisted. They aren't bad people, Horrocks believed. "I wrote them," she confessed.

"What was your purpose in creating 'Heaven Help You'?" Urpastor Martin inquired. A gaunt, twitchy man, forever knitting his fingers together.

"To topple the empire of nostalgia."

"Topple the *what*, ma'am?"

"Empire of nostalgia." What could she do now but explain herself as lucidly as possible? What other course was open? If the ambiguities added up to a crime, so be it. "I wanted people to start embracing the future. But that was sixteen years ago—now my goals aren't nearly so lofty. Lately I'd settle for getting through the day without screaming."

"Weren't you also aiming to found the Church of Uncertainty?" asked Urpastor Martin.

"No."

"But it got founded."

"I did not intend to start a church."

"So the error lies in those who came after you? In the Uncertaintist ministers and their congregations?"

"I can hardly blame them. You find meaning in this world, you seize upon it. People will take whatever deities they can get. Everybody has that need. I have it."

A soft smile crinkled Urpastor Dupree's acne. "Are you, as your followers believe, the daughter of God?"

"I suppose so. All right. Yes." How uncanny, the gentleness of their probes. She'd expected an inquisition, not a dispassionate quiz. "In this instance, however, I believe we're talking about a rather contemporary God. Outside the universe, know what I mean? Beyond the paradigms of both science and religion."

A pang of envy shot through Julie as Urpastor Martin poured sugar from a bullet-shaped dispenser into a coffee mug. She hadn't tasted coffee in weeks. "Assuming you are correct"—Urpastor Martin stirred the coffee with a gleaming silver spoon—"and God is unknowable, does that mean he didn't make heaven and earth? He didn't bring forth life?"

"In this century, better models for creation are available."

"But Miss Katz, if God has given the world a person such as yourself, then surely he has given us everything else—the birds in the trees, the worms in the ground, the very sun. Isn't that the truth of it?"

"What is truth?" said Julie. She pondered the three judges. Their faces beamed a glorious fascination, a blessed expectancy. "Study the problem in depth, as I have, and you'll find that the overwhelming bulk of the evidence favors cosmological and biological evolution. I'm sorry. That's simply the case."

"How can you be God's daughter and not believe in God?"

Julie pressed her index finger against her left eye. "Take the eye."

"The eye?"

"The human eye—any vertebrate eye. Instead of being linked directly to the brain, the optic nerve faces the light; the retina is wired in backward. No competent engineer, and certainly no deity, would ever design such a thing." Julie offered the bench a wry little wink. The urpastors leaned forward, radiant with appreciation of a point well made. "It's even starting to look like the very *idea* of reality had no actual beginning," she pressed on, merrily, "no moment before which physical laws didn't apply, no prime movement, no—"

"You see God as an engineer?" asked Urpastor Phelps.

"I don't see God as anything at all."

"An engineer, you said. An incompetent engineer."

"Incompetent, perfect, who knows? God is whatever we agree to pretend God is. God is our image of God."

Remarkably, the large red volume Urpastor Dupree now removed from behind the bench bore a title Julie recognized. *Malleus Maleficarum*—she'd once spotted the same book in Howard Lieberman's apartment; years earlier she'd seen it in Andrew Wyvern's lap in the doomed Deauville. *The Hammer of Witches, which Destroyeth Witches and their Heresy as with a Two-edged Sword:* everything the Renaissance priest ever wanted to know about the devil but was afraid to ask, Howard had gleefully explained. Have you any idea, Julie, what a terrible and insane era the so-called Renaissance was?

Witches. *Witches?* Oh, God, if you ever were a mother...

"I must say, we admire the audacity of your intellect, Miss Katz," said Urpastor Dupree, opening his *Malleus Maleficarum.*

"You have a subtle imagination," said Urpastor Martin.

"A unique perspective," said Urpastor Phelps.

"We'll be burning you to death not because your mind is weak or your will feeble," said Urpastor Dupree, "but rather because the Second Coming cannot happen until you, the Antichrist, are in hell." He folded his hands into a neat little bundle and rested them atop the bench.

"Burning? Antichrist?" Julie felt brutalized and betrayed, as if Phoebe had started drinking again, as if Bix had taken on a mistress, as if she'd been shot by a baby. "No, wait—"

"Guilty," said Urpastor Dupree.

"Guilty," echoed Urpastor Martin.

"All right, all right—maybe there *was* a prime movement, maybe there *was* something before the big bang. But quite likely the bang was generated by mere brute geometry, points in pre-spacetime, not by a divine—"

"Guilty," concurred Urpastor Phelps.

"Wait! Wait!" Julie splayed her phantom fingers. "Once you have space expanding—I'm talking right after the bang—you get organized energy appearing spontaneously, then comes your hydrogen, your helium, gravity, stars, organic molecules, eyeballs—"

" 'Wherefore that you may be an example to others,' " Urpastor Dupree read from his *Malleus Maleficarum*, " 'that they may be kept from all such crimes, we the said inquisitors assembled in tribunal' "—hunched with the burden of his office, he fixed her with his watery eyes—" 'declare that you, Sheila of the *Moon*, standing in our presence at this appointed hour, are dominated by demonic spirits, and by said judgment we pass upon you our sentence . . . of death' "—he sighed heartily—" 'by burning.' "

Julie gasped and wept. Carnivorous paramecia swam through her heart; the hammer of witches smashed her skull. Beyond, someone—herself, she sensed—released a loud squawl of anguish. She pressed her fish mouth suture against the bench, steadying herself. Implausibility, that was the New Jersey Inquisition's great strength, its total freedom from any impulse to be credible. The world was not prepared to move against Milk's mad enterprise because at some level the world did not believe it existed.

Then: an intervention.

It came as a sudden shout, a resounding "Stop!" It came in the person of Billy Milk's son hobbling across the courtroom.

"Stop!" he called again. Breathing raggedly, exuding an aroma of adoration mixed with silt and algae, he reached her side. "I *know* this woman!"

"You do?" said Urpastor Dupree.

Slowly, reverently, the archshepherd traced Julie's scar with his index finger. "I *know* her!"

She studied his moonish face. His freckled cheeks were like pointilist paintings executed by chimpanzees. How appropriate —for it was indeed he, Timothy the ape-boy, his clever pet made obsolete by an August miracle.

"It's she! The one who cured my blindness!"

"Is this true, Miss Katz?" asked Urpastor Phelps. "You gave our archshepherd sight?"

"His name's Timothy, right?"

"Yes!" shouted the archshepherd.

"I gave him eyes," Julie declared proudly. Complete with optic nerves on the wrong sides of the retinas, she thought.

"Eyes!" echoed Timothy.

Timothy! Dear, freckled Timothy! It was exactly like that wonderful legend, she decided, Androcles and the Lion. Androcles was spared by the beast he'd delivered from a thorn, and now Julie would be spared by the boy she'd delivered from darkness! Who said God didn't care? Who said God never got in touch? Forty years of silence, but now her mother was at her side, working through the grandpastor's son—poor Billy Milk, foiled by his own fertility, hoist on his own pecker, just look at the old dog, quavering there on his throne, sweating with awe, convulsed with epiphany.

"She gave me eyes!" Timothy shouted—and now, for the first time, Julie heard pain in his voice, sensed despair in his demeanor. "The Antichrist gave me eyes! I'll not wear Satan's eyes! If thy right eye offend thee, pluck it out! Out! Out! Out!"

Which he did.

Quite so. Plucked it. Out.

Julie screamed. It happened in a single unbroken movement: mad Timothy grabbing Urpastor Martin's silver coffee spoon and with the practiced nonchalance of a gourmet removing a wedge of grapefruit from a rind, the methodical efficiency of a mechanic stripping a tire from a wheel, de-eyeing himself. The noise suggested a thumb rubbing an overinflated balloon. Blood spouted from the ragged hole. The gouged organ rolled off the spoon and adhered to the floor like a wayward Brussels sprout dropped from a dinner plate.

Because this monstrous act seemed so complete in itself, Julie could not fault Timothy's astonished cohorts for assuming he would go no further. Had they realized he wasn't finished, they would doubtless have fallen upon him and wrested the coffee spoon away. Instead, when Timothy went after his remaining eye, the clerics simply stared, dumbstruck and incredulous, moving to intervene only after it stood poised on the spoon like an Easter egg leaving a cup of red dye.

"And if thy *left* eye offend thee"—shrieking in agony, weeping blood, Timothy collapsed—"pluck *it* out too!"

"Timothy! Timothy! Noooo!" Billy Milk rushed toward the shivering heap on the floor. "Somebody help him! Noooo!"

"Jailor!"

"Help him!"

"Grab her!"

"Move him!"

"Don't move him!"

"Jailor!"

"Find his eyes, find them! Noooo!"

"Get her out!"

"Find his eyes, they do transplants! *Noooo!*"

"Out!"

"Find them!"

Stunned, flabbergasted, Julie followed Oliver Horrocks out of courtroom and back into Parousia Plaza, though to her fractured psyche it was not the plaza but Andrew Wyvern's stomach, digesting her, melding her with his excrement, flushing her away, and while she arrived at the cosmic sewer not as a royal visitor this time, not as Satan's guest, still the imps and demons welcomed her, their old friend Julie Katz, former deity, condemned human, newest citizen of hell.

CHAPTER 17

♦　　♦　　♦

The Lord of the Underworld cannot return to New Jersey in clear weather. Hell has its protocols. As *Pain* cruises along Risley's Channel, Wyvern orders up a typhoon—"Rain, Anthrax! Tell them I want rain!"—and soon the angels are voiding torrentially. The devil tilts back his head and swallows. The fine brew dances on his tongue.

Slowly he shifts, taking on a pleasing shape. His horns retract, his tail disappears between his buttocks, his cloven hoofs become feet, and his odor, normally reminiscent of a whale corpse at low tide, becomes fruity and faintly erotic. Walking down the gangplank, firmly gripping his kittenskin valise, he adorns his cranium with golden tresses and covers his veined, leathery wings with overlapping tiers of waterproof feathers. Stepping onto the storm-swept sands of Dune Island, he makes a shimmering robe rush down from his shoulders like an eruption of silken lava. By the time Wyvern reaches the salt marsh, he looks fully the role he must play. He looks like Billy Milk's idea of an angel.

But the ruse has not been accomplished without cost, not without pain. Fighting for breath, Wyvern lowers himself onto a fallen tree trunk, slick and steamy with rain, and stares blearily at the swamp. An intolerable force squeezes his brain, as if God means to crack its casing and make an omelet of his thoughts. That lousy bitch. Her real hands: stopping the vigilantes, saving her friend, serving that soup. Her fake hand: highest of tech, warming that wog baby with its radiant fingers. Bitch.

He forces his spinning mind to focus on the immediate. History is going against him. Of all beings in the cosmos, Billy Milk is surely the last one a betting man would have cast as Julie Katz's savior. And yet it's happening. *Only a heaven-sent creature could have given my son sight*, runs the grandpastor's reasoning as far as Wyvern can fathom it. *Ergo, she's not the Antichrist*. And so, irony of ironies, Billy has determined to free her. It was true in Galileo's time, and it was true now: Christianity couldn't be trusted.

But the devil has a plan. He always has a plan. A sponge, a carousel, an ampule of venom. Cackling, he opens his valise and, taking care to shield his laptop computer and his stock portfolio from the gushing storm, draws out a small green bottle, its glass shatterproof, its face embossed with Julie Katz's *Moon* photo. He decides to test the bottle's contents, removing the stopper and letting a single dark dollop, no bigger than a raisin, roll off the rim and plunge into the briny water. On meeting Milk, of course, he won't call this venom by its names. He won't call it *Conium maculatum*, perdition's poison, or hell's hemlock. He'll lie through his fangs—he'll call it tetradotoxin, he'll call it zombie juice.

Absorbing the poison, the marsh begins to swirl and boil. The eel grass and spartina grow black as used lampwicks. The medusae and the moon jellyfish becomes piles of putrefaction. In short, the stuff works.

Cheers, Julie Katz. Bottoms up, child. Place the sponge of Matthew 27:48 to your fat lips and drink deep, Sheila of the *Moon*.

A thousand pipefish, alewife, polyps, shrimp, and hermit crabs drift to the surface and form a mat of corpses atop the rain-pocked water as, calling upon all his powers of drama, invoking all his affinity for spectacle, the devil takes out his laptop computer and begins scripting his enemy's death.

Doubt's worm, the parasite that had so often colonized Billy Milk's soul, was a mere itch compared to its opposite, certainty's scorpion, jabbing its barbed tail into his heart as, weary and heavy-laden, he shuffled past the Pool of Siloam toward the sacred canal.

Sheila: innocent.

Sheila: not the beast.

The facts rose before Billy, palpable, irrefutable. The holy river had not burned her. His phantom eye had found no locusts on her bones. But mainly there was this: over a quarter century earlier, Sheila had healed his boy. True, Satan's servants performed healings too, but nothing like the miracle that had brightened Billy's life for so many years, a cure for retrolental fibroplasia, eyes where there'd been no eyes. Billy loved Timothy dearly—poor stunned Timothy, sitting in a sunny ward at New Jerusalem Memorial, his gutted head encased in gauze— but the boy was wrong, *wrong*. Sorceress, shaman, adept, psychic healer: whoever this Sheila was, the gift she'd bestowed on Timothy that August afternoon in 1985 had come from above, not below.

A winged man sat on the riverbank, under the Tree of Life, fishing.

"Hello, Reverend Milk." His voice was at once lilting and firm, a voice like a harp.

"Good morning," said Billy woozily. Silk robe, golden hair, sleek white feathers. Hence...

"I'm afraid they aren't biting today," said the winged man.

"An angel?" gasped Billy. "You're an angel?"

The creature smoothed the feathers of his left wing. "Head to foot. Wingtip to foreskin."

"She's innocent, isn't she?"

"Innocent as Eden's first rose," said the angel, nodding. He reeled in his empty hook. "Favored by God, befriended by Jesus —and *you're* about to burn her."

"No. Please. I won't." An angel! He was talking with an angel! "I'll enter the arena. I'll say, 'Good citizens, I've torn up the execution order. Sheila of the *Moon* shall not burn—today or any other day.'"

"An admirable intention, Reverend. A laudable plan. However..." Like Aaron throwing down his staff before Egypt's royalty, the angel passed his fishing rod over the canal. "However, if you actually *do* that..."

The choppy waters froze, becoming smooth and glossy as a mirror. Silhouettes twitched on the surface like shadow puppets. The figures grew flesh, faces, clothes—breadth. Billy recognized himself, standing in the middle of the amphitheater, canceling Sheila's execution.

"Yes," he told the angel. "That's my plan."

And suddenly the believers were rising from their seats and stampeding across the sand, falling upon him. "You must give them their Antichrist," the angel explained. "Disappoint them, and they'll tear you apart." He cast out his fishing line. "Heaven can ill afford to lose you, Billy Milk. You've been a true and faithful servant, and we know you've got a few more cities in you. It's time to go international. Think of how wicked Teheran is. Tripoli cries out for the torch, Moscow's ripe for burning."

Relief gushed out of Billy like the fluids with which he'd christened the Great Whore—joy of joys, his campaign against Babylon, so controversial on earth, had been welcomed or high! "Then what am I to do?"

From his tackle box the angel produced a stack of fanfold computer paper. "The script for Sheila's execution," he explained, pressing the printout into Billy's hands. "I wrote it myself. You won't burn the woman, you'll drug her with tetradotoxin. Zombie juice." Reaching into his robe, the angel pulled out the green glass bottle embossed with Sheila's face and set it on the riverbank. "She'll fall asleep right there in the arena. The crowd will think her dead. Don't worry, it's just a mild case of suspended animation. Afterward, you can give her to ... whomever. Her husband. She'll wake up entirely alive. Thus will your cardinal sin—Billy Milk, persecutor of the innocent—be purged forevermore."

"Purged? Fully purged?" Billy's heart pirouetted with rapture.

"Your soul will become as clear as this canal."

"But is she really"—Billy glanced at the first page of the script: *A hay wagon rolls across the field,* he read, *pulled by a donkey* —"divine?"

"Hard to know. Ambiguous. Ah—a nibble." The angel worked his reel, soon lifting a great luminous starfish above the surface of the river. Holy water shot from its half-dozen arms as it flailed about, trying to unhook itself. "Some would say Julie Katz is definitely a deity."

Six arms, thought Billy, a six-pointed star: a Jewish starfish. "Then until the execution, we should be as generous as possible, right? We should treat her as God's own. Grant all her final wishes."

"Anything within reason," said the angel, swinging the starfish onto the grassy shore. "Allow her best friend to visit, that Sparks person."

"And her husband?"

"Yes, but don't let anyone go poking into his past. He used to be an Uncertaintist—actually preached it. Dreadful stuff."

Billy snatched up the bottle of tetradotoxin. A scheme conceived by God, a script authored by an angel! And yet... "We'll drug her."

"Right."

"They'll think she's dead."

"You got it."

"Suspended animation."

"Exactly."

"Fine. Good. Only—"

"Only—where's the drama?" said the angel. "Whither the spectacle? Trust me. My script is dramatic. Nails are involved, nails and wood. Perhaps you've read the Bible. Matthew 27:48. 'And straightway one of them ran, and took a sponge, and filled it with vinegar'"—the angel rested his soft white hand on the script—"'and put it on a reed...'"

"'And gave him to drink,'" said Billy.

"Likewise will your executioner give Sheila of the *Moon* a sponge filled with tetradotoxin."

"You mean she's to be...?"

"Crucified," said the angel.

Crucified? wondered Billy. *Crucified?* His flock would never accept a crucifixion, that holiest of chastisements—not for the woman they considered Satan's mistress. "Crucified. Yes, but—"

"Don't worry, your man will have plenty of time to deliver the drug. It takes hours for a crucifixion to work."

"But the audience—"

"Ah, the audience—they won't much like a crucifixion, will they?" the angel anticipated. "A crucifixion won't go over at all."

Billy's lips parted, his biggest smile since Timothy got his eyes. How marvelous having such rapport with heaven. "Only the Savior is worthy of crucifixion," he said, nodding.

"That's why she's to be anticrucified," said the angel. "An anticrucifixion for an antichrist."

"Anticrucitixion? As opposed to crucifixion?"

"You got it "

"What's the difference?" Billy asked.

"The difference is that you call one a crucifixion," replied the angel, "and the other an anticrucifixion."

An anticrucifixion for an antichrist, Julie mused as Oliver Horrocks led her through a massive cylindrical door into the dungeon's visitation room, its ceiling a jumble of floodlights and closed-circuit television cameras, their lenses poking into the air like possum snouts. An anticrucifixion for an antichrist: or so went the rumor from her jailor. Her enemies were going back to basics; tomorrow she'd be nailed up before the whole city and left to die. Nailed, not burned. A Pyrrhic victory at best, out of the frying pan and onto the cross.

The floodlights came on simultaneously, bathing the visitation room in milky luminescence, washing away the fact that outside it was late evening, still Saturday by a gentile's reckoning, Sunday by a Jew's. Along the left wall, seven grim-lipped and fearsomely armed corporals stood guard. As Horrocks guided her toward the center of the room, Julie clasped her real left hand in its ghostly counterpart and prayed to no one in particular that the next twenty minutes would go well, no awkwardness, no schmaltz.

Across the way, a series of interconnected cell doors opened and closed like canal locks. Her husband entered. Phoebe followed, cradling a scrawny, sleeping, terra-cotta bundle. Evidently Milk was honoring her last request. A kiss before dying. A hug before hell.

"We're trying every damn thing we can think of," Bix said, waddling uncertainly toward her, a flat cardboard box labeled *Pentecost Pizzas* balanced on his palms. "We're always on the phone, even Irene. We've got quite a list—a bunch of State Department people, both our senators, a retired ambassador I found in Bryn Mawr, Elmer West from the CIA . . ." His zebra-striped pajamas were several sizes too small. Domes of pale flesh emerged between the buttons. What a raving paranoid Milk must be, Julie decided: get them out of their street clothes, they've probably sewn cyanide into the lining. "Thing is, with Jersey so anti-Marxist and all," said Bix, "and the only record of your birth being in Trenton..." His eyes were red. Tears stained his cheeks like snail tracks. "Well, we're just not getting *support*."

"I don't expect you to save me, Bix. I really don't. I've been heading for the Circus all my life."

"Hey, the assholes took your hand!" whined Phoebe in a loud, icy, indignant voice. Her pajama top was open, breasts slung into an nursing bra. "They took Molly."

"No, I gave her to the Chaudrys."

"You're a good person, Julie Katz." Phoebe raked her fingers through Little Murray's hair, a mass of black spirals. His eyes popped open, dark brown disks haloed by pure white. "He sleeps through the night," she said. "Great disposition. I'd throw him in the Delaware if you could live."

"You don't mean that," said Julie.

"I don't mean that. Oh, Katz, honey..."

"Eighteen more minutes," said Horrocks.

"Want to hold him?" Phoebe asked.

"I'd probably drop him." Her brother seemed intelligent and well meaning, Pop's kid all the way. A contemplative astonishment lit his face, as if he'd arrived at the wrong planet and was debating whether or not to stay. "Is he circumcised?"

"Sure he's circumcised. It's what his father would've wanted. Take him, okay?"

"I'm afraid to. I'm...afraid."

The baby began squalling. His face reddened like litmus paper meeting acid. "You know, my mom used to nurse you sometimes, right from her own bod," Phoebe said, unhitching the left flap of her bra. She screwed her dark nipple into her son's mouth. The corporals' eyes drifted toward her. "You and I grew up on the same tit."

A silence descended, broken only by Little Murray's zealous sucking, a sound like Absecon Inlet lapping against a pier.

"Seventeen more minutes," said Horrocks.

"Be quiet, you little prick," snapped Phoebe.

"Take it easy," said Julie.

Bix sighed, a protracted bass note. "Listen, Julie, we heard they're not going to burn you. It'll be...different."

"I know." Julie cast a cold eye toward heaven. "An anticrucifixion for an antichrist. Good old God, always looking out for me."

"And afterward...tomorrow...they're going to give us. .I

mean, our pass is good till sundown, so we'll go home and come back, and they'll give us . . . you know." He exhaled, cheeks ballooning. "Your body."

"My flesh."

"Phoebe and I will do whatever you want," said Bix. "We'll sit *shivah*. We'll cremate you, give you a wake, anything."

Julie clenched her phantom fist. Had Bix and Phoebe actually been discussing her funeral? She was at once appalled and fascinated. She wished she'd been there. "Just drop me in the bay, darling. Bury me at sea."

"Absecon Inlet?"

"My old playground."

"Sure. Absecon Inlet."

"Something else. Before you sink me, I want a kiss."

"A kiss. Right."

"A kiss on the lips, Bix. Right on my dead lips."

"I promise."

"I'm scared."

"Of course."

"Sixteen minutes," said Horrocks.

"Why don't you shut up?" Phoebe snapped at the jailor. Her fingers drummed on the *Pentecost Pizzas* box. "Hungry?" she asked Julie.

Strangely enough, she was. "For pizza? Always."

"We made sure they got it right." Bix set the box on the floor, flipped back the lid. A divine cloud rushed out, the chemistry created as a mozzarella glacier migrates across dough. "Pepperoni, extra cheese."

Julie meditated on the topping. Was the plural *pepperoni* or *pepperonis*? God, the crazy data that pass through a condemned incarnation's mind. "Remember our picnic in the Deauville? You have any Tastykake Krumpets, Phoebe? Any Diet Cokes?"

"Nope," said Phoebe. "Sorry. Of course I remember."

"Are those things pepperoni or pepperonis? Is there such a word as 'pepperonis'?"

"What are you talking about?" said Phoebe.

"Those sausage things."

"Pepperoni, I think. Why?"

Julie shrugged. They dropped to their knees. Steadying the box with her stump, she tore an isosceles triangle free, lowered it into her mouth in a parody of French kissing. Her two hundred taste buds rose to the occasion, tumefying, relaying every nuance of the cheese, every glitzy detail of the pepperoni. Being so brave was oddly pleasurable. Smiling, she chewed her way to the crust.

Were it not for Little Murray, Julie felt, none of them would have finished eating without weeping or going mad. The baby was their mandala, the focus of their fragile truce with hysteria. Each random burp, gurgle, and smile sparked joyful chatter from the three adults, as if that particular action had never before occurred to any baby, anywhere. By meal's end, Julie was ready for him.

"Here," she said, existing palm out, soliciting.

Intoxicated with milk, he lay on Phoebe's shoulder like an outsized beanbag. "It's easy." Prying him free, Phoebe demonstrated something she called the football carry. "Take the hand I didn't blow off and tuck it under his head."

"Seven minutes," said Horrocks.

Julie liked the football carry. You never lost sight of the baby's face; you could simultaneously move him and teach him physics. "Gravity," she whispered. "Also magnetism, the strong nuclear force, the weak nuclear force..." She carried the baby toward the corporals. It must feel like flying, she decided, like backfloating down a river. His chocolate eyes were at their widest. "Earth orbits the sun," she sang to him. "Microbes cause disease." Such a new-looking thing, so unstamped. How sad that Pop and Marcus Bass hadn't survived to see this particular twist in their braided lives: the lighthouse keeper's son, the marine biologist's grandson. "The heart is a pump."

His mood swung, a sudden jagged screech. "Shut up," she whispered, pressing him to her arid right breast, the larger one. "Your problems are just beginning." It was not death that terrified her but, more prosaically, the nails. She feared for her flesh, its coming pain.

Pop's son shut up. His gums were spirited and wet, munching on her pajamas like a flounder taking bait, stiffening her nipple. The corporals pretended not to notice. Julie hated them. They were astonishingly handsome, impossibly clean-shaven: men with cauterized whiskers.

Little Murray stopped sucking and smiled.

"Six minutes."

Julie veered toward the cylindrical door, set the baby prone on the floor, and dropped to his level like a child flattening herself alongside her dollhouse, making it the measure of all things. What should one say to babies, what did they want to know about? "Well, first of all, there's your mother," said Julie. "A little flaky, but I think she's starting to be happy. Then there was your father—also a bit nuts, but I know you would've liked him. Your grandfather Marcus was a great biologist. Your grandmother Georgina was somebody I sinned against..."

"Five minutes."

Phoebe approached, pajama tops soppy with milk. "You okay?"

"No." Julie forced a smile. "I like my brother."

"Thought you would. Hey, Katz, guess what—I've figured out your purpose." A tear sat in Phoebe's left eye like a pearl in oyster flesh. She flipped open the nursing bra and gently lifted her son from the floor. "*Here's* your purpose, right? This guy. Little Murray. If you hadn't dragged his mother off a couple of battlefields, he'd still be living in a test tube."

Rising, Julie kissed her brother's nappy head. Good old Phoebe, never at a loss for bizarre ideas. "My purpose, huh? Why? Is *he* a deity too?"

"No." Phoebe grinned. "He's a baby."

"And he's my purpose?"

"I think so."

"Sounds rather..."

"Ordinary? Exactly, Katz. You were sent to be ordinary." Extending her tongue, Phoebe snagged the tear as it fell from her cheek. "Someday I'll write your biography. The gospel according to me. How God's daughter gained her soul by giving up her divinity."

"Four minutes."

And now here was Bix, waddling toward her.

Julie's stump tingled. Her phantom fingers seized Bix's pajama lapel, and he leaned into her like a wino grabbing a street lamp. They hugged more tightly than they ever had before; they crushed each other like colliding cars. Her libido blazed to life. She smiled, impressed by the party-crashing shamelessness of sex, its willingness to show up anywhere—a funeral, a sermon, a final farewell. This was the way to go out, all right, thumbing your labia at the cosmos.

"You were a good wife," he said.

"You were a good husband," she said.

Their embrace dissolved.

Throat swelling like a broken ankle, Julie sidled toward her best friend. "Good-bye, Green Enchantress."

"Two minutes."

"I can't stand this." Tears bubbled out of Phoebe as if from a medicine dropper.

"I said, 'Good-bye, Green Enchantress.'"

"I'm going crazy. Good-bye, Queen Zenobia. God, I hate this. Hate it, hate it..."

Slowly Phoebe melded with her, exuding an unfathomable mix of tenderness and eroticism, until the three of them—nursing baby, fecund bisexual, former deity—became a tight knot of bone and tissue, Little Murray trapped like a ship's bumper between the hull of his mother and the dock of his sister, and for a fleeting instant Julie was not afraid.

Brother and sister, Little Murray and Julie Katz, side by side, swimming through her petting zoo—so went the dream the policemen shattered when they barged into Cell 19, six of the usual smooth-jawed corporals, stroking the grips of their Mausers. Horrocks entered next, snipping at the air with a pair of steel scissors.

"I'm sorry," he said. *Snip, snip.* "I'm no barber, but..."

"Barber?" she groaned, rising from her straw pallet. She yawned. Slowly the world seeped into her. She slammed her palm protectively against her braids, always her best feature, still long and wild like Phoebe's old Wererat of Transylvania costume, still black and glossy like bundles of licorice.

"Let's get it over with," said Horrocks.

He made no pretense of finesse, attacking her hair like a selfish and stupid child cutting the twine from a Christmas package. The disembodied tresses floated to the floor like raven feathers, mingling with the damp straw. Her cranium grew progressively cooler. She pictured her gawky naked ears, her exposed S-scar; she imagined jagged tufts of hair sticking out randomly from her scalp. Thank God no mirrors were permitted in the New Jersey National Dungeon. She never wanted to see herself again.

"Done," her jailor said.

The policemen guided her upward through the maze of stairs

and corridors, Horrocks in the lead, unlocking doors, raising gates, opening the vertical Via Dolorosa.

"You're supposed to take a shower," he said. "You're supposed to start out clean."

He prodded her into the ladies' room, its walls gridded like drafting paper, the pattern marred where here and there tiles had fallen away like snapshots unglued from a photo album. A brand-new pair of zebra-striped pajamas drooped over the illustrated, three-panel Chinese screen standing between sink and shower. Julie stepped behind the mural—reviving Lazarus, stilling the waters, transforming the wine—and stripped. For the first time in her life, she was her ideal weight, a hundred thirty. There was no diet like terror.

She spent a full half hour scrubbing the dungeon's gunk from her body. The water ricocheted off her firm thighs, her milkless breasts, her scorched-earth head.

Dressing, she delivered herself to Horrocks and the police, who escorted her out of the dungeon and into the golden city. Citizens jammed the sidewalks of Eternity Place, men in white silk suits, women in pale yellow dresses, children in lederhosen and Bermuda shorts. Everyone seemed tense and confused, uncertain what to make of her; they'd never seen an antichrist before. Should they revel in Jesus' imminent return, or curse his enemy's flesh? For every low Wyvernian *sssss*, Julie heard a hosanna or a shout of joy. Perhaps they should even...love her? Ambiguous.

A tomato sailed out of the crowd and exploded against her shoulder. The police reacted instantly, spinning around, drawing their Mausers, but already more rot was in the air—stinking egg, mushy cantaloupe, soggy head of lettuce—a barrage of garbage, slamming into her fresh pajamas. When had she asked to be God's daughter? What sort of mother would allow this?

The crowd dispersed, breaking apart like a melting iceberg, and the death march continued, across the Advent Avenue intersection and past the Pool of Siloam, its sunbright waters reflecting the Tomás de Torquemada Memorial Arena with the clarity and fidelity of a mirror, doubling it, inviting Julie to project her inner life into the Rorschachian symmetry. What do you see, daughter of God? I see two arenas. I see two marble quoits, two lifebuoys from *Pain*, two doughnuts made of bleached dogshit.

Horrocks guided her through the narrow prisoners' gate and into the holding area, a gloomy granite dugout filled with about twenty criminals and heretics hunched on picnic benches. Beyond, an iron-toothed portcullis opened onto the execution field, a kind of landlocked beach, its rolling sands dotted with chunks of charred kindling. A dozen chopping blocks sat amid the dunes like tree stumps.

"*Moon* rising," a serene, aristocratic-looking prisoner greeted Julie.

"*Moon* rising," echoed another prisoner, a leathery old woman in ill-fitting pajamas.

"There are none so blind as those who see angels," Julie sneered in reply, dropping her thirty-nine-year-old ass onto the nearest bench. "None so deaf as those who hear gods," she added. The garbage had soaked through her pajamas, moistening her dark skin. "Screw the *Moon*."

"If you're not an Uncertaintist, what brings you here?" asked the old woman.

"Murder?" asked the aristocrat. "Adultery?"

"Bad genes," said Julie.

The tiers were packed, thousands of spectators waving pennants, focusing binoculars, buying hot dogs, perusing program books. At the far end of the field, a colossal statue of Saint John the Divine—legs splayed, hand gripping a quill pen—held aloft a thirty-foot television monitor while, higher still, banks of floodlights stood poised to illuminate the next nighttime performance. SUNDAY AFTERNOON AT THE CIRCUS OF JOY, proclaimed the video screen, the title gradually dissolving into the famous angel-with-sword logo.

Between Saint John's legs a massive wooden gate opened and out marched a brass band, their white uniforms glowing in the South Jersey sun as they played "Michael, Row the Boat Ashore" in 4/4 time, tubas bellowing, trombones blaring, drums thundering. A procession of motorized floats followed, bearing inflated rubber statues depicting what Julie, peering through the fog of her dread, took to be glimpses of the Millennium: lambs nuzzling lions, angels strumming mandolins and lyres, frisky multiracial children gamboling across grassy hills, a smiling middle-class couple harvesting beets and turnips from a pest-free vegetable garden.

"Sheila?" A familiar voice, dry and withered. "Sheila, is that you?"

Julie turned. Eyes wrapped in red veins, jowls slick with tears, Melanie Markson smiled.

"Melanie?" Good God: Melanie.

"Oh, Sheila, they've been hitting you. And your hair, they took your hair."

Hair, thought Julie. Hair, hand, ovaries. "Why are you...?"

"My last book," Melanie replied. "Full of errors, they said."

"Was it?"

"I don't know. You never got to America, huh?"

"I got there. Phoebe has a baby."

"Really? A baby? Who's the father?"

"*My* father."

"I remember that terrific thing he wrote about snapshots. I thought your father was dead."

"His sperm aren't."

"'Something of the Ordinary.'"

"Hermeneutics."

"Right. A baby, that's wonderful. Sheila, can you...?"

"Sorry, Melanie. I can't. You know I can't."

"I'm scared, Sheila."

The parade circled the arena twice and vanished beneath Saint John, whereupon the portcullis climbed groaningly upward. A thickset, overdressed man—red dinner jacket, red pleated cummerbund, white top hat—swaggered into the holding area and tapped a dozen prisoners, Melanie included, on their forearms with his riding crop. He raised a silver whistle to his lips and out came a sharp metallic shriek. "Get moving, folks," he said. "Right now, please."

ACT ONE: THY SWORD SHALL COMFORT ME, declared the video screen.

In the field below, an executioner with bounteous blond hair, wearing a white jumpsuit and red canvas gloves, strutted amid the chopping blocks. A chain saw sat on his shoulder like a beloved but mentally defective little brother. Julie shut her eyes. The portcullis dropped closed. She could feel her fear—feel it coiled around her spine like a snake entwining a caduceus. I don't want to die, Mother. I absolutely don't.

On the monitor, Melanie Markson knelt as if in prayer, her

pumpkin-colored hair flowing over the chopping block like a ta-blecloth. "No!" Julie screamed as the executioner pulled the starter cord on his chain saw. "For God's sake, no!" The motor kicked in. "Stop it!" The chain saw descended, grinding into Melanie's naked neck and swiftly severing nerve and bone—a deft move earning the executioner a standing ovation. "No! No!" The skillful camera operator caught it all, panning precisely as Melanie's head dropped free, turned over twice, and settled into a low dune like a cherry atop a mound of whipped cream. *"No! No!"*

For the next forty minutes, heads rolled and Julie wept, her sobs made inaudible by the chain saw's roar. Her tears were large, hot, and no longer for herself alone. She wept for Melanie. For Georgina. For Marcus Bass, for the slaughtered Boardwalk tourists, for every person who'd ever died for what somebody else believed in. When at last the act was over, a rawboned young man in a harlequin costume—black mask, diamond-pat-terned tights—trundled across the field collecting the heads and dropping them into his wheelbarrow. Julie pounded the bench with her stump. She rammed her bare heel into the dirt.

Intermission. As the harlequin wheeled the heads off the field—he looked like a farmer transporting a load of cabbages—a team of roustabouts in Torquemada Memorial Arena sweat-shirts lined the hippodrome with upright ladders.

ACT TWO: HIS LIGHT BURNS FOREVER, said the monitor.

The man in the white top hat strode into the holding area and blew his whistle, whereupon the remaining prisoners rose from their benches like schoolchildren participating in a fire drill and started onto the field. "Not you," he told Julie, his lips and nostrils quivering with contempt. But of course, she thought—Sheila of the *Moon* is a headliner, Sheila gets her own separate act.

In a series of elegantly composed longshots, a half-dozen har-lequins chained the heretics to the ladders and buried them to their knees in kindling.

Zoom in: straw, twigs, logs, gin bottles, cocaine spoons, zotz needles, feminist manifestos, Kurt Vonnegut novels, back issues of *Groin*, *Wet*, and *Ms.*, videocassettes of *Swedish Nuns* and *Bonnie Boffs the Vienna Boys Choir*, nude snapshots of the sort Pop's nut-tier customers used to bring to Photorama—piles of sin, stacks of iniquity, heaps of vice, dams engineered by leftist, druggie, prurient beavers.

Cut to: a line of trumpeters bleating out three sharp ascending notes.

Cut to: the grandpastor himself, Milk the holy arsonist, eye glassy, hands writhing around each other.

Cut to: the blond executioner, weaving among the ladders, lighting the pyres with a gleaming red flamethrower, spirals of fire gushing from the barrel.

The director covered the subsequent holocaust through tight close-ups. Mouths flew open and out rolled smoke and sparks, syllables of incineration. Faces writhed like beached eels. Thighs blackened, eyes exploded, hair ignited, muscles melted. The heat pounded Julie's shorn head. The air vibrated with screams. Bulbous and obscene vapors drifted over the arena.

Second intermission. The roustabouts carried aluminum pails filled with water—drafts from the sacred river, a subtitle explained—across the field and hurled the blessed liquid onto the flaming pyres, dousing them as emphatically as Julie had doused Atlantic City. Unchaining the hot bones, the roustabouts bore them away in rubber body bags.

ACT THREE: AN ANTICRUCIFIXION FOR AN ANTICHRIST.

This was it, then. No way out.

Alone on her bench, Julie shivered and moaned, suddenly aware that her bladder had split off from her brain. The warm pee dribbled down her thigh.

A hay wagon appeared beneath the portcullis, driven by the man in the white top hat and harnessed to a mangy, spavined donkey. "Get in, please," he commanded. "Antichrist Jew," he muttered under his breath.

"When I *feel* like it," Julie said, wrapping the words in spit The donkey brayed. Her soggy pajamas grew cool.

"Get in, Queen of the Jews."

Julie watched the monitor. A huge mechanism appeared, gliding between Saint John's legs, a thing at once frivolous and sinister, familiar and grotesque. Not just any merry-go-round, she realized, but an Atlantic City native, the famous Steel Pier carousel, a creation from which she and Phoebe had once stolen a wooden stallion. Whether any such animals remained, Julie couldn't tell, for the carousel had been boarded up like a condemned building, the entire span from cornice to platform sealed with a checkerboard of black and white plywood panels, giving the huge antique the look of a bass drum lying on its side. Round and round went the carousel, round and round to the rhythm of the Wurlitzer steam organ bleating out "On the Boardwalk in Atlantic City."

Two men in prison pajamas lay nailed to separate white panels. Two men, spinning, bleeding, crucified.

Laughing, Julie climbed into the wagon and sat on the sweet straw. The driver flicked his riding crop, producing a *snap* like a gunshot, and the wagon rolled forward, bouncing her up and down as if she were riding the stolen stallion of her youth. Laughing: for it was all quite hilarious, wasn't it, she finally saw the humor. She thought of the communications course she'd taken in her sophomore year, Crosscurrents in Popular Culture, the idiot professor finding Christ symbols in everything from *Superman* comics to Elvis. Tell me, Dr. Sheffield, when a woman gets nailed to the Steel Pier carousel, does that by any chance make her a Christ symbol?

The driver reined up within three yards of the mechanism, and immediately a quartet of black-masked harlequins scrambled into the wagon like tarantulas invading a banana boat. Their stares seemed to reach beyond that slice of the spectrum available to human vision: burning, hate-filled stares, looks meant to kill. Laughing, she turned away. The crucified men swept past, their blood patterning the plywood—river systems, root systems, nervous systems—half dead, half alive, once, twice, a third time, a bearded stocky man and a gnomish balding man, nose like a walnut, so close she could have touched their steel nails, licked their sweat. Now the blond executioner came aboard, cradling what looked like an amalgam of bicycle pump and power drill. Not a bicycle pump, of course, not a power drill: an electronic nailgun, a modern-day *malleus maleficarum*, state-of-the-art, for it was 2013, wasn't it, the future had arrived, supplanting hammer, supplanting iron spikes.

Julie laughed. The carousel slowed.

"Stand up!" the executioner screamed above the steam organ's bellow.

Laughing, Julie stood up.

The carousel stopped, framing her against a white panel, the bearded prisoner to her left, the gnomish one to her right.

"Lift your arms!"

Laughing, Julie lifted her arms. The harlequins held her fast against the wood. Plywood splinters pushed through her pajamas, pricking her skin. Hefting his nailgun, the executioner pressed the muzzle into her left palm. No laughter this time, no laughs left, no chuckles or giggles. "No!" Within and without, she shuddered; her bones vibrated, spleen rattled, liver trembled, pancreas shook. "Don't! No!" This couldn't be happening, couldn't—

Bang, a blast of searing pain—"No! Stop! No!"—and now, *bang*, a second fiery bolt, this one in her wrist—"Stop! No! Don't!"—and then, by way of dealing with her mutilation, the gap, *bang, bang*, between her ulna and radius, *bang*, a row of three steel nails pinning her right arm like tacks holding upholstery to a chair. The wagon pulled away, leaving all of her hundred and thirty pounds hanging on the nails like a pelt, the shafts cutting deeper and deeper, and still the executioner attacked, left foot, *bang*, right foot, *bang*, unbearable pain, made worse by uncertainty—how long would it take to die from this, an hour, two hours, the rest of the day?

The carousel started up.

She tried to distract herself with science, naming her pathologies, her hypercarbia, her tetanic contractions, the nail through her first intermetatarsal space, the nail through her flexor retinaculum and intercarpal ligaments, but it was no use, her muscles kept spasming, the hot knives continued to chew and burn. Breathing was impossible; the mass of her body on her outstretched arms filled her lungs to bursting. To blow out, she had to push up on her feet, placing all her weight on the tarsals and driving white-hot corkscrews through the damaged nerves.

The steam organ fell silent.

A voice said, "I . . . deserve . . . this."

"Nobody . . . deserves this," Julie replied, flopping her head to the left.

"I do," said the bearded prisoner. "Read Bible and . . . you'll see . . . Jesus favors . . . death penalty . . . for my kind . . . me."

"You're . . . guilty?"

"Raped . . . girlfriend . . . killed her . . . doctor said I'm . . . psychopath . . . but really . . . pornography . . . made me do it."

The pain was coming in waves now, as if her execution were some obscene version of childbirth. After each crest Julie's collateral torments broke through, the fiery sun, the vertigo caused by the carousel's spin, a thirst straight from a hadean iron mine.

"We are ... connected," gasped the other prisoner.

Julie pivoted her head. "I've ... met you?"

"Gabe Frostig ... told your father about ... he had ... embryo ... you."

"You should've flushed me ... down the ... "

"Almost did."

Pain, sun, vertigo, thirst. Pain, vertigo, pain. All she wanted was to die. There were truly fates worse than death, oh, yes ...

"I'm ... please ... w-water," said Julie.

"Thirsty?" said the executioner.

"Y-yes. Please."

"I've got just the thing." He held up a fat, dripping object hanging from the muzzle of his nailgun. "Drink."

A sponge. Matthew 27:48, Mark 15:36, John 19:29. Had they no shame? She opened her mouth, sucking the saturated tissues. The animal reeked of the sea. Its juices tasted like salted piss. Trickling downward, the liquid scored her teeth, burned her tonsils, and sent sharp bursts of nausea through her guts.

"How long ... been here?" she asked Frostig. Her impaled ligaments pulled her hand into a claw.

"Don't know ... two days ... in the end, it's the air ... no air ... gets you ... exhaustion asphyxia, they'll call it on ... certificate ... maybe hypovolemic shock, stress-induced arrhythmia, peri ... pericardial effusions ... if you're lucky."

Pericardial effusions. Like father, like daughter. Her heart was fated to collapse.

The steam organ started up.

"Drink," demanded the executioner, once more proffering the sponge.

She drank. A tingling arose at the point where her spinal cord entered her skull. Silver stars pinwheeled in her head. Sand castles exploded.

On the Boardwalk in Atlantic City ...

Someone sang.

Frostig? The murderer? The executioner?

No, myself, she realized.

We will walk in a dream.

She ascended. Julie Katz lay dying in the Circus of Joy, gasping bad lyrics, but she also soared high above, spiraling around Saint John, the video screen, the floodlights.

Glancing downward, she saw herself stapled to the carousel, bleeding, singing. *Saw* herself: vision, something eyes and eyes alone did, eyes, those soggy spheres of gelatin suspended in bone, wired in backward to visual cortex. "Dream," she repeated. Hence, a tongue, flapping in her mouth like a beached fish. So she'd left the ground—so what? This, too, was an incarnation, and even as her Doppelgänger glided past the towers and spires of New Jerusalem, across the roaring Atlantic, kicking clouds and terrifying gulls, she still felt its limitations, its vast potential for discontent. Time to return, then, back to her sad planet, back to the nails, the carousel, the exhaustion asphyxia, and so she fell, forsaking her wings and fusing with her singing self, not dead yet, oh, no, Mother, not dead yet, not yet...

On the Boardwalk in Atlantic City
we will walk
in a
dream
on the
Boardwalk in
Atlantic
City
life
will
be
peaches
and—

CHAPTER 18

◆   ◆   ◆

Perched on steel stilts high above the city's eastern wall, the video screen glowed with close-ups so obscene that Bix could barely bring himself to watch. Julie's left wrist: an oily gray nail burrowing into her flesh. Her feet: toes curled in rigor mortis. Her face: glossy and rigid like crystallized sulfur. While the average psychic, visionary, or *Midnight Moon* reader would doubtless have registered the exact moment of her death, experiencing it as an explosion in the skull or a sudden skewering of the heart, Bix did not. He knew only that at some nebulous moment between noon and now the Circus had done its work, taking from the earth his new wife, one-time god, and forever friend. So here they were, the two people who loved her most, huddled in the shadow of the Tropicana Gate, studying the pale, pearly faces of the bas-relief angels and awaiting the promised corpse.

Monitor and sky darkened simultaneously, the gray clouds seething like charcoal drawings made by a schizophrenic. The storm broke; a trillion raindrops clanked against the gold-plated causeway. Phoebe raised her umbrella, an old Smile Shop item with IT'S ONLY GOD PISSING on the canopy, and held it out, offering sanctuary. Bix flattened himself against the portal. Conventional sentimentality argued that loss bound people together, erasing old enmities, but such clumsy intimacy was the last thing he wanted, especially with her.

The gate parted with a deep, raspy grunt, like humping yaks

trying to disengage, and a police sergeant marched through the gap, his mirrored sunglasses beaded with rain. Two young urpastors in waterproof cassocks followed, a large tubular sack slung between them like a hammock.

"Mr. Constantine?"

Bix nodded. White and pulpy, the sack suggested the larva of some monstrous insect. Rainwater settled into its dents and sluiced down its folds.

He led the urpastors to the Green Tureen, and as they laid the flexible coffin in the kitchenette aisle his gaze wandered toward the city. Burnished ramparts, towers like titanic icicles, a shimmering, sinuous monorail track. A jokey umbrel.a sat by the open Tropicana Gate.

"Thanks," he told the urpastors. Umbrella, Bix mused. Open gate. "Go for it, Phoebe," he muttered as he got behind the steering wheel. "Shoot Milk and his whole crew. You have my blessing."

He headed into the broiling storm, across the crest of the city and over the bridge into Brigantine, his grief marching to the cardiac thock of the windshield wipers. Lightning zagged across the sky, gilding the refineries, flooding the apartments and condos with brief electric pallor. He swerved onto Harbor Beach Boulevard, glossy with rain, splotchy with puddles, and, turning sharply, drove down Rum Point as far as he could and braked. He shut off the engine, the wipers. Rain clattered against the windshield like fistfuls of marbles. IT'S ONLY GOD PISSING, Phoebe's umbrella had said, but this time Julie's mother was shedding all of herself, her urine, blood, lymph, sweat, amniotic fluid.

Opening the rear door of the Tureen, he found himself drifting from sorrow into a less expected emotion, a dull but undeniable anger. The fool—why had she given up her powers like that? Didn't she know that on this side of mortality the nails are made of steel, they don't bend, they don't budge?

Saturated, his William Penn High sweatshirt clung to him like papier-mâché as he lifted the sack over his shoulder and, carrying it to the end of the jetty, set it on the rocks. The rubber exuded the thick grim odor of a gas mask. Dropping to his knees, he tugged on the zipper.

Of *course* he wanted to deny the whole business, of *course* he wanted somebody to vouchsafe her a blissful eternity. He thought of the book his honors students were reading, Thomas Wolfe's *Look Homeward, Angel*—unbelieving Eugene Gant groping toward the divine. "Whoever You Are, be good to Ben tonight, show him the way," Eugene prays, singsong, over his dying brother. "Whoever You Are, be good to Ben tonight..."

Her face burst out and he groaned. What had he expected, Snow White on her bier? Certainly not this open-eyed shell, this bald husk, certainly not this *thing*. The corpse's inertia was unnerving. What, exactly, was it? When your car expired, it remained your car, but with death a new object evidently came into being, supplanting spirit, supplanting body as well, a vacant and degraded lump of nothing.

He kept pulling on the zipper. Raindrops pelted her, some collecting under her eyes, others rolling into the gorge between her slightly asymmetrical breasts. Leaning forward, he shielded her from the storm and dried her face with his shirtsleeve. Wrinkles and pouches, true, but still those heavy lips, that cute upturned nose. He'd never really looked at her before, not this way. He wondered whether each crease corresponded to some dark event in her life—there the imprint of her father's death, there the brand of Phoebe's dipsomania, there the mark of her infertility.

A promise was a promise. He kissed the corpse on the lips. Nothing. Not disgust, not fascination, not the merest sexual twinge. It was a corpse. It was nothing.

He zipped it up, nudged it gently, and sent it sliding downward along the slick, algae-coated rocks.

"Whoever You Are," he whispered as the sack hit the water, "be good to Julie tonight, show her the way. Whoever You Are," he said again as his wife disappeared into Absecon Inlet, "be good to Julie tonight..."

As Phoebe ran past the Tomás de Torquemada Memorial Arena, her yellow parka ticking with deflected raindrops, the last of the crowd streamed forth, their umbrellas blooming like black flowers, their Circus pennants limp and soggy. They seemed little different from Philadelphia basketball fans leaving the Spectrum. Judging by their smiles, you couldn't say for certain whether they'd just seen the 76'ers win by a three-pointer or a hundred sinners burn.

Across the street, the Holy Palace rose into the squalling sky, its golden pilasters cutting upward through a dozen balconies. Phoebe reached inside her parka, grabbing metal. Her plan might be ill-considered and vague, but her Smith & Wesson was loaded.

She let the night settle and, camouflaged by rain and darkness, hauled herself over the wrought-iron fence. In the rear courtyard a sycamore beckoned, and she climbed, quiet as stone, ever mindful of the guards and their Uzis, black and fearsome as her mother's bones. History pulsed through her. *Father cut in half. Mother burned alive. Best friend crucified.* Thick and wet as moray eels, the branches took her to the third floor. How naturally it all came: loosening the pane with Mom's old Swiss Army knife, unlatching the window—how easy to be the creature of history's vengeance.

Her charge to Irene had been simple. One: give him twenty to thirty ounces of formula a day. Two: put him in for his nap at noon. Three: if his mother is murdered, get married again. Every kid deserves two parents, more if possible.

Silently she wandered the gilded hallways—carpets as soft and warm as marsh muck, chandeliers like giant luminous crabs —eventually finding the floor where the clergy retired after a hard day's auto-da-fé. She peeked into the rooms one by one, just as she and Katz had done years before in the Deauville. Piety and luxury flourished side by side; for each altar there was a hot tub, for each portrait of Jesus a massage-bed. Not a bad life, grace.

At last, the grandpastor's chamber, it had to be—four-poster bed, solid oak writing desk, Oriental rug. Empty. She slithered toward the window, her boots marking the rug with mud and dead leaves. Raindrops clung to the glass like pustules. Draping the window curtain around her narrow body, she eased into the red velvet and waited.

When they were ten, a few weeks after Katz had cured that Timothy kid, the two of them had stolen a crucifix from Ventnor Seminary and pried off the Jesus. His arms were slightly raised —a perfect slingshot. After stringing rubber bands and a leather pouch between his wrists, they'd spent an unsuccessful afternoon hunting sea gulls on the Boardwalk, aiming to bring them down with marbles.

"I don't like this," Katz had said.

"Too disrespectful?" Phoebe had asked.

"Yeah."

"Of your brother?"

"No," Katz had said. "Of the gulls."

Milk entered, fur slippers flopping, silk pajamas hissing. Approaching his four-poster, he dropped to his knees, interlaced his fingers, and began talking to God.

"Oh, Lord, Lord, because of my sins he is stricken again, for it was I who brought Sheila into your city, Lord, I and I alone..."

Phoebe had read somewhere that after a person commits a revenge murder, he typically experiences excruciating regret. Not at his deed, but only at his failure to tell the victim two facts: who was killing him, and why.

"Hold it right there, Billy baby!" she screamed, thrusting the curtain aside.

Bastard. He allowed no explanation. He simply ran to the glass door, tore it open, and started onto the balcony.

He was halfway across when she caught him, springing onto his back like a lioness attacking an antelope. Together they arced over the balustrade, dangling toward the watery street. He spat in her face. She bit his hand, drinking his salty blood.

They fell. Fell with the raindrops.

Oh, shit, oh, God, oh, Katz, Katz, if you ever had a mother...!

The night air whizzed by and *splat*, exactly that, *splat*, a cartoon sound effect, and with it a redeeming ooze, blessedly soft. A sharp green stench cut into Phoebe's brain. She rolled over. Rigid fingers scraped her cheek. Lifeless eyes watched her; a crossbow bolt ran through the corpse's brow like a toothpick through an olive. She blinked. Another body, another. Corpses everywhere. Milk, dazed, lay wedged between two headless women. So much death, and yet these rumblings, these vibrant winds against her face.

Her mind cleared. Truck. Pickup truck, Circus truck: corpse removal. She laughed. Saved by the sinful dead. Already the vehicle was surging through the Tropicana Gate and onto the wet ribbony blackness of the expressway. Unmoving, Milk snorted and wheezed. Condos rolled past. Apartments, churches, farms. A solitary flame writhed and roared atop an oil refinery tower like a burning flag.

She made a fist, squeezed metal. Metal, glorious Smith & Wesson metal. Throwing herself atop Milk, she rammed the steel muzzle against his skull . . . ah, but there was a better entrance, wasn't there? She flipped back his eyepatch and slid the pistol into the socket until it bumped scar tissue, a sound like a doctor's rubber hammer striking a knee. "Know who I am?" she asked.

Milk seemed oddly pleased, as if the excitement of being under a woman compensated for her evident intent to murder him. "Babylon, is that you? You've grown darker, sister!"

Phoebe's mother had once told her every woman tries to imagine having a penis, every man a vagina. Well, Reverend Milk, she thought, twisting the revolver as if operating a screwdriver, here we have it.

"Ravage me, Babylon!"

The truck lurched to a stop. Steadying the revolver inside Milk's head, Phoebe leaned back in time to see the driver jump from the cab and, preceded by the beam of his flashlight, hurry through the rain to the nearest roadside exhibit, a mass of wired bones chained to a cattle fence. He inspected the skeleton carefully, as if to determine whether it needed replacing.

"Take me, Babylon!"

"I'm not Babylon, you crazy man."

"Ah . . . you're from the junta!" Milk cried. A pale light hit his face. Phoebe turned. Briefly the driver contemplated the two living corpses tussling in the back of his truck. "Colonel Ackermar sent you!" Milk persisted, pawing at Phoebe's parka.

Dropping his flashlight, the driver dashed into the stormy darkness like a frightened deer.

"You killed my best friend!" Phoebe sawed the Smith & Wesson back and forth. Why couldn't she pull the trigger? Why these spasms of hesitation? "Burned my mother! Cut my father in half!" Gunmetal ground against bone.

"In half?" Milk grimaced. "I remember. Your father died a saved man."

"You—" She smiled. Stopped sawing. Withdrew the revolver. The gospel according to Phoebe—she was really going to write it, really and truly. "Take a hike," she muttered, tucking the Smith & Wesson into her parka. The gospel according to Phoebe—and she didn't want a tawdry murder on page 301, no, she had more class than that, more style. "Out!"

Of the gulls, Katz had said.

Like a disappointed lover evicting her partner from bed, she levered Milk over the side of the truck and dumped him into a wet gunky ditch. The flying mud spattered her face.

Lightning exploded with flashbulb suddenness. The cranberry bog stretched in all directions, interrupted only by the expressway and its crop of ebony bones. A second flash: Milk, struggling to his feet. A third: Milk, hopping through the bog like an immense black cricket. Quite so, bastard, you are smart to run. Run your dick off. My mercy's not terribly reliable.

The smell, the pervasive unholy stink. And so she jumped, words pouring from her mouth, a speech heard only by the rain and the decaying sinners. "Katz, Katz"—she lifted her revolver heavenward—"you really got your hooks into me, didn't you?" She glanced at Milk's retreating figure. "Me, I would've shot the bastard. Oh, yes—"

Crack: a long, forking thread of lightning, slicing open the sky.

Whitening the bog. Striking Milk.

Phoebe blinked. Indeed: a running man, a bright zag, and— gone.

Lightning. Jesus. Wasn't that a bit much? Yet it had certainly done the job, a crisp, clean hit.

She sensed the regret spreading through heaven, and she laughed. One. he hadn't known who'd killed him. Two: he hadn't known why.

But Phoebe did. This was no fluke of nature, this was an assassination, plain and simple. Katz, no doubt, would've called it coincidence. "A universe without coincidence would be an exceedingly strange place," she'd said in one of her stupid columns. Stubborn Julie Katz, whose worldview did not admit of guest editorials by God.

Phoebe ran, rain washing over her face. Even before reaching Milk's corpse, she knew how the bolt had transformed him. God's punishments always fit: eye for eye, bisection for bisection. She gazed upon the miracle. A bisection indeed, only not at midriff as with her father but lengthwise, like a rail split by Abraham Lincoln.

Lightning. Perfect.

She staggered to the nearest tree and collapsed, curling her body around the trunk as if it were the core of her mother's womb, and soon the drumming rain carried her into a thick and dreamless sleep.

April's first sun rose fiercely, drawing steam from the cranberry bog. Gradually Phoebe gained her feet, jeans soggy with dew, chest heavy with milk. She slipped her damp fingers into her parka and, drawing out her ecclesiastical pass, noted that it had expired twelve hours earlier. What clever tricks would it take to reach America now, she wondered, what escapades, what lies? No point in worrying. She'd cross that bridge—that literal bridge, she thought with a quick smile, that Benjamin Franklin Bridge—when she came to it. The important thing was to get going. If Irene kept Little Murray on formula too long, he'd never go back to the tit.

The previous night was a hundred years in the past. Had it even happened at all? But then she started walking, and there he was, stretched out in the precise light of morning, his entire body a wound, the two halves cauterized. She felt sick, a sensation owing less to Milk's condition than to her incriminating proximity. If caught, she'd be blamed, no doubt about it. Phoebe Sparks, God's fall guy.

And so she began her furtive trek, sneaking from farm to farm and store to store like a marauding animal, living on pilfered fruit, stolen candy bars, and milk from her own fecund breasts. She shoplifted a backpack, the better to carry her plunder. She slept in cornfields, ate in Revelationist churches, peed in gas stations. On Thursday night a fresh thunderstorm arose, slashing a thousand creeks and ponds into the republic's face. She claimed someone else's umbrella from a bus depot lost-and-found and began looking for shelter, starting with the obvious—restaurant, laundromat—but in each case something made her lose heart: an armored van, a milling soldier, an Inquisition helicopter, a stranger's suspicious glance. The Smith & Wesson sustained her. A mere touch and she felt nourished, renewed. Every girl should have a gun.

A mile outside Cherry Hill she came upon a shabby and demoralized farm. A rusting John Deere tractor and two moribund threshing machines sat amid a grove of spidery apple trees. A battered windmill turned jerkily in the storm like a telephone rotor being spun. Phoebe slipped into the barn and, peeling off her parka, flopped down in the hay. To judge from the two dozen stalls, the owner had once raised horses or dairy cows, but now the place belonged wholly to hens and roosters, a fragrant, fidgeting kingdom, their clucks breaking through the howl of the storm like some animal Morse code.

Phoebe's stolen backpack held a feast. Swiftly she emptied it, setting out her imported Oscar Mayer hot dogs, an apple the size of a croquet ball, and a peanut-butter jar into which she'd expressed over a pint of breast milk. She devoured three weiners, washing them down with milk; her gastric juices sizzled. Satisfied, she stretched out in the cool, shit-sweet dark. Tomorrow afternoon she'd finally be back in America, kissing Irene, arranging a service for Katz, nursing Murray. God, how she missed that kid.

Sleep rolled across her like warm surf.

A peeing urge woke her. She'd had to urinate three times a night during her final month of pregnancy, and the conditioning lingered. She looked at her watch. Two A.M. Full bladder, full boobs, what a bloatoid she'd become.

"Hello, child."

Phoebe clutched her revolver.

"I see you finally got some tits." A male voice, fuzzy and thin.

Twenty feet away, a match flared. The tiny flame staggered through the air like a drunken firefly, alighting atop a cigarette.

"I'm armed," Phoebe announced.

"Nobody here but us chickens," the man replied, simultaneously coughing and laughing. A foul odor ripped through the air, rotten oranges soaked in rancid honey. "You remember me, don't you? Years ago we met on Steel Pier. We rode the carousel together. Same one they nailed Katz to."

A sudden glow suffused the barn as Andrew Wyvern ignited a kerosene lamp, a kind of miniature Angel's Eye suspended on a nail. Sallow and collapsed, his face suggested a jack-o'-lantern kept till Christmas. He sat propped against a cow stall, surrounded by nesting hens, a burning, filtertip Pall Mall wedged between his lips.

"You've aged," said Phoebe.

"So've you Want to hear a joke?" A small snorting pig—

round, pink, and bristled, a belly with legs—waddled across the barn and climbed into Wyvern's lap. "Billy Milk was planning to let your friend go free. Can you imagine?" With casual cruelty Wyvern dug his talons into the piglet and began skinning it alive. "I had to intervene."

Phoebe tightened her hold on the Smith & Wesson. "Know something, Mr. Wyvern?" The pig squealed horribly, bloodily. "You're sick."

"It was my poison that killed Katz, not the merry-go-round, not the spikes. *Conium maculatum*, a whole spongeful." Like a depraved potter, Wyvern molded the pig's red gooey flesh into a football. "Once again, the devil himself comes off the bench and throws the touchdown pass!" He lobbed the football into the adjacent stall, creating loud fluttery panic among the hens. "That's me, a winner all the way."

"You don't look it."

Wyvern mashed out his Pall Mall, lit another. "Her hand around your dynamite," he sighed. "Her lousy insulation. But I'm feeling much better, thank you. Give me some milk."

"Huh?"

"I want some milk." The devil aimed his clawed index finger at the peanut-butter jar. A large, empty swallow traveled down his throat. "Please."

"Thought you were a vegetarian."

"Lacto-ovo." He took a drag on the Pall Mall. "Bring it here."

"Come and get it."

"I don't walk terribly well these days." Wyvern exhaled a jagged smoke ring. "Temporary infirmity. Now that she's dead, I'll be back on my feet"—he snapped his fingers, and a luminous sphere of brimstone jumped out—"like *that*."

Rising, brushing hay from her jeans, Phoebe carried her milk across the barn.

"Thanks." Wyvern wrapped a mud-encrusted hand around the jar and, unscrewing the lid, took a huge gulp. "Great stuff, child. Nothing like home cooking."

"I made it for my baby, not you."

"Nevertheless, let me reciprocate."

"With what? Horse piss?"

"With this."

Scrabbling through the hay, Wyvern drew out a glass bottle.

Phoebe shivered, gripped by nostalgia laced with terror. Ah, the paradisiacal places rum had taken her, sun-kissed beaches, blue lagoons, Jacuzzis filled with ass's milk.

"Fresh from Palo Seco, child." He pressed the fifth of Bacardi into her palm.

Bacardi, the best. She studied the tense and slender bat on the label. Her old friend.

"Live it up," said Wyvern.

"Hi," Phoebe addressed the bat.

"Cheers," said the devil.

"Hi," said Phoebe again, breathing deeply as her mother had taught her. "Hi, I'm Phoebe, and I'm an alcoholic."

She scooped out a miniature grave in the hay and promptly reinterred the rum.

"I knew you'd say that, I just knew it." Wyvern puffed on his Pall Mall, coughing so violently Phoebe expected his ribs to separate from his sternum. "No matter. This has been a marvelous week for me. The Circus nailed her up real good. Why didn't you shoot him?"

"Who?"

"The grandpastor. Billy boy. You were supposed to shoot him."

"Yeah? Well, it started looking like a poor idea."

"You disappointed me, Phoebe. You hurt me."

"The whole thing would've looked bad in Katz's biography. I'm writing it. But then God came along and did the job."

"The biography?"

"The assassination."

"No, that was lightning, child." The devil coughed, a sound like a tubercular calliope. "If you're really writing her biography, be sure to get the facts right. She and I are two of a kind now. Obsolete. Even hell doesn't need me. Last I heard, they'd put in a fucking parliament." Again he coughed. "Time was, I could split open an entire Exxon supertanker with a wave of my hand. A simple nod from Satan and suddenly Mount Popocatepetl's dumping molten shit on Quauhnahuac. I'd just have to *think* about counterinsurgency, and—*bang*—a million Tanzanians are disemboweling each other. From now on, if people want evil and violence on their planet, they'll have to get it from sources other than me. From nature. From themselves."

"The usual sources," noted Phoebe.

The devil looked simultaneously insulted and amused. "The usual sources," he agreed, swilling down the remaining milk.

Beaming like Angel's Eye in its glory days, Phoebe packed up her incongruous belongings—her apple, umbrella, Smith & Wesson, peanut-butter jar—and strutted happily across the barn. She chuckled. Katz had beaten the devil after all! She'd actually done it!

In a sudden spasm Wyvern grabbed a chicken by the neck. "This isn't the end for me, you know. I've had plenty of job offers. I'm joining the circus." The bird twisted and squawked, kicking like a prisoner on a gallows. "Not Milk's circus, the regular kind. They're hiring me as the geek. I'm good at geeking." He jammed the chicken's head into this mouth and chomped, severing the neck.

"I think you've found your purpose," Phoebe told him.

The devil chewed slowly, grinding the skull against his rusting, roach-brown teeth. "Not bad for a vegetarian, eh?" He spat out a mixture of breast milk and chicken blood.

Phoebe opened the barn door. New Jersey dripped. Silvery moonlight poured down on the threshing machines, streamlining them.

"Hey—what do you get when you eat a live hen?" Wyvern called from behind her.

"What?" Shouldering her backpack, she stepped into the sopping yard.

"You get a feather in your crap," said the beaten devil.

It is harder to be alive than dead. The water seeps relentlessly into your coffin, stinging your eyes and burning your sinuses. Your esophagus twists like a hangman's rope. Your heart pumps panic and bile.

Why this supplemental torment, you wonder as your fingers claw at the rubber. Does the Circus never quit? Wyvern never sleep?

Your nails catch metal. The zipper moves—it moves, oh, God, oh, yes, it *moves*.

A foot, two feet.

Like a moth exiting a cocoon, you slither out and, lungs screaming, fight your way upward, wresting free of death—of death, of hell, of Morphean oblivion—with a single rapturous gasp. The water is frigid and choppy. Absecon Inlet? There's the spit, there's Angel's Eye, rising and falling in the distance like a piston. Alive. Unbelievable. A fiery web spreads across the sky, but nobody's razing any casinos today, it's merely the sunset Panting, coughing, you swim toward shore and pull yourself into the shallows, draping your body over the splendid rocks, their glorious slime greasing your bare abdomen and naked thighs. The tidepool is a carnival of life. Shrimp, scallops, pipe-fish, nereids. Two fiddler crabs mate within inches of your nose

You're alive. Incredible.

Rain slides across your back—and something else, something warm, soft, and rubbery, massaging your neck and shoulders. It creeps down your stubby right arm and bathes your three aligned wounds in salubrious salt.

A sponge. A familiar sponge. Her? Could it really be . . . ?

—Amanda? you inquire.

—Right, broadcasts the sponge.

Amanda! Amanda from your petting zoo!

She waddles onto your left arm and starts cleaning out the hole in your wrist.

—This is amazing, you say. I never thought I'd see you again, old sponge. They crucified me.

—I know, Julie. I saw.

—You saw the Circus?

—I can't blame you for not recognizing me. You were in great pain. But there I was, dripping with hemlock.

—You? I drank from *you*?

—Me.

—Poison?

—By the time it touched your lips, I'd transformed it: tetrado-toxin.

—*What?*

—Tetradotoxin. High grade, ninety-eight percent pure. Re-markable drug. Produces death's symptoms but not its perma-nence. It saved your life, Julie.

—*You* saved my life.

—True.

Delivered by a sponge! Heart saturated with love, soul abrim with appreciation, you kiss Amanda on what you take to be her eyes.

—I can't tell you how grateful I am, you inform her.

—You're entirely welcome.

—I'm confused, you let the sponge know.

A thousand smiles ripple across her porous facade.

—Some would say the miracle was entirely my own doing, Amanda notes. You were always kind to me, so I paid you back: Androcles and the Lion, right? But that strikes me as a hopelessly romantic and anthropomorphic view of a sponge's priorities. Others would call the whole thing a gigantic biochemical coincidence: under optimal conditions, sponges will metabolize hemlock into tetradotoxin. I am not persuaded. Still others would claim that God herself entered into me and performed the appropriate alchemy. A plausible argument, but rather boring. Then there is the final possibility, my favorite.

—Yes?

—The final possibility is that I'm God.

—You're God?

—Just a theory, but the data are provocative. I mean, *look* at me. Faceless, shapeless, holey, undifferentiated, Jewish, inscrutable . . . and a hermaphrodite to boot. Years ago, I told you sponges cannot be fatally dismembered, for each part quickly becomes the whole. To wit, I am both immortal and infinite.

—You're God? You're God herself? *You*?

—The data are provocative.

—God is a sponge? A *sponge*? There's not much comfort in that.

—Agreed.

—Sponges can't help us.

—Neither can God, as far as I can tell. I'd be happy to see some contrary data.

—I'm getting depressed.

—Look at it this way. God is not so much a sponge as she is the behavior of a sponge when confronted with . . . oh, I don't know . . . say, a middle-aged woman with a bad haircut who's recently been crucified. Turn over.

You turn over. The sponge traverses your chest and, waddling down your left leg, begins disinfecting your mangled feet.

—Are you saying God is more like a verb than a noun? you ask Amanda.

—I'm saying God is a sponge, doing what a sponge can do. Understand?

—I think so.

—Now run to America, child, before you get into trouble.

You sit up. You are at peace. It's only temporary happiness, of course, but you opt for a cheerier syntax: it's happiness, only temporary.

Twilight enshrouds Amanda. Not a particularly impressive mother, but evidently the only one you have. You sense she has forgiven your failings as a daughter, and so you resolve to forgive her failings as a parent.

—*Sholem aleichem*, you tell her.

—*Aleichem sholem*, the sponge replies.

She wriggles off your feet, hops into the surf, and is gone.

Mind reeling, wounds throbbing, you climb to the top of the jetty and head west. You feel immeasurably conspicuous. A woman with seven holes in her body limping stark naked down Harbor Beach Boulevard will not go unnoticed for long. "Send me some clothes," you pray to Amanda. "Something undramatic, something that doesn't brand me Sheila of the *Moon*."

No clothes appear. You aren't surprised. Your mother is a sponge. And where, exactly, does *that* leave you? Where you've always been, you decide.

The rain is slackening. Run home, Amanda has instructed you. You can't, of course, not with your feet torn to pieces—but by stealing a hideous red pantsuit from a Pleasantville clothesline and a bicycle from Pomona Junior High School, you do manage to reach Camden within four days.

Alive. Astonishing.

Slowly, like a photographic image materializing in a tray of developer, the Benjamin Franklin Bridge emerges from the dawn, its cables burnished by the rising sun, its macadam lanes blanketed with fog. Your only adversary is a lone, overweight policeman snoozing in the guardhouse. You leave the bicycle on the puddled steps of the Port Authority Building and limp onto the northern walkway.

The lanterns are still on, set on poles high above the road, their globes glowing through the mist. Gradually the land drops away, a scruffy, trash-littered neighborhood huddled against brick ramparts, and now comes the besmirched and clotted river. A Jersey Inquisition patrol boat and an American Coast Guard cutter pass each other in icy silence.

Ten yards away, a thin woman in a yellow parka walks briskly toward America, and you know right away it's her, *her*, and so you cry out.

"Phoebe! Phoebe Sparks!"

She turns. "Yeah?"

"Phoebe! Phoebe!"

"Katz? *Katz?!*"

"Phoebe!"

"Julie Katz?" She can't believe it. "Julie Katz! *Julie Katz!!*"

She bolts toward you like a dog being released from a kennel, and suddenly you're melting into each other, bones fusing, skin knitting, your blood a single organ pouring through shared flesh.

"Oh, Katz, Katz, Julie Goddamn Katz, how the hell'd you *do* it?"

"Do it?"

"You came *back!*" Phoebe smiles like an angel on cocaine.

"I came back. Don't let it get around."

"How?"

"There are several competing explanations."

Phoebe surveys your perforated arms, skewered feet, ravaged head. "Oh, God, honey, what a mess they made of you." She flashes her gorgeous Montgomery Clift teeth. "Listen. Good news. I ran into Andrew Wyvern, and he's in even worse shape than you. More good news—I didn't kill Milk, but he's dead just the same. Your mother zapped him with lightning."

"Lightning?"

"Divine justice."

"Secular coincidence."

"No, buddy." Phoebe places her hands defiantly on her hips. "God."

"God is a sponge."

"A what?"

"A sponge."

"What the hell are you talking about?"

"The data are provocative."

"A *sponge?*"

"Let's go home, Phoebe. Let's go play with the baby."

On the first day of September, 1974, a child was born to Murray Jacob Katz, a celibate Jewish recluse living across the bay from Atlantic City, New Jersey, an island metropolis then famous for its hotels, its boardwalk, its Miss America Pageant, and its seminal role in the invention of Monopoly. Forty years later, the woman that the child had become walked away from New Jersey forever.

Julie studied the Benjamin Franklin Bridge, her gaze lifting past the rivets bubbling from the girders, past the braided steel cords hitched like strings on a harp only an angel could play, past the stately sweep of the main cables, past the sky and the sun. So where was God—up there polishing her arsenal of lightning bolts, or in Absecon Inlet, sucking water through her dermal pores, straining out nutrients for her tissues and spicules?

She fixed on the path before her. WELCOME TO FLESH, the signpost said. UNCERTAINTY ZONE AHEAD. Yes, for another thirty or forty years, it was all hers again, the scarred forehead, pillaged womb, stumpy right arm—just as she wanted.

And this was only the beginning, Julie thought, for under the transforming power of the moment Vine Street did not end in the City of Brotherly Love but flowed like a river, ever westward. This morning she and Phoebe would get out of Camden, next month they'd all leave Philadelphia—she, Phoebe, Bix, Irene, Little Murray—then Pennsylvania, then Ohio, mile upon mile, moving against the planet's spin, the sun always at their backs as they passed through Chicago, St. Louis, Denver, Phoenix, Los Angeles, and perhaps even the South Seas island they'd discovered in the Deauville.

Her best friend loved her. Her husband loved her. She had powers. She could clothe the naked, feed the starving, water the thirsty, insulate the freezing. Then there was this child-hunger business. Would Little Murray satisfy her, or would she and Bix adopt? This too: she wanted a job. Julie the high-school physics teacher, Julie the advice columnist. Or maybe she'd get a doctoral degree. Dr. Katz, the fighting middle-aged theology professor.

Forty: not too late to start her deferred but promising life.

Julie Katz looped an arm around her best friend, who promptly gave her a wry wink and a quick kiss on the cheek, and together they crossed the warty old bridge and entered the world.